S0-BPR-339

THE FRUITS OF WINTER

"*Strong, thrilling, hard, human, with a vividness which is wholly genuine.*"

"*Solid, well written, honest, not contrived.*"

These comments by two members of the jury which awarded France's most prestigious literary prize, the Prix Goncourt, *to Bernard Clavel's novel, are typical of the overwhelming words of praise which greeted its original French publication. Now for the first time this book is available in English.*

Gaston Dubois and his wife, Fernande, live in their own small world, where the events of World War Two mean little to them. Their cares are focused on their home and children: Paul, the materialistic son who trades with the Germans; Julien, who is a Communist and lives the life of a bohemian artist.

This realistic novel provides a moving portrayal of human beings trying to understand themselves, one another, and the world around them. It is a powerful story, rich in both characterization and incident.

The Fruits of Winter

by

BERNARD CLAVEL

Translated by

ANNIE MYGIND

in collaboration with

PATRICK HENRY

GEORGE G. HARRAP & CO. LTD

LONDON · TORONTO · WELLINGTON · SYDNEY

To the memory of all the mothers and fathers whom work, love, and wars have silently killed, and history not recorded.

B.C.

Published in France 1968

First published in Great Britain 1970
by GEORGE G. HARRAP & CO. LTD
182–184 High Holborn, London, W.C.1

ISBN 0 245 59904 5

Composed in Linotype Granjon type and printed by Western Printing Services Ltd, Bristol
Made in Great Britain

CONTENTS

Translator's Note

In the French original Bernard Clavel almost invariably refers to Gaston and Fernande Dubois as "le père" and "la mère", except when addressed in direct speech. It was impossible to use these words in English—they sound faintly ridiculous, certainly stilted. But in French they have the effect of constantly reminding the reader that it is this parental relationship with which we are concerned.

. . . it is the words they never spoke
that make the dead so heavy in their coffins.

H. de Montherlant

PART ONE

The Cart

1

On the morning of October 1st, 1943, Gaston Dubois woke up some time before dawn. He had slept badly. A dull ache bound his head like a band of iron, tightening now and again. He lay still for a few minutes, listening to the night. No sound came from outside; the west wind, which had been blowing for three days, seemed to have passed without bringing any rain. The old man sat up slowly, eased towards the side of the bed, and stuck his feet down on the cold floor, searching for his slippers.

"You getting up already?" asked his wife.

"I thought you were asleep."

"No, I've been awake some time. Why are you getting up so early? It's not light yet."

"I've got a headache."

"Stay in bed. I'll go down and get you an aspirin."

"No. I've got to get up anyway."

She sighed. He was already getting dressed in the dark. She asked, "Are you worried about the wood again?"

"No, but I've got to make room for it. I should have done it yesterday, but I thought it was going to rain, and I had urgent jobs to finish in the garden."

The bedsprings creaked, and he realized his wife was getting up.

"You don't have to come down now."

She did not reply, and he groped his way towards the door. There was a dim light in the corridor from the dormer-window leading to the roof, but its outline was still obscure. He had not blacked it out with paper, like the other windows. It was above the staircase, where there were no lamps, and they only used it on their way to bed. The few moments' glimmering of a candle was hardly likely to attract any planes. Besides, the window could not be seen from the street, and no-one seemed to worry much about an isolated house at the bottom of a large garden. Moreover, Gaston Dubois did not really believe in all that Civil Defence nonsense. What on earth could aeroplanes find to bomb at Lons-de-Saunier? The Germans at the Michel barracks and the *école normale*? There were Germans everywhere—even in the smallest villages. The Americans could not bomb everything.

When he reached the kitchen he lit a candle. It would be light in half an hour. It was not worth putting a match to the oil-lamp. As his wife came down he asked, "Are you going to light the stove?"

"It's hardly worth it just for two bowls of coffee. There's only a little meths left, and they haven't given me any more this month."

"Oh, the misery of it! They'll just let us die."

"I'll light a few beanstalks. That should be enough to heat the coffee."

"Yes, but it's bad for the chimney."

"You and your chimney! It'll bury us both."

"That's all you can ever talk about."

"And it's true."

She had begun to clear the grate, raking the bars to make the ashes fall through and putting aside two pieces of charred wood. She then put half a sheet of crumpled newspaper in the front of the grate and broke up the dried stalks on which there were still a few leaves.

He followed all her movements as he dissolved his aspirin in a small glass of water. It had come to this—saving a bit of old newspaper and warming themselves with what they used to throw on the compost-heap. No doubt the chimney and everything in the house would survive them! Especially at the rate things were going. At seventy you cannot work from dawn till dusk on three wretched meals a day.

The fire was crackling under the little iron saucepan, and soon the coffee began to simmer gently.

"Don't let it boil," he said.

"I haven't moved—I'm standing right here. There's no risk of it boiling over. Go on with you!"

"I'm not allowed to say a thing."

She stayed in front of the stove, stooping slightly. Over her white nightdress she was wearing a large black woollen shawl which reached the floor. When the coffee was hot she took the saucepan off and replaced the iron ring on the stove, where a few remaining embers glowed. He went to his seat, his back to the window, while she put two bowls, two spoons, a knife, and a piece of grey, dry bread on the table. Before she sat down she asked, "Do you think we could open the shutters? There should be enough light by now, and it would save the candle."

"True. And we wouldn't risk missing our aim with the butter."

He got up and opened the shutters, while his wife blew out the candle. A faint dawn was breaking behind the roofs and trees of the *école normale*. Over on the right he could just make out the little hill near Montaigu. The sky was like a piece of grey cotton cloth slung low from one end of the horizon to the other. The more luminous grey from the east drew no trace of real light, no outline of shapes, however dim.

As he closed the windows again he said, "The west wind has dropped without bringing any rain—but it might still come. It's not far off."

"I know—I can feel it in my back and kidneys."

He had begun to eat. He, too, had aches and pains. Mostly in the wrists, shoulders, and ankles. At times it was almost unbearable. They were like vicious thrusts, as though metal wire had been shoved through the bone-marrow. He never mentioned them; he was worn-out. What was the good of talking about it? His wife was worn-out too. She was fourteen years younger than he, but toil and privation had left their mark. She often accused him of being selfish. Perhaps it was true, but when he complained, when he gave vent to his wrath about the difficulties of keeping alive, it was as much for her as for himself. After all, she was only fifty-six. At her age he had been a lot stronger. Was she not a little too self-indulgent? Women were always over-sensitive, and by talking so much about their ailments they ended up believing in them. Of course, one could see the rheumatism in her deformed joints and twisted fingers, which at times she could hardly bend, but all the same, had she the right to feel old at fifty-six?

"D'you want another drop?" she asked.

"No. It's terrible coffee. You used nothing but barley?"

"Of course. You know I haven't yet taken up the October ration."

"They'll kill us, I tell you."

He pushed the rest of the bread towards the middle of the table.

"When I think of the bread I used to make!"

"You're always saying that, and it's not—"

He interrupted her. "Yes, and I'll say it again—and I'll say it as often as I like. I baked bread for more than forty years—bread that people would come over six miles to buy, and now, at my age, to have to eat this synthetic rubbish. I don't—"

A fit of coughing seized him. He slumped forward for a moment, hand on his chest. Then, as he got up to spit in the grate, he said in a choking voice, "You work your guts out all your life and then come to this—"

"You're not the only one. People without a garden are worse off than we are."

"The garden doesn't grow itself."

He emptied his bowl, which she stacked with her own and the spoons. They both got up.

While they had been eating, the day had trickled into the room, and now it was as though its troubled waters had spread laboriously around the black cast-iron stove with its brass fittings, the wooden staircase leading to the floor above, and the plain little chest with its four large drawers set one above the other.

"Would you like me to help you clear a space?" she asked.

"No. I'll manage. I only hope this Picaud won't let us down."

"But he promised you."

He made a tired gesture. "Promises! These days! If it had been the old man it would have been all right. He'd have remembered that I used to be one of his best customers when I had the bakery, but the son doesn't give a damn. He'd rather sell his wood to people who've got tobacco or wine."

"That reminds me—I'm going to get some of the tobacco ration this morning."

He went out grumbling that he had not had a smoke for three days.

2

As he opened the door of the big cart-shed at the other end of the garden Gaston turned round to make sure that his wife had not come out behind him. Then, moving the work-bench to one side, he opened the shutters of a little window he had made in order to be able to do odd jobs in peace on rainy days. Returning to the door for one more glance up at the house, he took a garden chair over between the bench and the window, stood up on it, and reached for a biscuit-tin from the shelf above the window. There was a whole row of boxes where he kept bolts, hooks, screws, and nails—things he did not use very often. He got down, brushed a cobweb off the tin, and, holding it against his chest, opened it. In the tin were four packets of shag tobacco, several packets of cigarette-papers, some lighter-wicks, three little packets of flints, and a smaller, blue cardboard box. He opened this box and leaned over towards the light to examine the contents. He still had about fifty butt-ends. He chose three, which he put on the corner of the work-bench, and then put everything back carefully. When he had moved the chair he sat down facing the door by a beam that supported the roof. Though hidden in the shadows, he commanded a view of the path and the house from this position. He broke up the butts, taking great care not to lose a single shred, rolled a thin but perfect cigarette, and began to smoke slowly, relishing each puff. His headache seemed to ease at once.

He let his cigarette go out twice so that he might have the pleasure of waiting a little before relighting it. He thought about the tobacco he had been able to save. It was a good little stock. If his wife discovered it she would almost certainly insist that he forgo some of his ration in exchange for eggs or butter. But he felt quite safe. She would not find his hiding-place. She had never come nosing around here where she had no business to be. This was his own private territory. When Julien had been at home he might have come occasionally to mend his bicycle; but now Julien was far away, and the bicycle was stored in the loft, of no further use. The tyres were still good though, and Gaston knew people who would give several tobacco rations for one single inner tube. He had often considered it, but he felt he had no right to use the bike this way when it belonged to the boy.

Fernande and he forced themselves to talk as little as possible about the boy to avoid arguments. This morning he thought about it because of the possible exchange of the useless tyres for tobacco. He thought about it, but that was as far as it went. Besides, there were more important things to think about. To begin with, this business of the wood. Here it was, October already, and he was still waiting for the winter supply—this was really too much. Before the War he had always started the winter with an extra year's supply. Because of this they had been able to manage quite well up till now, without having to stint themselves too much; but now there were hardly enough logs to last another month—perhaps two, if the winter did not set in too quickly.

He looked at the logs over on his left, cut the right length for the stove and piled against the open fencing of the shed. Two heaps. Two heaps that had already been broken into, and had hardly been a man's height to start with. Before, when they had got down that far, there would be other piles next to them, six times as deep and at least six feet high.

The forester had promised delivery in August. That was two months ago. Then the wood would have to be sawn and split, and it would probably be unseasoned, pissing with sap. That would wreck the chimney all right.

This problem had been his greatest worry ever since last August. He never spoke about it, but it was there at the back of his mind, and rankled his thoughts as soon as he took time off to relax a bit.

That shed had been built way back in 1912. He remembered it clearly. He had hired four men to help him—massive fellows they were. It had taken two months. He himself had only worked at it in the afternoons, when he had finished his baking, which he started at eleven the previous night. That made an eighteen-hour day—four hours' sleep, two for meals, and that was that. He had good reason to be worn-out now, having led such a life, living through four years of the other war, and now again hoping anxiously for a small load of wood and counting his fag-ends.

Good God, people no longer had any conscience. They forgot all but evil things. He had built that shed especially for the firewood. The wood was for the bakehouse, of course, because in those days he only baked with wood, which meant quite a few loads a month for the forester. He was an honest forester, just as Gaston was an honest baker. They had never had the slightest misunderstanding. Forty years that way they had naturally become good friends. He had known the son when he was no taller than the wheel of his father's first lorry. Would he remember all that? Of course not. There was nothing left but thought for profit, barter, the black market. Come to think of it, it was the all-corroding sin. The greed that perpetually set man against man for a crust of that filthy rubbish they dared call bread!

Gaston sighed deeply, several times. He growled, shrugged his shoulders, pulled a wry face. Then he stopped, motionless. Every time he thought of the past and considered what he had suffered since the beginning of this War he felt overwhelmed; anger always got the better of him. It was a useless sort of anger, there was nothing to be done about it. It was deeply rooted. He had to choke it back and repress it, but it was always there, ready to break loose again, twisting the pit of his stomach like a cramp, and nothing could loosen its grip.

Having lived through the other war, he had feared this one. He had feared it as everyone else had, but he had never imagined it would be like this. It seeped into everything, without ever really being there. It did not kill in the way the first war had; it crushed the whole of life, it wrapped you in a sort of endless night, darkening everything. Every week, every day, brought another batch of news that was difficult to understand. But it was never good news.

Several things had happened that one no longer dared discuss. Dubois kept these painful things to himself and tried to avoid thinking about them.

His wife often reproached him for being selfish. She was astonished that he could be so interested in what she dared to call his own comfort: food, tobacco, wine, warmth, relatively quiet nights, and a well-ordered garden. He would let it pass, but it hurt him.

He had not been unaffected by the boy's disappearance, but he saw it in a different light from his wife. It could well be true, after all, that he thought too much about the garden, the rabbits, and the like. But that was life. You could not let yourself be done in because . . .

He stopped suddenly. A black figure had just passed behind the boxwood-tree at the corner of the house. He had finished his cigarette some time ago, but his fingers still grasped the sodden, flattened butt, which had gone out of its own accord. He flicked off the ash, twisted the paper so as to save the remaining tobacco, took a small tin, shiny with constant use, from his apron pocket, and put the butt in it. Fernande was coming down the path facing the wide-open door. He went over to the left-hand corner of the old shed and began to gather up the onions which he had laid out on an old tarpaulin on the ground. When she entered he turned round, asking, "You off already?"

"Yes. I don't want to queue for too long, so I'll have to be there before they open."

He had come up to the threshold only a couple of paces from his wife. She moved forward slightly and hesitated for a moment, frowning. "I thought you hadn't got any tobacco."

"No, I have none left."

"Well, you've been smoking."

"Of course I've been smoking. I happened to find a butt on the work-bench, and I smoked it. Here, see for yourself if I have any left!"

He was angry. When he took the little tin from his pocket his hands were shaking. He opened it and proffered it to his wife.

"There you are. Look for yourself, seeing that you must inspect everything that goes on."

She shook her head and sighed. "Poor old Gaston! How excited you get over nothing! I had no intention of prying. I just thought you had been smoking, that's all. If you have any tobacco left, so much the better."

"No, I have none left. Satisfied?"

She had already turned and was setting off, a tiny figure, shrivelled beneath her sombre clothes and her black hat whose broken brim completely hid the back of her neck.

He was left alone with his anger. Its bitterness spoiled the taste of the tobacco.

3

Alone again in the cart shed, the old man went back to his work. He finished gathering the onions together, putting them into three big baskets, which he then took up to the loft. It was not easy. After each journey he stopped to regain his breath while looking at the garden, still shrouded in the morning mist. On the third trip he had to stop half-way up the ladder, his knees pressed against a rung. Clutching the side of the ladder with one hand, he leaned the basket on his shoulder against the other side. The load had almost tipped him backwards. He felt his cough coming on and made an enormous effort to control it.

"Thank you very much," he groaned. "And this only weighs forty pounds. To think that I used to carry the flour sacks up to the store—thirty, forty of them, one after the other. What's become of me?"

He waited, listening carefully to his heart-beats, and staring at the luminous dots that flew like fire-flies trapped under his closed eyelids. After a while he felt a cramp coming in his right arm, and his hand clenched the basket, which he was afraid of dropping. Slowly, gathering all his strength, he continued upwards. When he reached the top he had difficulty in letting the basket down gently on the loose floor-boards. This done, he slumped on to a big black trunk and took off his cap. The air suddenly chilled the sweat on his bald head, and he quickly wiped it with his handkerchief, which he also passed round the inside brim of the cap. His back, too, was drenched, and his hands shook. He realized that this sudden sweating was more because of fear of falling than physical strain. A grim smile drew his lips thin as they pressed together over his toothless jaws. For a moment his white, tobacco-stained moustache nearly met his protruding, stubbled chin. He had been afraid of falling when only six feet from the ground. To think that long ago, when he left Joinville, he could fling himself from one trapeze to the next in the gymnasium, with only a thin layer of sawdust on the ground. His vision clouded over again, but this time it was neither fatigue nor fear. Like the time when he dived into the freezing water from a bridge on the river Ain, he drew in a great gulp of air and stood up brusquely. His knee cracked like a breaking twig.

What a wreck he was! His body was like a stubborn animal. He really ought to control it better. Make it feel the whip! Make it forget the harness and still keep it lively! He leaned over towards one of the baskets and seized a big onion. He prodded the reddish-brown dried skins with his horny thumb. There were four layers. The winter was going to be hard and might come quicker than expected. This apprehension made him remember the wood he was waiting for. He would have to saw it up and split it as quickly as possible, so that it would have time, if not to dry out, at least to spew out some of its water.

Before the War he had sent for a motor-saw, but now the only people who could use it were those who managed to get petrol. So it would all have to be done by hand. And there was still the garden, where the beds must be finished before winter.

Gaston put the onion back in the basket and went down below. There was still a pile of empty boxes to clear, which would make good kindling, and some bundles of bean-sticks, which might still be used a year or two longer. He had ordered both pea- and bean-sticks from Picaud, but could one rely on him?

He interrupted his work several times, and went up the path leading to the road that ran between his back garden fence and the wall encircling the grounds of the *école normale*. There he stared down the street and listened hard. No, it was not the forester's lorry, but the German vehicles manœuvring in the school courtyard. So Picaud was late—two months late—in spite of his promise to come this morning.

He was on his way back to the cart-shed when he stopped at the top of the path. His wife was coming down the road. She had hardly had time to get there and back. Perhaps she had been the first to arrive? Or perhaps there had been no tobacco.

She seemed to be walking more quickly than usual. Had she forgotten the ration-cards? The old man wanted to get back to work, but his wife must have seen him. He waited till she had gone a bit further, then set off to meet her.

As they approached one another he could see more of her face under the brim of her hat. It looked hard and tense as on days when the news was bad. When she was level with the house, instead of continuing in his direction, she turned right and went up the little path that led to the front-door steps. He hurried after her, turned up the same path, and reached the bottom step just as she was entering the kitchen.

"Well, what's the matter?" he asked.

She turned round on the threshold and snapped, "You can come up here, can't you?"

By her tone the old man realized there was something very

wrong, and that it concerned him. He went up the steps without hurrying, left his clogs outside the door, and went in.

His wife was sitting on the second step of the staircase, elbows on her knees, leaning forward with her head bent. She had not even taken off her hat. By the movement of her shoulders he could see that she was out of breath. He stood still for several minutes without saying a word. All he could hear was his own wheezing breath. He looked at his wife and did not dare speak. It was only when she straightened herself slightly and put her hand on her chest that he asked, "What's the matter? Aren't you well?"

She lifted her head slowly towards him. Her face looked distressed, her chin trembled, her eyes, more grey than blue, looked full of reproach. He sensed that only anger prevented her crying. With his hands wavering, not knowing what to do with himself, he took a step forward and said in a very unsure voice, "Well, then, say something. Don't you think I've the right to know?"

A sad smile deepened the wrinkles on either side of her mouth. Her lips moved several times before she made up her mind what to say. "Let me recover. Besides, I can never know how you'll react."

He lifted his arms and let them fall again, his hands flat against his apron. "That's right, take it out on me. Obviously—"

"There you are," she interrupted. "You are getting angry already without knowing anything about it."

He did his best not to shout, and said, "I'm not getting angry. But you must admit you're behaving very oddly. You come back, I don't know what's the matter, and now you are getting at me for no reason."

"No reason!"

She looked overwhelmed, unable to continue. Her body seemed to shrink again, and then suddenly, as though she had regained all her strength, she got up, took off her hat with an irritated gesture, pulling with one hand at the elastic that had caught on a hairpin in her bun.

"Your tobacco!" She threw the words at him. "You can go and get it yourself if you want it!"

She put the hat on the wooden knob on the banisters, and began to unbutton her woollen jacket. He was going to question her further when she started again: "Oh, yes, you were ashamed of showing yourself in town because they say Julien has gone to join de Gaulle. Well, now it's all right. You can go there. The shame is blotted out."

She laid strong emphasis on those last words and looked so hard into his eyes that his throat tightened.

"What else are you going to make up," he stammered. It was not really a question, but as soon as he had finished he realized he had said too much.

"Make up!" she cried. "So I'm making it up. Well, then, you just go to the tobacconist's. And you ask the people in the queue if I am making up stories. And if you dare stay with them and wait for your tobacco it must be because your craving for smoke is stronger than your self-respect."

This attack released his anger. As his wife approached the window he also advanced and struck the table with the flat of his bony hand.

"I would have been most surprised," he shouted, "if you didn't immediately begrudge me my only pleasure. It would have..."

"Keep quiet! That's exactly what it's about!"

As always when he got angry, Gaston began to cough. Half choked with phlegm, his eyes streaming, it took him a long time to recover his breath. His wife had gone into the scullery to fetch him a glass of water, which he drank slowly as he sat on his chair, one elbow on the table. He had not brought on this fit of coughing deliberately, but he felt it had come to his aid in the nick of time. When he was fit enough to listen again he said, "There we are. We get angry instead of speaking calmly, and we do ourselves harm."

Peering out under the grey peak of his cap, he saw that his wife was still standing up between the table and the stove.

"Do you want another drink?" she asked.

"No. I'm all right now."

He was well aware that this interlude was not the end of his wife's anger. In any case, she would tell him what was on her mind sooner or later. However, time had been gained, peace restored for a moment. He listened. No, it was not the sound of a lorry. If only Picaud would come . . .

He tried hard to breathe more deeply. "This sort of thing kills me," he muttered.

His wife drew up a chair, and she, too, sat down. "It hurts me too. And the blow I've just received in front of more than twenty people, I can tell you quite definitely that *that* hurt me even more!"

He wished he could have sounded more self-assured, but it was only with great difficulty that he managed to give voice to the words as he asked, "Well, what is it then? Tell me what it is, and let's get it over and done with."

"Done with? How can you talk like that? These disasters will only be done with when the War is over—or when we're finished."

He was struck by the fact that she had hesitated over her last words. There was something in her voice as well as in what she said which disturbed him, in spite of himself. She did not usually speak lightly of death. On the contrary. If he should happen to say, for example, "Better be six foot under than live in these times," she would rebuke him sharply.

"It's not all that far off," he said. "I've never felt so drained of strength."

Now she seemed to hesitate, as though reluctant to put her reproaches into words, frightened of reviving her own anger. He did want to know what had happened, yet for a moment he hoped she would resign herself to silence.

"When I think," she said at last, "when I think of the scene you made after the gendarmes came here that day." She raised her voice as though he might interrupt her, and went on, "And which you stir up again every time they call."

"So it pleases you, does it, to have them in the house every month? And the neighbours asking questions."

She laughed mockingly and hurled back at him, "And now they may put some questions that'll please you even less. When they ask if you have joined the Militia, for example, I wonder what you'll think of telling them."

"I've never been involved in politics. Those who know me are well aware of the fact." He had spoken loudly in a firm voice, but without shouting.

"That doesn't stop your son from being involved, or from selling photographs of Darnand in the street."

"What on earth is all this about?" His voice was already less firm. He knew it and searched desperately for something else to say. Fernande got in first.

"That's just it!" she said. "There he was, with two Militia men, and selling photographs. He offered them to everyone in the queue. When he got near me he actually said, 'And you, wouldn't you like one to send to your communist son?' That's what he said. And I—I wanted to spit in his face!"

She began to tremble. Her face was deathly pale, and when she had finished two big tears rolled down her hollow cheeks. He felt his forehead become burning hot. He had difficulty in swallowing, and only after a long silence did he manage to say, "Is anything really known about this Militia?"

"If you don't know you must be the only one—because you do all you can to ignore the War and set yourself apart from everyone else."

"I don't live like a hermit, in spite of what you keep telling me all day, but I don't want to get mixed up in politics. As far as I can see, this Militia is a—is a kind of Government thing, and I have never in all my seventy years stepped outside the law."

Now it was she who tried to intervene, but he raised his voice in order to carry his idea through. "It's no concern of mine what my lad does. He is over forty, and he's free to do as he likes. As for you, you've said often enough he's not your son."

"I delighted in that fact more than ever today."

She had shot this at him like an arrow, which took him by

surprise. There was a very short silence. Then they both shouted at the same time.

He: "You'd do better to concern yourself over what has become of Julien since the gendarmes started looking for him."

She: "I'd rather die of sorrow wondering whether Julien is still alive than die of shame—"

Gaston finished first. She had shouted the louder, giving vent to her feeling as she leaned towards him, short of breath, her hands trembling with excitement. The door had been left half open and someone was calling from the bottom of the steps. Gaston got up as his wife went to the door. She went out, and he recognized young Picaud's voice asking, "What about it, then? D'you want this wood, or shall I take it back to the forest?"

Gaston realized he was utterly exhausted by the scene. He saw his wife disappearing down the steps, and before he could follow he had to stand still for a few moments, leaning with one hand on the door-frame, on the brink of succumbing to the same dizziness he had experienced earlier in the loft.

4

Young Picaud was a great big fellow with a ruddy face and a balding head dotted with a few grey hairs. He smelt strongly of wine, tobacco, sweat, and that particular smell which clings to people who spend most of their lives felling trees and working in sawmills. Gaston shook the great rough hand that Picaud held out.

"*Old people, like lovers, squabble in front of all-comers,*" he said.

Gaston forced a smile. "Where have you put the lorry?"

"In the road."

"You should have driven right in. You know the way."

"Not possible this year. I've brought the big lorry. It would be a tight squeeze, and I'd risk getting stuck."

Gaston had some difficulty in understanding. He still felt dazed by the quarrel. He did not react, so the forester explained in his rough voice, "I haven't any petrol left. The big lorry runs on gas."

Gaston took off his cap and wiped his forehead. "Thanks very much—I can't drag two loads of wood right down there with a cart, just like that!"

Picaud was torn between laughing and some other emotion, which seemed to tug at the corners of his mouth. But probably, because he had an expansive nature, he put his big fist on the old man's shoulder, and, towering above him, he burst into laughter, and explained, "Well, then, it's a good thing I haven't brought you all that much! It won't be so hard for you."

It was Fernande who intervened. "What do you mean? All that much?"

"My dear lady, wood is like everything else. We have to make do with what we can get. I've brought you six cubic yards, and, believe me, that's because you are friends."

"You don't care about me!" Gaston shouted.

"Come on," said the forester, "I must unload. I've got deliveries to other customers."

He went up the drive with long strides, followed by Gaston Dubois and his wife. Gaston was grumbling. But the man calmly insisted, "Quite impossible. I can't give you any more. But the coal ration should see you through."

"We can't burn coal," explained the old man. "Our stove isn't designed for it, and it's too old to be adapted. God, if we can't keep warm it's the end of everything."

When they reached the road Gaston, not used to walking so fast, was too out of breath to speak. He leaned against the garden fence, wiped the top of his head as he looked at the huge lorry filled with wood. The forester and his assistant had already begun to throw the logs on to the pavement. Gaston looked on as each one fell. He no longer knew what to say. It hurt. That was all.

When the unloading was finished he pointed at the logs still left in the lorry and asked, "Couldn't you just let me have a little bit more?"

The man took a tobacco-pouch out of his pocket and filled his big, stubby pipe. Then he said, "No. Quite impossible."

There was no point in going on. Gaston lowered his eyes, following the man's movements as he closed his pouch. The other must have felt his gaze, for he offered the tobacco to him, saying, "Here, roll one for yourself."

Gaston took the pouch and fetched his little tin from his pocket, opened it, and took out the cigarette-papers.

"You see, I just can't refuse. I've got to the end of my ration."

"Take some more for later on."

Gaston hesitated.

"Go on—take some. I've got a friend who's a customs officer—he brings me some from Switzerland."

They went back to the house, where Fernande counted out the money for the logs while the three men drank a glass of wine. Gaston could not very well plead again with this man who had just given him tobacco. Nevertheless, without really complaining, but in a voice that trembled a little, he began to talk about the time when the foresters would come crying to the bakers for their custom. "Never in my life did I buy a single log except from your father," he finished. "Never!"

"Listen," said Picaud, "I'll make you an offer. There are two clearings above Pannessières where I haven't yet finished trimming the branches. They are not kindling, you know. They're good and thick. If you'd like to go up there you can help yourselves."

Gaston turned to his wife, who was standing leaning against the brass rail of the stove. They looked at each other for a moment, then it was she who asked, "Where exactly is it?"

The man explained by drawing on the oilcloth with his big, creased finger whose nail looked like a badly shaped tool. Taking the short cut, it was not all that far. Five, six miles at the most, but, of course, the hill was quite steep.

"And you'd fetch them for us?" asked Fernande.

"Oh, no, that's impossible. I always come back with the lorry full. But you've got your lad—the grocer. He's got some lorries which must go quite near there from time to time."

Gaston looked down. There was a deep silence. The man emptied his glass and stood up. "It's up to you," he said.

The assistant went towards the door, and Picaud was about to follow him when Fernande asked, "Could we get there with our cart?"

The fellow looked at the two old people as though sizing up their strength. "Yes—you could; but if you have no-one to help you up the hill—" He stopped, and then said in a firmer voice, "When I go up there the lorry's empty. If you've finished with the cart tonight I could put it on the lorry, and I'll leave it up there for you."

They again discussed the exact spot and whether there was any risk of the cart being stolen.

Gaston was a little alarmed at the prospect of the work involved and of the long walk, but he dreaded the departure of the two men even more. They had brought their own live atmosphere into the house, and it had filled this part of the morning. Their departure would leave a void. He glanced at his wife from time to time, and made every effort to prolong the conversation. However, the forester had the rest of his wood to deliver. He reminded them of this several times as he edged towards the door.

"And you—you've got your logs to move. If you'd like me to fetch your cart tonight you'll have to get it done."

He again said that he would leave the cart near the woodmen's hut, and that there would be no risk at all. He also explained where they might find the key to the hut, and added, "You're welcome to stay the night. It's not exactly comfortable, but it might be useful."

As he went off behind his assistant Gaston followed him with his eyes. He felt his wife standing next to him. Without turning his head, he could see her out of the corner of his right eye, looking at the forester, who had now reached the end of the long drive lined with fruit-trees.

The old people now stood side by side as though immobilized by the silence of the morning. This was soon broken by the rumbling of the lorry. They stood there, alone, separated from each other by one thing, yet drawn together by another.

When the sound of the lorry had died away Gaston turned to his wife. "I don't think we've reached the end of our troubles."

"No. But we have to take it or leave it. That's the position. Otherwise we run the risk of freezing without a fire if the winter is long."

"Right; I'm going to see to the logs."

"I'll help you."

"It's no work for you. The logs are too heavy for you with your hernia."

"There aren't many big ones. Besides, with the two of us, each load will be so much lighter."

Gaston knew she was right. He also knew that she would help him, as she always did. Nevertheless it gave him some sort of pleasure to go on defending himself, pretending that he could do the work on his own, though he knew very well that it might wear him out completely. He always went on like this, but this morning, more than usual, as he went towards the shed where the cart was kept, he felt the need to keep on saying, "My poor wife, it's no work for you. You'll do yourself in—that's all you'll do."

Fernande said nothing. She walked beside him to the shed, and when he pulled down the shaft of the cart she was already at her place, her hands on the cross-bar, ready to help with all her strength.

5

They worked on till midday. It was no easy task, as the drive was only just wide enough for the cart. When a wheel hit a protruding stone Gaston was occasionally taken by surprise, and would be wrenched to the right or the left by the jolting of the shaft against his arms and shoulders. Once a wheel struck a flagstone bordering the plot. That gave him a very hard knock. Gaston swore, stopped, and started again, pressing his lips together hard over his toothless gums.

At first they had used the road parallel to the garden. It was not so narrow, but the surface was more uneven. It was muddy in places, and they slipped and the wheels would get stuck.

They managed about ten logs on each trip. It was impossible to load more than that because of the slope between the house and the shed. Normally the slope was hardly noticeable, but with the loaded cart it was another matter. As they approached the hillock Gaston would shout, "Forward!"

The word was as though torn from the depths of his being. They would make an enormous effort, quickening their pace and straining forward like whipped animals. If the wheels caught on a bad hump they would lose the impetus they had gained with such great effort. Gaston groaned, closing his eyes that burned with sweat, groaned once more, and threw his full weight forward.

This slope was more exhausting than all the rest of the way put together—and it was a good hundred yards long.

Just before midday the baker's assistant, who had come out on the front doorstep for a breath of fresh air, came over and offered to help. He was a big, fat fellow from Bresse. Gaston liked him because he knew how to listen appreciatively to stories from his younger days.

"Perhaps you could give us a hand with one or two loads—that would be a great help."

The baker's assistant grinned.

"We shan't need your good lady," he said. "She can go and get your soup ready."

Fernande thanked him. Gaston watched her going away, and said to the assistant, "It's no sort of work for her, but what can I do? She's even more obstinate than I am myself."

The rest of the wood was taken in two loads. The assistant

threw himself at the shaft and went so fast that Gaston had to give up. The cart, creaking under its load, left him behind, and Gaston followed, thinking to himself, "If he hits one of the flagstones he'll break my cart!"

The lad would lean well forward on the slope, head and shoulders disappearing behind the load so that the cart looked as if it were rolling up the hillock of its own accord—the same hillock that had given the old people so much trouble—and it did not lose speed at all. When Gaston came into the shed the man had already begun to throw the logs on the pile.

"Leave it to me," he cried. "I'll finish this in next to no time!"

"Twenty-five is a good age to be," said Gaston.

The work was like a game for this stocky fellow with arms so fat that his muscles were hidden, though this in no way lessened his strength.

If only he could come with them to the forest, if only he could spare a couple of afternoons to help them getting in the wood. Gaston felt like asking many times: he would pay him. Perhaps not as much as he would get at the bakery, but if he did it in his spare time it would be a bit extra. The old man did not dare. He might ask him about Julien and what had become of him, why he was not there to give him a hand.

When the cart was unloaded Gaston merely said, "And now it's all got to be cut—and by hand. I'm still sweating."

"Wood warms you twice, that's a fact."

The baker's assistant laughed.

Gaston went on: "Wish I could find a strong fellow like you who'd like to make a bit on the side. . . ."

"I'd come and do it if I had the time. But I haven't."

"I know. We all have our work cut out."

Gaston did not sound gloomy. He had been fantasizing about the boy sawing his logs, while he himself split them and Fernande stacked them. In his imagination he had seen the work finished in a couple of days, and the shed cleared to make room for a big load of good, thick branches from the forest. He had an uneasy feeling in his chest as he told himself that none of this was done. He would have to do the job on his own, and get it done in good time, before the first frost set in.

"Well," he sighed, "let's work out what I owe you."

"You're joking."

"No—no. I've never had people work for me for nothing."

He was about to mention the days when he employed assistants himself, but the young man interrupted.

"I'll have to run," he said. "The boss will be wondering what's happened to me."

"At least come and drink a glass of wine!"

The big fellow had already picked up his white apron and was passing it under his belt. Without turning round he cried, "Another time!" Then he began to run towards the road.

On his own again, Gaston sat down on an empty box, took out his little tin filled with the forester's tobacco, and slowly rolled a cigarette. He had been working the whole morning, paying no attention to his body. He had turned a deaf ear to the aches in his back and limbs. Now that he was sitting still the pain swept through him. It started at each joint and ran like an acid between bone and muscle, which it pierced wherever it found a weakness. It was like an inexhaustibly welling spring. This spring fed on the thousands of bits of waste which time had accumulated imperceptibly in his whole body. The least movement made them pierce like needles, gave them a new strength, which made them advance and enlarge the path already formed.

His elbows on his knees, his head bent, and his gaze lost in the expanse of grass outside and the grey dust which covered the floor of the shed, Gaston thought about himself. He drew tiny puffs on his cigarette, and held them for a long time in his lungs. The tobacco the forester had given him was good—a pleasant taste and aroma, much better than the one the Government distributed so sparingly.

The old man thought about himself, and the sort of man he had formerly been, and what had become of him after all those years of sorrow and labour and want.

6

Time flowed by. Gaston's exhaustion was dulled, though it did not lessen. It was like water turning to ice in the frost—every now and again an eddy stirred, but the main current no longer had its previous force. Now he had other things on his mind. His wife would soon be coming down the front-door steps to call him in for the meal. They would sit down to table, would eat their soup, talking of nothing more than the trouble they had had that morning and the help given by the baker's assistant. But inevitably they would come back to the argument interrupted by Picaud's arrival. Fernande would not stop there—that was certain. Either his anger would exhaust him, or else he would be no less exhausted with the effort of holding it back. What was the use of arguing when so much effort was already needed just to keep alive, to keep going, sustaining an existence entirely filled with work, which only yielded just enough to eat, without forcing them to sell any of their property? This war had made money worthless—at any rate, the money belonging to small investors. Fernande went every six months to cash the dividends on bonds which were now worthless. They had bought those bonds with sound money—money that had been saved from nights spent at the dough-trough and at the maw of the oven. Every centime was probably the equivalent of a whole batch of good white bread. Nowadays, when Gaston mentioned the matter to informed people, they would smile. A lifetime of work worth no more than a few pieces of paper which no-one would exchange for a pat of butter or a sack of wood. But the authorities responsible for this disaster didn't give a damn. They probably had gold in Switzerland or shares in the armaments factories. No-one could touch them. They lived comfortably on the backs of the small investors.

Gaston let his thoughts wander along this tortuous path, channelled with ruts where the water was stagnant and bitter. Sometimes he would clench his fists. They had stolen everything from him. They had torn away his right, so bitterly contested, to end his days in peace, and he could do nothing about it.

Not only did he have to struggle and slave for a crust of vile bread, but the War brought its crazy strife right into his own home. The other war had made him unhappy enough. Two years in the trenches, and the rest behind the lines making bread for the front-line troops. In 1915 his first wife died, and he had had to close the bakery. In 1919 he had remarried, opened the business again, and got back into harness. Then more years slaving away in order to save up enough to retire and live off the garden and the tenants of the bakery. It was not exactly paradise, but it was good enough, with the work in the open air, which was better for his weak chest than the dust in the bakehouse. Besides, he would not have known what to do with himself without some kind of work. He had never shirked from doing his best. But since the beginning of this new war the end was no longer in sight. The more you wore yourself out, the more there was to do and the less there was to show for it.

He always came back to that point. This anxiety obsessed him, as did his fear of the moment when his wife would call him to table. He had no difficulty in imagining what she was going to say. He thought up some replies, but knew quite well that at the crucial moment completely different words would occur to him. He had just put his cigarette-butt in his tin when he heard a footstep by the cart-shed door. Gaston raised his head. It was M. Robin, one of the tenants of the house behind the shed.

"I was coming over to see you and I heard you coughing," said M. Robin.

Gaston got up. M. Robin was a man of about thirty, with curly blond hair and a childlike face, a little on the pale side.

"We had to fetch in the firewood," said Gaston, "and so we haven't eaten yet."

"I've brought you the paper, but I don't think there's much in it. But I listened to the Swiss radio, and the Allies have reached Naples."

At the beginning of September, when the Americans had landed in Italy, M. Robin had come in saying, "This time the Jerries have had it." Gaston had been full of hope, but he had since realized that the War might last a long time yet. The Germans would not be beaten so easily. His greatest fear was that the front should come near them. The collapse of 1940 had saved his house, but there could be no guarantee that the War would end without involving the Jura. But for the moment he thought more about his immediate danger, and his neighbour's arrival presented a new means of putting off the reckoning.

"Come up into the house," he said.

"If you've not yet eaten I shouldn't want to disturb you."

Gaston insisted, and M. Robin went with him. Fernande had already laid the table and served the soup. "I was about to call you," she said, after replying to M. Robin's greeting.

Gaston sat down, saying, "Sit down for a while; you are in no hurry."

The neighbour sat down, and while the two old people began to eat he told them what he had heard on the wireless.

"The Russians have advanced too," he said. "And it looks as though the maquis in Haut-Jura have got hold of some weapons."

"I thought as much," said Fernande. "I heard planes a couple of nights ago."

"I didn't hear anything," said Gaston. "But if things are moving up there, then there'll be more people shot, like at Besançon last month."

"We now know," said M. Robin, "how many they shot—sixteen. They executed them on September the 26th. There was a young man of twenty-one, who came from my wife's part of the country. We saw his mother. I don't know how that poor woman is going to get over it."

There was a silence. Only Gaston went on eating. Fernande stared at M. Robin, whose disturbed face expressed grief and anger all at once.

"How old were they?" Fernande finally asked.

"I believe the youngest was seventeen and the eldest twenty-nine."

M. Robin was silent again. There was a certain awkwardness in the air, and Gaston wondered whether M. Robin had seen his son with the Militia men. He tried to think of something to say to break the silence. But M. Robin spoke first. "One day they'll pay for all this."

"In 1914 we said exactly the same," sighed Gaston, "and they did nothing of the kind."

"For heaven's sake, don't always talk about the past," said Fernande. "There's enough to do with all that's happening now." She had spoken in a firm, almost hard voice, and Gaston was afraid she was going to taunt him about his son's behaviour. For a moment he regretted bringing M. Robin into the house, but he recovered very quickly. No. It would not happen. His wife would not talk about it in front of a stranger. He could not imagine her doing such a thing. In spite of this he felt almost relieved when M. Robin got up. Fernande got up too and went with him to the door as she said, "I'm not listening in to London tonight. We have to get up very early tomorrow and—" she hesitated—"and finish some work."

"If anything important has happened I'll let you know," promised M. Robin.

She shut the door, fetched a plate with a piece of cheese, dry and grey like old plaster, and put it on the table. Gaston helped himself, saying, as he did at every meal, "Call that cheese!"

She waited a few seconds before replying, "Yes. But *your* grocer probably eats the best gruyère."

He had not foreseen that she might broach the subject from this angle. He reacted more violently than he would have liked. "What!" he cried. "You're not going to start that again. Whatever Paul does is no concern of ours. And, besides, that's your story, but . . ." He stopped. He had tackled it the wrong way. He felt this, and his wife's reply hurt him more than a pistol-shot.

"Up till now there was reasonable doubt. But now that he has the Militia men in his pocket he'll be able to deal in the black market as he pleases. He won't have to account to anybody. He'll not be short of petrol for his lorries. He doesn't care that his father has to half kill himself dragging in firewood on a cart!"

Her voice had become louder and louder, and her last sentence rang out clearly. Gaston felt himself turn white. His stomach heaved with nausea, and he had to make a great effort not to rush out banging the door. He felt it would be a foolish reaction. His wife might come after him, and if they quarrelled in the garden the neighbours would hear them. He suffered, not only because of her shouting, but above all because it seemed unfair to him that his son should be accused in this way. After all, he was not the only one supporting the Vichy Government. Were they the only ones in the wrong? Gaston had suffered too much in the War not to hate the Germans, but what about the English who bombed French towns? For a long time now he had refused to take sides. He could not see this involved situation at all clearly, and he had other fish to fry.

"I've already told you that I don't want to hear any more on that subject," he said in a firm voice.

"Oh, don't give me that! Haven't I heard you often enough saying that Julien has deserted? You're in no position to tell me to shut up."

Gaston sighed. "There's strife in every house that has children from different beds. And they expect nations to agree with each other!"

"Don't you try to turn the subject."

He suddenly felt his anger giving way to an immense weariness, which had nothing to do with the aches and pains brought on by the morning's work. "I'm not trying to do anything of the sort," he mumbled. "I know that you always end up having the last word."

His voice sounded weak. Fernande must have taken pity on him, for she seemed to hold back what she was about to say. She coughed, hesitated a moment, and then, putting her elbows on the table, she tossed her head and pulled a wry face, before replying, "You are right. There's no point in stirring up all this resentment. But at least you must admit that what happened this morning was not exactly pleasant."

All he could do was to raise his hands and let them fall again on the oilcloth as he whispered, "My poor wife. What do you want me to do about it?"

"Nothing. There's nothing we can do but forget the shame and hope that it won't go any further."

"And where would it go?"

She looked into his eyes. Her anger seemed to fan anew, and he regretted the question. However, she did not raise her voice as she explained, "Just now, when M. Robin was here and he spoke about the executions at Besançon, didn't you notice that it was as if he was holding something back?"

"I don't understand," Gaston declared.

"Do you know who arrested those poor people?"

"How should I know?"

"Well, it wasn't the Germans who took them. It was the French—the Militia . . ."

From the movement of her lips Gaston could see she had stopped short in the middle of a sentence. No doubt she had refrained from adding, "like those Paul was with this morning." He was grateful to her for being able to check herself. Come to think of it, she wouldn't hurt him for the sake of doing so. If she had lost her temper it was, no doubt, because the scene at the tobacconist's had upset her so much. On the other hand, what was Paul up to? He should not get involved in politics when he was in business. Could it really be true that he had spoken to her like that? Gaston wanted to ask his wife exactly what Paul had said when she had gone without buying a photograph, but he was afraid of provoking another outburst. He only said, "He shouldn't have done that. And you shouldn't blame me."

"It gave me such a shock."

Gaston thought she was going to cry, and he dreaded her tears as much as he feared her anger.

"You're overtired with hauling the wood," he said, "and

I'm exhausted too. If we're going to this place tomorrow we'll have to rest."

"You go on up. You know I can't sleep in the afternoon."

He had longed for this moment when he would at last be able to retire without looking as though he were running away, and now that the moment had come he no longer had the strength to leave his chair. He looked at his wife. There she was, quite near him, as tired and no doubt also as unhappy as he. What would she be thinking about? Normally, as soon as they had finished their meal she would get up and clear the table and wash the dishes. Today she was sitting there motionless, as though flattened by the silence that thickened around them, filling the room and seeping out through the walls to envelop the house and overflow into the town. Were they going to live like this, paralysed by the weight of their suffering, which was harder to endure than the work ahead?

He took a deep breath, pushing back his chair as he slowly got up. "If I shouldn't wake up, call me about four. I have to oil the cart before they come and fetch it. And then I'll have to find something to tie up the branches. And I must sharpen the billhook."

"My poor Gaston, I wonder if we should have accepted. It's not the sort of work you should be doing now."

Gaston suddenly felt comforted. The work reassumed its importance. It would always be less troublesome than any other aspect of life.

"Bah!" he said. "We won't be able to manage much, but it'll help."

He went towards the staircase. As he was about to put his hand on the banister he saw his wife's hat still there on the knob.

"Shall I take your hat upstairs?" he asked.

"No," she said, "leave it there. I'll go and get your tobacco at about six. Most people will have been, and it won't be as full as this morning."

7

Gaston Dubois had kept the habit of going to bed after the midday meal from the days he was a baker. He did this the whole summer season, preferring to get up at dawn, and then using the day until nightfall. On this particular afternoon he could not sleep. He kept dozing off, only to wake up with a disturbing sensation of coming up suddenly from the bottom of a dark and narrow pit. The shutters were half closed, and daylight, still subdued, came into the room picking out the metal bar of the bed with a green reflected light. His eyes half closed, his head sinking into the two pillows, Gaston stared at this reflection, which softened out of focus as his eyelids drooped. His tiredness was lulled like water becalmed, but he knew that as soon as he got up it would again be stirred into a mire.

His wife was probably in the garden. No doubt she would clear the beds he had decided to dig and sow before winter set in. She must be thinking about Paul and that stupid incident that morning. She had never been very fond of the boy, who had not liked her either. That was how it was. Paul had never been really unkind to her. He just lived his own life! True that his table was better provided than their own. It was to be expected, after all. His business was successful; he knew how to manage his affairs. How could you begrudge him that? He never helped his father. But did Julien ever think of them? Had he ever made any attempt to come and give them a hand? After all, he was a man now, twenty years old. Fernande protected him. She did not love him wisely. She had always spoilt him. She was too good. Perhaps she was too good to everybody, but her love for this boy sometimes blinded her and made her unfair. When she got angry she always put the blame on her husband. What had he had to do with it? Nothing! He just worked and made no demands. His life had been spent working, just as he used his spade through the seasons, always turning the same earth. Since he was twelve he had been no more than a beast of burden working for its food. He had started with his father, and since then he had never been out of harness. The only pleasant experience in all his life was his two years' military service. Called up in '93, there had still then been a chance of drawing better stakes.

Only two years. In the 44th Infantry Regiment. Because he was the best athlete in the regiment he had been sent to Joinville. He could have re-enlisted, made a career as an instructor. That sort of work did not ruin your health, and led peacefully towards a secure retirement. He had thought about it, but when his father died there had no longer been any choice. His mother was alone. As soon as he was discharged he had taken up the bakery and the rounds. Penal servitude! Since then he had had no leisure. He had never been in charge of his own life. Work had always taken charge of him. Year followed year, each with its tasks chaining him down, each bringing nothing unexpected, unless it were unpleasant. Nevertheless he had found pleasure in his work. If there was one thing he missed from his younger days it was the long nights at the bakery, shaping and baking the bread that people came to buy from miles away. And the brioches on Sundays! Suddenly the room seemed to fill with the hot and mellow smell which streamed from the oven door the moment the golden orbs were taken out, baked in thick paper cases on which the women burnt their fingers as they peeled them off. His mouth watered. He had never been greedy, but the thought of that bread and the brioches really excited him. Who then would have dared tell him that one day they would be baking bread made of bran and sawdust in his oven? He was glad he was no longer a baker. At least he could grow real vegetables and pick healthy fruit in his garden. If he had had to handle that grey putty and then sell it as bread he would have died of shame.

As this word came to his mind he remembered what his wife had said about Paul.

Did he really feel that his work was more important than what his son might do? A wave of anger seized him as he asked himself whether she had not turned against him. Yes, she had! What harm was there in liking your job? He had always striven to do his best. No-one had ever been able to find the least fault with his work. How many bakers could say as much? He had had assistants who had been with other bakers and who had laughed at him to his face because he would not use any methods that were not strictly beyond question. There are no two ways about being honest!

He was well aware that others grew rich by cheating wherever they could and diddling everyone. Nowadays that sort did it with money, and were without a care both in war-time and winter. Honesty was no substitute for bread and warmth. Nevertheless it was an achievement to have been able to get your body through seventy years without owing a penny to anyone. The opposite was true in his case. If all the people who still owed him for a loaf of bread were to come and pay there would be some crowd in the garden. He still met a few in the street. Some of them went to church more often than to the cafés, and were held up as models of virtue. As for himself, he had never had any need of religion to lead a righteous life. He had never gone off the rails, because any idea of behaving otherwise had never entered his mind.

So here he was today, worn-out and miserable, trying to sleep so that his tired body might regain enough strength to carry on a bit further along his inflexible path; to carry on alone as he had always done without expecting help from anyone—not that it had ever occurred to him to expect it.

8

It was six o'clock in the evening when the forester's lorry came back and stopped outside the garden. Gaston was filled with anxiety the moment it had driven off with the cart, heading for the clearing where it was to spend the night with no-one to mind it. He said to his wife, "We didn't consider the whole thing carefully enough! I could have gone with them. There's a hut where I could have slept."

"No," she said. "It would have been too cold. It's bound to be a ramshackle and draughty old place."

"All the same, leaving a cart like that in the middle of the woods."

"Poor Gaston, don't worry so much about a cart. Who d'you think would want to lumber themselves with that old thing?"

She had already put on her hat and taken her basket.

"I'll go and get the tobacco," she said, "and then I'm going on one or two errands."

"Good. I'll go and see to the rabbits."

He watched her going away. She really was a bit odd, making a fuss about a few little jobs, and then not being in the least concerned about a serious matter. He was well aware that his cart was not new—it was almost as old as he—but it still worked. It was strong, not too heavy, and when you fixed on the extra rails it could hold a sizeable load of hay or branches. Fernande was definitely wrong if she thought there was no risk in leaving such a cart for the night in the woods, three miles from town. It might prove a great temptation to a farmer or a woodman. Then there was the rope. It was a strong and supple piece of rope, seven yards long, that could not be bought nowadays. No, he had most definitely been wrong in letting the cart go. He should at least have removed the rope. One never considered such matters with enough care. Gaston now felt he would not be able to sleep. He had already missed his sleep that afternoon because of the scene about the Militia. Tonight he would turn and twist in his bed again—and they had to get up early in the morning. Something always happened to make a mess of his life!

He took a folded sack from the top of one of the rabbit-hutches under the little wooden shelter at the side of the house, and went towards the cart-shed to fetch some hay. In the shed he saw the empty space where the cart usually stood. For the first time in his life the place looked empty. Normally he did not see it in this state. As he was the only one who ever used it, he would never be there when it was out. For years it had been like that—the one pulling the other. They had made many a journey together—the vegetables they took to market, the fresh grass and hay they went up to fetch from the hillside at Montciel, journeys with logs, potatoes; not to mention the daily carting of wood from the shed to the bakehouse when he was still a baker. Never, until this evening, had he thought so much about his cart. It had played an important part in his life. Come to think about it, it had done as much work as he had—like him, without ever complaining. He had spent half a century pulling it around all over the place, greasing it, repainting it so it would not wear out, and now today, without giving it a thought, he had let it be taken away on a lorry to spend a night in the open forest, a prey to all-comers. He had behaved like an irresponsible youngster.

The more he thought about it the more he was convinced he would never see the cart again. Tomorrow morning they would go up into the forest, they would find it had disappeared, would look for it everywhere, and there would be nothing further they could do but come down here again. There would be no hard work cutting the wood, as there would be no means of getting it back. And Fernande would be sure to say, "There you are, if your boy had helped us with his lorry this would never have happened. You would still have your cart." It would be her victory. Basically she would be right. He realized that. But how could one ask a wholesale grocer to sacrifice his driver's time, and then run the risk of getting his lorry smashed up in the forest for the sake of a few logs? If he had gone and asked him Paul would probably have replied, "My drivers have bloody well got other things to do. Why don't you burn coal like everyone else?" Would he understand what their life was like? Would he see that the expense of converting the range was too great for them?

Gaston had taken down his sack of hay and attended to the rabbits. Now, as the evening slowly rose up from the earth, he was standing at the corner of the house, completely absorbed by his thoughts about the cart. The lorry should be in the forest by now. Only a short while ago they had had to ask the baker's assistant to help lift the cart on to the lorry. With the four of them, each taking a wheel, they had had some difficulty as the lorry was tall. A good cart is light when it is rolling along on its own wheels, but when it has to be lifted, that is another matter. Picaud would be alone with his assistant when it came to unloading. They had promised to use the rope to steady it and to take very great care, but they were young, both of them. A cart was of no great value to people like that. It was strong enough, even if his wife did call it antique, but if it fell on one wheel it would be sure to break. On the other hand, if it had a broken wheel no-one would bother to steal it. But what was he going to do tomorrow morning with a broken cart? And then, if people saw a broken cart lying around in the forest they might think it had been abandoned and help themselves to a wheel or to the brakes or to the rails or to seven yards of good rope.

He had had all day to think about it, and only now when it was too late had he seen the risk. The cart, no doubt, was already on its own in the forest, perhaps with a broken wheel or a shattered shaft. That shaft was not very strong any more. The bolts that held it had worn the wood a little. There was some play in it, and the pegs which he had driven in so hard would scarcely hold it. If the shaft let them down when they had loaded the logs they would be in a right mess! This adventure was quite unsuited both to their age and strength. They had not considered the matter carefully enough before committing themselves. It might possibly prove more expensive than buying coal and having the range converted.

Gaston Dubois walked slowly over to the corner where the two paths met, and took the tin with the tobacco that young Picaud had given him from his pocket. He rolled a cigarette, which he held between his lips for a moment before lighting it.

It was growing darker. Shadows were advancing across the black earth of the plot. They slipped round the edges of the piles of red-brown leaves blown through the bordering flagstones by yesterday's wind. The piles lay on the earth like neglected islands of light. The peach-trees too, as yet with yellow leaves, were brighter than the heavy sky. Gaston turned towards the setting sun.

Behind Montciel the sky was lighter, turning red. There was still no breath of wind, yet there was a fair hope that the dry north wind might rise during the night and clear the weather.

9

It was almost dark when his wife came back.

"We shall have to light the lamp now if we're going to eat," said Gaston.

"I can't help it. I wasn't able to get done any quicker. I had to find something for us to eat when we go up to the forest tomorrow."

"Did you get anything?"

"Yes, I got a little pâté and some brawn. We'll take hard-boiled eggs and fruit."

"Why don't you just heat up the rest of the soup for tonight? I don't want too much. I'd sooner go to bed early."

"If you'd rather, but we'll have to eat something more substantial tomorrow morning before we leave."

They were now in the kitchen, and while she lowered the oil-lamp to light it he closed the shutters and windows. When the wick had been adjusted and the lamp pulled up again Fernande lit the fire and put the soup on.

"Did you get the tobacco?" asked Gaston.

"Yes, I've got two packets out of your ration and two out of mine. If we saved one of them I could try to get some butter for it."

He did not reply. There was nothing he could say. His wife had every right to do as she wished with the tobacco that was part of her ration. She had never smoked, but he knew of some women who smoked as much as a man. Last month M. Robin had given him a packet of cigarettes. Perhaps he would give him another this month too. Then, counting his little store . . .

The soup was now simmering on the stove, and Fernande put two plates and two spoons on the table as well as the grey bread that made your stomach turn just to look at it.

"Did you remember bread for tomorrow?" Gaston asked.

"Yes, it's in my bag. I'll get it all ready tonight."

"We'll have to take the big haversack. I'll put my billhook in it too."

"Won't all that be a bit heavy?"

"No—because you are going to carry the roll of wires."

Gaston was still thinking about his cart and the whole venture which seemed to him increasingly foolish. However, he dared not speak about it for fear that his wife might mention Paul and his lorry again.

She dished up the soup, and they began to eat in silence. Between mouthfuls he would occasionally stop and listen. If the north wind rose the chance of rain would be negligible.

They had almost finished when Fernande put down her spoon and leaned back in her chair.

"What's the matter?" asked Gaston.

"You heard nothing?"

"No. It's the wind rising. That means we'll have—"

She interrupted him.

"No, it's not the wind; it's someone coming."

"But I locked the gate."

"It must be one of the neighbours coming round the back way."

"They never leave us alone," grumbled Gaston.

He heard the footsteps when the visitor turned the corner of the house and was approaching the front door.

"It's not M. Robin," said Fernande, "and it's not M. Durelet either."

She got up and went to the door. The feet were coming up the steps.

"It's bound to be someone who knows their way," said Gaston.

He suddenly felt disturbed. A visit at this time of night did not augur well. It flashed through his mind that maybe the forester's lorry had turned over in a gully, and they were now coming to tell him that the cart had been smashed to pieces.

Fernande opened the door as the visitor reached the top of the steps. Gaston could see by her face that this visit was unwelcome. Her eyes were hard, and she frowned as she stepped back without a word to let Paul in. He greeted them breezily. "Good evening! Hope I'm not disturbing you?"

"Oh, it's you," said Gaston. "You came the back way?"

"Had to. You lock yourselves up pretty early."

By the tone of his voice and the unnatural brilliance of his eyes Gaston could see that his son had been drinking. He knew this was happening more frequently, and it pained him. Several friends had said to him, "Here, your son's not exactly teetotal, is he?" They laughed as they said it, but Gaston, who had not in all his life drunk more than a moderate amount, had never tolerated any drunkard amongst his friends. However, he had tried not to listen to the gossips.

From the moment his son had crossed the threshold he had felt his heart contract as he realized that the battle with his wife would now start up again. He had forgotten about it till this moment. He looked hard at his son as he said to himself, "He has been drinking. So it's true. My boy has begun to drink. Oh, my God, my God!"

Paul, who had pulled up a chair, sat down as he said, "Finish your soup. It will get cold."

Gaston swallowed a spoonful. Fernande was about to sit down when Paul asked, "Look here, Mother, aren't you going to offer me a glass of wine before you sit down?"

She stopped, and was about to turn round when Gaston cried, "No! You've had enough to drink!"

Paul looked embarrassed. His thin face screwed into a grimace, showing up the uneven redness of his prominent cheekbones. Gaston looked at him more closely, and noticed that his eyes were bloodshot. That meant he really had been drinking.

Fernande was still standing and seemed to be waiting, not knowing what to do. Gaston looked at her. He had spoken with some passion. Now he wondered if it had not been a mistake putting her in the right about this boy whom she already detested. Paul had pushed his little brown hat with the turned-up brim to the back of his head, uncovering some of his thinning hair. "Well, that's it," he sighed. "When my father refuses me a glass of wine I've seen the lot."

"I refuse you nothing," said Gaston. "But you've already had enough to drink. That's all too obvious."

"I've been drinking because we've been meeting people all day long who've insisted on inviting us to drink with them." He looked at Fernande. "People whose opinions are different from yours, who are not in favour of selling France to the English!" As he spoke his voice grew louder. Fernande, still standing, turned towards her husband. The anger in her eyes gave way to a flash of distress which quite shocked Gaston.

"Shut up, Paul!" he cried. "If you've come here to talk politics it would be better if you went home to bed!" His voice was trembling, and he knew it. He fought hard against the anger boiling inside him. He looked at his wife and Paul in turn, and then he shouted at them, "Neither of you ever leaves me alone. I spend all day working myself to death, and then you come and mess up my few hours of peace!"

As though reassured when he realized his father was not blaming him alone, Paul seemed to relax. He settled down in his chair. He pushed his hat back a bit further, so that it looked like a dark halo around his face, and took out a packet of cigarettes and a lighter from his pocket. He tapped a cigarette on the edge of the table, lit it, and then flicked the packet towards his father so that it slid across the oilcloth. He said, "If it had been my idea to bugger things up for you I wouldn't have come. I came to do you a favour, and you welcome me as though I were a dog in one of your seedbeds."

Gaston looked at the packet. He fought against his hand, longing to reach out and take it. His glance shuttled from the blue packet to his son's face, and then to his wife's. Paul asked, "You given up smoking?"

"No, except in the evening."

"Go on. Take one."

Gaston made a reluctant gesture. He took out his packet of papers, broke a cigarette in two, and opened one half as he said, "I roll my own. The paper's not so foul."

Fernande, who was still standing, cleared the plates without finishing her own soup. When she came back she placed a half empty bottle of wine and two glasses on the table. Gaston looked at her. Was she going to be more tolerant than he? Was she behaving this way because Paul had said he was going to do them a favour? What did he mean by that, anyway? Had he heard about the logs in the forest, and was he going to offer to fetch them in a lorry? If that was the case Fernande would no longer be able to say that he and Micheline were completely selfish.

Gaston had finished rolling his cigarette. He lit it and drew on it. He had hardly touched his ration today.

Fernande poured the wine. She half filled Paul's glass, and Gaston said, "Just a drop for me. You know I never drink apart from meals, especially in the evening."

"You're wrong, you know," said Paul. "Some days, if it wasn't for wine—"

"You know I don't like to hear you talk that way," said his father. "What is it you have come to tell us?"

Fernande had just put on the table a small brass ashtray which Gaston had made out of a shell-case in 1916. She sat down again, but looked as though she were half-perched on her chair, fearing it might break under her weight. Paul drank half his wine, blew a cloud of smoke across the table, and said, "I've come about what happened this morning."

"Now listen—" Fernande had started to interrupt him, but Gaston stopped her.

"Let him speak," he said sharply. He saw that his wife was making a great effort to keep quiet and remain seated.

"Yes," Paul continued, "I told Micheline the story at lunch-time. She told me off. She said, 'I know Mother well enough to realize that she's the first to be annoyed and worried by it all. Just because Julien has made a mess of things, there's no need to take it out on her.'"

Now Fernande sat up in her chair properly. She straightened up fully, and Gaston saw he would not be able to stop her.

"Julien has done nothing foolish," she cried. "He joined the Army at the time of the armistice because he felt it was the right thing to do. When the Germans invaded the free zone and he realized they were going to be picked up or made to work for the Germans he left. That's all there is to it."

As soon as she had finished Paul began to laugh. "Left!" he said. "What a way of putting it! He deserted, and that's quite a different matter. And he probably deserted in order to get to England, like a lot of other idiots who don't know what's in store for them."

"If you know where he is," cried Fernande, "then how fortunate for you! I'm his mother and I, for one, would like to know."

Her voice faltered. She was not crying, but she must have had a lump in her throat and her eyes were full of tears. There was a short silence. Paul, in his drunkenness, had to search for words, and Gaston took advantage of this to interject, "I thought you said you'd come to do us a favour."

"Exactly. And it concerns him. If he is still in France it'd be better if he showed up now, rather than wait for the police to pick him up. It would be best for him as well as for you."

Fernande got up. Her whole body began to shake, and her hands on the table were like two wild beasts ready to pounce. Gaston was frightened. There was no time for him to get a word in.

"If you have come to ask me to denounce my son to the Militia," she cried, "then you can arrest me, you can shoot me, but you'll never get a word out of me!"

This time she had swallowed back her tears. A terrible anger lit up her face. She turned towards her husband as she continued, "And you let him talk like that under your own roof! You let him threaten us without lifting a finger to stop him!"

Gaston felt very small and lost. He was weary and sick. He wished he were far away on the other side of the world, or even under the earth, where you find everlasting peace. What should he do? What should he say?

Fernande fell back on to her chair. She looked exhausted, but her hands still trembled on her knees, and her eyes were suddenly devoid of all expression.

"You haven't understood me," said Paul in a calm, almost gentle voice. "You know quite well they are looking for Julien, and not without reason. You're welcome to think I dislike him. You're too stubborn to convince otherwise, but do you really believe it'd give me any pleasure to see him arrested? Do you believe it would suit us any more than it would you?"

"In other words," sighed the old woman, "you're thinking of yourself."

"You're being unfair," said Gaston gently.

Paul stopped him with a movement of his hand. "Even admitting that I'm only thinking of my father and myself, if it is still possible to save Julien from going to prison we mustn't wait for him to be arrested. He must come back of his own accord and say, 'I've been stupid, I admit it, I was carried away.' And then, I'm not sure how, but it should be possible to find a way of saving him from his mistake."

Gaston was looking at his wife, who had turned towards him. She looked lost. Paul must have seen his advantage. He went on, "Politics apart, don't you think it's better to stay within the law?"

The two old people were still looking at each other. Paul waited a few moments before concluding, "Believe me, it would be much better to tell him to come back while there's still time."

"But I told you," said Fernande, "I told you. I assure you that no-one knows where he is."

"You're not going to tell me you've never heard from him?"

It was on the tip of Gaston's tongue to explain that all they had heard was when they received a postcard last August from Toulon, with no address on it. It said no more than "All's well." Since then, silence. An endless silence which tormented them both. He restrained himself. The look his wife had just sent him prevented him uttering another word.

"Well," sighed Paul, "you alone can judge."

"But we've told you we've had no news at all," said Gaston. "Do you think we like not knowing where he is?"

Paul smiled disbelievingly. Raising his hand to stop them talking, he said in a superior tone that annoyed his father, "I have done my duty. I have warned you. I had no wish to be accused of not caring about Julien. He is only my half-brother, but that's no reason for letting him down."

He got up, picked up the cigarettes and lighter from the table, put his hat on properly, and said again, "Well, that's all I wanted to tell you."

As Paul made for the door Gaston got up and said, "Wait, I'll get the key to the garden gate and come with you. It'll be easier than going the back way."

Fernande had already opened the door. Their eyes met, and Gaston could see that she was disturbed. As Paul was already outside at the top of the steps he said loudly enough for him to hear, "You see, everyone thinks we've heard from him. But there's been nothing—nothing. If only we knew where he is!"

10

The night was very dark. After closing the door Gaston groped about looking for the banister. He heard Paul's feet shuffling on the steps. "Take care," he said. "You can't see a thing."

"I don't come here often, but I still remember the way."

At the foot of the staircase he knocked against his son's shoulder. As he drew level he smelt the drink on his breath. They walked on a little without speaking, and then, after much deliberation, Gaston asked, "Why do you let yourself drink so much? You'll ruin your health."

"It doesn't happen often, but today we've been running all over town getting rid of those photographs."

"I wanted to talk to you about that. Do you really think it's the sort of thing you should be doing?"

He was aware that his son stopped. He stopped too. Now that his eyes had grown accustomed to the dark he was beginning to make out his face—a lighter blob under the dark hat.

"Now see here," said Paul. "You're not going to tell me that you're in favour of de Gaulle and revolution?"

"I'm not in favour of anyone. I'm in favour of trying to live and getting the buggers to leave me in peace."

The tone of their voices was hard, although they did not raise them much.

"Exactly. You want to live in peace, and that means living with those who are strongest."

"Do you think they'll always be the strongest? Look at what happened in Italy."

"Italy? That doesn't mean a thing. Don't you remember how the Ritals pissed off to Caporetto in 1917! Hitler was wrong to trust them. They collapsed at the first serious attack, but the S.S. drove the Americans back into the sea quickly enough."

"In 1917," Gaston remarked, "there were also those who didn't believe in the Americans. And yet—"

Paul interrupted: "You really don't believe that Stalin will get on with Roosevelt and Churchill in the long run? Sooner or later they'll come to blows, and it'll be Hitler who wipes up the mess. Otherwise we stand a good chance of having the communists down our neck. And then you'd soon see what would happen to your few shacks and the twopence-ha'penny you've saved."

Gaston had always been aware of the threat of communism. During the Popular Front days he had trembled for his few possessions, and the boy's words had reawakened his old fears. "You know," he said, "I'm not a big capitalist."

Paul's hard, mocking laughter grated on him.

"Big or little, you'll still be good for a fleecing, and end up in the old people's home."

"Sometimes I think I'd be better off in there. At least the food is put in front of you, and you don't have to kill yourself working and still go short."

Paul took out his packet of cigarettes. Gaston understood the gesture.

"I've enough for my tobacco, though," he said.

"Take it," said Paul, as he held out the packet. "It's all right, keep the lot."

Gaston thanked him. Paul was not as selfish as Fernande made out. He wanted to bring up the subject of the logs, but he did not dare. He merely said, as he took a cigarette from the packet, "You know, life isn't easy for old people like us. Money has become worthless."

He leant over the lighter that Paul held out. For a moment their two faces were quite close, separated from the darkness by their hands raised round each side of the flame, and as though sheltered under the peak of Gaston's cap which almost touched the brim of Paul's hat. When the lighter went out the brilliant after-image lingered a few moments in the black void.

"If you need money," said the son, "why don't you sell one of the houses?"

"Sell?"

"You don't get much rent, so why not sell, and you'll be able to eat till the end of your days."

Gaston was dumbfounded. It was almost as if his son had given him a violent blow in the pit of the stomach.

"God Almighty," he sighed. "How can you suggest such a thing! Does this mean you don't care if everything goes to strangers?"

"Of course not. But if you are short of money . . ."

Gaston started coughing, and when he had regained his breath he said slowly, emphasizing each word, "I haven't got much. But I still have two hands. They've kept me alive for sixty years, and they'll do so until I die."

They walked on in silence, and after a dozen steps or so the son said in an offhand way, "You know we'd look after you if you needed help. But if you decide to sell a house sometime we could perhaps arrange it so that it doesn't leave the family."

Gaston did not reply. He understood perfectly what Paul meant, but the idea had taken him by surprise. It is not an easy decision to sell property that has taken a lifetime to build up—even if it was to a son. Besides, there was his wife to think of, as well as Julien.

They reached the gate, and Gaston groped around trying to find the lock. He opened it and stood back to let Paul out. As he went Paul said, "Anyway, I mean what I said about Julien. If you can contact him see that he comes back as quickly as possible."

"I will, if we hear from him—"

Paul cut in, "I've no reason to doubt your word, but you must admit that his disappearance looks odd to everyone; and if the police get the idea of hauling him in . . ."

He did not finish. Gaston thought he had gone, but in fact he had taken only a couple of paces along the pavement when he turned and said, "Besides, if you did hear from him the police would know. They're sure to be watching your mail."

11

When Gaston got back to the kitchen, having first put out the half-smoked cigarette with his fingers and clumsily put it in the tin, Fernande had already prepared the haversack for the morning.

"Now all we need is the hard-boiled eggs," she said. "And the fruit. Remind me in the morning. It's better to leave it in the cellar till then."

"The billhook?" asked Gaston. "Did you wrap it up in paper?"

"Yes. What shoes are you wearing?"

"My walking boots."

"It's a long time since you wore them. Are you sure they won't hurt your feet?"

"No, I don't think so. I'll wear two pairs of socks."

"That's all very well in winter, but when the weather's warmer the feet swell."

"What about you? What are you going to wear? Remember your corns."

"There's no choice. Apart from clogs and my best shoes, I've only got one pair strong enough."

"Will they hurt your feet?"

"I hope not."

Gaston thought hard of something else to say. He was glad that the conversation had turned around the next day's expedition, as this kept him safe from another subject. As he could think of nothing more to ask, he hurriedly said, "We ought to be going to bed."

"You go on up. I'll get undressed and be with you."

He was surprised that she had not tried to say anything about Paul's behaviour. He hurriedly fetched his chamber-pot from the little cupboard under the stairs, then went up, saying, "We're sure to wake early, but perhaps you had better bring the alarm-clock. You never know."

Fernande agreed, and Gaston went on up the staircase, which, as he turned the corner, was engulfed in darkness. When he reached the bedroom he slid the pot under the bed in its usual place on the left and undressed in the dark, after he had closed the shutters. As his wife had said nothing downstairs, perhaps she was going to say something once she had got to bed. He dreaded this. He would have liked to go to sleep quickly, but he knew this was impossible. Too many things had happened during the day. They were all inside him like a sea in perpetual storm. He thought about the wood he had got in, which would certainly not last them through the winter. He thought about his cart taken away in the lorry, about his son's visit, about his other boy—he would at least like to know whether he was alive or dead. It was all whirling around in his head, adding to the exhaustion of a hard day—too hard to let him feel drowsy now. He was worn-out, but felt no sign of relieving sleep.

Fernande came up and went to bed without a word. For a long time the silence was broken only by the sound of their breathing and the creaking of the bed-springs when one of them moved in search of a better position for a tired body.

Gaston tried to lie quite still. If he did not move, then perhaps sleep would come more quickly, or at least his wife would think he was asleep. At all costs he must avoid any conversation. He knew that she would go on and on, or else become bitter. He wanted to go to sleep. To rest, to escape from all those things that were not part of his life and had nothing to do with his work. For a long time he pondered over what Paul had said: "Why don't you sell one of the houses? Then you'll be able to eat till the end of your days." What a thing to say! Selling property at his age in order to live! And his own son making the suggestion! Would Paul really think of buying one of his houses? And why? As an investment? Perhaps it was true he was making a packet. Fernande had been right. Ah well, if he was making a lot good luck to him. No need to be ashamed of that as long as he was honest about it. As it happened luck had favoured his business. Why should that be held against him? No reason for that at all. Now that times were more difficult he had to try and hang on harder, and he was right.

He was accused of black-market dealings. But who could boast they had never done the same? Who could throw a stone at him in these times when every single person was struggling to survive? Evil tongues told tales of him selling to the Germans. What about it? How could one refuse them goods when they paid for them? Last year, when so many of the wounded lodged at the *école normale* had died, some Germans had come here to order flowers. Fernande had to make up bunches all day. Would it have been possible for her to refuse? And this Militia. M. Robin said many terrible things about it, but then M. Robin condemned everything to do with the Government.

After all, it was only a new police force. It was accused of many more crimes than it could possibly have committed. At Lons it was obvious it had not enlisted the pick of the bunch. There were all sorts in it. But did M. Robin know the sort of people there were in the Resistance? He who only listens to one bell hears but one sound. Besides, Paul had not joined the Militia. If the Militia men had asked him to come and sell photographs of this Darnand, perhaps he could no more have refused than Fernande had been able to refuse flowers to the Germans. No, it was not very serious. Paul was not a bad citizen. Not as selfish as Fernande made out. The packet of cigarettes he had given him proved it. Almost full, it was. He had not given it to impress Fernande, because she was not there to see it.

The more he thought about it, the more he regretted that he had not spoken to his son about the logs. He was now sure he would have offered a lorry. What had finally prevented him asking was his wife. She was always so assertive, although she did not know a thing about it. It was an obsession with her. And now, because of her, the cart was perhaps already stolen—or broken or lost somewhere in the woods. Those were the woods where they said the young deserters from labour service hid themselves. Perhaps they might take the cart away. Not that they would need it. They would more likely sell it to some farmer, and then drink up the proceeds.

Fernande heaved over in bed, changing her position. Gaston, who had been forcing himself to lie still, had pins and needles in his right leg. He moved too, and Fernande asked, "You're not asleep?"

"Not yet, no."

"Try to sleep," she said, "or else you'll be too tired for the journey tomorrow."

Gaston sighed. She did not attempt to say any more. He moved about, trying to find a comfortable position for his head, and then, more relaxed, he at last let himself drift into sleep.

12

Gaston woke up and groped for his lighter, which he always put on a chair by the bed. He had only just lit it when his wife said, "You want to know the time? It's just struck four."

How lucky for her to be able to hear the dining-room clock from her bed! They both got up at the same time, and he hurried outside to look at the weather. The sky was clear, the stars were shining. A gentle wind was blowing through the leaves.

He came back into the kitchen, already filled with the smell of coffee.

"I still had a little of the real stuff left," said Fernande, "and it's ready. If there's any left over I'll put it in a Thermos."

Gaston rubbed his coarse hands together. They had become numb from lying still during the night.

"That's a good idea. It'll go down well after a cold meal."

This morning he felt less tense, almost happy about the day ahead, which looked promising and which would take them into a forest where he had not been for a number of years. Before the War he would sometimes go up as far as the first rise looking for mushrooms. Seeing the haversack on the table and his walking-stick hooked on the banisters, he had the illusion for a moment of being much younger and ready to relive a particularly pleasant time of his life. He had never taken a holiday, had never had much spare time, only a few simple pleasures, like a walk to Montciel on a Sunday afternoon. Or a school outing. And mushrooming with a few friends. Their greatest luxury had been to stop at a village inn and eat an omelette which was prepared while they knocked down a few skittles in the square. It was not much, but when he recalled these memories suddenly at the sight of a haversack, a walking-stick, and a pair of boots, a little warmth and strength spread through him.

They ate, drank their coffee, gave the rabbits a large pile of hay, locked the cellar doors, the cart-shed, and the house shutters, and set off. As he turned the key in the lock of the garden gate Gaston remarked, "It's many a year since we left the house empty for a whole day."

"It will be all right."

"Yes, I know, but—"

"I told Mlle Marthe that we were going away for the day. She's keeping an eye on it."

He looked up at the shutters, still closed, on the first floor of the house opposite. Mlle Marthe spent a lot of time by this window every day. Gaston did not like it much: she sat so still for hours on end. He could not understand how a woman, even if she was elderly, could live like that without doing any work. It seemed to him that without working life must be meaningless. He did not like the look on her face as she followed his movements to and fro. It seemed to imply: "All this work makes me feel quite tired, M. Dubois!" However, this morning he felt reassured at the thought that no-one could come to his house without Mlle Marthe's knowledge.

Walking in step, the two old people went up the rue des Écoles. The ferrule of his walking-stick and the hobnailed boots grated on the tarmac. There was hardly any sign of dawn. The street was empty, and when they passed the portals of the *école normale*, where a German soldier stood on guard in a sentry-box, they did not even look at him.

The haversack thumped against his buttocks with each step. His walking-stick felt light in his hand, and by the time they had crossed the town and left the park behind he was surprised to find he was not out of breath. They had kept up an even pace, without talking or leaving the middle of the road. It was not at all unpleasant, this walk before sunrise. It was good to breathe the fresh, sharp air, and as they turned in on the road to Pannessières his head rang with the old marching-song of the Sambre-et-Meuse regiment. Without realizing it he quickened his pace, throwing his stick a little higher at each step.

"You're walking too fast," said Fernande.

"You tired already?"

"No, but at this speed you'll get out of breath, and we shall have to stop and rest."

He slowed down and looked at her. Her features were already a little tense. Her left hand was clutching the roll of wire, which she had now placed over her shoulders. Now and again her right hand would go to her stomach and with a quick movement adjust her truss.

"You should perhaps rest for a moment," he suggested. "You know the way. As long as you get there by midday you could come on quite slowly."

She shook her head.

"Give me the roll, then."

"No, it's not heavy."

They now began to climb, following the road, which began to wind gently. Gaston looked at the clear sky getting lighter ahead of them, sharply outlining the wooded crest where the tracery of leaves shook in the wind. Soon they were high above the town behind them. They passed villages in the valley below on their left. He did not speak. It seemed to him now that his breathing came less easily. However, he kept up the rhythm, turning towards his wife more frequently, watching for signs of fatigue in her.

When they had passed the village of Pannessières and reached the main turning that overlooked the plain, the light broke through fully and shone on their faces. The sun had just risen above the forest. Gaston pulled the peak of his cap over his forehead, exposing the back of his head. It was as though an icy wet cloth had fallen on his neck. He had not even noticed that he was sweating.

"Would you like to stop for a moment?" he said.

"If you like."

"I want to piss, anyway."

This was not true, but was a way of not admitting that he needed a break. While he went over to the edge of the wood Fernande sat down on a rock at the roadside. When he came back he explained, "In the 44th, when we went on manœuvres in the hills, we always made our first halt here. Then we'd go as far as Vevy. And after that we—"

She cut him short. "Don't talk so much. Get your breath back. And wipe yourself a bit. You look soaked."

He took off his cap and dried his head with his handkerchief.

"I should have brought a spare vest. Then you could have changed when we got there."

"Don't worry. Once we're inside the forest we won't get cold."

As soon as they had left the main road and taken the one into the forest the air was not so sharp. When they came to a clearing the sun burned their skin as though it were a summer day. The ground varied. Sometimes it was uneven rock worn by the cart-wheels. Then there were deep ruts in the earth. Elsewhere it had been surfaced with pebbles which rolled underfoot. The track would rise upwards, then go downwards again, run along a higher level or a dip, only to go down and up again. The going was now hard, and Gaston had to stop several times in order to cough and spit.

"There you are," said Fernande. "We've been walking too fast. You're exhausted."

"Not at all. It's the change of air."

"It would have been better if we'd gone by the main road. It's further, but it's easier to walk."

"No. This way we save at least a mile and a half. But on the way back we'll take the road. I'd be afraid of the cart letting us down on this one."

They set off again at a slower pace and with frequent stops. Gaston walked in front as the track was narrow in places. He had shifted the haversack to the other shoulder, but refused to give it to Fernande, who still carried the roll of wire. In the undergrowth along the way scores of lizards, mostly out of sight, would scuttle under the dead leaves. During one of their rests Fernande asked, "Are there many adders around here?"

"That's the least of our worries!"

"You must be careful when you are cutting. They often hide under piles of branches."

"Don't you worry. I may be a bit hard of hearing, but I can see perfectly well."

The north wind was still blowing, but as though it feared to penetrate the woods. Instead it just combed the tops of the trees as it passed, tearing off huge armfuls of reddish-brown leaves on which the sun sparkled as they fluttered on their long way down to the ground.

When they reached a fork in the track Gaston stopped. "That's odd," he said. "It didn't look like this before."

"Have we gone the wrong way?"

"No, of course not. But it looks to me as though this road to the left turns back on itself after the bend ahead."

He said no more. He was trying to focus on his memory of the place, and now suddenly felt completely uncertain. Fernande looked at him anxiously, her face puckered in wrinkles under her old, loosely-woven straw hat, which she used for gardening. Her forehead, dotted with tiny specks of sunlight, shone with sweat. She wiped it off her eyebrows with the back of her hand.

"You are hot," said Gaston. "I thought this was no sort of work for you."

"Don't you worry about me. You just make up your mind which is the right way."

When she repeated that it would have been better to go by the road Gaston shrugged his shoulders and set off on the road to the right without being really sure that he was not mistaken.

"Are you certain this is the way?" she asked.

"Yes, don't worry. I shan't get lost in a forest I've known for fifty years."

In spite of this, without slowing down at all, he tried to get a glimpse through the tree-trunks of the track that had turned left, but the undergrowth was thick and he lost sight of it. He tried to estimate how long ago they had left the main road, but it was difficult. They had not walked at a steady pace: they had

had endless breaks, and so it was impossible to judge. According to the forester's directions he had been quite clear on how to find the place in relation to the main road, but from this angle it was not so easy. It had all seemed simple enough in his mind, but the forest was becoming more and more unfamiliar to him. He had thought of it as being much more level. The hours passed, and the sun rose, growing stronger and stronger.

Gaston took a long time to make up his mind before he stopped and took off his jacket, which he refused to hand over to his wife. He slung it over the haversack and shifted the strap over to the other shoulder. It hurt him a bit.

At each stop Fernande asked, "Are you sure we haven't made a mistake?"

Gaston was not sure of anything, but he persevered. They had gone too far to turn back, and he hoped that the track would eventually take them to the top of a high ridge where he might at least see the end of the road and get his bearings. He was now wondering whether they might not be going towards Briod. The position of the sun would indicate as much. After a while this idea took root, but he still hoped to find somewhere he could get a bearing on the main road. He had assured his wife too often that he would never get lost in the forest to retrace their steps deliberately, just like that, merely saying, "I was wrong."

As time passed, fatigue crept up his legs and tightened round his chest. His hand clutched the hard wood of his big walking-stick, the haversack got heavier, and the air thickened, almost impossible to breathe.

He stopped near a rock, sat down, and said, "We'll have a drop of wine. It'll give us new legs."

He began to open the haversack when Fernande raised her hand, saying, "Do you hear something?"

"No, only the wind."

Loudest of all he could hear the beating of his heart and the wheezing in his chest.

"There are some woodmen over there on the right, not far away."

Gaston listened, but could hear nothing but the moaning of the wind and the snapping of branches.

"I'm quite certain," said Fernande. "I'm going to have a look."

Gaston got up. "No, you'll get lost away from the track. I'll go." Although he said this, he was scared of climbing up the slope over rough ground.

"I can't get lost," said Fernande. "It's straight up the hill, so to get back I've only got to go downwards and I can't help but find the track."

Gaston tried feebly to restrain her, but his tiredness robbed him of all will-power. Sitting on his rock, he watched her going off with faltering steps, supporting a hand on a tree-trunk, lifting her foot high to stride across undergrowth. When she had disappeared he felt very much alone, utterly alone in this forest, and he blamed himself for not having stopped her going.

Since they had set off he had completely forgotten the sad thoughts of the previous evening. He had walked with pleasure at first. Later the going had been hard, but walking was all that mattered. And now he was beginning to feel lost again. Not because of the forest—after all, he knew well enough there was nothing to fear—but because of a mounting anxiety.

He would never succeed in getting in this extra wood. They had made so bad a start there were bound to be unexpected difficulties ahead. When he got there he would be sure to find his cart broken or gone. And then firewood did not cut itself. If the trees had been felled several months ago they would be half dried out and difficult to cut. He was no longer a youngster, nor was Fernande. What could they accomplish in a day? Ten, fifteen bundles at the most. It was a lot of hard work for very little gain. They must not leave too late and find themselves on the road in the dark. What was the track like from the clearing to the road? Picaud had said it was usable, but then he had oxen to draw his wood.

He left his rock to sit on another in the sun. The wind was not strong in the depths of the forest, but now and again a cold caress would reach down and chill his back. The few steps he took showed his fatigue was greater than he had realized when he had stopped. His knee-joints burned, and a shooting pain thrust from the back of his neck, breaking across his forehead. He deliberately breathed more slowly. This was no time to be ill. His wife would go out of her mind. A fine state of affairs.

What was she doing? She thought she had heard some woodcutters, had gone off impetuously, and would no doubt get lost, fall over a tussock, or go round in a circle and finish by coming down the wrong slope.

He forgot his fatigue. Now it was a mental anguish that tortured him. It was as though an eternity had passed since his wife had gone. This detour of hers would make them lose precious time. She was always so intent on her own ideas, always making idiotic mistakes. It had been like that for over twenty years. For Julien, as with everything, she always did exactly as she wanted. He should never have let her leave the track by herself, running after the sound of an axe that she had probably imagined. She did not know these woods. Anyone would get lost unless they were used to them. She might have fallen in a pot-hole, trodden on an adder. Heavens above, how stupid she was with her obstinacy!

Gaston fought against his anguish for a long time. He took the bottle of watered wine from the haversack and drank a gulp. Then he rolled a cigarette, which he lit and began to smoke, savouring each puff, forbidding himself to think of anything but the pleasure tobacco gave him. Truly his only pleasure. A pleasure that was worn a bit thin with rationing and the need to keep some of it back for barter.

He felt he was getting more and more numb, so he got up and went a little way into the copse where his wife had disappeared. The shadows, alive in the wind, were moving continually. Patches of light ran across the ground or stretched up against the tree-trunks. He listened in vain, could hear nothing but the continuing music of the wind.

"I've had enough of this wind," he moaned. "If she calls me I won't even be able to hear her."

For a moment he thought of going up to look for her, but he told himself that with even ten yards between them they might miss each other in the denser thickets. If she came back and found nothing but the haversack and the jacket lying abandoned on the rock she might get very frightened, go back up again, and so they would lose even more time.

He stood leaning against a large beech-tree for a time, his eyes tired from looking for his wife through the moving patterns of light and shade. Then, almost in spite of himself, he put his hands to his mouth and shouted, "Hey! Hallo there! Fernande! Fernande!"

He kept on shouting in several directions, but felt that his voice carried no farther than he could see. So he stopped and went back to sit on his rock.

He had no strength left. The shouting had emptied his head, had no result other than awakening the dormant pain in his chest. He had to stand up in order to cough, hands on his breast, head dropped forward, throat filled with phlegm, and his vision blurred with tears.

13

"Good God, you've been a long time," sighed Gaston when he saw his wife coming out from amongst the trees.

"It was farther than I thought," she said as she sat down beside him. "Sounds are deceptive in the forest."

There was a deep silence. Gaston had only just finished coughing and had difficulty in recovering, but he noticed that Fernande looked completely exhausted. Her face was running with sweat, her chest heaved in quick rhythm, and her back was bent as though all the weight of the forest were upon her thin shoulders.

"Well then, did you see anybody?"

"Yes," she said. "We took the wrong turning."

He had already guessed as much, but his fatigue was so great that this piece of news could make it no worse. He let a few moments pass before asking, "And is it far?"

"We have to go back to where the road forked, take the other track, and go right to the end of that."

He was tempted to say, "It's too far. Let's go back home." But there was the cart. He only had to think of that to recover the strength to go on.

"You've had enough," he said.

"I'm all right. Come on, let's go."

He got up and began to walk behind her. As he went his eyes were fixed on her thin legs and the hem of her grey skirt. So they would have to retrace their steps, and there would still be some way to go after that.

They had been walking since daybreak. All to no avail, because he had stuck to his track even after he had realized that it was not the right one. His wife had followed him. Then she had walked even farther, much farther, away from all paths while he had been resting, and on her return she had said, "We took the wrong turning." She had not said, "You were wrong." She had not uttered one word of reproach, nor had she implied any, and there she was in front, uncomplaining, without even saying that she was tired herself. True, she was younger than he. She did not have the chest trouble that clawed his lungs when he tried to breathe, but then she had a hernia which must drag her down at every step.

Gaston walked, drunk with exhaustion, his head slowly filling with a stupor that allowed the rest of his body to function like a piece of machinery, a little worn, perhaps, but continuing under its own momentum. Now and then he woke up enough to say to himself, "You ought to be in front. That's where you belong. She's already done more than you." But he said nothing. Walking now seemed easier, and he felt if he made any sort of change, if he broke the silence and the rhythm for only a moment, he would not be able to continue.

When they got to the fork Fernande stopped, and Gaston walked straight into her. "I'm going in front," he said in a voice scarcely audible.

She turned round, looked at him, and appeared horror-struck. "You can hardly stand up. We must stop."

"If we stop again we might as well give up." His voice was broken, and he was overcome with a fit of coughing, largely because he had tried to repress a kind of sob. Good God, he was not going to start crying. That would be the end. Then he would really be finished, not even a shadow of his old self.

Fernande made him sit down on a tree-stump a little way from the track. "Now we're going to eat," she said. "I'm sure it's long after ten. Then we'll feel better. I'm a bit giddy myself."

He realized she was lying. She did it for his sake. He knew this, but said nothing. He had no energy left, no strength to argue. The thought of the time wasted, the wood to be cut, the cart standing all by itself in the forest, was still with him, but far away, still and heavy like a stone at the bottom of a well—a stone sinking slowly into the mud, soon to be covered, and there would be nothing left but his own heavy fatigue.

She opened the haversack and set out the meal. At first he had difficulty in eating. His tongue was half paralysed, the saliva had almost dried up. He had to make a great effort to swallow and suppress a disgust he had never felt before. But when he had managed the first few bites and drunk half a mug he admitted that his wife had been right. She had realized that he was tired because he had had very little to eat before they left. He no longer felt as weak and exhausted as a short while ago. When you have been the best athlete in the regiment and have spent half your life hauling two-hundred-pound sacks, a few miles carrying a miserable haversack are not going to floor you. No, at seventy you cannot expect to be like a twenty-year-old, but that does not mean you have to collapse like a silly woman. You still have a bit in reserve.

As for work, there was no doubt he could not manage as much as in his youth, but he could still cut wood. He would prove it when they reached the clearing. He looked at his billhook. There it was, lying at his feet, its edge worn with chopping and being sharpened on the sandstone. He had made the handle himself. It was so polished with use that when he grasped it in his hand it seemed as though his fingers and palm were moulded to it. This old billhook would be good for a long time yet. He liked it because it was well balanced—not too heavy, but heavy enough to add its weight to that of the man who used it. A billhook made for woodcutting. Between them they would do a lot more work. Well-cut, straight pieces such as few youngsters nowadays could manage. He had wasted over an hour taking the wrong turning, but he would know how to make up for it.

The coffee, which was still hot, gave him back his enthusiasm. Now all they had to do was to find the clearing and hope the cart was still there with its four wheels intact, ready to carry the load as he himself felt ready to tackle his piles of branches.

When Fernande had gathered everything together he picked up the haversack. He walked with a firm tread, no longer like an exhausted old man.

14

No doubt because he was sure he was now on the right track, Gaston did not find the way to the clearing long. As soon as he saw the black roof of the hut in between the bare trunks of the ash- and oak-trees he hurried his pace.

"You're going too fast," panted Fernande.

"But we're there already."

He could feel his heart beating. He wanted to run. He saw the tarred felt roof, the board and timber construction of the walls, the piles of huge logs, the enormous tree-trunks lying amongst branches, and still no cart to be seen. His heart beat wildly, and not only because of the long distance they had covered.

"The cart. Oh, my God, my God, the cart!"

"What's that you're saying?"

He had spoken out loud without realizing it. "Nothing—it's nothing," he said as he strode on.

Now he completely forgot his weariness. His limbs no longer felt heavy with the effort of getting there. There was only one thing on his mind—the cart. He left the track as soon as they reached the clearing and made straight for the hut. He took great strides across tree-stumps, stumbled, got caught in branches. Blast those woodmen leaving everything in a clutter. He would have liked to leap across the piles of logs as he did in his youth. He went round them. His fear both spurred him on and held him back. The nearer he got, the more certain he was that his cart had been stolen. He tightened his grip on his big stick, while his other hand clenched the strap of the haversack. Heavens, what sort of men had felled these trees? The bastards! Would he dare go all the way? Go right round this hut on the edge of the forest?

"You must be mad," shouted Fernande. Her voice already sounded far away. "Don't go so fast!"

He took no notice. In fact, he pushed on even faster. Now there was nothing between him and the hut but a pile of wood which he passed. Nothing there. In front of the hut the ground was clearer. The earth was well trampled down. He paused, but his anger lashed him forward again. He went down the side of the hut and turned the corner. There it was as though all the air of the hills and mountains swooped into his being.

He stopped.

It was there—there in front of him, only a few paces away. He did not dare move. His eyes flew from one end to the other, from one wheel to the other, clambered like a squirrel the length of the shaft that lay like a luminous cross on the shadows of the undergrowth.

It was there, undamaged.

His eyes only just had time to take it all in before they filled with blinding tears.

Gaston took out his big checkered handkerchief and wiped his eyes. Fernande was behind him. He sensed rather than heard her.

"You were running like a greyhound," she said after a while. "What's the matter with you?"

Gaston thought she meant his eyes which he was wiping. "It's the sweat. It stings my eyes."

He took three paces forward, unhitched the haversack, picked up his cap, which had fallen off as he passed the strap over his head, and slowly walked round his cart. His right hand never left the edge of its floor. He leaned over each wheel as though performing an ancient rite. His eyes inspected the hubs where the pinkish grease glistened in the sun. He did not give a damn that Fernande was watching him. He wanted to ask the cart whether it had had a good journey, whether the foresters had not been too rough, whether it had been cold during the night. His mind was split in two, one half saying, "Gaston Dubois, you're an idiot. Here you are, seventy years old, and you're talking to a cart as though you were a little four-year-old talking to a clockwork train," while the other half was totally absorbed with the cart and did not listen.

After this close examination Gaston stood back to take it all in with a single look, and then turned towards his wife. She was sitting on a tree-trunk, not even looking at the cart. She had turned her back. She was no more concerned than she might have been if they had brought it up themselves. He found her indifference quite monstrous. Really, the woman had no understanding. To her, a cart was nothing but an old bit of rubbish, of no interest. If she had slept badly last night it was certainly not because of the cart standing all alone in the forest.

She got up. To begin with as her legs straightened, they pulled at her body, which looked as though stuck in a sitting position, the back seized up. It must have been her hernia pulling her forward, because her hands were holding her stomach. Slowly she straightened and then turned round. Her face wore a grimace of pain which slowly gave way to a painful smile amid all the wrinkles.

"Well," she said, "here we are. They put your cart behind the hut so it couldn't be seen from the track."

Gaston pretended to look unconcerned. "Nowadays, you know, people are too bone idle to go looking for a cart this far out."

Fernande's smile turned into a grin. Was she making fun of him? He shrugged his shoulders, and, taking the billhook from the haversack he had hung on the shaft, went towards the felled trees, saying, "There's more to it than that. But now it's time to get to work."

She took the haversack over to the shade by the hut, took off her cardigan, and picked up the roll of wire. Gaston had already stopped in front of a pile of branches. He spat into his hands, rubbed them together a little, took the billhook from his belt, and attacked the first branch.

15

They worked for a long time without talking. Gaston felt completely at ease. His legs firmly planted on the ground, he pulled the branches out of the pile one by one and cut them cleanly with his billhook—one or two well-aimed blows always at the correct angle right through the bark, giving a clean finish. They needed good, solid logs, not sticks. There would be enough kindling with the prunings from the fruit-trees. So he selected the best branches as thick as his arm. He had the size of his cart in mind, and that was the length he made them. He cut and trimmed and threw them. Fernande picked them up as they came and made them up into bundles.

"Don't make them too big," said Gaston, "or they'll be too heavy to load."

When the bundle was assembled she did up the wire roughly. "I'll tighten them later," Gaston had said earlier. "You won't have the strength."

When she had assembled half a dozen he hung his billhook on his belt, took the pincers, and came over to tighten the wire. He put his foot on the bundle by the loop through which the other end had been threaded. He pulled at it with all his might, heaving at the bundle when a branch appeared to be out of place. Before he went back to his cutting he took out his tobacco and contentedly rolled a cigarette.

"At this rate we'll soon have a full load."

"Would you like a drink?"

"No, I don't need one yet. We'll drink later on."

He lit his cigarette and said, "As you walk around you could be finding out what state the rest of the track leading to the road is in."

She gave him a sour smile as she observed, "Walk around! You know, I've done plenty of walking this morning."

"There's no need to go straight away. There's plenty of time. I'd rather know now so that we don't set off with load that'll get stuck in a bog."

She left the wires on a finished bundle, found a branch the length of a walking-stick, and went off. Gaston sat down for a moment to finish his cigarette and watched her retreating figure. She looked as though she found it heavy going, although the ground in the clearing was hard and dry. Her age was certainly no advantage to her. She was not as strong as he. He considered this with a sort of pride which made him forget the pain she must be suffering. He put out his cigarette and put it back in the tin, and set to work again.

Fernande was away for some time, and said when she came back, "It's a good three-quarters of a mile to the road. The track is in a worse state than the one we've come by. The oxen must have been through with some big and heavy carts when they took away the tree-trunks. There are ruts over a foot deep, and in one of the hollows there is deep mud."

"Oh, we'll get through that all right."

"I was thinking it might be better to go back the way we came."

"With a loaded cart? You don't know what you're talking about."

She made an ineffectual gesture. Gaston thought she must be exaggerating. Being tired, she was in no state to judge.

"The muddy patch—wouldn't it be possible to avoid it?"

"No, it wouldn't. There's no other open ground except the clearing here. The rest is dense forest. You can't get off the track. In this particular place it's thick with leaves. They keep the earth wet."

"If it's only in that one part, then we'll put down some branches and get across it that way."

"I really think you ought to go and have a look."

Gaston was enjoying his work. He had such strength in his arms and was so happy wielding his hook that he did not even reply. He had not come here to go for a walk, but to cut his firewood, and that was what he was doing. He had seen many a load in his time with this cart of his. The important thing was to get a well-trimmed load and not be distracted by anything. As it was, he was annoyed with himself for having wasted time on the way up. Now he had to do all he could to make up for it. He was also ashamed of his momentary weakness, and had decided to work so hard that he would forget it. Women always got worried before there was any need. If you listened to them you would never get anything done. Besides, his wife knew nothing about the forest. She was no judge: neither of the value of a good cart nor of his strength; she took him for a doddering old man. She had only to look at what he had done in her absence to realize how much he could tackle.

"Come on, now," he said sharply. "You get on with piling them together, and I'll tie them up."

He was now in a good working rhythm. He went steadily on, aiming each blow, sizing up with one look what to let fall, what was worth keeping. He imagined how much heat he would get from each trimmed branch. A good small log would give a lively heat and then leave enough embers in the grate on which to put a bigger one which would burn slowly with the draught shut down. This would make the logs Picaud had delivered last out. What a splendid idea that fellow had had!

The sun shone brightly in the sheltered clearing; the wind

kept up its autumn dance and sang through the tree-tops. They were lucky with the weather, which could not have been better, and must make full use of it.

He turned round. There were already a good dozen bundles.

"There you are," he said. "We're not lagging behind."

"Perhaps we should load those up now," suggested Fernande. "Then we can see how much it fills."

He began to laugh. "Don't you worry about the cart. It will take twice as much."

"That may well be. But what about us?"

"You don't think we're going back with only half a load?"

"Have it your own way."

She did not smile. She was always accusing him of being depressed, and now today it was she who was pulling a face, while he felt more alive and happy than he had for a long time.

He went back to the job. He was not working so fast now because of an ache in his wrist. It was not serious, but it still hindered his enthusiasm. It now took him two or three blows with the hook to get through a branch. Earlier it would have yielded with a single cut. Perhaps the wood here was too dry. He stopped for a moment and cast his eyes around, examining the other piles. Over there there were more leaves on the branches. They must have been felled more recently.

"You're moving on?" asked Fernande.

"Yes. The wood looks better over there."

"It will be further to carry the bundles."

"It's not more than twenty yards. You get me something to drink. And while you're about it, get me the stone in the haversack. I'll have a go at the hook."

While he waited for his wife he sat down on a tree-stump and put the tool on the ground. Grasping his right wrist hard with his left hand, he began to bend and stretch his fingers. He felt the ligaments moving. The ache lessened slightly, spread up his arm, and disappeared.

"Is your wrist hurting you?"

He had not heard her coming. "No, no, I was just loosening up my hand a bit."

"You've grazed your left hand."

"Bah, that's nothing."

He rubbed it against his trousers.

"You'll get it infected."

"There's nothing to be afraid of. Everything is clean in the forest."

They each had a mug full of watered wine. It had got a bit warm.

"The sun's beginning to go down," said Fernande. "The haversack was not in the shade any more."

He looked up at the sky. His wife must have guessed his thoughts, for she said, "You really should have brought your watch. One can never be sure—"

"It can't be much after three. I'll do what I planned, and then we'll load up."

When he got up he had to clench his teeth to stifle a groan. It was as though a blade had cut through his loins. He cringed, and the blade continued its cut up the length of his back, meeting the pain from his hands which mounted through his bone marrow to the back of his neck. Here these three powerful forces joined together, twisted themselves into a lash like so many thongs which pulled with a terrible strength as though to break his spine.

"Christ," he moaned, "I've dislocated something."

He hardly dared breathe. The rest had chilled his body. All his fatigue had been reawakened by this attempt to move once more. He made an enormous effort, grasped his wrist with his hard hand, and spat on the stone to sharpen the hook.

"Should never have stopped—never."

He put down the stone and attacked a branch. He was torn by brambles and stung by nettles at each stroke. He was a battlefield of various pains, each one vying for his muscles. Even as he struggled with the wood he had to fight against this continual torture.

He soon realized that the wood was no easier to cut here

than it had been elsewhere and that sharpening his tool had not brought back his skill. However, he steeled himself, clinging to the idea that he had not come so far only to go back with half a load. He had told Fernande that they would take back two dozen bundles. That was what he had said, and he was not going back on it. Nevertheless he turned more and more often to count the piles that she had lined up behind him. He had just counted eighteen when she asked him, "Isn't that about enough now?"

"I said two dozen," he moaned, hardly moving his lips. His face and body were covered in sweat. He put down his hook and took off his cap and shirt.

"Don't take your clothes off," said Fernande quickly. "You'll get cold."

"No, I won't. In fact, I'm taking off my vest, and it'll get dry, and I can put it on again when we go back."

She took the soaking-wet vest and laid it out on a woodpile in the sun. She said, "Poor Gaston, you ought to stop."

He put on his shirt and set to work. Next time he looked round he noticed that his wife was making the bundles a lot smaller. He felt like telling her it was a waste of good wire, but said nothing. He thought of cutting two extra bundles, if only to show her he was no fool, but when she told him they had got the number he wanted he drew a deep sigh and stuck the hook into a log near his vest.

"Couldn't we manage two or three more?"

He said it, but his tone did not invite a response. He knew in advance what his wife would say: "Let's load on what we've got first. Then we'll see."

He tightened the wires. That, too, was a painful job because, with its temporarily forgotten movements, it reawoke numb muscles with their dormant aches. It was like a huge and hungry fire rekindled. They came back, sharper and sharper. Gaston felt them coming. He anticipated their progress, watched for their climax. It was a sort of game, but the dice were loaded. All the rules were broken. No use him saying, "This time you won't get me," because one after another they tore into his flesh, which refused to give in; and he still went on working. He was not one of those whom exhaustion overtakes because they are not used to work. But the daily tasks in his garden were quite different. First, there had been the unending walk that morning, and now this job which he had tackled much too quickly. He had wanted to do it the way he used to. But then he used to be much younger, and when he went up into the forest it was only to get bean-sticks or stakes for the fence. He had thrown himself into work today in a frenzy just to prove to himself that he was still young. His body had let him down. In the excitement all had gone well, but exhaustion had accumulated, and now it was suddenly overflowing, adding to his fears for the return. He remembered what Fernande had said about the track that lay between them and the road. Had she really been exaggerating? Would the two of them be able to get the loaded cart out of the clearing?

When the bundles were finished they dragged them to the edge of the track and went off to get the cart.

At first, loading up was almost a rest. Lifting these firmly-tied bundles cheered him up. He took pleasure in counting them once more and in finding that they were not too long for the cart. It was a load to be proud of. Old people seeing them go through the town would surely say, "M. Dubois is still good at making faggots. He has the knack. And his cart is really loaded."

As the pile got higher he had to make a greater effort, stretching his muscles to the utmost. When he had hoisted the fifteenth he began to cough, and had to stop. Fernande rushed off to get him a drink, but it took some time before he got his breath back.

"We've taken on too much," she said. "There are far too many."

He knew she was right, but still he would not listen. "We'll put the cart alongside this pile of wood," he said. "I'll get up on top. You have only to lean the bundles against the pile, and I'll take them from there."

"You'll break your legs."

"Don't you worry."

It was as difficult for him to talk as it was to work, and he dreaded another fit of coughing. Fernande had to help him bring up the cart, which was already heavy. He put one foot on the hub of the wheel and climbed up on the woodpile. The logs were big, and it was easy for him to keep his balance. He was glad to see that the cart was already full up to the slats. He had truly made a good load. He had reckoned just the right amount. He got down, threw the rope across with a fine gesture, and tightened it until the cart itself squeaked. "We'll tighten it up again when we get to the road. The load will have settled by then."

Fernande pointed up at the sky as she said, "We mustn't be too long about it. It'll soon be getting dark."

It was true. The sun was going down, and the shadows were getting longer in the clearing.

"I'll put on my vest when we reach the road." They hung the haversack on one of the slats. Gaston went to the shaft and Fernande to the back.

"Right then," he cried. "Off we go!"

He threw his weight forward, pulling with all his might, and ignoring with a curse the pain that began to seize his back and arms. Once it had started the cart rolled joltingly over the dry ground. There was a slight dip, and all they had to do was to avoid the ruts and the bigger roots to keep it going without too much trouble.

When they got to the track itself it was much darker. The air was not so fresh, and he had difficulty in breathing. He would have liked to stop for a moment to get his breath back, but he noticed that the incline had changed. They were getting to a small hillock, and it would be better to make use of their impetus to get to the top. It was not a very steep slope, but nevertheless the pace slackened, and he cried:

"Hey-up!"

Maybe Fernande was not pushing as hard as she had to begin with. Now was not the time to stop and have a look. He pulled harder, but the track was narrow, and it became impossible to avoid obstacles. The front wheels struck so hard against a great big root partly worn away by other carts that Gaston felt for a moment as though his arms had been pulled out of their sockets. They might have cleared it, but they had lost so much speed that the rear wheels could not get there. The load wavered, Gaston stiffened himself, throwing all his will-power into the effort, but the dead weight of the bundles was the stronger. There was a slight recoil, and he cried, "Hold on!"

They let the cart run back till the front wheels were wedged against the root when he shouted, "Put on the brakes! I'll hold it."

She turned the handle, and when the iron brake-shoes had engaged he let go of the shaft. "Dirty great root," he moaned.

Fernande held on to the side of the cart with one hand, the other on her stomach, as though wanting to knead it. Her face was red and shone in spite of the shadow cast by her hat. There was a long silence filled only, for each of them, with the storm of their bodies. "We'll never get through," she panted.

Gaston, who was frightened by the approaching dark, was obstinate. "We've got to, dammit!" He looked around and walked a few paces to pick up a branch. He broke off the thinner end and slid it down between the slats and bundles of wood at the rear. "If we should stop on a hill again, prop this against the wheels. It'll be quicker than putting on the brake. Come on now. We'll try again."

He held on to the shaft like grim death while Fernande took the brake off, and when she had told him she was ready he cried, "Hey-up, let's go!"

With a big and well-timed effort they got over the obstacle and reached the top of the hillock without stopping. In spite of the half-light he was aware of a greater unevenness ahead, but the rise on the other side did not look too rough. If only they could get up a good speed all would be well. Pushed by the load, he began to run. The cart jolted about, the shaft shook his arms, but he knew that all would be well, for the cart as much as for his old body.

When they were a few yards from the bottom he realized

that this must be the place where Fernande had noticed the boggy ground, but they were going too fast to stop. They would have to take advantage of their speed to get through.

"Hey-up!" he shouted again.

It was as though Fernande was not pushing at all. As soon as they got to the level part the cart seemed to be loaded with lead. It slowed up, slowed up, and stopped, in spite of all the old man's efforts, though he felt the ground was more or less firm under his boots.

"Blast it!" he roared. "It's not bloody well possible." He let go the shaft and turned to see the four wheels bogged down in the sides of the track, where the earth was very much looser than in the middle.

Anger flooded through him, and he began to shout, "Now we're in a right mess! Why didn't you tell me it was here that we might get stuck! I'd have come to have a look and put some branches across this dungheap!"

His cough seized him, and he had to stop. When he was able to hear again Fernande explained, "This wasn't the place. There's a much worse one further on."

Gaston threw up his arms. "It must be a swamp, then. You might have told me—"

"But I did tell you."

"You didn't tell me a thing. You wanted me to come and have a look. As though I had time to waste. If I'd come it wouldn't have been worth both of us going wasting our time. You wouldn't have wanted to cut the wood! You've got us into a proper mess, you poor woman—and it won't be you that gets us out of it."

He realized he was being unfair even as he spoke. It had been wrong of him not to listen to her, but this was the second time today she had been right, and that was too much for him—especially when it concerned things that he knew more about. He knew he was being unjust in blaming his wife, but his anger had got hold of him. He had energy for nothing but to feed this anger. It spoilt so much, but would need a far greater strength than the flood of his anger to stop it.

Fernande said nothing. She waited as always, staring straight at her husband. All her look expressed was total submission. She accepted everything. She seemed to be saying, "Why don't you stop? If you want it this way, well, I agree that I made a mess of things. But don't exhaust yourself shouting or you'll make yourself cough again." He knew quite well that his anger would end that way, but without admitting it he relied on the cough to protect him from an unkind reply.

This time the fit went on for so long that he had to sit down by the side of the track to get his breath back.

When he raised his head dusk had penetrated the track. The sky still looked light between the branches, but several stars were already out. He murmured, "What are we going to do?"

She walked round the cart several times. "Do you think if we put some branches—"

"Branches have to be put down beforehand. Now that we're in it, we're really stuck. We can't move forwards, much less backwards."

"Well, then?"

"I don't know."

He was quiet. Everything was too much for him. His exhaustion, the emptiness left in place of his anger, the swiftly approaching night, and this coldness that attacked his shoulders and glued his soaking shirt to his skin.

"We ought to go back home," suggested Fernande, "and then come back again tomorrow."

The thought of covering all that distance twice made him indignant. He began to shout, but this time the fear of tearing his lungs stopped him.

"God Almighty, I'd rather die here," he sighed. "Lie down and die like an animal. It shouldn't be allowed at our age—living this kind of life. What have we done to deserve it?"

He withheld a sob, but his body shook, and he got up shivering. There was not only the cold of the evening, but the ground where he had been sitting was cold too. He had just remembered the suggestion about using the hut, and the key that

Picaud had told him where to find. He did not dare say it in so many words.

"I haven't the strength to go back. And you can hardly stand up either."

"Well, then," she suggested, "we had better go and see if it's possible to sleep over there."

He thought of his house standing empty for the night, of his rabbits which might be stolen, but he had reached such a state of exhaustion that he pushed the idea away. "We'll have to unload the wood to get out of this. It's the only way."

Fernande took the haversack and the clothes, and they began to walk.

"Give me my jacket," Gaston said. "It's not exactly warm."

She turned round and put the jacket over his shoulders. And so, laboriously, they got back to the clearing where there was still a little daylight left.

16

The woodmen's hut consisted of one large room with a long table made of rough planks nailed on to six stakes that had been driven into the ground, two uneven benches, and a kind of partitioned section with a layer of straw. Holding his lighter at arm's length, Gaston examined the whole room, brushing away the cobwebs here and there with his free hand. A smell of rotting wood rose from the ground.

"It's very damp," said Fernande, "and we haven't even got a blanket."

At that moment Gaston was thinking about his house and his bed, where he would have liked to lay his aching body.

"Do you want to try and go back home?" he asked.

"No," she said, "it's too late. We would never get there."

He found an old iron stove in a corner. The chimney pipe went straight up to the roof and through a hole that had been made twice as large as need be. The light filtered in.

"Better make a fire."

First they burnt a handful of straw to make sure that the stove worked. It drew almost at once. The light from the flames revealed a pile of bark and sticks that the woodmen had left there.

"A bit of warmth will do us good," he said.

"Poor Gaston, we're behaving like a couple of children. Here we are without even a blanket, and nothing to eat but a hunk of bread."

"I'm not hungry."

"Eat some, anyway."

She handed him three-quarters of the piece.

"What about you?" he muttered.

"I've got enough."

They were sparing with their words. They looked at the fire, stretching their hands towards its heat. Their faces leaned into its light, showing the marks of dust and grime drawn deep with sweat.

"We're not much to look at," Gaston said.

They sat there like that for a long time, gradually becoming numb with heat. Gaston was sitting on a chopping-block that he had rolled over next to the stove. Fernande was on a rickety box. Gaston had no thoughts in his head. His exhaustion filled him, was the only reality in his body and brain. In the end he raised the bread towards his mouth: he had been holding it for a long time in his hand, which was so utterly spent that it had no feeling left. He began to chew slowly, and as though she had been waiting for this signal Fernande began to eat too. There was no coffee left, but they still had some wine and water. Fernande poured it into a mug, which she held out to her husband.

"What about yourself?" he said.

"I'm not thirsty."

She was sure to be lying, but he had no courage left to insist. He drank slowly. As he handed back the mug he sighed, "Now there's nothing left."

Fernande shook her head. The fire crackled. Long flames

danced from the grate and roared up the flue, which was full of little holes.

"With that broken-down thing," said Fernande, "we're likely to be suffocated."

"As long as there are flames there's nothing to fear. It's afterwards, when there are only embers left."

He sketched a vague gesture with his hands and then let them fall back on his knees. If they died here, the two of them together, all their problems would be solved. They would be found in a few days. No doubt people would say, "This happened all for the lack of money." They would also say, "They did have a little property, though. And children. And there they were, like a couple of tramps, without even a drop of water."

Gaston took out his tobacco-tin.

"If you smoke," Fernande remarked, "you'll be thirsty."

"No, a cigarette will help me relax."

She laughed bitterly. "If that's so I'd have to smoke a whole packet."

"My poor wife! When I think how we should be quietly at home with some good soup and a comfortable bed. Oh, my God! Here we've slaved away like convicts and come to this. We've half killed ourselves bringing up children and now feel so utterly alone!"

"If you work yourself up like that," Fernande stated calmly, "you'll make yourself cough. And there's not a drop of water left."

He restrained his anger. They sat facing each other, the fire lighting up one side of their faces with its intense heat. As they sat there something more alive than the fire burned between them. They looked at each other. Gaston knew that she was thinking about Paul and his lorries. He was thinking about Julien, who was young and strong, Julien, who could have pulled the cart out of the mud and taken it up to the road. That was it. They were both right. Paul was hard, selfish, and Julien did not care what happened to the old folk. He was never there. He only came back when he wanted his clothes washed and mended. Paul spent all his time on politics.

Those children were a harder burden than their fatigue and misery. Worse than all their poverty. This evil burden lay between him and his wife, as live as the fire which they fed continually with sticks. But he could not even speak about it. If he did his anger would get the better of him and make matters much worse. So they would have to stay like that, looking at each other, not speaking except with their eyes. They would sit there brooding over their fatigue and distress, waiting for the dawn which would bring them nothing but work beyond their strength.

Had they really come here to die without even being able to talk openly to each other?

As the fire died down Fernande got up and put on another two or three pieces of bark. The hut had become considerably warmer.

"You should lie down for a while," she said. "Even if you can't sleep you'll get some rest."

He looked at the partition. Seventy years old, and stranded on a handful of straw already flattened by other sleepers. It was worse than the time with the regiment, worse than the bivouacs in 1914, where there was at least water and fresh straw. And they had had blankets and a greatcoat for a pillow.

As though she had guessed his thoughts, Fernande took the haversack and emptied it on to the table. Then she went over to the partition and filled the haversack with straw. "Here, this'll make a good pillow," she said.

"What about you?"

"I don't want to lie down just yet. I'll stay by the fire."

He got up. He was immediately assailed by the swarming anguish of his pain. He walked over to the door, opened it, and went out.

The sky was still light, and the stars shone as brightly as though there was a frost. It was cold. He went to relieve himself a little way from the hut and then hurried back. The cold had hit him. He shivered so hard that he was out of breath. The thought struck him that if they both went to sleep the fire would go out, and the hut would get cold again. He took off his boots and lay down on the straw that Fernande had gathered together at the end of the partition. When he was lying down she put up the collar of his jacket and did it up with a safety-pin under his chin. Already submerged in his pain, which was diluted and mixed up with his overwhelming tiredness, he allowed her to do it. He just said, "When you want to lie down wake me up, and I'll look after the fire."

"Yes, I will," she said. "Don't you worry."

His head on the haversack, he stared into the fire. He stopped thinking, and soon he was asleep.

17

During the night he emerged several times from his sleep, and each time he had seen his wife, either sitting by the fire or putting more wood on the stove. He had opened his eyes, he had tried to find the strength to get up and say, "You come and lie down now. I'll look after the fire." But he had not moved. Each time his fatigue had nailed him down. He was unable to move, at the mercy of a sleep into which he sank without resistance.

However, he got up a good hour before dawn. For a long time he had held back an urgent need to relieve himself. Fernande, who was sitting leaning against the wall of the hut, lifted her head.

"Haven't you lain down at all?" he asked.

"Yes, I have, don't you worry about me." Her voice was hoarse and faint.

"You take my place. I don't need any more sleep."

She got up, went over, and lay down without a word. Gaston went outside. There were no stars now, and the wind was not so strong. The sky must have clouded over, but it was still very cold. When he came back he said, "If it rains we won't be able to do a thing."

Fernande must have been at the end of her strength. She

hardly moved her eyelids. Gaston was frightened. Her face was like that of a dead woman. He looked at her for a moment, then went back to the fire and threw a few pieces of bark on it. She must have been awake the whole night while he had been asleep. There was hardly any wood left. He had been asleep while she had kept the fire going. He felt guilty, but told himself that she was younger and had not worked as hard as he. He was thirsty. His tongue was coated. He hesitated a while before he finally rolled a cigarette. The first few puffs were unpleasant, but soon he felt the smoke livening him up. His aches had not completely disappeared, but he had nevertheless regained his strength. He went on stoking the fire, and from time to time he would get up and open the door to look at the sky. As soon as he saw it was getting light through the branches he went back to the partition. Fernande opened her eyes.

"Haven't you slept?"

"I've dozed a little."

"It will soon be day."

Her hands, which had lain crossed on her stomach, moved as she drew a single, deep sigh. She turned over and sat up on the edge of the bunk. When she had put on her shoes she got up and whispered, "Let's get on with it."

She emptied the straw out of the haversack and packed the billhook, the grinding stone, the Thermos, and the empty bottle. Gaston made sure that the fire was out, closed the stove carefully, and went on ahead.

"And we haven't even a drop of coffee," said Fernande.

Gaston reproached himself for having let her stay up the whole night. From now on he must make sure that everything went smoothly and that she did not have to do too much. When they reached the cart they could hardly see under the dense trees. Gaston had already taken hold of the rope to undo the load when Fernande suggested, "What if I went to Pannessières to see if I could find a man who'd come and pull us out with a horse?"

"If we pay for a man's time as well as for a horse this wood is going to be too expensive. Let me do it. We've got the day ahead of us. I only hope it's not going to rain."

He felt strong in himself. Not that his fatigue had vanished with the night. But he had stopped thinking about it at all. He had only one idea in his head—to finish the job without help from anyone. Everyone had let him down. Even his children would not mind if he died. Well, he was not going to! He would get the wood back home, and he would do it on his own. Fernande had lost her strength and will-power, so he would show her what a seventy-year-old could manage. He had an idea. When you have not much strength a good idea will get you out of a difficult situation.

He undid the rope and climbed up on the cart. The bundles were strong, which was good. He could at least throw them down without running the risk of the wire coming undone.

"Get out of the way!" he shouted.

She moved away. There were twenty-four bundles. He threw sixteen on to the side of the track as he counted them. When there were only eight left in the cart he got down. "We can manage that lot. Let's go."

"Are you going to leave all those behind?"

"Don't worry. You'll see. We are going to pull it, and all you have to do is to let me know when we get to the bog you mentioned."

He took up the shaft, found good support for his feet, and shouted, "Right then, off we go!"

Fernande was spent. He knew that. He would have to manage on his own. His wife had no more than a tiny little strength to be added to his own.

He pulled, turning the shaft to the right and left, but the cart only rocked slightly. He straightened himself as he cried, "Hey there, don't kill yourself!"

"We'll have to take some more out."

"No, it moved, so it will come. You come up here. All you have to do is to guide it as you pull a little. I can push harder at the back."

She obeyed. He realized she was like an animal with no

mind of its own, and this was enough to make him stop listening to her. Her weakness increased his strength.

When she had taken her place at the shaft he leaned firmly against the back, his legs flexed, one shoulder against the floor of the cart, as though he wanted to heave up the whole load. "Hrey-up!" he shouted. Eyes closed, teeth gritting, he bent his body and began to push with his legs. He felt the cart moving slowly. The wheels were gripping on the muddy track. A cry came from the depths of his being, sounding like an animal. "Hrey-up!"

The cart suddenly came unstuck, went at least half a yard, and then came to a halt as Fernande cried, "Stop!"

Gaston straightened up, ran to the front as he shouted, "Good God! Don't stop! We've made it."

She was on her knees, her hands on the ground. She could hardly get up, and he had to help her. "When it got going," she panted, "I slipped."

He wanted to abuse her, but the sight of her ravaged face stopped him. "Did you hurt yourself?"

"No, I'll be all right. I'm sorry, I'm such a nuisance to you!"

This word made him feel good. He wanted to take her in his arms, but it was a long time since he had forgotten how to make such a gesture. Instead he said, "Now that it's free of the mud we'll be all right. But I'll take the shaft at the front. It's too dangerous for you. If the wheels knock against a stone it could easily throw you to the ground, a thing like that."

Fernande went round to the back, and they were ready to start again.

The track was not easy, but they reached the boggy patch without too much difficulty. Gaston stopped the cart before the gentle slope that led down towards it. "I think we'll get through, but it won't be so hard if we put some branches across it."

He took his billhook and began to cut the lower branches from the trees near by. Fernande dragged them over to the mud and put them down across the track. When the patch was covered with a good layer they tried again, and were able to get across without difficulty. The rest of the track to the main road was in a much better state, and they reached it with only two pauses for rest.

"And now," said Gaston, "we've only got two more journeys."

His wife had possibly guessed his intention, for she expressed no surprise at all. Instead she looked at the sky where some big clouds were scudding over, then she sighed, "As long as it doesn't rain."

"Come on, now. Once we've got the lot out of the forest we'll be all right." He felt he had strength enough for the two of them. They had managed the first run, so there was no reason why they should not manage the others. And they did—successfully. It was not exactly a restful job, but the cart went well, and the old man felt fully in charge. It seemed to him that if they had had something to eat and drink he could easily have managed to cut more wood. But he was plagued with hunger and thirst.

When they had loaded and settled the whole lot he asked, "Did you bring any money?"

"No, I didn't. It wasn't worth it. It was too much of a risk losing it."

"That's silly. We could have bought something to drink at Pannessières."

"Yes, but how was I to know we'd need it?"

The road went downhill on the return journey, right to the edge of the town. All they needed to do was to guide the cart and apply the brake according to the steepness of the hill. As he walked Gaston leaned on the bar of the shaft, which knocked into his back. Fernande was at the side of the cart, ready to tighten or undo the brake as necessary. At Pannessières they stopped to have a drink of water at the fountain. The water was cold, and they washed their faces.

"You are hot," said Fernande. "Don't drink too much."

Gaston took up his position again, Fernande undid the brake, and off they went once more. To begin with, Gaston had turned round to inspect his load several times. Now it was no longer necessary. All was in order, and he knew it. There, jolting his back from behind, was his cart, safe and sound, and a couple of dozen bundles of good firewood which he had cut with his own hands, with his old billhook.

It was a beautiful job, a job well done by a man who had never skimped his work. Bread, earth, firewood were all handled in the same way—with his heart as much as with his hands. Nowadays people had forgotten how to do this, but he would not fall in with this fashion for laziness and half-measures. He had a sense of what was right. He had never allowed himself to cheat, and he was not going to start after sixty years. What the youngsters did was nothing to do with him. Were they on their own, Fernande and he? Ah well, if that was how it was they could manage alone. They did not need either Julien's youth or Paul's money. It was not in his nature to beg for alms. He had been right to hold out against his wife. If he had gone and asked Paul for help he would have run the risk of refusal, and that would have hurt. If Paul had agreed to help the work would have been a lot easier, and they would no doubt have brought home twice as much wood, but still, it was better this way. He was not sure why this should be so, but he was convinced of it. He believed this in spite of the overwhelming tiredness which drove him towards the bottom of the hill with even greater force than the heavy weight of this cart. He still hung on to this idea when he reached the bottom and had to start hauling at the load again.

In the town there were several upward slopes and no-one there to give him a hand. That was because it was nearly one o'clock, and people would be at their midday meal. This gave him a kind of satisfaction, almost a passionate one. All alone. They would go all the way alone.

They had reached the top of the rue des Écoles when he felt the icy stinging of the first drops of rain. It was as if the heavens faltered and then, like a sudden shower in spring, the down-pour burst upon them. The street was filled with a strong smell of wet dust. The German flag with its swastika over the entrance to the *école normale* flapped in a gust of wind, and Gaston saw the sentry in his green uniform take shelter in the black-and-white sentry-box. It seemed to him the sentry was laughing at them as they passed, but Gaston did not care. "The brake!" he shouted.

The iron brake-shoes grated against the rim of the wheels, and the cart slowed down. He stopped it by the garden-fence and put the brakes on fully.

"We'll take it in when the downpour is over," he said as he took the key to the gate out of his pocket.

They walked as quickly as they could to the house, but before going up the steps he went along to count his rabbits, and gave them a handful of hay.

When he came into the kitchen Fernande had already opened the shutters. She brought two glasses and a jug of water from the scullery. They drank slowly, relishing every mouthful.

Now there was only the fire to light and a meal to cook, but the two old people remained seated without moving, pinned down by his exhaustion which united them.

They looked at each other from time to time. There was no need to speak. They sat opposite each other, back in their own house, with the rain beating down so heavily on its windows.

They looked at each other without speaking, but they both knew that the labour and misery they had shared had brought them together much more than a common joy could ever have done.

PART TWO

A Long Winter Night

18

One evening, just before nightfall, a strong wind blew up from the north-east and made the fire roar. Gaston went to the window and watched the dead leaves chasing across the black earth in the garden. He came back and sat down, leaned one elbow on the table, put his feet in their coarse, grey, woollen socks on the open oven door, and sighed, "Now winter is really here."

For a long time he listened to the wind. He looked at the big pear-tree, stripped of its leaves, tossing against the grey sky; then at the bright flames dancing in the grate.

At last, when the wind had settled down to a steady rhythm and blown the chaos of its first anger beyond the horizon of the dark hills, Gaston got up again and put two knotted logs in the grate and adjusted the damper. When he had hung the poker on the brass rail he sat down again and said once more, "Now winter is really here."

"Do you think it's going to snow?" asked his wife.

"As long as the wind holds, it's hard to tell. But if it dies down we might well get a packet. The sky is overcast. I've felt it coming since this morning. My shoulder is twinging. A little while ago, when I went to close the shed, I covered the rabbit hutches with sacks. That shows I thought as much."

He got up again and placed himself in front of the window, standing on top of his slippers. He stayed quite still for a moment, one hand on the window fastening, the other hidden in the pocket of his big, blue apron. The peak of his cap touched the glass where his breath was slowly spreading condensation.

"I think you can light the lamp," he said. "I'm going to close the shutters. What we lose in the way of light we'll gain in heat."

When he had pulled in the big wooden shutters, which were lined with black paper to cover the chinks, he closed the window, fastened the flower-patterned curtain, and came back and sat down again. The effort involved and the cold air he had inhaled made him short of breath. He stayed quite still for a few seconds, one hand on his chest and the other clutching the corner of the table. Fernande finished adjusting the wick, hauled the lamp up slowly, chains squeaking, then looked hard at her husband as she observed, "You seem to be short of breath tonight."

"You know the first cold of winter always has this effect on me. I'll have to start taking the cough-mixture again."

"There's no more cough-mixture to be had. We have to have a prescription. And then they sell that filthy stuff with no sugar in it, which makes you feel sick."

"There's nothing left for it then but give up. It's only just the beginning of December. What'll we do when it gets really cold!"

He said this without anger. It was just a statement. Everything seemed to conspire to hasten the end of old people like themselves, deprived of all means of struggle. He always used the same words, and they always drew the same response. This evening his wife again said, "Poor Gaston, everyone is in the same boat. Everyone suffers the same."

"Yes. And everyone will end up dead."

"In that case, what do you want to do about it?"

Fernande showed no sign of anger either. There they were, both of them, with their poverty and no desire to rebel. All their energy had been used up in their long struggle for existence, and they had just enough strength left to hang on to the dwindling life within them. He cursed the cold, and yet he sometimes felt that winter was the season, in spite of everything, that was easiest to bear. The nights were longer, the days a continual twilight, making him stay quietly in the corner by his fire, curled up like a lamp whose wick has been lowered to save paraffin. Even the War had fallen asleep. It was all going on in distant countries whose names meant nothing to him. Even the Germans were behaving more quietly, and when they ordered a curfew at six in the evening it was not as irksome as in the summer. Altogether, there were long periods during the day when everything seemed normal. Most of his time was taken up with the past, and for hours on end Gaston lived his life over again or chose an incident to picture in every detail.

Fernande had pulled a little casserole over to the corner of the stove. The escaping steam smelt of good, cooked vegetables. She took off the lid and reached for a dish, on which she placed her mincer and began to put the vegetables through. The mincer was old. It stuck a few times, and she had to bend over with the effort needed.

"Don't force it," said Gaston. "Try going backwards. If you force it you might break the handle, and you'd never get it replaced. Then—"

She turned round and stopped him with a movement of her hand. He was about to raise his voice and say that he did, after all, have the right to express an opinion, but he could see by the look on her face that that had not been the reason for her stopping. She had almost turned her back to the stove, one hand in the air and the other holding her draining spoon dripping into the casserole. She was staring at the door. Her face looked tense.

Gaston made an effort to listen hard, but he could hear nothing but the steady roar of the fire and the kettle simmering. "It's the wind," he said.

"Keep quiet. I'm certain someone banged the cellar door."

"Right; I'll go and have a look."

"No, you'll get cold."

As she was putting down her spoon and Gaston was putting on his slippers there was a tap on the shutters.

"I didn't imagine it that time," she said.

Gaston had heard it. His heart began to beat very fast. It seemed to him that all the peaceful warmth of the kitchen was about to be swallowed up by the cold night air surrounding the house. Nothing good ever happened like this. Was someone after his wine? Or his rabbits? Or his wood piled up in the shed?

An endless minute went by. At last Fernande took the torch

—its battery was almost worn out—and opened the door a little. Turning its orange beam towards the balcony, she stuck her head out and shouted in a wavering voice, "What is it?"

Gaston was behind her. On his way he had seized the poker, which he grasped in his right hand.

There was a knock against the handrail, and the metallic noise seemed very loud in the night: they no longer even heard the sighing of the wind.

"Is that you, Mother?"

Fernande opened the door wide and took a step forward. Gaston was not sure whether it had been Julien's voice. Nevertheless he went out. The torch showed nothing but the stone steps and the corner of the wall. Another question rose up to them, "Are you on your own?"

"Yes, of course we are, my love. Come on up. Come on, quickly."

Gaston stepped back and stood aside to let his son enter. But Fernande did not wait for him to reach the kitchen before she flung her arms round his neck and kissed him. The icy wind cut like a blade through the open door. In spite of the lamp-glass the flame quivered. Gaston controlled himself awhile, and then said with some urgency, "Come back indoors. You're making the house freeze and the light can be seen from outside."

He had not seen his son's face yet, but when they came into the light Gaston could do nothing but mutter, "Oh, good God! Oh, good God!"

Julien had grown a chestnut beard—just a fringe outlining his jaws and chin—and his hair, which used to be cut very short, was combed to the back of his head, reaching the collar of his overcoat, where it turned up like a duck's tail.

"Oh, good God!" Gaston said again. "I wasn't expecting this!"

What could be seen of Julien's face was brown and made his blue eyes look lighter.

Gaston turned to his wife, who remained speechless, her hands stretched out, her chin crumpled, and tears in her eyes.

Julien kissed his father on both cheeks and took his mother in his arms again, lifting her up and holding her tight for a moment. Gaston took off his cap, scratched and shook his head, and went slowly back to his place. There was a long silence while Julien took off his overcoat and hung it on the wooden knob at the foot of the banisters.

"You've—you've not got a case?" asked Fernande.

"Yes, it's down by the cellar door. It'll be all right there for the moment."

Gaston could not take his eyes off that bearded face. At first his heart had missed a beat, and there was a kind of contraction in his whole chest. Now a great emptiness spread through him. Nothing. He could think of nothing to say. Nothing to ask. Fernande must be feeling the same as she stood between the stove and the table, staring at the boy sitting on the stairs and taking off his shoes.

Turned to confusion and driven far beyond the borders of the garden, the winter night came back gradually, more intensely, the wind whistling in the pear-tree, the fire roaring in the grate, and the small, brass-lidded kettle singing monotonously.

Gaston settled down slowly. His body, a little overwhelmed with the excitement, found its customary position in his chair. His elbows on the table, he relaxed, opening his hand on the oilcloth, while his feet abandoned the slippers and found their usual place on the oven door.

19

After those endless minutes, during which Fernande wiped her eyes many times, there was a moment of feverish excitement. She began to whirl around the kitchen, asking questions and giving the replies as well. "Have you eaten? Of course not. You must be hungry. What can I get you? There's some soup. There should be a few eggs left. If it wasn't so late we could have killed a rabbit. I can at least peel some potatoes. Gaston, will you finish making the soup?"

Gaston pulled on his slippers and got up. She was mad! It was always the same performance when Julien came back after a long absence. But this evening there was also the fact that they had not been expecting him.

Every now and again, as he ground the vegetables, he turned his head to look at the boy still sitting on the staircase. Fernande was still dancing around, opening the cupboard, going to the scullery, pulling at a drawer which got stuck and which she then shook to push it back in with a noisy clatter of jumbled-up cutlery. Gaston felt increasingly irritated. He tried hard not to shout at his wife to calm down, but in the end he turned to Julien and asked him, "What on earth made you grow a head like that?"

The boy began to laugh. "It's a bit of a joke," he parried. "I don't want to get arrested, so I had to take precautions."

"You know the gendarmes are looking for you," said Gaston.

"That doesn't surprise me!"

"It doesn't seem to worry you."

"Well, I'm not the only one, you know."

"Come on now," said Fernande. "At least let him tell us where he's come from."

Gaston choked back his anger. His son's slightly ironic tone had hurt him. The boy had deserted. The police were at his heels. They had thought he was in England, and here he was back home, all smiles, with a ridiculous beard and hair like a girl! That was the situation, and Fernande seemed to imply there was nothing unusual about it.

He fished around for the rest of the vegetables at the bottom of the casserole, while Julien explained, "I've come from Marseilles. I've been staying with a friend, a painter. He's a nice fellow. I haven't written to you because it might have caused trouble. The Militia are all over the place, even in the post-office."

"But what were you doing in Marseilles?" asked Fernande.

"I was painting with my friend. I could have stayed there, only it was difficult to get food. I had no ration-book." He stopped. Gaston turned round again. Fernande was no longer laying the table as she listened to her son. "You've got no ration-book!" she said.

"No. I was able to get a forged identity-card, but it's another matter with ration-books."

Gaston thought to himself, "That really does it. We haven't even got enough for ourselves!"

He said nothing, and it was Fernande who asked, "My poor boy, how did you manage?"

"There were ways and means. But it wasn't always fun."

She went up to Julien, who rose to his feet. "Yes, you are thin," she said. "You don't see it at once with your beard, but when you look more closely. . . . My goodness! It's lucky you were able to come back!"

"It's about time we had some supper," said Gaston. "He can talk just as well at table."

He noticed that his wife shrugged her shoulders. However, she said nothing, threw her black woollen shawl over her head, took the key to the cellar, switched on the torch, and went outside. Gaston had gone back to his seat, but he sat stiffly, without leaning back, looking at his son sitting at the opposite end of the table. He was trying to think of something to say, a question to ask, when he jumped up. Fernande had screamed.

"What's that?" he asked.

Julien got up, appeared to hesitate, and as he went towards the door he laughed and said, "Oh, blast, I'd forgotten. She must have come across Seraphin!"

"What on earth are you talking about?" asked Gaston.

But Julien was already on his way out, saying over his shoulder, "Don't worry, I'll see to it. He's not a scoundrel!"

Gaston did not dare get up, neither did he dare sit down properly. He stayed on the edge of his chair, ears straining as he tried to make out his wife's and Julien's voices. He could hear they were talking down below, but with the wind it was no more than a confused mumble. So Julien had not come on his own. What could that possibly imply? Good God! To be so peaceful at home, with all the doors closed and in front of a good fire, then suddenly to find yourself in the midst of this uproar, with the doors constantly opening and the winter howling in—and a stranger coming any minute? Who? What sort of person? An artist, perhaps? God Almighty! Here he had spent his whole life slaving away, only to find himself robbed of a few hours' peace. There was nothing he could do about it. One hapless word, and his wife would be angry. He knew it. She would call him selfish again.

Something knocked against the railings outside, then there was another bump against the door, which opened slowly. Fernande appeared. She was carrying three eggs in one hand, the torch in the other. "Bring your case inside," she said, "but leave the rest on the landing." She looked paler than usual. Gaston got up and heard Julien saying, "You're joking. You should have let me leave it in the cellar then." Julien managed to open the door fully, pushing it with his foot, and Gaston stood there with his mouth open, holding the peak of his cap with one hand, the other resting flat on the table. He just looked. That was all he was able to do. He could not utter a word. He could not even think.

Julien came indoors clutching a skeleton of a man in his arms. There was a skull, arms, all the bones tied together with three pieces of coarse string which also held a roll of white paper, as though the skeleton were clutching it to its chest.

As the boy put down his case and Fernande was about to shut the door Gaston cried in an unsteady voice, "You're not going to— Would you please do me the favour of chucking that outside!"

Julien looked surprised. "Why? It's quite clean. This is Seraphin. It's at least thirty years since he took leave of this world!"

"But you're not going to keep that in the house!" This time Gaston had shouted loudly. The son hesitated. "I could put it in my room, after all. It's one of the tools of the trade."

"Tools of the trade," stammered Gaston.

For several seconds the words rang through his head. A tool! That was the limit! He looked at the skeleton, and at the same time he saw a dough-trough, a shovel, his billhook, his wheelbarrow. That thing wasn't a tool!

"Now listen, Julien," said Fernande, "your father is right. We don't keep things like that in the house."

The boy did not seem to understand. He looked from one to the other in astonishment, an unsteady smile hovering above his beard.

"Good heavens!" he said at last. "He can sleep on the balcony if you insist. He won't catch his death there. But I think I'll remove my papers first—the damp will ruin them."

He put the skeleton down on the floor and took a table-knife to cut the string. In spite of himself, Gaston exploded, "Not with that!"

"What?"

"It's disgusting, that's what. Take the old pair of scissors."

Julien sighed and obeyed. He said, "I don't understand you. Here's a bloke just like the rest of us. Right then, he's dead. He's been cleaned up. Since then he's been in my friend's studio."

He put the roll of paper on the sideboard and picked up the skeleton, its dangling arms clicking against its sides.

"If he were made of plaster," said the boy, "it would look exactly the same."

"Leave it on the balcony for tonight," said Gaston. "But tomorrow morning you'll have to take it to the shed first thing. If someone should come . . ."

Julien came back. "You know," he said, laughing, "it's a long time since he bit anyone. When he was alive he may well have been an honest fellow. On the other hand, he might have been an assassin. It's mostly people they've executed who end up like this. But this one hasn't had his head cut off. His neck is in impeccable condition. He's well preserved, you know—"

Fernande interrupted him. "Go and wash your hands. And don't talk any more about it. It worries your father."

"Yes," sighed Gaston, "he does worry me. Here we've been

so worried about him, and look at him, coming home like that. With—with that head on his shoulders, and a dead man."

Julien was in the scullery. He had left the door open in order to be able to see. Cold seeped into the kitchen, just as if it had come directly from outside. This was a bad sign. Gaston thought about it, then came back to the skeleton. "You took it on the train with you?" he asked.

"Of course I did. And I didn't have to pay for his ticket."

"For someone who's being sought after and doesn't want to be noticed, you're setting about it the right way."

"Precisely. The police never suspect anyone looking so flamboyant. Besides, on my identity-card I'm described as an art teacher. As my friend said, I have to look and act the part."

Gaston said no more. Fernande asked, "Art teacher? You? At your age?"

"My identity-card says I'm twenty-nine."

Julien came back to the table and sat down. The old people were still standing up, not daring to look at each other, but watching this stranger whom they did not understand and who had just arrived with the night and the first frost.

Gaston shook his head. His boy was home. He had a beard and the sort of hair you see on some pictures of Christ; he had come from Marseilles, he called himself a teacher, he had a dead man with him; he was his own son; he was called Dubois, like himself . . . He had a beard . . . He carried a dead man . . .

20

That was how the boy arrived, without warning, looking like an artist and with that dreadful skeleton. He arrived, and Fernande went mad, as though someone had set the house on fire. She turned everything upside down. She gave him two big plates of soup and then still urged him to have bread. As though bread were not rationed. She fried three eggs for him. As if eggs . . . and he had not even got a ration-book. What if he objected? Gaston took care not to. He knew what the answer would be in advance. "It's your own son! Anyone would think you weren't happy to see him!" Happy? Of course he was. All the same, seeing him in this state had given him a bad shock. Was Fernande blind or something? She was swallowing him up with her eyes. She drank in his every word. That boy would be able to come back one day saying he had committed a crime, and she would still welcome him like this. And they had thought he had enlisted with de Gaulle! Oh, not even that. What had he been doing since he deserted? He was telling them about that now as he ate the soup and the eggs and the huge pieces of bread. He had been living with a friend in a bohemian sort of way. He said that without blushing. It seemed entirely natural to him. He had left Marseilles only because his friend had gone away and he did not feel he could manage on his own.

Gaston remained silent for a long time, leaning over his empty plate, stealthily watching his boy talking, and his wife listening so foolishly, as though she admired everything that annoyed him. At last, unable to stand it any longer, he asked, "And now what are you planning to do?"

Julien made an evasive movement and pulled a face, distorting his beard. "I don't know exactly. I could lie low here for a while."

There were questioning looks between the three of them. The boy hesitated for a long time before adding, "I have some work to finish. I could do it here."

"Some work?" asked Gaston.

"Yes."

"What sort of work?"

"Oh, I can't explain. It's too complicated."

"I see. We're not intelligent enough to understand."

Fernande intervened. "Now don't get angry, Gaston," she said. "If it's painting, it's true that we don't know much about it."

"Painting?" said Gaston. "Where can he paint in this house? Besides, painting's not work."

"No," admitted Julien, "it's not painting. It's—er—something I have to write. So—"

He stopped, looked at his mother, then at his father. He sighed, pushed his empty plate away, and took a packet of cigarettes and a box of matches from his pocket.

"What's this? You've started smoking?" said Fernande.

"Why, yes. I'm old enough." Before taking one for himself he handed the packet to his father, who hesitated. "I don't smoke in the evening."

"Go on, just for once."

A crowd of contradictory thoughts jostled through Gaston's mind. If he accepted this cigarette he would not be able to speak his mind. On the other hand, how could he refuse a cigarette? Almost against his will, his hand reached out towards the packet.

"It'll make you cough all night," said Fernande.

"What makes you think that? Cigarettes don't do you any harm. You know that Father coughs because of his asthma."

"Precisely," she said again.

Gaston had already put the cigarette in his mouth and taken the lighter from his pocket. Fernande went on, but without conviction, "You know he already smokes too much."

Gaston enjoyed the smoke. It was pleasant this way, not having to hide or go outside in the cold or down to the lavatory. There was a silence almost good enough to inhale, living like this with the good taste of tobacco. However, there was a question nagging his mind. He pushed it back several times before letting it slip out between two clouds of smoke. "If you've got no coupons, how do you manage to get tobacco?"

Julien laughed. "Oh, tobacco's easier to get than bread or potatoes on the black market in Marseilles. There are boys selling cigarettes in all the cafés. I should think it's the same here."

"I don't know," said Gaston. "I never go to the café. Anyway, they probably cost more than I can afford."

"Besides," Fernande said quickly, "your ration is enough to make you cough."

Gaston felt like answering his wife sharply, but he had something else on his mind. When he had been speaking about the café he had had an idea, but he had wanted to talk about prices first, and he had not been able to get it in. However, it was still there, and he had to say it. "No," he sighed, "I've never been one for going to cafés, but sometimes I used to have a drink with friends when we met in town. Nowadays I go out as little as possible." He thought Julien was going to ask him why he no longer went out, but the boy remained silent, staring at the cigarette between his fingers. Gaston avoided looking at his wife and went on, "I don't want to blame you in any way. You arrive here and you must be tired, but all the same, we'd still like to know what has been happening? You were a soldier, you deserted, and here we are with the police at our heels."

Julien was about to speak, but Fernande got in first, "You can't say the police are all that bad."

"They're not bad because they know me. All the same, it's no easy state of affairs, and now that he's here—" He had raised his voice, but Fernande interrupted him by talking louder than he did. "They don't come every day, and they've never searched the house."

"Why, have they been here a lot?" asked Julien.

"A lot!" Gaston said vehemently. "I'll say they've been here a lot. Have you any idea—"

This time it was his cough that interfered. While he went to spit into the grate Fernande gave him some water. "Your lime tea will be ready in a few minutes," she said.

"I suppose that means I can go to bed and leave you two on your own."

"Poor Gaston, I can't say a thing without you getting angry. I mentioned your tea because of your cough, and then—"

Julien began to laugh. "I see you haven't got out of the habit of bickering over trifles."

Gaston felt the conversation was drifting into channels that would prevent him getting to the point. He would have to stop getting angry; things had to be clarified. "Anyway," he said, "you will have to realize what's going on. You're running a risk—and so are we."

"Risks. Well, at the moment there are thousands of young people going around with forged papers and avoiding labour service."

"But you, you're a deserter."

"A deserter from an army that sold out to the Germans. There's no shame in that, after all."

Gaston looked at his wife. He could see that she was not on his side. That was natural. If he got angry she would talk about Paul and the Militia. Then there would be more anger and a quarrel, leaving him torn and distressed, a prey to his cough while the others went on talking. "My tea should be ready," he said.

Fernande fetched a bowl and the sugar. As she began to pour Julien got up, saying, "Don't put any sugar in. Wait a minute."

He opened his suitcase, took out crumpled clothes, some papers, and then a pot of honey, which he put on the table.

"Heavens, where did you get that from?" asked Fernande.

"From my case."

"But where did you get it?"

"My friend had an uncle from Provence. He would bring us some occasionally. My friend told me, 'Here, take this for your parents.' He's a good sort, you know."

Gaston looked at the pot of honey. For over a year it had been impossible to find any at a reasonable price.

"And it's lavender honey," said Julien. "Take some. It's good."

"There you are," Fernande remarked. "You are lucky to have a son who thinks of you."

By the look on her face and the way her lips moved Gaston could see that she had not finished the sentence. He could easily guess what she had meant to say. If she had not checked herself she would have added that Julien, who had nothing, nevertheless found something to give his father, while Paul, a wealthy grocer who never went short, did not make the slightest effort to help them. That was what she had thought.

Gaston resented it, but at the same time he was grateful that she had said nothing. Why had she kept quiet? Was it really to spare his feelings? Was it not rather to avoid a discussion that might go on for a long time, to make him go up to bed so that she might be alone with Julien, whom she would then tell everything? She would be sure to tell him about Paul and the Militia. She would take the opportunity as soon as they were on their own. Julien would be delighted to have a chance to insult his half-brother, whom he detested.

He had come home with that weird head, with his skeleton under his arm, and there he was, offering cigarettes and putting pots of honey on the table. It was one way of shutting up his father. Then, to show how really generous he was, he was now saying, "It should last you some time, a pot like that, if you only use it for your tea."

"What about you?" asked Gaston. "Don't you like it?"

"Oh, I've had so much of it recently. And I've always heard that it was good for your throat."

"That's right," said Gaston.

He took some, stirred his tea slowly, breathing in the smell of lime flowers that rose with the steam. This honey must be especially good. It enhanced the aroma of the tea. He drank a mouthful.

"It's a very good honey," he said. "And sugar is so scarce too."

They all three sat looking at each other without saying a word. Slowly the aroma of the tea filled the narrow room, replacing the smell of vegetable soup and fat from the fried eggs.

"You know, we've been worried about you," said Fernande. "We thought you might have gone to England by way of Spain. I've often been over to M. Robin's in the evening to listen to the broadcasts from London. I thought that if you were there you might send some sort of message."

"A message? What kind of message?"

"I don't know. Just something I could have understood."

"I don't see how. Besides, you don't go to London as though it were Montmorot."

"Well, anyway, when you de— when you left the Army, you must have had some idea of what you wanted to do?"

"Yes, of course. I joined the maquis in the Black Mountains, but it wasn't very successful. A friend of mine was killed, and I got picked up."

Gaston said quickly, "Yes, we heard what happened. You were imprisoned at the Carcassonne barracks and escaped after knocking down an N.C.O. I don't know if you realize—"

Julien interrupted him. "He was a bastard. An out-and-out collaborator. What they didn't tell you was that it was thanks to the captain that I managed to get out. He was a fine fellow. He only stays in the Army to help the maquis and send information to the British."

Gaston deliberated. Should he go up to bed or go on with this discussion, which was sure to end in an argument? He drank another few mouthfuls of lime tea. Then, trying hard to stay calm, he said, almost timidly, "A spy, in other words."

"If you like. But it's necessary."

"I don't know about it being necessary, but I'd rather see you in different company. That sort of adventure never leads to any good. I well remember the Dreyfus affair—"

Fernande interrupted, "But that's ancient history. You are always harping on things that happened a long time ago. You refuse to look at the situation realistically, and when you do look at it you never take an optimistic point of view."

"You're not going to start that again!"

It flew out before he had time to consider, and Gaston regretted it at once. His wife had already straightened herself up in her chair, ready to retort. However, she said nothing. They looked at each other hard for a moment. Was she going to say something about Paul? Would she understand that her husband was sorry for what he had just said? There was a silence. Then, as she slowly leaned back in her chair with no sign of anger, she said softly, "This war makes everything beastly. It divides people from each other. It causes mischief even when people are not fighting each other."

"The only thing to do," said Julien, "is to pull out without getting hurt."

Gaston wanted to ask him if he regretted deserting, but he did not dare. Perhaps he had already guessed the answer from what Julien had just said, but he preferred to cling to his hope. He contented himself with asking, "But you can't go on hiding indefinitely?"

"I'll have to keep out of their way till the end of the War. When the Germans have gone back home I'll be able to show my face again."

"Do you really think that—"

Gaston could not finish because Fernande cut in, "Your father knows nothing about what's going on. He never goes over and listens to the wireless. We don't have a newspaper, and at the moment he's reading old copies of *L'Illustration* from before 1914."

"There's no need to read the paper. You keep me informed. You always know everything, you do!"

"I try to live with the times."

It was worse than a real argument, this conversation that balanced its way along a thread stretched between anger and the tenuous peace they had known for a short while when the son had taken out his cigarettes and that jar of honey. Gaston struggled against his desire to go up to bed, at the same time suppressing his longing to give vent to the feelings that cramped his body.

Peace. That was all he wanted. Oh, yes, when he thought about peace it was the kind he could still feel when he sat here quietly, or when he was in his garden. That was the kind that exasperated his wife. But what harm did it do anyone, trying to live as far removed from events as possible? If everyone had behaved like that, would not a lot of trouble have been avoided? Curfew and restrictions apart, did the Germans give much cause for complaint? All you had to do was ignore them. Not tread on their toes, so that they left you alone. Anyone could see that. But Fernande just would not admit it. She always had to interfere. She involved herself with what went on outside the house as much as with the essentials of their life. And what were they going to do from now on with this boy for whom the police were looking?

Gaston suddenly felt a great weariness come over him. It was not like the tiredness which possessed him in the evening after a hard day's work. Neither was it the kind he felt when he thought of days gone by, the strength he once had, and his vanished youth. It was a sense of emptiness, as though Julien's homecoming had driven something out of the house, something which he could not name, which had no substance, but nevertheless was there helping him to live, just as the hot air that rose from the oven all day gave the kitchen an even warmth, where he could doze gently, allowing the cruel season to run its course.

21

Gaston decided to wait no longer and went up to bed. He had finished his tea, taken his chamber-pot and lamp up to his room, where he noticed there was frost sparkling on the wallpaper in places.

"If this weather continues," he grumbled, "we'll have to light a fire in the room before we go to bed—which is no way to save wood."

He undressed as quickly as he could and slid in between the sheets, where his wife had put a hot-water bottle wrapped up in an old stocking. After a while he slid it down his body, pushing it slightly over to the right where Fernande would be sleeping. But tonight she would not be coming to bed early. Now that he had left them on their own they would undoubtedly go on talking for a long time, the two of them together, and he knew well enough what they would be talking about. In deciding to go to bed he had succumbed to his fear of a quarrel. He had told himself that he always went to bed around nine o'clock, but that was only an excuse. Now he blamed himself for having withdrawn. His behaviour implied he had abandoned Paul, whom Fernande was no doubt going to drag through the mud. Had he been a coward? Paul was his own son, after all. Should he allow his reputation to be sullied without saying anything in defence of his attitude?

He had been afraid of getting hurt by accepting the challenge, and now he was tortured by remorse.

For a moment he felt like getting up and going quietly to the door at the top of the stairs to listen to what they were saying. He might even go into the kitchen to fetch an aspirin, pretending to have a headache. His right hand pushed the hot-water bottle down along his thigh. The bed had been pleasantly warm for a while now. His nightcap was pulled down over his forehead, the bedclothes were tucked under his chin, and Gaston felt comfortable. The slightest movement would make the bed cold again. He thought about the icy floor, the floorboards creaking underfoot, the lamp he would have to relight. Anyway, if he heard them speaking ill of Paul, what could he do? How could he defend his son, he who knew nothing about politics or the international situation? No, whatever his wife and Julien might say was of no consequence. The only thing that mattered was keeping the peace. On the whole, he was not the only one to think like this. A little while ago Julien had said that the important thing was getting through the War without running any risk. And Fernande was already talking about him as though he were a hero! A fine hero, with his hair done up like an artist and staying in Marseilles! Just like those servicemen in 1939, vying with each other to be the first to reach the Spanish frontier. The men of 1914–18 were of a different calibre. They had known how to stick it out!

Gaston gave a deep sigh. He moved the hot-water bottle again; already it had ceased to burn his hand. He took care not to let the icy air get under the bedclothes. He stayed flat on his back, his head sinking into the soft hollow of the two pillows.

All the same, his son was strange. Painting pictures and wandering from Marseilles to Lons-le-Saunier with this skeleton under his arm was unconventional. All the members of his own family, as of his wife's, had been sensible people, normal people, who worked hard. That boy had never been quite normal. Where could he have got this odd streak from? A dead man. Wandering around with a real dead man under his arm. There should be a law against it.

Now he could only think about the skeleton, which had been stowed out on the balcony. Had Julien put it down behind the balustrade? Had he left it standing up in the corner? The thought worried him. Who could this good man have been, skinned instead of being put in a coffin? It was the first time that Gaston had seen the like at close quarters. He knew such things existed in museums and medical schools, but it was different having one in your own home. No, it was beyond comprehension.

Was it wise to leave it on the balcony? If the police got the idea of calling early in the morning, what would they say when they came face to face with the skeleton?

Without realizing it, Gaston began to feel ill at ease. Although he would not admit it, it was the idea of death itself that tormented him. Not only death in general, but his own death. The skeleton below had been a man like himself, had led a life full of work and struggle. He might even have been a baker. Who knows? Or perhaps a farmer who had loved his land. Maybe a man who had never been away from his own district when he was alive. Had anyone asked his permission to treat him like a gadget to be traipsed around with no more care than an umbrella? Seraphin. Julien had called him Seraphin. So he must have known who he was. He treated him without any respect or care. True, you no longer suffer once you are dead. Looked at from a certain angle, it came to the same thing, being like this or rotting in a hole in the cemetery. And yet after a long working life would it not be more natural to have a bit of quiet? A stone over your chest, your name engraved on it? Even if no-one ever stopped by it, it was still something solid left behind. Besides, there was always someone to remember you. Gaston only went to the cemetery on the eve of All Saints and for funerals. For All Saints he would cut the grass on his parents' and first wife's graves and bring some chrysanthemums in pots which he had grown especially for this purpose. And every time he told himself that that was where he belonged—with them—and his wife too, eventually. There they would all meet again. There might be no-one left to bring them flowers, but there would always be the gravestones with their names. For many years people would walk past after a funeral in twos and threes, and would read their names as they went by. They would say, "Gaston Dubois. Now there's a man who has earned his rest. He moved quite a few sacks of flour around during his sod of a life." People of his own age, or perhaps a little younger than he, would talk about the bread he had made. "There aren't any bakers like him nowadays." And their mouths would water just at the thought.

It did not amount to much, that thought, but it was enough to make the prospect of leaving feet first a little less sad.

Gaston conjured up all these thoughts, and they always returned to the dead man, who had never been buried, who slept so far away from the other dead, so lonely out there on the windswept balcony. Since his life ended he must have heard only art students' jokes and songs. That was no company for someone properly dead.

When Fernande came up to bed Gaston was still not asleep. First he heard a movement in the little room which Julien was using next to theirs, then the door opened and she came in quietly.

"Haven't you got a light?" Gaston asked.

"No, I left the candle with Julien. You're not asleep?"

"No."

She got undressed and slipped into bed. The movement of the bedclothes chilled it again with the cold air of the room.

There was silence for a while, broken only by the creaking of the bedsprings when Fernande moved to find a more comfortable position. Before he fell asleep Gaston mumbled, "All the same, it's a crazy idea bringing a dead man with him."

22

The next day Gaston realized that from now on his life was going to be turned upside down by Julien's return. He had woken up several times during the night, always with the image of the skeleton on the balcony before his eyes. In his drowsy state the feeling came over him that Death was standing at his door, waiting for the moment when he might enter the house.

As soon as he was up he put on warm clothes and went out to remove the skeleton. There was hardly any daylight—only a slight greyness emerging from the dark winter night. Gaston went up to the cart-shed loft and hid the skeleton behind a heap of empty boxes which he had saved for kindling. Nothing made any sense to him. He must be mad as a March hare, going about with these old bones under his arm. Like everyone else, this dead man had a right to his corner of the earth, and it was not at all seemly leaving him on the rough floor of the loft.

He used the opportunity to carry back a basket of logs to the house, and when he reached the kitchen Fernande had already lit the fire and made the coffee. Without saying a word he sat down at his place near the window, drank his coffee, and began to wait. He could not see clearly enough to read yet. He did not want to, anyway. He looked at the garden. He waited.

He waited for the boy to wake up, mentally preparing what he had decided to say. The words came easily. He congratulated himself on not having said anything the previous night. He must see it through, find out what the boy had in mind. He told himself Julien could not have come back without a clear idea of what he intended doing. Did he want to mend his ways? Try to square himself with the authorities? What did they do with deserters? Did they always put them in prison? He thought about Paul's suggestions—perhaps an opportunity for reconciliation there? If Paul helped Julien now, Fernande would no longer be able to say anything against this son who was not her own, no longer be able to criticize him for his attitude to the Militia. Perhaps there would be peace in the house at last.

Everything was still this morning. There was no sign of Julien having been in the kitchen. The first thing Fernande had done was to empty his suitcase of some books, two boxes of paints, and no small quantity of dirty and crumpled clothes. She had crammed the clothes into a bag and put the paint-boxes in the dining-room. Only the books had been left on the table. Gaston, after some hesitation, drew the pile over to where he was sitting. He took one and began to thumb through it. It was called *Les Fleurs du Mal*, by someone called Baudelaire. He took out his glasses, but the book contained nothing but poetry, which he did not even try to read. He put it down, looked at the others, and then pushed the whole lot away. There was nothing but poetry, and on some pages there were only a few lines, some of them very short. As far as he was concerned, that was not very serious work. Not unlike a baker giving short weight. He found it stupid to buy books containing so much blank paper. The more he thought about it, the more strange his boy seemed to be, quite different from the world in which his family had always lived.

Fernande said nothing. She did her work in silence, trying to open the door as little as possible so as not to let the warmth escape. Gaston looked at her from time to time. He felt she wanted to say something but did not dare. The idea had struck him just like that, but without any real foundation.

When she had finished the washing-up from the previous evening she brought to the stove an iron pot full of vegetable peelings intended for the rabbits. She then emptied a small bag of lentils on to the oilcloth and began to pick them over.

"Would you like me to help you?" asked Gaston.

"No, there aren't that many." Again there was silence. Then Fernande resumed the conversation. "I wasn't very warm last night."

"No, the cold has really got a hold on the house. Tonight we'll have to light a fire to dry the walls out a bit and air the room."

"It's so damp, the room should be heated all day."

"All day! That would be insane. It needs heating at night, as we used to do before the War when there was a heavy frost. Anyway, with the amount of wood we've got, we can't afford even to think about it."

Fernande said nothing, and Gaston thought that was the end of the matter. They had already spoken about it the previous winter, but Fernande knew as well as he that wood was in too short a supply to heat the room properly.

For a long time there was only the sound of the lentils being drawn across the oilcloth and dropped into a salad bowl which Fernande had on her knees. At last, after a deep sigh, she said, "All the same, those branches we fetched amount to a good deal of wood."

"The branches haven't been cut yet. And you know that I haven't been able to finish sawing up the big logs."

"That's it! Julien could do it. With care, he should be able to go down to the shed without being seen."

Gaston did not know what to reply. He agreed it would be good if Julien could saw and split the wood. But if Fernande was talking like this it meant that he must have said he wanted to hide here, live secretly in this house which was only separated from the town by the garden. Fernande must have realized that her husband was tempted by the prospect of the boy helping him cut, for she continued, "You understand, if he hides here for some time he will not be able to work in the kitchen. Three people in this little room—and someone might walk in at any moment. As there's no fireplace in his room, he'll have to take a table into ours. The only thing is—the only thing is, he'll have to have a fire."

Gaston gritted his teeth. His hand worked the corner of the table. A flood of words rose up in his throat. None came out. He opened his mouth several times, but he could not express them. What Fernande had just said was far removed from his hopes, and even from his fears. None of the sentences that he had been turning over in his mind for so long were of any use to him. He would never be able to understand either his wife or Julien. When he was on his own with her life was not always easy, but the work they did together gave them a close understanding. The labour got them over their quarrels. But as soon as Julien came back his world was turned upside down until he did not know where he was.

So the boy had thought of living here, doing nothing, hiding in a corner by a fire that would have to be kept going for him alone, because they were already managing without heating themselves! And Fernande approved of this. She was ready to support this good-for-nothing who had been unable to stay quietly in the Army! Good God! If he could not even be a soldier he would never be able to undertake anything with any chance of success!

The news had taken him by surprise, with the result that he was unable to give vent to his anger. He stayed where he was, speechless, looking at his wife, and wondering whether she was giving all her attention to her task or whether she kept her head down to avoid meeting his eyes.

23

It was after ten o'clock when Julien came downstairs. Gaston remarked as he forced a smile, "You must have needed that sleep. You've nearly slept round the clock."

"He must have been glad to be in his own bed again," said Fernande. "Did you have enough over you, my boy?"

"Yes, I was very comfortable."

Julien sat down in front of his bowl, which Fernande filled as she said, "There's not much milk, and it's impossible to get any more."

"As with everything else," said Gaston, "there's nothing. Nothing at all. It's as simple as that."

There was silence. Julien began to eat, and Gaston watched him. After all, this thin, bearded boy was his son. He wondered whether he had really believed this last night when he saw him coming in. He had been mulling over a speech that morning since he had got up. He had decided to persuade Julien to live like other people, to return to the way of life he considered right. Now he could remember none of the ideas so carefully prepared. As he watched him he thought about the months that he and Fernande had spent waiting. A hundred times they had believed him dead, and every time they had suffered. They had never talked openly about it, but Gaston had learnt to guess what was going on in his wife's heart. Hundreds of times he had felt like saying, "I suffer too. I suffer just as much as you at the thought that he might be dead, but you think I don't love him, that I have no feeling." He had suppressed these words so often that he would never be able to say them. He knew this. He also knew he would find it almost impossible to lecture Julien. Why? he asked himself. He found it difficult to understand what happened to him when he found himself facing the boy. The anger he nourished when alone vanished almost entirely as soon as Julien appeared. If he managed to rekindle it he still had to make an effort to shout, and things nearly always turned out wrong because his words never expressed exactly what he felt. It was so complicated trying to understand a fellow of twenty so different from himself!

Still, he must not give up so easily. Not for his own sake alone, but for the whole family's peace of mind. Fernande must be completely blind if she could not see the danger of harbouring a deserter whom the police were after. They must not let him settle down here without knowing what he planned to do.

In an effort to bolster his purpose Gaston tried to imagine what might happen. He saw the police in the house, the Militia, even the Germans; the trial, the shame, the house searched, plundered, burnt down. He filled his mind with the most dismal prospects until suddenly, unable to bear it any longer, he asked in a slightly trembling voice, "Well, then, what do you intend doing?"

Julien, who had finished his breakfast, lit a cigarette, and went over and offered one to his father, saying, "Well, I told you, I've some work to do."

"But look here. Staying in this house is like sticking your head into the lion's jaws. You can't live like a prisoner, never going outside the house."

"If I install myself in your room and work I won't have any complaints."

Gaston hesitated a moment. He felt that what he was about to say might put Fernande's back up. She had not spoken till now. She was in the scullery, the door was ajar, but no doubt she was listening.

Gaston forced a laugh. "You'll have no complaints, but we might complain about our stock of wood."

"A wood shortage in these parts, it's not—"

Gaston was about to reply, when Fernande came out of the scullery and said, "Your father is right. We can tell you what we've had to do to get an adequate supply for the winter. It's not easy, you know." She hesitated. Then, turning to Gaston, she said, "All the same, there's ample for the winter. You must see that he can't spend the day in the kitchen hiding every time he hears someone coming. If he has to work he'll have to do it in our room."

Gaston looked away. What she meant was: "This is your son. He's come here to hide. You're not going to let him freeze. You're not going to throw him out. Even if it kills us going without food because he hasn't any ration-book, we have got to keep him with us for as long as possible. He's my own son. He's here now, and I am not letting him go. As for you, you're nothing but a selfish old man. I've told you that hundreds of times, and I'm telling you again."

Yes, that was what Gaston felt. He could read it in her eyes as though they were a wide-open book. There was much more in her look. There was the threat of mentioning Paul—how they had had to fetch firewood from the forest, the food that Paul and his wife sold and bought on the black market, Paul's friendships, his connections that Julien, who had left the Vichy Army, would no doubt despise.

"What I'd like," said Julien, "is for you to keep me here for a month—that's how long it will take me to do my work—and then I'll piss off."

"My poor boy," sighed his mother, "that means you'll be leaving again. And God knows where you'll go!"

"Don't worry," said the boy. "Don't you worry."

There seemed to be an understanding between them. Perhaps Gaston sensed it the moment he was about to give in. They had used the previous evening to get all their arguments ready, and decided they would easily get round him. This provoked his anger.

"Well," he cried, "I'm perfectly willing, but you don't suppose the police are going to give up looking for him!"

He was almost shouting, and Fernande looked surprised. Her eyes were sad rather than angry. "If you think he'd be safer with strangers or tramping around the countryside we should tell him to leave."

She had spoken calmly, but Gaston could guess what more she might say. He suddenly felt conflict between the peace he had enjoyed since the beginning of winter and the war which might explode in their midst and turn all into chaos. One ill-considered word from him, and Fernande would shout, "So you want him to die—to die so that Paul becomes your sole heir and gets everything." She had never spoken like that before, but Gaston knew she would go so far in order to defend Julien.

Alone.

Once more he was alone. Once more his peace was threatened. He looked at both of them separately, lowering his eyes, and, turning away, he put his right elbow on the table and muttered, "So help me, you do as you like. I was only thinking of Julien."

You could only just hear the end of his sentence. He had already put his feet on the oven door, and his body slumped into its normal position of rest.

24

Time began to pass slowly again, as though winter had regained the rhythm that had been broken for a few days. Julien hardly ever got up before nine. He came down to wash and have breakfast, then went up to shut himself in his parents' bedroom, where he lit the fire. He did not come down at midday because that was the most likely time for unexpected visitors. His mother took him a meal, and sometimes went up two or three times. In the evening, once the outer gate was locked, the boy would come down to the kitchen, but they all kept on the alert.

What was he doing all day, sitting at the table he had pushed over in front of the window? Gaston would have liked to know. Every evening when he went up to bed he looked at the table, but Julien left nothing there but his pad of paper, a pen, some pencils, a dictionary, and an ashtray that was often full of cigarette-stubs. Gaston would help himself to a few, putting them in his tobacco-tin and, shaking his head, would go to bed. The bedroom smelt of cigarette and wood smoke. When he had put out the lamp he would lie for a long time with his eyes open, watching the light dancing on the ceiling. There was still a log burning in the stove behind the blackened, cracked mica windows. There were crackling noises, and the characteristic sound of green wood oozing its sap on to the embers. As he listened Gaston thought about the forest, about the trouble they had had getting this wood which the boy was burning all day long.

But Gaston took great care not to talk about it. He knew his wife would not take kindly to such a remark. All he had asked on the second day was: "But what is he doing?"

Fernande had replied, "I don't know. He's working."

"But he's not doing any drawing?"

"No, he's writing and studying books. We must leave him alone. He's certainly not wasting his time. We have to remember that he left school when he was fourteen to become an apprentice. He has not had much study. Some boys study till they're over twenty."

Gaston had not replied. Her words were clearly meant to indicate that a son might be dependent on his parents for much longer than Julien had been. There was nothing he could say. He could not even ask his wife how she managed to get enough food, how she bought bread without coupons, nor by what magic Julien was able to smoke so many cigarettes when he had no tobacco card. Fernande was spending no more time shopping than usual, and nothing had changed in her routine. He decided to wait, to let time roll by, showing neither bad temper nor astonishment. Times were odd. Nothing was done in the normal way, so it was quite natural not to be surprised at anything.

On the fourth day after Julien had arrived the weather suddenly turned milder, and the wind dropped, bringing heavy rain.

"I thought it was coming," said Gaston. "My shoulder has been hurting for the last two days."

"I'm going to take advantage of this and go and saw some wood," said Julien. "No-one will come down to the bottom of the garden in this sort of weather. I'll put on the cape with the hood up to get to the shed. Even if a neighbour should see me they won't recognize me."

"I'm coming with you," said his father.

"You'll get cold," said his wife.

"No, it's not cold. I'll split the logs and stack them. If someone should come you tell them to wait here, and then come and fetch me. Julien can hide in the loft down there if necessary."

They worked all morning, and Gaston tried asking his son several questions about his life in Marseilles. But Julien only talked about his friend the painter, whom he admired very much.

After that particular morning all was quiet again. Now and then a neighbour would visit them, stay a while for a chat, and then leave, having given them news of the War, of people who had been arrested, others who had been shot, and others who had disappeared without a trace. It was mostly M. Robin who brought them information because he listened to the B.B.C. every night. But to Gaston all this was but an echo of far-away events. The names of most of the countries were unknown to him. When M. Robin told them about the formation of the Tito Government, for example, Gaston wondered how that could possibly affect them. M. Robin had said to Fernande, "You no longer come and listen to the wireless, Mme Dubois?"

"No, it's too cold to go out in the evening."

Every time he came M. Robin asked, "Still no news of Julien?"

"Still no news."

From time to time M. Robin would bring them a little butter or a small piece of cheese, or yet again a packet of tobacco for Gaston. Then Fernande would go outside with him, saying, "Let's go down in the cellar, and I'll give you some onions and apples for your little boy."

M. Robin also brought newspapers which Gaston tried to read, thumbing through them to look at the pictures.

Life went on in this fashion, with visits from neighbours and the weather alternately cold, foggy, or raining.

One afternoon, as the grey day was darkening, Paul Dubois arrived.

"I was passing by," he said, "and I saw that the bedroom chimney was smoking. I was alarmed. I thought my father must be ill."

"Oh, no," stammered Gaston, "it's only, you see—"

Fernande interrupted. "With all the rain these last few days the bedroom has become dreadfully damp. The walls are so wet that the paper is peeling off. So we have to light the fire for a while. Besides, we do that every winter."

"I know," said Paul, "but usually you only light it in the evening, that's why I thought my father was in bed."

"This evening," said Fernande, "I lit it a little earlier to try and dry the walls out."

"That's what I must have seen. When I went up to the station at about two o'clock it was already smoking. I didn't think about it at the time, and then this afternoon it came to my mind again. I said to myself, if they are lighting the fire during the day there must be something unusual going on."

He had sat down, opened his raincoat, and pushed his brown waterproof hat to the back of his head. He was half smiling, looking from one to the other. He took out his packet of cigarettes, selected one for himself, and slid the packet across the oilcloth towards his father.

"Here, have one."

Gaston hesitated. He felt ill at ease. His son's look seemed to pierce right through him.

"I'm smoking less and less," he said.

There was a slight creak upstairs. Fernande coughed, but Paul had looked up. He began to laugh. Then he said, "Drying out the house makes the floor creak."

"It's time I went to put another log on the stove." She said this on her way to the staircase.

"Wouldn't you like me to do it for you," suggested Paul, "then you won't have to go upstairs. It must be a lot of work keeping the fire going all day."

"I'm used to it," she replied drily.

She went up. The staircase creaked. Gaston's throat tightened. He looked at his son through the smoke from their two cigarettes. Had Paul guessed the truth? Was he going to say anything? Would he do something? What exactly was the Militia? No. It was impossible. He would not dare. He would not be able to do it. But perhaps they should have asked him for advice if his wife would have agreed. Now it was too late. Too late? Perhaps not.

Everything was whirling round in Gaston's head. He realized that his hands were trembling, that his face was cowering. Paul must have noticed. Paul smiled. Was he enjoying himself? Was he laughing at his father's difficulties? Still smiling, he said, "It must be very hard work for Mother, keeping that fire going all day. You should have a coal stove. You fill it up in the morning, and that's all. I've got one I could lend you."

Fernande was already coming back. She must have warned Julien. But Gaston had not heard her shutting the bedroom door, and he had been listening. Could Julien hear what they were saying?

She seemed calm. She offered Paul a glass of wine, which he accepted. She poured it out. Her hand was certainly not shaking, and Gaston wondered how she managed. Paul drank half his wine and asked, "Don't you think coal would be better for you? I've got a small stove I could lend you. I could send one of my drivers to install it for you."

"No," replied Fernande, "it's unhealthy with coal in a bedroom, and there's the risk of being choked by the fumes."

"I was only trying to help you."

"Thank you," she said, "but we are managing all right as it is."

"One thing you could do to help us," said Gaston, "is to fetch some sacks of firewood if one of your lorries should be going up into the mountain. There should still be some offcuts left at the sawmills."

He had spoken without thinking, without preparing what he was going to say, and he was quite surprised with himself.

"I'll remember that," Paul promised. "Next time we deliver to Morez or St Claude I'll tell my driver."

He said no more. It was as if he had something else to say. He glanced from one to the other. He was still smiling, but not in the same way. At last he continued, in a voice more serious and low, "But I promise nothing. When the lorry goes up that way we never know if it will come back. Some of them have been attacked by terrorists. They not only steal the goods, but they keep the lorries as well. There was even a driver who had to be carried back because he resisted. I don't like my staff having to take those risks. So we only deliver up in the mountains when we have protection."

He was becoming uneasy as he spoke. His voice was pitched higher, and the delivery was more abrupt. He stopped for a moment, but no-one breathed a word. He drew on his cigarette twice, and then went on: "That's it. I'm asking for an escort. We are working so that people shan't die of hunger. If we weren't there to deliver they wouldn't even get what their ration-books entitle them to. So it would be reasonable for the police to give us some security. When the police are not able to do it, well, then, the Germans have to. That's for sure. I know there are some who don't like it. But I don't give a bugger for them, I don't. I am doing my duty. Whether it pleases them or not doesn't matter."

The smile had gone. His face was tense, his eyes hardened.

The light was fading, and it was time to light the lamp. But Fernande did not move. She was sitting straight up in her chair, her hands flat on her knees. There was only light on the right side of her face. Gaston turned his back to the window and he found this a relief. Paul was facing the light, but his features were becoming less sharp. Only his eyes were still bright. There was a long silence. Then, in a voice that was less strong, but still rang like steel, Paul added, "I'm a businessman. I follow my trade. Believe me, it's not all fun and games. Nowadays no-one takes any action against the rabble. Ask anyone. You'll find out that those who have joined the maquis from Lons are the worst layabouts. Little tramps who were just waiting for a chance to find an outlet for their instincts for robbery and murder. That's what the Resistance is. A beautiful lot, indeed!"

His voice was rising again. Then he stopped suddenly and began to laugh. "But I didn't come to talk about that," he said. "I came to see how you were because I saw smoke coming from your bedroom chimney. But it was of no significance."

"No," said Gaston firmly, "no significance at all, as you say. As for those stories, they're no concern of ours." He did not shout, but his voice was decisive, almost hard.

The words came because they had been on the tip of his tongue for a while. They came out with a sudden force, like the bung spurting out of the barrel when his fruit was fermenting into wine. Now he sighed. Then added as he got up, "It's time to light the lamp and put the soup on."

Paul got up, buttoned his raincoat, and said before he went, "I'm not asking you for news of Julien. I know you would have told me if you had any."

25

As he went out through the door Paul gave a scornful little laugh. He had been slow about leaving, and gusts of cold night air had filled the kitchen. When the door was shut again the two old people listened to his footsteps down the stairs. They faded as he crossed the flagstones in the courtyard until they were lost in the drive. Gaston felt as though the cold air that had invaded the room had sprung from that unpleasant laughter. It was an odd and painful impression. He wanted to shake it off, but it persisted until Fernande lowered the lamp and said, "If you'd close the shutters I'll light the lamp."

When he had closed the window he turned round. She had finished trimming the wick, which she then lit. Julien was standing at the bottom of the stairs. Because he had been leaning out of the window and been completely taken up with the effort of unhooking the shutters, Gaston had not heard him coming down. Their eyes met. Julien's face looked both severe and ironic.

"You shouldn't come down before I've been up to lock the outer gate," said his mother.

Julien laughed. "There's no reason for me to hide any longer," he replied. "The whole town will know I'm here within the hour."

Gaston had feared this reaction, but still the words were a blow.

"What are you on about!" he shouted.

"It's the truth. If you haven't understood that you really must be thick."

"Julien!" cried his mother. "Please!"

There was a silence. Fernande had pulled the lamp up again, and the flame had stopped flickering. They were all three standing in the light reflected by the lampshade shining down on the table which separated them.

Gaston was breathing hard, but more because of anger than the effort he had just made and the cold air.

"You have no right to speak like that," he said, controlling himself. "Your brother doesn't know you are here. Even if he did know, why should you think he'd go and shout it over the rooftops?"

"He won't shout it over the rooftops, but he'll know how to drop a hint in the right quarters so that action is taken."

"But why should you think he'd do such a stupid thing, you young idiot!"

Gaston could control himself no longer. Something shouted inside him that he was wrong to fly into a passion, but his anger was choking him. He did not even know against whom it was directed, but a force over which he had no control made him lose his temper. Julien shouted louder than he, "Why? Because he told you. Because he's hand in glove with the Germans. Because he needs them! Because without them he wouldn't be able to grow fat in the black market!"

"Julien, you're going too far!"

A fit of coughing overcame Gaston just when Fernande intervened. "Be quiet, both of you. Someone might come, and they'd hear you half-way up the garden. Julien, go upstairs again. I'm going to lock the outer gate."

Julien shrugged his shoulders. He stayed where he was for a moment, hesitating. Then, as his mother took a step in his direction, he turned on his heel and went quickly up to his room.

His father stood rooted between the window and the table, staring at his wife's back. At first her back was rigid, but gradually slow movements shook through her, and he at once understood that she had begun to cry. He sighed, looked down at the floor, and slumped into his chair.

He was still angry, but he knew that he would not lose his temper again. He was making no effort to hold it back. It was as though his anger, having been part of the very fibre of his being, was now separating itself out like a writhing animal and hardening into a cold, unwieldy lump. It was hardly alive, but it prevented him from breathing freely all the same.

Without looking at him, without even a word, Fernande

threw her shawl over her shoulders, took the key to the gate, and went out quickly.

As soon as she had shut the door behind her there was a deep silence. Gaston felt himself plunged into an unfathomable emptiness like black fog, where, should he attempt to challenge it, his voice would be lost without even an echo. It was completely hostile. Paul's words threatened him, Julien's words threatened. He was in the middle, not knowing where to turn. While he was alone he could only keep on saying, "It's the War . . . it rots everything. Nothing good will ever come of it."

26

As soon as Fernande came back she put the soup on to warm. Gaston looked at her guardedly, daring neither to question nor to look long enough to meet her eyes. Shortly afterwards she went up to the bedroom. Gaston listened, but he heard nothing. He waited. The atmosphere of the house lay like an oppressive weight on his shoulders. Upstairs his wife and his boy were talking together. Whereas he, alone in the kitchen, was left completely outside.

Without knowing why, he suddenly thought of the loft in the cart-shed and the pile of boxes behind which the skeleton was sleeping.

Was that dead man more alone than he? Had he had children too? Who was it who had been able to give him away or sell him to be carted around like this in the world of the living?

The door closed upstairs, and Fernande's footsteps could be heard on the creaking wooden staircase. When she appeared Gaston asked, "Isn't he coming down to eat?" His voice sounded quite normal.

"No," she said, "he's gone to bed."

"Doesn't he want to eat, then?"

"No."

"He's in a bad temper."

"It's best to leave him alone."

"Heavens above . . ." He sighed.

His wife waited a short while before saying, "I know what you're thinking."

"Oh, do you? Well, then, tell me."

"All you can think about is not having a quiet life any longer since the boy came home."

Gaston made a great effort not to shout. He stroked his chin twice before he replied. "Yes, it's true that life isn't peaceful any more. You're also right to call him a boy. His behaviour is no better than a youngster who can't see beyond his own nose. As for us, it's because we're concerned for him, thinking of what might happen, that we're no longer able to live quietly."

Fernande sat down slowly. She crossed her arms on the table and fixed her gaze on Gaston's eyes. He realized at once that she was going to get at him.

"Nothing will happen if no-one gives him away," she said slowly. She showed no sign of anger and appeared amazingly calm. Even this was disturbing.

Lowering his eyes, Gaston muttered, "No-one will give him away."

"I hope not," she said.

Then she got up to get the plates and brought them to the table. When she had laid it they began to eat in silence, and it was not till she had finished her soup that she announced, still very calmly, "He wants to leave again."

Gaston felt as though a great draught of air had filled his lungs, making it easier to breathe. He tried hard not to show his relief. He was successful because a bitter feeling rose to spoil his sense of wellbeing. He had difficulty in understanding this, and his fear of giving himself away increased. He swallowed three spoonfuls of soup before asking, "Leave again? But where does he want to go?"

"He won't say. And I don't think he knows himself. But I . . ." She had to search for words. She spoke slowly, hesitating before each sentence. "I am very worried indeed," she went on. "I don't think he'll find it easy to hide. After all, he could have stayed here until we'd found him a better hiding-place—in the country, for example."

"No-one is forcing him to leave."

"No . . . of course not . . . no-one . . ."

The word vibrated in the warmth of the room. Gaston could still hear it although it had already died away.

Fernande had stopped talking. No doubt she supposed that Gaston guessed her thoughts. When people have lived together so long there are times when silence is enough. One single word is a key, and the rest is easy to surmise.

When she had cleared the table she fetched a bowl and the pot of honey from Provence. She made the lime tea in a small pan of water. As she sat down again she said in a very low voice, glancing over at the staircase, "He's very unhappy, you know."

"No-one's happy these days."

"I know. Circumstances are difficult, but there are other things that he won't tell us about."

She was still speaking in a low voice, hesitating over her words. Gaston had to concentrate hard to be able to hear her, realizing that she had a lot to say and that she intended saying it all.

"You know," she went on, "when he joined the maquis his friend who went with him was killed. . . . He broods a lot over that, I believe . . . and then . . ."

At this point she waited so long that Gaston thought she had given up. "Well, then?" he asked.

"I think he was in love with a young girl, and it didn't work out. So, you understand . . ."

"Has he spoken to you about it?"

"No, but I felt things weren't going well for him. The other morning, when you were both chopping wood, I read what he is writing."

Gaston shook his head. He began to tap the oilcloth with his hand. "Good heavens . . . good heavens!" he muttered.

What else could he say? Nothing. There was nothing to add.

He too had seen his friends dying. By the dozen. He remembered their names and their faces. But that was a long time ago. As to this girl his son had loved—but then, what exactly did it mean, to love? That he hoped to marry her and she had refused him? There would be others. Anyway, what could he have done with a wife, the state he was in at the moment? His own youth had been nothing like Julien's; he could not understand what went on in the boy, so different from himself. When he was young he had had to spend so much time working that there was little left over for anything else. He got married. He had a son. His wife had died, leaving him on his own with the bakery. It had not been much fun, admittedly, but he had not shut himself away on that account, taking refuge alone in a room, writing about how sad he was.

His wife had probably expected a different reaction. After a long silence she poured his tea and asked, "I would like to try and see Vaintrenier. What do you think?"

He was still thinking about the boy's sentimental despair, so he was surprised. "Vaintrenier?" he said. "But what has he got to do with it?"

"He used to be deputy mayor. He resigned when the Pétain Government was formed, which proves he doesn't agree with them. If he doesn't agree with them he might well know how to hide Julien."

Gaston raised his hands. Such ideas frightened him.

"How can you?" he said. "If you begin telling people Julien is here—"

He stopped suddenly. He regretted what he had said, but the reaction he had feared did not materialize. Fernande said nothing about Paul, and he decided she wanted to avoid at any price an argument that might complicate matters. He was about to continue when she said, still in a low voice, "Listen to me. Without giving anything away I've spoken to M. Robin. He said to me, 'If you should hear from Julien one day, why don't you go and see M. Vaintrenier. I'm sure he would be able to help him.'"

Gaston looked at her for a long time. She did not flinch, but nevertheless he felt she was not speaking the truth. No doubt she had already told M. Robin that Julien was back. Gaston had no reason to distrust his neighbour, and yet he was suddenly frightened. Without intending any harm, M. Robin might be indiscreet. He could tell his wife in all confidence, talk in front of his little boy. A whole sequence of events tumbled through Gaston's mind explosively. Fear made him think quickly. He saw his house ransacked, burnt to the ground, he saw himself dragged off by the S.S., in a prison-cell while they shot Julien. The only unbearable thing in all this was the vision of his boy being executed. Had he brought bad luck on himself in bringing the skeleton of the old man with him?

As surely as he had refused to admit that Paul might even inadvertently give Julien away he feared that a stranger might do it. He knew that Paul was in with the Germans, while M. Robin was not afraid of condemning them, but it did not alter his opinion. One ill-considered word, and all would be lost. They might even believe that Paul had been responsible.

His head was ringing. He felt completely confused. It hurt, trying to get his ideas in order, controlling this fear which twisted his stomach. His fear slowly changed into anger. Unaccountably it turned against M. Vaintrenier.

"God Almighty!" he exploded. "If Vaintrenier refuses to help he's a bastard! After all I did for him when people were leaving town!"

"You made bread because all the bakers had left town and people were starving," said Fernande calmly. "I know you didn't have to, but I don't see why you should be angry."

Gaston felt his rage had been ridiculous. "I'm not getting angry," he grumbled, "but I know people. When they want something they're there. When it's a matter of them doing a favour they disappear."

"Wait at least till we've asked before talking like that."

"Asked! We can't go asking him tonight."

"It might be a good time. I'd be sure of finding him at home."

Gaston almost felt comforted. Fernande was going to go and find Vaintrenier herself.

Looking at the alarm-clock, she said, "There's more than an hour left before curfew. I'll have plenty of time to go there and come back again."

Without even waiting for a reply she got up and began to put on her coat.

27

Fernande got herself ready very quickly. Gaston vacantly watched her every movement as she bustled around. She went out. She was going to try to persuade Vaintrenier to help them. That was all.

As soon as she had gone Gaston had muttered, "There she goes. God in heaven above, I'm the one who should have gone. She won't know how to press the point. But it's difficult for me to walk at all at the moment, so what else could I have done?"

But another voice inside him replied, "You didn't go because you don't want to get mixed up in all this. You don't want to have anything to do with Julien. You're just carving another stick to beat your own back. Serve you right!"

Was he responsible, after all, for the boy's folly? Who had brought him up? His mother. Fernande had done it on her own. She had always disagreed with anything he had done towards the boy's education. She had corrupted the boy by spoiling him.

The result was there now. It was not only Julien who risked going to prison or even the firing-squad for his impulsive behaviour. He had endangered them all by coming here to hide. They might all end up like that, and the house as well! But what mattered most? Oh dear, there he was again, thinking only of himself and his tired old body. The most important thing was to enable Julien to hide. To escape from being found. The rest mattered little.

He repeated all this to himself, but another idea tortured him. Paul. If Paul succeeded in getting a German escort for his lorries it meant that he was on good terms with them, had an understanding with them. It was possible, just possible, that a word from him could settle the matter. But Fernande would never agree to this; and yet it would mean peace and security for them all. What would the neighbours think? Well, the neighbours need never know. But what would they think if...

Gaston turned the thought over in his mind, but the more he let it mull the more sour it became. Everything became foul, took on a disgusting aspect. He thought about Paul's suggestion. He could see his son becoming annoyed as he expounded, "What! The Germans. What have you all got against them? They conquered us—so? We shouldn't have declared war on them! What are you afraid of? That they'll steal your property? If anyone will steal your property it'll be the bolsheviks. The Germans are protecting you from bolshevism. Do they get in your way here? They buy. They pay. They have set up Trade Commissions when they could quite well have pinched what they liked because they are the stronger. I work with them because I'm a tradesman. You've been one all your life. Did you ever refuse a customer? I've never seen you go to Mass, but that didn't prevent you making bread for the priests and their schools. If it wasn't for those idiots who stab them in the back the Germans wouldn't have to make all these restrictions. Of course they have to shoot hostages when their men get killed. It's to be expected. Pétain signed the armistice. One has to accept that. You were in the '14 war. You know who Pétain is! You can't tell me he was a traitor. But do you know de Gaulle? You've heard of him? Who is he? An adventurer, that's all. So there are young people who follow him, and it's our duty to enlighten them and make them see sense!"

Oh, yes, that was how Paul spoke. Others who spoke with equal reason looked upon Pétain as a traitor and de Gaulle as a saviour. What was he to believe? Here he had spent his life kneading bread, and now he was tilling the earth again, and that did not leave much time to think about politics. Gaston found it very difficult to see things clearly for himself.

Up till now the War had not affected him apart from these troubles and the restrictions. It was bad enough, but it was nothing compared with what he had seen in 1914 where the fighting was going on.

Gradually he began to feel as though no-one could ever touch his garden or his house. This little plot of land had been cultivated up till now, and it seemed to him that that was how it would go on until the end of the War. For it would have to end some time! The main thing, if they were to enjoy a peaceful life, was not to take in a barrel of gunpowder. That was what Julien seemed at the moment—an explosive that would send everything sky high.

Gaston had to stop thinking several times. It made his head ache. Occasionally he would look up at the clock. Time was passing. The fire was dying down. Should he put another log on? Could he go up to bed before his wife came back? Would she accuse him of not caring if he did not wait up for her?

There he was, one elbow on the table and his feet on the oven door. He tried to keep calm, to tell himself that everything would be all right again, but he was shivering from the sweat on his back and neck. It was worse than the kind that soaked his shirt when he was working in his garden at the height of summer.

He was used to long, hard, and sometimes disappointing work. Strain had always been part of his life, but the evil that dug through his mind was a thousand times more painful.

The night lay heavy upon him. Here he was. Julien was sleeping right above the kitchen. Fernande was walking through the darkness. Nothing seemed to be alive, and everything seemed to be preparing a great disaster for them.

28

When she came back Fernande had said that M. Vaintrenier had received her extremely well. He had listened to her without seeming at all surprised, and then he had just said, "Right, I'll come and see you early tomorrow morning."

Gaston was not completely reassured by this promise, and he had a bad night, disturbed by nightmares that woke him continually.

He was up before daylight.

"Early morning for Vaintrenier," said Fernande, "is sure to mean about nine o'clock. It's not worth turning everything upside down."

"We must get Julien up. If only he'd shave his beard off he'd look a little more respectable."

"Now listen, don't start that again."

Julien got up. Fernande told him about the impending visit of the former deputy mayor, and Julien just said, "Oh, that's good."

They had breakfast in silence. An awkward silence which seemed to ooze out of the atmosphere like a dull day from a dawn over the edge of the horizon.

The only live thing was the fire, where an acacia log crackled without stop.

"There was a time," said Gaston, "when a good forester wouldn't dream of putting acacia with the firewood. But nowadays they don't give a damn."

"Still, we should be glad to have something to warm the room," said his wife.

And that was all. Silence again.

Gaston looked at Julien, who was smoking, having finished his breakfast. Forearms on the table, hands crossed, and his head inclined, the boy seemed abstracted.

A little while later Julien got up and went upstairs. Gaston heard him moving about and realized that he was lighting the stove. He wanted to tell his wife that it was perhaps a waste of time, but he restrained himself. He felt it would have been ridiculous. Vaintrenier was coming, but he was hardly going to say to Julien, "Come with me. I'll take care of you."

Gaston heard every sound. He imagined the boy stuffing the stove with logs so that it would be roaring away. It was amazing what a stove of that sort could consume in the course of a day! A month of this, and they would be through the first pile.

The hours passed slowly. The dead calm of the grey morning obscured the hills as though drowning them in dirty water. Vaintrenier arrived shortly before nine. As soon as he came in he took off his hat, put it on the chest-of-drawers, and unbuttoned his black overcoat.

"I'll take that," said Fernande.

She took the coat to the dining-room. Vaintrenier sat down by the table. He must have been walking fast, because his face was red. He wiped his forehead and grey, wavy hair with his handkerchief. "Well," he asked, "and where's this prodigy of yours?"

Gaston pointed to the ceiling.

"I'll go and call him," said Fernande.

Alone with the former councillor, Gaston looked at him for a moment before saying, "I'd like to thank you for coming, Hubert. It's very kind of you."

"It's not kindness that makes me come. It is natural that we should help each other. When I asked you to make bread during the crisis you did it."

Gaston raised his hand to interrupt. "Ah, but that's finished and done with. You didn't ask me to do it for yourself, but for all the others. And they don't seem to have been very grateful to you."

"Why do you say that? Because I'm no longer a councillor? Make no mistake. No-one's thrown me out. I resigned of my own accord because I wasn't going to take orders from a government I disapproved of!"

His voice had hardened slightly. Gaston felt that his few words implied some sort of reproach directed at himself. He muttered, "You know, at my age, politics—"

"Of course," said Vaintrenier, "but it's not only to do with politics . . ."

Then he stopped. Gaston felt there was still something he wanted to say. Before the War Vaintrenier had been elected by the supporters of the Popular Front. He was not much older than Paul Dubois, and Gaston knew that they did not see eye to eye. The former councillor probably wanted to speak about Paul. If this was his intention it would be better if it happened while they were alone together, but if the presence of his wife was going to restrain him she had better come down quickly. Very quickly.

Gaston listened hard. He felt a mounting anguish. Vaintrenier said, "We live in terrible times, my friend. War is no joke. But I wonder whether a real war is not somewhat less unhealthy than this situation where Frenchmen are tearing each other to pieces."

There was a noise on the staircase, Vaintrenier stopped, and Gaston breathed more freely.

When Julien appeared the councillor got up to shake his hand. He began to laugh as he said, "Bless my soul! Your mother told me you were painting, but she didn't tell me you had already acquired the professional headgear."

Julien shrugged his shoulders. "It's really so that I won't be recognized," he said.

"I'd like him to shave that beard off," said his father.

"No, don't do that," said Vaintrenier. "I'm not saying that he won't go unnoticed, but I swear that if I met him in the street I wouldn't have recognized him. When you have known him with short back and sides, looking like a healthy sportsman, it's different."

Gaston still insisted feebly, spoke of bad taste, but Vaintrenier interrupted, "Even if he wanted to shave it off I'd advise him not to at the moment. He's very sunburnt, and it would show if he cut off his beard. Then he would really look like a boy who'd wanted to disguise himself."

Gaston gave up wearily. No doubt at all, nothing was normal these days.

Julien went to fetch a chair in the dining-room, and they all sat down round the table. Fernande poured a small glass of brandy for Vaintrenier, who drank a mouthful before saying, "We don't drink this very often these days."

"I had a few bottles in stock," said Gaston, "but I'm afraid they won't last as long as the War."

"Who knows!" said the councillor. "Things aren't going so well for the Germans in Italy and Russia."

He waited. Then he sat forward in his chair and looked at Julien as he asked, "Well, now, what were you thinking of doing?"

"For the moment, I'm all right here."

Vaintrenier shook his head slowly two or three times before saying in a very gentle voice, "No, my boy. That's not possible. No-one could live in a house as small as this without being noticed sooner or later. You could hide almost anywhere, but not here."

"It will be all right if no-one denounces me!" Julien said, almost aggressively.

Vaintrenier smiled sadly and shook his head again. He sighed, "Yes, I know, but that's another matter. You mustn't believe in miracles."

As Julien was about to speak Vaintrenier raised his hand to silence him and went on in a firmer voice, "I'm not saying there's a risk of your being denounced deliberately, but through carelessness. Or because of jealousy. You forget there are thousands of boys of your age who have gone to Germany on compulsory labour service. You forget that others are conscripted to guard the railways or work here in the factories. Their parents probably don't agree with their going, but if they know that others are hiding, then, without intending any harm, they might drop a careless word."

He hesitated, looked at each of the parents in turn, and in a low voice, speaking slowly as though he regretted having to pronounce the words, he added, "Besides, there's the police, and the Militia as well. They've got their eyes and ears everywhere."

Gaston looked down. The only sound for a while was the crackling of the fire. Gaston wanted to shout at Vaintrenier, "You don't really imagine that Paul would denounce him!" However, he did not dare. He contented himself with saying, "And if he let them know . . . If he went and said—"

The former councillor interrupted him. With a scorn that cut Gaston like a knife, he said, "Oh, no, my friend. It's quite in order to keep out of things, but you can't shut your eyes to what's going on. I'm not saying that all the supporters of the Vichy Government are bastards—there may be some who deceive themselves in good faith. But the ones in the Militia . . . No, no, and again no!"

He must have kept something back for fear of hurting the old man. But Gaston had understood. He had difficulty in restraining his anger. He wanted to say that all this was no concern of his, that he no longer felt responsible for his sons' actions. One of them was too old. The other had never belonged to him. And then he had been a soldier. There was the War. It was the governments, it was society, that was responsible for all this mess!

The words were inside him, tumbling and jostling like nuts in a basket; the tumult was painful but they could find no way out. He knew he would never have the last word with a man like Vaintrenier, who was used to politics and involved discussions. He felt paralysed. His back sagged. He fixed his gaze on the faded blue-and-white squares of the cracked oilcloth. That was what the world was like, cracked and threadbare, and nothing could be replaced.

Gaston's anger subsided, but before it froze completely it came up once more in spite of his efforts, and he cried, "Damn it all! There's nothing left for us but to die!"

Vaintrenier did not appear moved or even surprised. No doubt he understood what was going on in the old man. Gaston realized this, and in a way he felt uneasy. Vaintrenier's frank look went right through him. He lowered his eyes and sighed, but felt better for his simple outburst. He realized that his remaining anger would now leave him alone. He knew that everything that was going to be said and done from now on would have no relevance to his life. After all, Vaintrenier had come because he might be able to help Julien, and it was best to let him speak and act.

The councillor drank another mouthful of brandy, smacked his lips, and said, "This is getting us nowhere. The important thing is that Julien can't stay here."

He stopped. He frowned. He looked questioningly at Fernande, then at Gaston, and finally stared hard at Julien. "Now it's up to you," he said. "You must know what you want to do."

Julien looked vague and pulled a face so that his beard stuck out.

"The possibilities are limited," he went on. "Either you join the maquis or else you go and live in a big town where no-one knows you."

"The maquis," muttered Gaston.

Vaintrenier looked at him, but Gaston had nothing more to say. But the councillor had guessed what was on his mind.

"It's not what you imagine it to be or anything like what people say," he explained. "It's an army—underground—but an army all the same. You know my opinions. I've never been a militarist, but nowadays there's only one thing that counts, and that's sending the Germans back home with a kick in the arse—the sooner the better. Some people are trying to do this, others don't agree at all, and—and then there are some who hope it will happen, but wait for it to happen without their help."

He stumbled slightly over the last few words, and when he had finished he was silent. As no-one spoke, he emptied his glass, put his big hands flat on the table, and leant over towards Julien. He seemed to have made a decision on his behalf.

"Right," he said, "I know what happened to you when you tried to join the maquis in the Black Mountains. It's a sad story, and I'm not going to dwell on it. I don't want to influence you in any way. You'll have to think about it. When you've come to a decision you know where to find me."

He leaned forward on his hands for a moment longer, rocking slightly, then slowly stood up.

When he had put on his overcoat, which Fernande had fetched, he appeared to think again and asked, "Show me what sort of identity-card you've got."

Julien went upstairs. As soon as he had left Fernande asked, "The maquis, M. Vaintrenier, you know, it frightens me—"

"Your fear is understandable and perfectly normal, Mme Dubois. But in the towns, you know, there are constant raids. They arrest anybody, they put people in prison, and if they need hostages they just help themselves. So, you understand, when it comes to risk—"

Julien was on his way downstairs, and Fernande interrupted the councillor, asking him quickly, "And on a farm . . . ?"

He raised his hand. "Yes, that's one solution. But I wouldn't be able to help you there."

Julien gave him the identity-card, and he examined it at length. Then he asked, "Have you got some spare photographs?"

"Yes, there's one left."

"Give it to me."

Julien searched through his wallet and gave a photograph to the councillor, who slipped it between the pages of a dog-eared notebook.

"I'm calling again tonight. In the meanwhile take care you're not seen."

Turning towards the old people, he added, "If anyone asks you why I came here tell them my wife owed you for some vegetables, and I came to settle with you."

He had already shaken them by the hand and was going to the door when Fernande said, "M. Vaintrenier, he has no ration-book."

He turned round. His voice was almost hard as he rapped out, "I know. You already told me twice last night."

He crammed his hat on his head with an incisive gesture and left quickly. Fernande went outside and waited till he had reached the bottom of the steps before she closed the door again.

29

When M. Vaintrenier had gone they all three stood for a moment without speaking, as though expecting a command that never came.

Gaston looked at Julien. He was wearing an old pair of paint-stained trousers and a thick brown polo-necked sweater—the collar came right up under his blonde beard. He was drawing hard on his cigarette and stood with his back bent, like an old man. Gaston thought he was going to say something, but, having stood quite still for a while, he turned about and went up the stairs.

Fernande followed him with her eyes, seemed to hesitate, then with a tired gesture said almost inaudibly, "My God, what are we going to do!"

It was not a question. Even so, Gaston would have had nothing to say in reply. He went to sit down, and Fernande went upstairs to Julien.

On his own, Gaston poked the fire, sat down slowly, and looked at the garden. The earth, dug over for the winter, was black. Bare. Waterlogged.

He stared at the earth without seeing it, because between it and him there was Julien. Thin. His face bearded, his hair too long. A sad, poverty-stricken look. Not the poverty of people without house, food, or money, but an indefinable poverty. That's how it was. As far as he was concerned, Julien was poor. He imagined him rich again. Rich in all the things he had had in the past. Strength. Health. A look of substance. Moulded by sport and manual labour. It seemed to the father that his boy had been changed. True, they had not always understood each other, there had always been a gulf between them, preventing any easy exchange of words. And yet, when Julien came back after his apprenticeship with his trade learnt and the strong arms of a worker, then, in spite of all his faults and quirks of character, the father had felt much closer to him. And now, today, he was a different boy. A boy who was going away again, not knowing what direction to take.

"Would you rather see him joining the maquis or know that he's leading a dauber's life in town, as he did in Marseilles?"

The question was there, as though asked by the dead earth in the garden or the fire that sighed so gently behind the bars. It was there, but Gaston refused to answer. It seemed to call for the kind of judgment that he had no right to make. The idea he had formed of an artist's life was such that slowly the certainty had grown in the depths of his being that nothing could be worse. It was like water finding its way through the earth and suddenly hitting upon a rock. As soon as he had rejected the prospect of a life in town for Julien he came up against the idea of the maquis. And there he stopped. The maquis was illegal. The risk of being taken, condemned, shot, or killed in a fight in the mountains. The Germans set out, they shot whoever they could take, and in reprisal they burnt down farms whose owners were mostly innocent farmers. Could a father advise his son to take such a path? Vaintrenier was a brave man, but his opinions were very much to the left. The maquis was a bunch of communists!

So there remained this other solution of sending Julien off to a farm.

The effort of going over all the pros and cons made his mind buzz like a hive, and in the end Gaston could only see the earth. The earth was still the cleanest thing left. The War had even soiled the bakers' trade by making the bakers knead that filth that could no longer be called flour. It had forced the best artisans to cheat their way and the most honest tradesmen to sell the worst rubbish at enormous price. True that in the towns they accused the farmers of profiteering by selling their produce on the black market, but if he went into the country Julien would only be an agricultural worker. He would have nothing to sell. He would have to plough the earth—and the earth remained the same. The only thing that resisted all the defilement of war.

Without even realizing that his brain was working exactly as if Julien had already taken the decision to find refuge on a farm, Gaston began to think about all his old friends who lived in the country.

He remembered them in all sorts of places. At Courbouzon, at Gevingey, at Cousance, at Saint-Maur, at Vernantois. A whole map of friendship took shape slowly. Half-forgotten faces emerged from the past; others came to mind suddenly, as though he had seen them only the night before. Comrades from the regiment or the War, customers from the time when he had delivered bread with his horse, wine-growers from whom he had bought wine for many years. They all came, bringing with them memories of their first meeting and later encounters, the whole lot bound up with a thousand insignificant events, every detail of which he had kept in the depths of his memory. A life was made up of such things. His own was full to bursting-point with these contacts that register on your mind. They are forgotten. Then one day, for some reason, there they are, all coming back at the same time. The whole crowd fills your brain and heart as it would the town square on the day of the big fair.

And the morning, so begrimed by the ashes of winter, grew light. This crowd from the past began to live all around him, like a lake widening with the melting of the snows. It created an uproar of sound. It poured a brilliant wine into him. One of those wines that have kept the sun prisoner in the cellar's darkness.

His face relaxed. He surprised himself by suddenly breathing in deeply, as he used to on holidays when he had just uncorked one of his better bottles.

30

The room was now comfortably warm. Gaston sat there a long time without moving. He withdrew into himself. He let his memories flow through him, and only feared the moment when the present would insist itself again.

That moment arrived when Fernande came back downstairs. He tried to hang on to all that had sprung to life around him, but it was no longer possible. The mere presence of his wife was enough to terrify the people who had come from so far afield to see him alone.

"Well?" he asked.

"He's leaving."

"Where's he going?"

"He says he knows enough people in Lyon to find himself a lodging. He's sure he'll be able to work there."

Gaston was about to ask what sort of work when Julien came down for a suitcase he had put in the dining-room. He had heard the question and said, "I've got a trade. There's no reason why I shouldn't manage as well as anyone else."

Gaston felt a great warmth surging up. So Julien was going to start working again. Go back to his work as a pastry-cook which he had learnt and then abandoned? One thing worried him though. "Are you sure you'll find a job? There's not much call for pastry-cooks with the rationing."

At first the boy looked completely put out, then his face relaxed suddenly and he began to laugh. "Who said anything about that? My trade is painting. Baking cakes! Sod that. Is that what you call a trade!"

He picked up his suitcase and climbed the stairs, still laughing.

Gaston had no time to reply, and he probably would not have known what to say, the laughter had hurt him so much. A simple word can wound you so deeply that you lose all your resources. A trade! That's what you call a trade! Julien had said it with such scorn and disgust that his father was stunned.

Fernande looked away and said, "I must get his clothes ready."

She disappeared before Gaston had been able to utter a word. He still felt overwhelmed. His hands trembled. His throat hurt. Slowly something opened up within him, liberating a rising flood of words in his mind.

The trade. Good God! What about it? He despised it that much? Then he must despise them all. Including the one his father had practised so lovingly for the best part of his life! There he had been, ready to talk about the land. The possibility of the boy going on a farm. What a situation! Was it because of the times or because the boy was simply a monster?

Would his mother at last understand that her boy possessed neither common sense, reason, courage, nor any of the virtues that make a man live an honest life. Paul? At least he had a trade. He had succeeded.

Painting, a trade? Nothing but dabbling on a bit of canvas and being seen around with a skeleton under your arm?

Gaston went on grumbling. This released some of his anger, and as it disappeared he became convinced it was best to say nothing. There would be no point in provoking an argument before Julien left. Juliet was going to leave, and then perhaps peace would be restored to the house.

31

Julien's departure was quicker and easier than Gaston had expected.

The same evening M. Vaintrenier brought his identity-card and ration-book. He did not mention the maquis again. He had realized that neither the mother nor the son liked the idea. He explained in a sober, almost mournful voice, "Your name and age have been changed. The cards are registered here because you have lived in the town after the defeat, but you were born in Philippeville, which you left when you were quite small, and your parents settled here. So you remember nothing, which is natural. We do it this way to make it impossible to check up."

"And what name have you given him on the card?" asked Fernande.

"I'm sorry, Mme Dubois, but I think it would be better if no-one knew. I know you wouldn't shout it from the rooftops, but it's a security precaution."

Fernande did not flinch. Gaston looked at Vaintrenier, but his expression revealed nothing. He just seemed to be doing a routine job.

"You know," he said, "it's a precaution that even married couples accept. You won't be able to write to your son, but there's no reason why he shouldn't write to you. He could send you a card every time he moves."

Vaintrenier waited a second. Then he said in a rather dry voice, "Julien is not wanted by the Gestapo or the Militia, like some who are suspected of being in the Resistance. He's only a defaulter from Compulsory Labour Service, and the police are interested in him because of his desertion. With things as they are, no-one's going to put a brigade of policemen on his heels. As long as he doesn't do anything stupid he's in no danger at all. I don't even think that your letters are censored."

He said this in a slightly mocking tone. Gaston looked at Julien, but the boy seemed unmoved. He held the documents in his hand and looked at them occasionally without daring to open them.

Vaintrenier wasted no time. He refused a drink, shook hands with all three of them, and as he went out he said to Julien, "All the same, I think you're a shit."

Outside he turned round again and added, "I take it I can trust you about those documents. I run a considerable risk, you know."

It all happened so quickly that Gaston had no time to speak. Fernande had only just managed to thank M. Vaintrenier. They all three found themselves as though turned to stone, speechless. Julien, though that was no longer his name, still held the documents in his hand without opening them. In the end he slipped them in his pocket and said, "Good. I'll leave tomorrow morning. There's a train at six o'clock. It will still be dark, and no-one will see me leaving."

Fernande sighed, "God in heaven, the things that can happen!"

Gaston coughed, got up to go and spit in the grate, and then sat down again.

After that there was silence—a silence broken only by the noise Fernande made as she prepared the meal and laid the table. Julien was smoking with his elbows on the table. Gaston sat opposite, sideways, as usual, with his feet on the stove, and also smoking a cigarette that Julien had just given him.

This was their last evening together. Silence enveloped them. The night enclosed the house. The wood burnt quietly in the hearth. There was no wind. Nothing.

And when the meal was over and the table cleared it felt really empty.

Gaston drank his tea, got up, and said, "Good night."

Julien got up too and said, "I'll say goodbye then."

"No, I'll be up before you leave."

"I wouldn't bother."

"Yes, I'll get up."

Gaston was at the bottom of the stairs. He adjusted the wick of the little lamp in his right hand, took the chamber-pot in his left, and said "Good night" again.

The others replied, and he went slowly up to bed.

32

Gaston had dozed only two or three times that night. He had heard the boy and his wife going to bed more than two hours later. He had said nothing. The entire night he had felt that his wife was not sleeping either. She must have realized that he was not asleep, but she said nothing.

They had lain next to each other, trying not to move. So near each other, and yet separated by the silence into which they had both withdrawn.

In the morning Fernande had got up quietly long before the usual time and gone down to light the fire and prepare breakfast for the boy. Gaston waited till Julien was up before coming down.

Now they were all three in the kitchen. Fernande had lit the lamp; it might just as well have been evening.

There were two suitcases by the door. The smaller one had a roll of papers done up in newspaper tied to the handle. It must have contained drawings. Julien's coat was hanging on the banisters. Gaston looked at it all. Then he looked at his son, who was slowly eating bread soaked in barley coffee into which his mother had grated a square of chocolate. The kitchen was filled with the smell of chocolate.

Gaston drank his bowl of wretched coffee, then he took out his tobacco-tin and rolled a cigarette.

"It's too early for you to smoke," said Fernande.

"I won't be smoking any more because of this one," he said. "You know that I don't keep more than a day's ration in my tin."

They did not go on. Julien had not even raised his head.

"When he goes to the station," said Gaston, "he ought to go through the boulevard. It's longer, but he's not so likely to meet people who know him."

"At this hour of the morning—" said Julien.

"Your father is right. It's safer."

"Right, I'll go any way you like."

He had a dejected look about him, an air of resignation which seemed like a burden on the whole house. Gaston wanted to say something to comfort his son, but he could think of nothing.

Fernande said many times, "My poor boy . . . my poor boy!"

She told him several times to be careful and sensible. Julien said, "Yes, yes. Don't worry about me."

All this was interspersed with seemingly endless periods of silence.

When the time came Gaston asked, "You've got some money?"

"Yes, I've got enough."

Gaston knew that Fernande would not have let him go away with empty pockets, but this was the only thing he could think of saying. When the boy approached him to say goodbye he added, as he kissed him, "Don't leave us for too long without news. And try not to do anything silly."

That was all. Julien picked up his cases, went out behind his mother, who was going with him to the gate.

When he was alone Gaston took the scallop-shell that served as an ashtray, emptied it in the stove, and put the stub that Julien had left in his tobacco-tin. Then he opened the shutters and put out the lamp. It was still dark, but the firelight flickered on the lino. Gaston sat down, put his feet on the oven door, and looked into the fire.

So Julien had left. He had gone away towards the town. The old people were left behind alone. The War affected everything. It was invisible, but its presence could be felt even in the midst of this night which seemed as though welded to the earth. Gaston tried to imagine the unlit streets, the station with its few lights shaded blue, but the pictures he conjured up were from the other war he had known when he was still in the prime of life.

Now he was an old man, his strength waning. Never had he felt it as much as this morning and during the previous night when he had wondered whether it would ever end, dragging the dawn from under the earth—an earth he could hardly fathom.

When Fernande came back she only said, "What's this? You've put out the lamp already?"

"Yes, there's nothing to do that can't wait."

"I suppose so . . . for the moment."

That last word hung in the air, caught up in suspended time.

Fernande had sat down in her place between the range and the table. They did not see each other. Gaston knew she was staring into the fire, as he was. She too was probably trying to follow their boy in her thoughts.

Time passed, and he lost count. Perhaps it was half an hour, then she whispered, "That's it, now the train's gone."

"You heard it?"

"Yes."

Gaston had not heard a sound. "He had plenty of time to catch it."

"Oh, yes. The trains are always late," she said.

Still no daylight came and silence filled the room. One lot of logs burnt down without either of them saying a word. When there were only a few embers left in the grate Fernande got up and put on two more logs.

"All the same," sighed Gaston, "we do live in curious times."

"It's nothing for us. But for young people . . ."

Gaston did not reply. Fernande closed the grate, sat down, and went on, "He could have stayed here if we could have been sure no-one would give him away."

Those simple words stirred a bitterness in Gaston's heart. He tightened his lips against the biting words which rose to his mind. His hand grasped the edge of the table tightly. He clutched so hard that his finger-joints cracked. Pain shot through his arm as far as his shoulder.

Nothing. He said nothing. Neither did Fernande add a single word.

His eyes left the hearth to look at the window for signs of the day that had not yet appeared. From now on he knew that his wife and he would live like this, side by side, but more apart from each other than they had ever been.

They were going to live and wait, but what was there to look forward to in this endless night that opened up before them?

The black sky, crushing the cold dawn, gave no hope of light.

It was winter.

There was silence.

The earth was filled with an insipid stench, like the one that chills you on entering a room where a corpse is lying.

PART THREE

Summer Flowers

33

Winter passed slowly, dark and damp. Then spring arrived, but brought no real joy and held only a faint promise. Would the War never be over? Who could predict the end? For it was still being fought in a way which grew more terrible as days went by.

People discussed it without knowing what was really happening. But one thing was certain: senseless and haphazard killing was going on everywhere. There were also many arrests. Men from the Militia or the Gestapo would arrive one morning and take away people who would never be seen again. Sometimes the curfew was enforced at six in the evening, and once a pensioner from the Village Neuf who was in his garden was beaten up by a patrol. You had to shut yourself in, lock the doors and the windows, stay in the shadows, and never venture outside. There had been the arrival of the Mongols from Vlassov, the burning of several villages in the hills; not a week passed by without hearing of the death of someone you knew. The Germans had assassinated Dr Michel in April just because he had attended some Resistance fighters.

Gaston never left his garden except to fetch water at the fountain. When Fernande was out buying the few provisions to which their ration-cards entitled them Gaston was worried.

The police had called three times to ask whether they had news of Julien, but it was not too alarming.

The officer said, "It's just a routine matter, so we have to do it, but the authorities know that he won't come back here to pass the time of day until the War is over."

Gaston and Fernande made the same declaration each time, which they both signed. It only amounted to the following: ". . . declare not to have seen their son Julien since his disappearance and have no knowledge of his actual whereabouts."

This was almost the truth. They did not even have to lie, because no-one asked them whether they happened to have heard from him. Besides, could you describe as news the few hurriedly scribbled words signed with an illegible name, posted once from Lyon, another time from Saint-Étienne, and yet another from Marseilles? It was as good as silence. Scarcely more than an occasional reminder that Julien was not dead.

Paul had visited them at the beginning of January. He had come to wish them a happy New Year, and had drunk a cup of very inferior coffee with them, said that he still believed the Germans would win, left his father two packets of tobacco, and then cleared off without mentioning Julien's disappearance.

For Gaston the War was a long silence and a loneliness without respite.

The old people had even stopped bickering. They carried out their small jobs in the garden, and it yielded enough to prevent them starving.

The neighbours still bought their vegetables and brought news of the War. But the War never broke through their loneliness until the day when they knew for certain that the landing of the Allies in Normandy had been successful.

A breath of hope swept over the country and freshened the sultry air of early June; it reached right into the garden. M. Robin brought them the news. There was a broad smile on his face, and he said they would soon see the end of all this misery.

But a biting wind of agony followed. The Germans became increasingly harsh, and it was feared that the War would sweep through every country.

"In 1918," said Gaston, "it was also the Americans who struck the final blow, but not without damage wherever they fought."

And Gaston's apprehension grew when, on the 16th of August, they heard that troops had landed at Cavalaire. For the first time in years he pored over the map of France on the back of the calendar.

"If they come up from the south," he said, "there's a serious risk we'll find ourselves in their way."

They had not heard from Julien for four weeks, and Fernande reconciled herself by saying, "If only I knew where he is."

Gaston did not flinch. They had never talked much, but in the last few months they had learned to understand each other. He knew that his wife's simple sentence meant: "As for you, you'll never be anything but selfish. All you can think about is your garden and the house, which might be destroyed. You only think about your own life. But these things are of no consequence to me. All that matters is my boy. He would have been safer here with us. But he's on his own. He might be killed in an air-raid, arrested, tortured, and we don't even know where he is."

Gaston saw this in her eyes or in the way she shrugged her shoulders when he spoke about their property. She was completely aloof, even from him. She looked after him, she shared the awful black bread they were sold, she also shared those endless nights they spent side by side, pretending to be asleep. All through force of habit, because it had been laid down that they continue this way until death parted them.

This existence had a bitter taste. It was not even attuned to the seasons, where you know that the hardest winter will be followed by brighter, warmer weather. Summer had come without change for the better. They had hoped so often in vain that now even hope was exhausted.

"You're too pessimistic," said M. Robin. "The Allies are advancing. We'll be liberated in a few weeks."

Gaston shook his head. "They said the same in 1917. I know the Germans. They don't give in quickly."

What frightened him most was that fighting should come to their district and settle on a line near the Jura. That would be the end. The house destroyed, the garden ruined, flight into unknown and hostile country. They had been spared in 1940. For a long time Gaston had clung to the idea that this corner of the earth where he lived would remain untouched, but now, without knowing why, he was afraid. He saw himself dispossessed. He imagined this dreadful end to his life's work, everything destroyed and plundered.

He kept on working, but felt his strength ebbing, and he often looked at his garden in disgust. Grass grew high along the drive, it even invaded some of the vegetable plots, and all he could say was, "It's useless trying any harder. I can't go on. I can't do it all any more."

When someone came he would sometimes have a fit of pride as he showed them his neglected garden, and, making angry gestures, he would say, "I'd be able to manage. I've still got the strength, but there isn't enough time. When there's a curfew from six in the evening till six in the morning the days aren't long enough. At my age I can't get much done in the heat of the midday sun. I grow tired so quickly."

One afternoon, in the second week of August, when he was working near the road, Gaston heard the gate click. He straightened up and leaned on his mattock. A young girl had come in. She appeared to hesitate. She looked around amongst the trees, searching. When she saw Gaston she came up the drive till she was level with him and called out, "Where can I find Mme Dubois, please?"

Gaston had never seen her before. She was small, with long chestnut hair, and wore a simple, short-sleeved dress. She was carrying a small leather case.

"Why do you want to see her?" asked Gaston.

"I've come for some flowers."

There had been less demand for flowers since the War started, and Gaston had cut down on space for them to make more room for vegetables.

"Go down to the bottom of the garden. She's probably somewhere near the pump. But there aren't many flowers, you know."

The young girl went off. Gaston followed her with his eyes for a second, and then went back to work. He went on working for a few minutes, but the presence of this stranger disturbed him. Where could she have come from? He was sure he had never seen her before, and it was rare to get customers who were strangers. He leaned his mattock against the pear-tree, walked down slowly along the fence, taking care to keep behind the line of trees.

When he was about twenty yards from the pump he stopped. He saw the visitor, half hidden by Fernande, through the branches of the peach-trees. He moved over to the left. Fernande was reading. The young girl was standing in front of her. After a while Fernande looked up. Her face was shadowed by her hat, and he could not see her expression. However, he could see that there was something serious going on when she thrust the paper into her apron pocket and buried her face in her hands.

For a minute Gaston fought against the temptation of joining the two women, but he did not move. The air was heavy and still and filled with the sound of insects. A German lorry was manœuvring on the other side of the wall of the *école normale*.

The lorry stopped. Now Fernande was talking, but he could not hear what she was saying. As he could not approach any nearer without being seen, he went back to where he had left the mattock. Something had just happened. Something serious, it seemed, and Fernande had not even called him! Was it to do with Julien? Probably. But why did Fernande want to keep it to herself? Did she reckon he had lost the right to know what had become of the boy? What had he done to deserve such treatment?

He had started working again, and, because of his anger, at a pace beyond his strength. His shirt soon became drenched. Beads of sweat appeared on his forehead and ran down his nose. When he straightened up he had an attack of coughing and he had to drop his mattock. His eyes swam with tears as he saw the girl walking past. She nodded her head to him, but he was in no state to respond.

All she carried were a few peonies.

34

Gaston had only just got his breath back when Fernande joined him.

"You're coughing," she said, "and you're hot and sweating. You ought to stop for a while."

He was thirsty. Above all, he wanted to know who the girl was. Nevertheless he said, "No. I want to finish this border today."

"All the same, you'll have to come indoors for a minute. There's news from Julien. Then you can change your vest."

He followed her. His throat was burning and he had to wipe his eyes again. His wife had been calm as she spoke, but he noticed deep lines round her mouth, and she had red eyes and a tense look.

Had something serious happened to the boy? He found she was walking far too slowly, and yet he was afraid of learning the truth.

The shutters were closed and the blinds down in the kitchen, and the air was almost cool. There were flies buzzing around under the lamp.

Gaston drank a glass of water while Fernande went upstairs to fetch dry clothes. When he had changed and sat down in his chair Fernande came over to the table and took Julien's letter from her pocket. She put it on the table and slowly smoothed the crumpled sheet with the flat of her hand.

As she could not make up her mind either to speak or read, Gaston asked her, "Well, what does he say?"

"Oh, dear, I don't know where to start. . . ."

She said no more. Her mouth was moving; her lips seemed to mouth the words she could not utter.

"Well," grumbled Gaston, "read me the letter. He has written more than he usually does, from what I can see."

"Yes—that's because he has a lot to tell us—and he has been able to write more freely because his letter did not come through the post."

"Do you know her, the girl who brought it?"

Fernande shook her head, waited a few more seconds, and then raised her eyes full of tears and whispered, "I don't know her, but—but they are engaged."

This was the one piece of news that Gaston had not expected. He had imagined the best and the worst, but this was miles away from anything he had imagined. All he could do was whisper, "She's engaged to him, did you say?"

"Yes, they are going to get married."

"But who is she?"

As though this question eased her mind, Fernande replied very quickly in a more confident voice, "She comes from Saint-Claude. You don't know her, I realize that. Her name is Françoise—Françoise Jacquier—the family is well known in the district. Her father is a mason. She met Julien at the gymnastic displays that were held at Saint-Claude. They hadn't seen each other again, and then they met at Lyon. She works there."

She stopped. She must have told him everything she knew about the girl. She breathed deeply and looked down. Gaston felt she was hiding something that was not so easy to tell.

"He sent her all this way to tell us this? After all, I don't suppose they're going to get married at once!"

As Fernande did not reply, he went on, "How was she able to get here? Only the Germans have been able to go by train for the last ten days. M. Robin told us that this morning."

"She didn't come by train. Anyway, she's going on to Saint-Claude. That's why she didn't stay longer. If she can she'll look in again to see us on Monday when she goes back."

"Well," sighed Gaston, "I hope he doesn't get married without having a job first. Especially in these times!"

"According to what he says in his letter and what the young girl told me, he's been doing quite well up till now."

"With his painting?"

"Yes, with his painting."

Gaston saw a triumphant gleam in his wife's eyes. But she lowered them quickly and added, "Of course, since the invasion, people have had other things to do than buy pictures."

"At any rate, it's not a job. And even if the War ends he'll have to wait till he's found work before he gets married. I hope this girl can understand that."

While he was speaking Fernande had turned over the letter on the table twice. Gaston noticed her hands were trembling. He was going to question her, but she got in first in a faltering voice: "They can't wait. They—they've been silly."

It was obvious that she had difficulty in keeping back her tears. Gaston felt a flood of anger, but Fernande looked so distressed that he found the strength to control himself. Without raising his voice, he said, "Good God! That's the last straw!"

She must have been expecting him to be angry because she looked at him in astonishment. She must have seen that he was still quivering with his barely suppressed anger for she hurriedly said, "Don't be angry, Gaston. Please don't be angry. I feel bad enough about it already."

"I'm not getting angry. It would do no good."

It was comforting to Gaston that she had confessed her weakness and sorrow so spontaneously. If he began to shout, if he accused her of being responsible, reminding her that she had always spoilt, supported, and protected Julien too much, she would be incapable of defending herself. He hesitated for a moment, but the burden of these last years they had endured together made him keep silent.

Further battles between them were impossible. All around and above this house, which was their only refuge against the stupidity of the outside world, was already enough evil, threats, and misery to bear. They must at least be able to look at each other without hatred and speak without wounding each other.

"My poor wife," he sighed, "what can we do about it?"

Silently, her body hardly shaking with her sobs, she began to cry.

Gaston waited patiently for a while before asking, "He told you that in his letter?"

Fernande wiped her eyes and read slowly, "'My dear Mother, Françoise is bringing you this letter. She will explain to you that we shall have to get married as soon as possible. I know that you have always wanted to have a daughter. I would like you to welcome Françoise as though she were your own daughter.'" Her voice faltered. After a long silence she added, "After that he talks about his job—and he says that the War will be over before the end of the month."

"Over!" said Gaston sardonically. "And what'll happen in the meanwhile? What will become of us between now and then?"

"Little Françoise told me exactly the same as M. Robin did. The Germans will collapse as we did in 1940. All they'll think of is to save themselves as quickly as possible. She says many of them have already left Lyon."

The situation was getting complicated and taking on a completely new aspect. There was no longer just anxiety about the War. They knew that Julien was alive, but now there was this girl from Saint-Claude messing things up and giving them other reasons to worry.

"And the young girl told you that they would have to get married?"

"Yes."

"She dared tell you that?"

"Julien had written it in his letter. I asked her if it was true. She blushed, but said yes, it was. And . . . and—I don't know how to put it—but I had the impression she wasn't really embarrassed at telling me."

"Good Lord, what an extraordinary time we live in! I've told you often enough, and there's no mistake about it."

Fernande replied in a subdued voice, "That's just it: it's the times we live in which can make this kind of thing happen. If Julien hadn't had to live with a false identity they would already have been married."

"All the same—all the same—to come and tell you a thing like that. This girl can't really be—she must be without any shame."

He had meant to say, "This girl can't really be much good," but he stopped himself.

"I didn't see her for very long," said Fernande, "but she made a good impression on me."

"Did—did you—" Gaston stopped. Fernande guessed what he had been unable to say and explained, "I know I should have called you. But—but I would rather have talked to you first. And then she was in such a hurry—and she was already overwhelmed at having to talk to me."

Gaston's anger had subsided, and he made an effort to raise his voice. "Julien must have made her think I was an ogre—though I've never eaten anybody."

Fernande's eyes were still damp. However, she smiled, and, leaning over in his direction, she whispered, "Oh, good heavens, when I think of the kind of news we might be getting just now . . . good heavens, don't you think we're still very lucky?"

35

This piece of news, coming so unexpectedly, had not changed the course of events, and yet the oppressive anguish of the past few weeks eased a little for Gaston. Without knowing why, he felt that nothing of further importance could happen—as though the War held a certain amount of misery in store for every separate person, and Gaston had had his share. His full burden was already there, and he could look forward to carrying on more or less undisturbed till the end. It was all rather hazy, but he felt that the girl's visit had made things move forward again. They had been on the edge of an abyss for so long, and neither he nor Fernande had dared look more closely and discover its full depth.

As he had shown very little animosity, Fernande often spoke about Julien and Françoise and what they ought to do for them. Her ideas irritated Gaston, but even so he kept his temper to himself. When she spoke it was as though life stirred again in the stagnant waters of their solitude.

This time the rout of the Germans was real enough. They felt it in the district. Convoys came rumbling through the boulevard or the rue des Salines. There was a constant coming and going at the *école normale*. Gaston often watched through a slit in the bedroom shutters. M. Robin came over with news four or five times a day. At ten o'clock he announced that the Allies had reached Lyon. At midday he arrived to say they were only at Valence. At four o'clock he declared that Paris was going to be liberated during the night. Then, a few minutes before curfew, he ran over to announce that a battle was being fought that would put an end to the War.

"The man's mad," said Gaston.

"It's we who aren't like the others," Fernande maintained. "We've shut ourselves up in here without knowing what's going on. Everyone else is on edge."

"And what good does that do?"

When he thought about the War Gaston was torn between wishing it would end before there was a battle in the area, and hoping that the Germans would at last experience war in their own country.

He knew that the Russians were already in Poland, but that was so far away. Too far for him to appreciate its significance.

M. Robin often spoke about the maquis fighting in the Haut-Jura. When he had gone Fernande said, "I only hope the young girl doesn't get caught up in that kind of thing!"

"But what an idea to travel around at a time like this!"

"She had to."

"I'd like to know why."

"She didn't tell me, but I believe it was important."

"Anyway, she can't go back to Lyon now, that's for sure."

As Gaston said this he saw Fernande wince. She sighed a few times, and then whispered in a low voice, as though she did not really want Gaston to hear, "I haven't seen much of her, this young girl, and yet—I don't know—I feel that if I knew she was near him I'd have been happier."

She added a few words under her breath. Gaston could

almost guess them by the movement of her lips. "She seems to be so much more sensible than he."

36

The nights were endlessly long because of the curfew, which started at six in the evening, when the sun was still high in the sky. Gaston and Fernande ate in the shadows of the kitchen, the shutters barely open. When they had finished their bowl of soup they would sit still for a long time, alert to every sound and scrutinizing the narrow strip of light where the leaves were still heavy in the heat, but livened by the zigzag flight of insects and the singing of the birds. They would sit like that for more than an hour, without moving or speaking; an occasional sigh sounded like a refusal to admit the oppressiveness of the evening. When there was a shot somewhere in town or in the surrounding hills they would listen harder, they would look at each other, and then wait again as the silence closed in more thickly.

One evening they heard shooting near the house. The next day M. Robin told them that a man living on the Boulevard Jules-Ferry had been wounded when he had opened a window slightly on to his garden.

After this endless waiting Gaston and Fernande would go up to bed. It was still light. Gaston pressed his eye to a small hole in the shutter where a knot had fallen out. In this way he could see a large part of the park and grounds of the *école normale*, where the twisted shadows of the trees and bushes stretched across the reddish sand paths in the setting sun. Soldiers on guard in their caps, boots, and green uniforms stood silently at the corners of the buildings. Others were walking along the walls below by the dairy. This meant that there would be others walking not less than thirty yards from the house, beneath the wall that separated the garden from the park of the *école normale*. Every evening, as he pondered over this, Gaston recalled scenes from the other war. He was thirty years younger, the world was different and so was his life, and he tried to go to sleep thinking about what happened in those days. But often he did not fall asleep till very late, having first exhausted this fund of memories many times over.

During the night between the 24th and 25th of August Gaston was woken simultaneously by Fernande shaking him and by a crackling like a huge bonfire of green wood.

He sat up in bed. They were shooting.

Machine-guns. Sharp explosions. Others more heavy. Bursts of mortar.

Fernande clutched his arm hard.

"Gaston! They're shooting everywhere!"

A continually increasing gunfire split the night.

"We must get up," he said.

"Don't talk so loudly."

"What difference do you think that makes?"

After his first fear Gaston felt quite calm.

"Get dressed," he ordered. "And above all don't light any lamps."

"I'm not stupid."

He noticed that her voice was more confident than when she had woken him. He pulled on his trousers, adjusted his braces, and put on his slippers, and then groped his way towards the shutters.

"Don't go near the window, Gaston. Stay where you are."

"Leave me alone. I'm not going to open it."

He found the hole with his hands and put his eye to it. The explosions were following each other at an ever-increasing rate, and he saw flashes near the station and at the foot of the Montaigu hill.

"It's near the station," he said. "They must be attacking the railway."

"Or the Gestapo headquarters."

"That's possible."

They were quiet for a moment. The noise was coming nearer.

"You'd think it was coming from Montciel as well," said Fernande.

Gaston listened. It could be an echo from the hillside, but it seemed as though the explosions were coming from all sides. There were no windows on that side of the house, and there could be no question of going outside to see what was happening.

"Let's go downstairs," he said. "We'll be safer down below."

"But if they came into the house . . ."

He laughed at her. "If they came in it wouldn't be worth hiding. What we have to fear is a mortar hitting the roof and setting the house on fire or making it collapse. If there's a fire we'll be able to get out more easily from below."

He went ahead first, feeling his way with his hands and feet.

"If only we didn't have to go outside to get to the cellar," said Fernande.

"Yes, but we'd better not try."

Gaston used his lighter in the kitchen.

"No," said Fernande, "don't light that."

"What on earth do you mean? You know nothing can be seen through the shutters. Come on, don't be silly. I just want to see what the time is."

He held it up to see the clock. His hand was not trembling at all. He noticed that Fernande was pale. She looked distressed. Fear had deepened every line on her face. She had put her shawl over her shoulders and now drew it tightly across her chest, her hands clenched.

Gaston put out the lighter. It was a quarter to three.

As soon as the flame was extinguished the darkness seemed deeper, yet it held the after-image of the light, making, as it were, a colourless hole in the night. The gunfire did not stop, but was like the sound of the sea broken by crashing waves, a sea surrounding them, approaching, retreating, coming back faster and nearer.

"I think they are fighting on all sides," said Gaston.

"Do you think they have attacked the town?"

"Probably."

"The Americans?"

"How should I know?"

There had been a lull. Then suddenly the explosions burst much nearer the house.

"We can't stay here like this," said Fernande.

"If they're fighting in the streets that's the end of everything!"

Gaston had practically been shouting. He felt no fear, but an anger that made him clench his fists.

"Don't shout," implored Fernande. "Don't shout."

"But we're finished," he snapped. "You don't understand that it's all coming this way!"

"Oh, my God! My God!"

They stayed where they were for a little while, standing up in the dark at the foot of the stairs. Then Gaston suddenly looked for his wife's arm and said as he grasped it, "Come on, you never know."

"But where do you want to go?"

"To the cellar."

"And go outside?"

"No-one will see us. It's too dark. They've got enough to deal with."

"You're mad."

"On the contrary. I know where it's safest."

"My God!"

Gaston pulled his wife towards the door. He searched for the lock, turned the key, pulled back the bolt, but before opening he had second thoughts. "Is there any money in the house?"

"Yes—and the papers."

"We must take them all."

They went to the dining-room. Gaston flicked his lighter. Fernande opened the left drawer in the dresser and began to search. Her hands were still trembling. She took out some papers and things which she put on top of the dresser in wild disarray. The draught caused by her movements made the flame flicker, and it went out three times. Gaston swore. It would not light again. "We'll have to get a candle."

"You know there's one in the kitchen, and there's another lighter too."

Gaston looked for them, groping and knocking things over.

"God in heaven! We're losing time."

There were three explosions, much heavier than before, which shook the house and made the windows rattle. A crackling of machine-gun fire came nearer. Gaston lit the candle and went back to Fernande, who had not moved.

She held the papers up to the light, which flickered in the draught.

"Don't blow the light out," Gaston mocked. "The papers will see to that without any help from us!"

"What shall I put them in?"

"Haven't you got your bag?"

"My bag?"

"Yes, or anything you like."

They were both getting nervous. Gaston heard the battle coming nearer. If they did not leave now it would soon be too late. The garden might be full of soldiers either attacking or defending the *école normale*.

He went back to the kitchen, opened the scullery door, and took a string bag hanging on a hook.

"Put the lot in this," he said.

He also took his watch, which was hanging near the window, and crammed it in his pocket.

"We ought to take some clothes," said Fernande.

She took out the coat she had made for herself from the soldier's greatcoat—the one they had sheltered at the time of the capitulation—and threw the cloak over his shoulders. They went as far as the door, where Gaston put out the candle, slipping it in his pocket along with the two lighters.

The gunshots and explosions were coming nearer.

Gaston listened hard, slowly opened the door a little, and turned round again to ask, "Can you hear anyone moving about?"

Fernande stepped forward. "No."

"Then we must go. Keep as low as possible. If they start shooting near us lie down flat and don't move."

He opened the door just enough to let them slip outside. He bent double, recalling an old, forgotten movement. He took one step out on to the landing and felt that Fernande was clutching his cloak.

Just as he was turning round to say, "Shut the door and don't bang it," a whole series of explosions tore the night apart as though fired under their feet. Gaston saw flashes on the fronts of the houses along the rue des Écoles. He pushed Fernande as he turned round and roared, "Christ! It's too late!"

They had knocked into each other. Gaston felt that Fernande had lost her balance, and clung to her. He tried to hold on to her, but he too had lost his balance as he had turned. They both fell into the kitchen, flinging the door wide open so that it banged against the frame.

Grenades exploded even nearer, and four red flashes lit up the room.

Gaston raised himself to his knees, helped his wife to sit up on the floor, and shut the door again.

37

"Oh, Christ," moaned Gaston, "oh, Christ, this is the end!"

The door was shut again. There they were, the two of them, next to each other on the cold kitchen lino. Fernande did not speak.

"Are you hurt?" asked Gaston.

"No, are you?"

"No. The bag didn't get left outside?"

"No, I'm holding it."

"We can't—stay here."

The noise was so close they had to speak loudly, waiting for moments when the firing died down.

"But where are you going?"

"Not behind the door. I'm going upstairs to get a mattress. We shall have to go into the dining-room by the dresser. Then we'll be as far as we can from the window."

He felt Fernande was moving away. He went with her to the dining-room. They were on all fours like children playing.

"There. That's the best place. Lie down against the dresser. I'm going on up."

"No, stay here."

"There's no risk at all. I'm going up to get a mattress." His voice was firm. Authoritative. And still Fernande persisted, "I'm coming with you."

"No, stay there!"

He went off. He found his way without difficulty, as he knew every nook and cranny of this house. He could hardly have been quicker in daylight. He felt neither tired nor breathless.

Once in the bedroom he went up to the window. In passing he searched with his hand for the cold marble of the little table on which he put his tobacco-tin every night. He slid it into his trouser pocket and leant towards the window, pressing his eye to the hole. Flashes were still streaking through the dark night. There was shooting near the station. There was shooting by the dairy and the Village Neuf. The brief flashes outlined the silhouettes of the trees and houses.

Gaston went back to the bed, and it was only then that he realized that the cloak was going to be in his way. He threw it clear of his shoulders, pulled the bedding to the foot of the bed, folded the mattress three times, and lifted it up in his arms. He was as strong as he had been at thirty. He lifted it easily and walked without staggering. His arm knocked against the door-handle, but he felt no pain, and walked steadily down the stairs.

"Do you want me to help you?" asked Fernande.

"Get out of the way."

For a moment there was silence.

"Put it down," she said.

He let the mattress slide down and laid it alongside the dresser.

"We can lie on that for the moment," he said. "If the fighting comes too near we'll sit against the dresser and put the mattress in front of us."

They sat down side by side with their backs against the doors of the dresser and their legs stretched out in front of them. In this way they were not facing the window. There was the whole length of the room between them and the very thick wall. Behind them, the dresser, then the wall, then the kitchen, and another thick, outer wall. Next to the wall behind them was the cast-iron stove. Gaston had noticed only a very few explosions sounding like mortar shells. But all the rest were rifle-fire, machine-guns, and grenades. The bullets might pierce the shutters, but not the walls. There were only the shells to fear, but at the moment there was no artillery-fire.

"You got hot," said Fernande, "bringing this mattress down. Wrap yourself up in your cloak."

"Don't worry."

Most of all he feared the house catching fire. He knew that a bullet could set fire to the roof. There must be a lot of inflammable dust in the inaccessible space between the tiles and the ceiling. And the shed with the hay and the dry wooden boxes. Good God, it might all burn up like a torch!

Gaston was surprised that he had been able to keep so calm. He felt he must remain so. He took the candle, the lighter, and his tobacco-tin, and put them down next to himself. He struck the lighter.

"You're lighting it? But what do you want to do?"

"Roll a cigarette."

"Heavens above!"

He lit the candle and held it out to Fernande. "Here, hold this."

Fernande's hand was trembling.

"You know nothing can be seen from outside—absolutely nothing. Now, hold the light so I can see what I'm doing."

She leaned over with the light. While he was unravelling

two half-smoked cigarettes and rolling them into one their faces were very close to each other, lit up by the flame that gleamed on the polished metal of his tobacco-tin. Gaston closed the tin again and put it down on the mattress. It was not unlike being at the front again, the two of them in a trench. He lit his cigarette on the candle.

"I am sure there's fighting in front of our house," said Fernande.

Gaston listened for a while. They must be shooting on the boulevard as well as in the rue des Écoles—which meant on both sides of the house.

"But what's happening? What's happening then?" sobbed Fernande.

"Now there's no doubt at all. It must be the maquis. If it were the Americans there'd be artillery. They must be feeling strong. There are barrages of gunfire at each road into town."

"But I told you, they're already in our street."

"Perhaps it's the Germans firing from here."

They were speaking quickly. For a period they stopped in order to listen, trying to follow the fighting in their mind's eye.

"If only I knew what was happening in Lyon," said Fernande. "If only I knew whether the little girl was able to get back."

Two mortar explosions shook the house. Gaston stood up.

"Don't move!" shouted Fernande.

"Let me be. I'm going to open a window. All the glass will break if I don't."

He went and opened the kitchen window, and the uproar was suddenly much louder. He shouted from the kitchen, "Is there any coffee made?"

"Yes, but it's cold."

Gaston came back for the candle. Fernande was crouching in the corner between the wall and the dresser.

"Don't move," he said to her. "I'm coming back."

He brought in the meths burner and a small saucepan into which he had poured the coffee.

"You must be mad," said Fernande.

"No. If they're coming this way I'd rather drink my coffee first."

There were probably men in the garden already. Everything would be trampled down or destroyed. Gaston had seen villages where fighting had taken place during the last war too often to hope that his garden, his house, and his shed stood a chance of being spared. What could he do about it? Nothing. Go out and shout at them that they were mad? That they had no right to fight on his property? That it was nothing to do with him, and there were plenty of other places where they could go and fight?

There must have been hundreds of men in every war who had wanted to do just this?

As long as the War went on gnashing its teeth and pulling faces at you only at a distance, there was always hope left. But when the circle closed in, when it came into the garden and trampled everything down and laid siege on the house, what could be done?

Gaston clenched his fists. He pulled nervously on his cigarette. He wished to God he had a rifle and could place himself by the window and at least kill a few before he died!

He felt alternate waves of hatred and tenderness rising within him. He wanted to say thousands of things to Fernande, who was clinging to his arm, sobbing.

"My poor wife, we've seen a lot of each other during our lives. Sometimes we've sworn at each other. We shouldn't have done that. I've had some faults, I know."

"Don't," she whispered. "I've had some too."

"In the place where we meet again we'll get on well together all the time."

A round of fire cracked so close it was like a raging hailstorm whipping down on the little house from all sides.

They kept quiet.

They pushed the mattress away, lay down on the cold floor, and pulled the mattress over themselves as though it were a big eiderdown.

Now there was nothing they could do except wait.

38

They lay there for a long time. The floor was hard, and Gaston felt colder and colder, till at last he stood up. The shooting was less intense.

"I don't know where it's coming from," he said, "but I'd say that it's further away now."

"We don't even know the time."

Gaston took his watch from his pocket and flicked on his lighter. It was nearly five o'clock.

The noise died down still more, and soon there were only a few occasional shots.

"Stay here," said Gaston. "I'm going up to see what's going on."

"Take care."

He went up to the bedroom and looked through the hole in the shutter. It was daylight, but the sun had not yet risen above the rooftops. On the paths in the garden of the *école normale* the Germans were either lying or sitting on the ground by their weapons. They were chatting. Some wore their helmets, but others were bareheaded or wearing forage-caps. One of them got up and walked over to a plum-tree, which he climbed. Gaston thought he wanted to see what was going on beyond the wall, but soon realized that he was only concerned with picking plums. When his helmet was full he climbed down again, took some of the fruit over to his friends, and strolled back towards a bren gun whose barrel was lying on a tree-stump where another soldier was sitting. Occasional bursts of fire could still be heard, but during long intervals the silence was broken only by the rumbling of engines.

The two soldiers ate the plums, throwing the stones at another group of soldiers, who were laughing. Once his helmet was empty the man who had been over to pick the fruit stuck it back on his head, lay down behind the stump, and shifted his weapon. The barrel began to spit out little red flashes, and instinctively Gaston crouched down on the floor. There had been one initial burst. Gaston rose up again and saw the man who was next to the one shooting calmly reloading his weapon. Gaston did not move when the second burst came. The Germans were shooting towards the slope by Montciel. They emptied four barrels like this. Then the one who had been shooting went back to pick plums. He did all this calmly, as though it were a routine matter involving no risk whatsoever.

"What are you doing?" shouted Fernande from downstairs.

"I'm coming." Gaston went downstairs.

"They were shooting so close I was afraid they were shooting at you."

"No, they don't give a bugger for us. They're shooting at Montciel."

"At Montciel?"

"Yes, and this means that if they really were attacked the attack wasn't successful. You should have seen them. They carry on as though they're completely hardened to war. It takes more to make them afraid. People say they've had it, but it doesn't look like it."

Gaston had been deeply impressed by the calm of these soldiers. Everything about their manner made him think they would be here for a long while yet.

As they were hardly shooting any more, Fernande asked, "What are they going to do now?"

"You'd have to be bloody clever to tell."

Gaston had scarcely finished speaking when there was another burst of shooting quite near, and almost at the same time shouts and crackling. They listened for a moment. Then Gaston said, "There's something burning."

They still did not dare open the shutters. They went up again through the darkness to the first floor. His eye to the hole, Gaston saw a thick cloud of smoke rising over the sun. Another cloud was blackening the sky over towards the station. There were only a few soldiers left in the garden of the *école normale*. Gaston appreciated this in a few seconds, and then stood back to let Fernande take his place and said, "God Almighty, the whole town's on fire!"

"Oh, God, the whole of the rue des Écoles is burning."

They stood there dumbfounded for a moment. Then they made for the stairs. There daylight was pouring through the dormer window opening on to the roof.

"If I could get up there," said Gaston, "I'd be able to see."

"It's impossible. The ladder is out in the shed."

Gaston measured the distance with his eyes.

"If the window wasn't above the stairs, then a table—"

He stopped. He had just thought of the dormer window in Julien's little room. Fernande had thought about it at the same time. They ran in and pushed the desk under the window. Julien had left some books and papers there, and Fernande put them on the bed. Gaston climbed on to the table and tore away the flowered curtain and black paper on the window. Standing on tiptoe, he could just see the tops of the houses opposite the garden. In order to see the street he would have to open the window and stick his head outside.

"Give me the chair," he said.

"You're not going to open it!"

"Give me the chair, I tell you."

"Gaston, it would be most unwise."

"No-one can see me!"

He had been shouting. Fernande put the chair on the table. Gaston climbed up. Now he was too tall, and he had to lean sideways and bend his knees. Slowly, steadying his nerves, he grasped the metal ratchet lever and freed it from the pinion. It squeaked. Gaston stopped for a moment, then gently lifted the frame and hooked the lever on to the second notch. He waited about ten seconds. The crackling of the burning houses sounded nearer. The smell of smoke was already coming through the narrow opening. When he had counted ten Gaston cautiously advanced his head until his forehead touched the glass pane. He could now see part of the street and some of the garden.

It was not the houses opposite that were on fire, but the ones farther over to the right, level with the school. The flames were very high, ripping and slashing the eddies of grey and black smoke that covered a whole section of the sky. Bursts of tommy-gun fire mingled with the noise of burning.

At the top of the garden the street was deserted. The fence was intact, and the gate still seemed to be closed. The shutters on all the houses were closed too.

No-one.

"Well?" asked Fernande.

Gaston was unable to speak. He looked at the fire once more. Then he got down.

"Get up," he said. "Then you'll see."

Fernande climbed up. When she was up there Gaston moaned, "They are quite capable of setting fire to the whole town."

Fernande said nothing. Her hands clung to the iron frame and were trembling. Suddenly, at the same time as he heard the raucous barking of a bren gun, he saw her right hand let go of the frame and clap to her mouth. "Oh, my God!" she cried.

"What's the matter?"

She climbed down so quickly that Gaston had to hold on to her to stop her falling. Her pale face was covered in sweat.

"I saw him . . ." she stammered, "I saw him fall—his hands clutching his stomach . . ."

She imitated his action and let herself fall on to Julien's bed. Gaston climbed on to the table, then on to the chair. When he was up there Fernande went on, "The baker's assistant—I've forgotten his name—the one who helped us bring in the logs. In front of the door to the passage—I saw him . . ."

She repeated this phrase again and again. Gaston looked over towards the house that stood opposite the garden and belonged to him as well. A white figure was curled up in front of the door, but the trees partly concealed it. Without moving, Gaston asked, "But what did he do?"

"I don't know. I saw him coming out. Then all at once there were gunshots, and he fell. I saw him—he put his hands over his stomach and he fell."

"He's not moving. They bloody well got him."

"And if he's not dead, is he going to lie there?"

"I don't know, poor boy...."

Gaston kept staring at the white figure and the open door leading to the dark passage. The wind, still light, carried an occasional cloud of smoke as far as the garden. The smell was stronger and stronger. Through the smoke Gaston could just discern another white figure coming out of the shadows of the passage. It bent down, and Gaston saw the baker, whilst keeping out of sight, pull his assistant back inside. Soon the passage door was shut again.

Gaston climbed down and described what he had just seen. Then he sat down on the bed next to Fernande.

Now his legs were shaking. He felt sweat standing out in beads on his face and running down his back. Fernande sat quite still, her elbows on her knees, eyes staring, and whispering again and again, "My God . . . poor boy . . . poor boy . . . I saw him fall—he put his hands on his stomach and he fell!"

39

The morning dragged on. They spent most of it in Julien's room—the only one that had any light. Fernande only went downstairs to fetch the spirit stove, bowls, and coffee. She also brought up some bread, but neither of them could eat anything.

Gaston was well aware that he was overcome with fear. That strength which arose in him when he was dragged from sleep by the shooting had drained away, leaving his body bruised and his head empty. His legs could hardly carry him. Now and again he would pull himself up to the dormer window to see if the fire was spreading. For a long time he thought the whole street might burn, but by mid-morning his mind was at rest. The fire was decreasing in intensity, and its core was more or less limited to the area around the orphanage. The street was deserted. Once, having heard some shouts, he climbed up, but as he looked out he could only see a group of German soldiers running towards the end of the street. Shortly afterwards there was a salvo of shots, and that was all. There was a droning of cars and lorries. When he had got down again he could see that the garden of the *école normale* was empty.

At midday Fernande warmed a small pan of soup on the little meths still left. She did not dare light the fire. When the flame had gone out they slowly ate the soup. The vegetables were completely cold. Later Gaston stretched out on Julien's bed. He did not want to fall asleep, and yet he submitted. When he woke Fernande was no longer in the room. He sat up on the bed and listened. Someone was talking in the kitchen.

He got up quietly, and only when he was halfway downstairs did he recognize M. Robin's voice. He came into the kitchen saying, "What a night we've had!"

Fernande had half opened the shutters. The door was wide open and the bead curtain drawn across.

"You were able to go out?" asked Gaston.

"Yes, just to get over here, because there's no road to cross. Otherwise I would not have risked it."

M. Robin told them that the maquis had attacked the town. The Germans had been forced back into the centre, then they had made a counter-attack, and the maquis had fled. When they had gone the Germans had set fire to a number of houses, killing anyone trying to get out. They had rounded up about twenty people, whom they had shot in front of the old people's home at the foot of Montciel.

M. Robin had learnt all this from an attendant there who had been able to move around.

"We're not out of the wood yet," sighed Gaston.

"No-one knows, but it seems the Germans are leaving by the road to Besançon. At any rate, there's not a single one left at the school.

It was good to be in the kitchen. They stayed there a while without speaking. Then Gaston said, "I'd like to go and have a look from the top of the garden."

"No," said M. Robin, "don't go there. It's not at all wise to go there yet."

Fernande handed M. Robin half of the bread she had left.

"There'll be plenty of people doing without bread tonight, I think," said M. Robin.

"Who feels like eating?" said Fernande.

They again talked about the baker's assistant who had been killed because he had wanted to see what was going on in the street. Then M. Robin left.

"I'll come over tomorrow morning," he promised, "and tell you whether they say anything about Lyon tonight on the wireless."

When he had gone Fernande went down into the cellar to fetch fruit and a bottle of meths. Then they took chairs over by the door and settled down without talking.

In this way they were able to see, through the bead curtain, a part of the garden and the street where nothing living moved.

It was summer. There were birds and insects, but in the sunshine the wounded town lay still.

40

Once again the town seethed with excitement. The occupying troops had left, and flags blossomed from every window. There they stayed for a day and a half. Gaston went to look at the rue des Salines, where there were flags at every house, on every floor. Then on the second day the rumour spread that a German armoured column on its way north was heading straight for the town. Within a few minutes the flags disappeared. The streets emptied and shutters were pulled to in every house. A few members of the F.F.I. took to the woods again.

Gaston had come running back to take down the flag which Fernande had hung from the bedroom window.

Not a single German came, but the town kept withdrawn in fear until the first American contingents arrived.

Suddenly life was changed.

For a time Gaston spent half the day looking at the lorries, armoured cars, and all sorts of vehicles passing through. He came back with his pockets stuffed with cigarettes that he never managed to smoke.

"It's not tobacco," he said. "It's spiced cake. But it doesn't matter. They've got a bloody good army. There's nothing they haven't got. It'll be like in 1919. We were still selling stocks of American goods ten years after they had left."

Fernande had managed to get hold of some coffee, chocolate, and tinned meat, which they could not eat, it was so sweet.

"They're not a bad lot," Gaston said again. "All the same, they've got some peculiar ways."

M. Robin told them that Lyon was now fully liberated. All the bridges had been blown up, but not many people had been killed. In spite of this Fernande was still anxious, and talked endlessly about Julien and Françoise.

"He'll come on a lorry, perhaps," she said.

Gaston did not reply, but he went as often as possible to the corner of the rue des Écoles and the rue des Salines to see the convoys arriving. Sometimes civilians would get down. Others would climb on board the lorries. And the Americans laughed as they kissed the girls and slapped the men on the back.

Several regiments of French soldiers wearing the same uniform as the Americans also passed through. They were more reserved, and people welcomed them less enthusiastically.

Gaston talked to other people standing around and watching, but his eyes never left the vehicles coming in on the road from Lyon.

When he returned home he made a point of passing by the place where the houses had been burnt down. As a rule there was no-one there. Now that the War was more distant, people tended to ignore disaster. Nevertheless people had died in these houses, burnt alive or shot down the moment they tried to get out. Those who had escaped had lost everything.

Sometimes Gaston stopped by the corridor leading to the bakehouse, where he had made bread during the best years of his life. He did not go inside. He looked down at the pavement. There was a large and very clean area. The paving-stones had been washed down where the assistant's blood had flowed. Before they had been able to wash it someone had spread ashes. There were still some left in the gutter. The first rain would carry them away and leave no trace of the clean patch, and then there would be nothing left of the assistant but the memory of a large young man, full of strength. He had left the bakehouse just long enough to get himself killed on this spot. He was neither a Resistance fighter nor a collaborator. He just worked so that people might go on eating bread.

He must have been about the same age as Julien. At Lyon, too, they had killed people who were not involved in the War.

One evening, near the burnt houses, Gaston saw an old woman coming along. She was thin and withered, her back was bent, and she walked with little hopping steps like a bird, her arms hanging loosely in front. He had often seen her in this part of town. She had been widowed for a long time; her husband was someone called Hurtin, who was killed when he was employed at the salt works. The old woman came up to him. She said in a cracked voice, "It's a sad sight—yes, indeed!"

Gaston shook his head. The old woman was looking at the end house. Part of the walls, the roof, and the floors had collapsed. The remainder was black, but here and there the wallpaper was still intact. A porcelain sink was still in place, hanging out in empty space with a dangling end of pipe. The old woman pointed at it. "Have a good look," she said. "My kettle's still there in the sink. I'm sure it's still all right. A man could get it down for me with a ladder."

"It wouldn't be safe," said Gaston. "The walls might collapse."

"It's a good kettle," she went on. "Aluminium. It boiled very fast. I bought it the year before the War. Nowadays you'd have to go far to find one like it."

"When they come and clear up you'll be able to get it back."

"If no-one steals it in the meanwhile. I've already been along to look for a few things. I'm sure there are some left, but the roof collapsed on top of them, and I can't move the beams and all these tiles."

"You were lucky to get out," said Gaston.

The old woman gave a short, grating laugh.

"You call that lucky—to be left without a thing at seventy-six? We lived there from 1906. The year my poor Firmin went to the salt works, where disaster was in store. We came here because it wasn't too far from his work. And it was easy for me to find cleaning jobs in the district. Would you believe it, I've been working for some people since before the First World War. When my poor husband died I wanted to leave. And then—you know how it is—years go by, and it's not that one forgets, but I got used to things. And then I had so many ties here that I was afraid to move away."

Her unpleasant, mirthless laughter rose again.

"The move's been made now!"

She drew nearer, looked around, and, lowering her voice, she said as she pointed towards another half-destroyed house, "That one there—that was a young family, you know—called Pernin. The husband had joined the maquis. The young wife was killed along with the baby. The husband, he came back. He went mad. Then he went off again, it seems, saying he was going to kill the leader of the maquis. He said, 'If they'd waited till the Americans came it would have been done without a shot fired. The Germans would just have left, and that would have been all.'"

She stopped, seeming alarmed by what she had just said. As Gaston did not reply, she asked, "Do you believe it's true, M. Dubois?"

He made an indefinite movement. "I don't really know any more about it than you do."

The old woman spoke about her kettle again, and Gaston promised he would come along with his ladder the next morning and try to get it down for her. She thanked him, and then told him she was staying with some people for whom she had cleaned for over ten years. "But it's not like having your own home," she said. "It's nice and they are kind, but it's not one's own home."

She came up close to him again and lowered her voice, asking, "Do you know why I'm not dead like the others?"

"No."

"More than twenty years ago the owner promised to install lavatories inside the house. He never got round to it. We had to go downstairs, across the yard, and use the ones in the other house—the one that faces out on the rue des Salines. Well, when the shooting started I was so scared that I got a stomach-ache. So I went there. And the people there—they're called Champeau, you know—they made me stay with them. It was just next to the toilets. There you are, as easy as that. When I saw what was happening I didn't even cry. You should have seen how it burnt. If the other houses had been like mine with a door out the back they could all have escaped. But no such luck. You should have seen how it burnt."

She repeated this several times over, still with that unpleasant, jarring cackle.

She had nothing left except a few odds and ends she had been able to salvage from the ruins. All the rest had burnt except this kettle, which she kept glancing at with longing.

As it was getting late, Gaston said, "You ought to go home now."

"Tomorrow morning, then, you'll bring your ladder?"

"Yes, I'll come."

She walked off with her hopping little steps, and Gaston heard her sniggering again.

When she had disappeared he went back to the garden slowly. His house stood there, without a scratch, without a broken window. The War had passed close by, but had not even trampled on his garden.

41

The next morning Gaston took his ladder and went over to the burnt houses. Fernande went with him. The old woman was inside the house, rummaging around in the debris, which she was turning over with a poker. She had brought a big basket with her.

"You should be more careful," said Fernande. "You never know when it might collapse."

The old woman laughed scornfully and implied with a gesture that her life was of no importance.

Gaston moved a few tiles and propped up a charred piece of rafter to make a level site. Fernande helped him get the ladder in position and kept holding it while he climbed up as far as the sink. The kettle was neither dented nor broken. There was still some water in it. There were also a ladle and two spoons in the sink, which Gaston brought down.

The old woman emptied the kettle, put the other bits in her bag, and began to laugh again.

"My kettle," she kept saying. "Not a dent. It's a good kettle. You've no idea how quickly it boils."

She thanked them, took the kettle in the crook of her arm as though it were a baby, and hurried away, clutching it to her breast.

"All the same, poor woman," whispered Fernande. "We can count ourselves lucky."

They went back with the ladder, and Gaston said, "I'd like to go for a walk right into town. You never know, I might meet someone from Lyon."

"Oh, heavens, if only we had some news!"

Gaston put on a clean apron, changed his cap, and went off towards the centre. He had hardly been out of the immediate district these last few months, and he looked carefully at everything, trying to see what had changed. Apart from the burnt-down houses, there were others marked by the battle in the streets, but this was superficial.

There were lots of people gathered in the rue Lecourbe, in the square, and under the arcades. A crowd had formed at the beginning of the rue du Commerce. Gaston thought they were selling food without coupons, and he regretted having no money on him. However, he went up and, being unable to see above the heads in front, asked, "What's going on here?"

"They're cutting the hair off the girls who've been friendly with the Germans."

There were shouts and bursts of laughter from the crowd. Names were passed from person to person along with remarks about the families.

"They're going to put them in a lorry and show them all around the town," a woman said.

"No, they're going to make them walk barefoot, I've been told."

"Shave it right off!" screamed a woman.

There was a gale of laughter, and several voices took up the cry, "Shave it off! Shave it off!"

The crowd became restless. Now it was up to anyone to suggest further ideas.

"Shave her pussy off too!"

"Tattoo a swastika on her titties!"

They were jostling each other in order to see. Everyone shouted louder than the rest. Gaston was still some way off, but though not trying to move nearer, he found himself in the middle of the crowd as the numbers grew. All around him people kept on talking. "The whores! That's just the first course, but tomorrow they're going to parade all the collaborators."

"Then there's still a whole lot left to pack off to clink."

"All those who traded with the Germans and made a fortune at our expense."

"And the councillors."

"And the Militia."

"They've all buggered off."

"They'll be found, even as far as Berlin!"

Gaston suddenly thought of Paul. He felt as though imprisoned by this crowd, and he was afraid. Had his boy been arrested? Had he gone away? If Paul had disappeared, would they take it out on his father? Show him up like a strange animal before throwing him in prison and setting fire to his house? Why had he come here? For several months he had been burrowing into his corner, and now today he had stupidly stuck his head right into a hornets' nest.

It seemed as though all eyes were turned towards him, trying to place him.

Pushed from all sides, jostled, breathless, and sweating, Gaston used his elbows, and at last succeeded in breaking free from the crowd. No-one paid any attention to him. Nevertheless he avoided the main roads as he made for the rue des Écoles, taking a devious route through lanes and alleyways. It occurred to him to call on Paul and hear the news, but he had not the courage.

He walked as quickly as possible, scanning the street, looking behind him, convinced that a hand would seize him by the collar as a voice cried, "This is Dubois' father. Just look at the old bastard. He didn't lift a finger to stop his son trading with the Germans!"

On reaching the garden gate he hesitated. Perhaps they had come to take him while he had been away? He had thought that once the Germans had gone there would be nothing more to fear, no more misery or obsession with losing all he had, and here again he faced another terrifying prospect.

He went inside, handling the gate carefully. Fernande was not in the garden. He walked slowly up the drive where the shadows of the trees moving in the wind appeared to push swarms of golden insects before him.

At the corner of the path leading up to the house he stopped. Someone was talking in the kitchen. He felt unable to breathe. His legs had begun to shake again. Nevertheless he went on, listening hard.

At last, when he got to the foot of the steps, he recognized the voice. It was Julien.

42

When Gaston came into the kitchen Julien and his fiancée were sitting by the table. A good smell of smoked pork being fried permeated the room. Julien kissed his father, and then, bringing the young girl forward—she had kept in the background—he said, "This is Françoise. You're allowed to kiss her, you know."

Gaston kissed the young girl.

"You look hot," Julien remarked, "and exhausted, too."

"I'm not used to walking." Gaston sat down.

"I've made them something to eat," said Fernande. "They left at five o'clock this morning, and they had to change lorries three times to get here."

Gaston looked at the table, where there was a small piece of butter put out on a plate, bread, jam, and a basket of fruit.

"Julien brought some American smoked pork," said Fernande. "Would you like to try some?"

"Do some eggs for him, like you did for us," suggested Julien.

Gaston hesitated. He looked at Françoise, then at his son, then at the table.

"It's not smoked pork," Julien declared. "It's bacon."

Françoise said, "It's still smoked pork, you know. Just a different name."

"All things considered," said Gaston, "I don't think it'll do me any harm to have something to eat. Besides, it's gone eleven o'clock, so we can call it an early lunch."

"Would you like one egg or two?" asked Fernande.

"Are there enough?"

"There are four left, but Julien said he would go and get some tomorrow."

She had already put two slices of bacon in the frying-pan. The smell spread throughout the room. This was already sustaining, and Gaston felt his mouth flooding with saliva.

"If you can do me two," he said, "just for this once—"

He stopped, looked at the table, and asked, "What about you. Aren't you eating?"

"No," she said. "I'll have some jam and fruit."

She broke the eggs. The fat sputtered. Gaston followed every movement she made. He was breathing quickly, relishing the atmosphere of this kitchen, where for months there had been no other smell than that of vegetable soup. Eggs and butter had become so scarce that Fernande had mixed them into the mashed potatoes.

Gaston ate slowly, taking a delight in each mouthful. For a while that was all he could think about—the eggs and the peaceful kitchen, the young girl, who was peeling a pear from the garden, Julien eating jam, Fernande who was looking at them. It was the stillness, peace . . . The eggs and bacon were very good, and if there had been a piece of real, white bread, crusty and well-risen to go with them . . .

Julien described how they had managed to get there. Gaston listened, but the image of the crowd he had seen that morning came back to him by degrees. He had meant to tell his wife about it when he returned. Now he no longer dared. It was not Julien's presence that embarrassed him, but that quiet girl, about whom he knew nothing. When their eyes met the girl smiled shyly. Gaston tried hard to respond to her smile, but he felt ill at ease.

Fernande asked about everything: How had the girl been able to get home, and then get back to Lyon? Why had she made the journey, and what had happened when Lyon was liberated?

Julien gave nearly all the answers. He laughed. He ended up telling them that Françoise was in the Resistance. "She was doing an important job," he said. "She was the contact between an organization in Lyon and the maquis in Haut-Jura. It was dangerous. She always carried ten times the material needed to make the Germans shoot her had she been arrested. But she couldn't tell you that when she first came."

Fernande looked as though she was full of admiration for

this young girl. However, she asked, half angrily, "Were you afraid I couldn't keep my mouth shut?"

"No," said Julien. "But it was a strict rule. Even I knew nothing about what she was doing."

Fernande looked incredulous. "Weren't you in the Resistance?"

"No."

Françoise intervened. "He didn't belong to a group, but he worked for us all the same. And the risks he took were as big as anyone actually fighting. Perhaps—"

Julien interrupted her. "Shut up. It's not worth talking about."

There was a silence. Gaston emptied his glass. Julien offered him a cigarette as he said, "Have one. They're not American."

"That reminds me," said Fernande. "If you'd like some of those—the American ones—your father brought some home, but he can't smoke them."

"No, keep them. Just give me a few packets, and I'll use them to get eggs and butter for you."

There was silence again. Gaston thought he felt a hidden menace in this silence.

"What did you have to do to join the Resistance?" asked Fernande.

Françoise raised her eyes. She looked at the two old people in turn, and then in a calm yet firm voice she said, "My eldest brother was a member of the Communist Party. So I didn't have to go far to join it too."

43

It was only just after twelve o'clock when Gaston went upstairs to rest. He had excused himself, saying he was tired after his walk into town. That was true. He felt as though the morning had broken his legs, but not because of the walking they had done. And then, worst of all, there was the blow he had sustained when they were at table.

God! How he had fought and slaved and suffered the whole of this bitch of a life, and now come to this! A son going communist!

He was lying down. He had suffered two bouts of coughing, and felt drained of all strength and more dejected than he had been for several weeks.

Communist! The word was like an iron cannonball weighing him down. Right in the pit of the stomach, crushing him slowly.

Paul had told him hundreds of times about communism. So he understood it quite clearly. As soon as the Germans were beaten all the communists would come back. With their weapons. They would be the masters. They would come into his house and say to him, "Dubois, nothing belongs to you any more. Here is a certificate of admission to the old people's home. Your house belongs to us. So do your securities, and your garden and tools. Everything. As for you, you can go to the old people's home. You don't need all this any more."

They would come. And amongst them would be Julien and that girl. That youngster with her innocent look. A little saint who went to war. And to bed with his son before they were married, and pushed him into communism once she had got him in her clutches. Some inclinations he had, that boy!

Was it inevitable that politics and war contaminated everything? You thought you were through with all the misery, but nothing had changed. The evil had come into the house. There, down below. Prepared to steal everything.

Gaston thought about the old woman. The fire had left her the kettle. Would Julien and his mob leave him as much?

No. It did not look like it! What had he done to deserve being dogged by such bad luck? Nothing. A life spent working. That was all. Perhaps he had worked too hard and not thought enough about himself. If he had lived like some other people he would have been dead years ago, but he would have lived a pleasant life and never known this disastrous war.

However, his work had always given him more pleasure than anything else. What was the answer?

Gaston questioned himself. He turned over on his right, then on his left, then on to his back again, rearranging the pillows. He had left the shutters slightly ajar. He caught sight of a strip of bright sky. Warm air floated in from the garden sleeping in the sunshine. Nothing stirred. Fernande must have been on her own, because Françoise and Julien had said they ought to go and visit some friends. Communists, probably.

And now the War was over there was another one brewing. It was already here in this house. It rose up between them and set them against each other. But would Fernande still support the boy with his crazy ideas if they were forced to give up all their property? When Julien had come home after his apprenticeship and was already playing about with these ideas Fernande had said, "If his boss hadn't taken advantage of him and treated him like a slave he wouldn't have become like this."

But today he no longer had a boss to take unfair advantage of him. There was only this girl going to his head. Perhaps that was worse.

What was he going to do? What were they going to live on? On his painting? Or politics?

The more Gaston went over this ground, the more his sorrow, which gripped him to the point of stopping him breathing, rose into anger. It was the injustice, making him feel a victim, that hurt him most cruelly. He who had never taken part in politics, he who had ignored all the arguments and parties, there he was caught between two sons who already disliked each other and who were going to hate each other even more.

And all this was happening out of his control. It was as though an enormous wheel had started to roll. It revolved, and there he was, caught up and dragged along, unable to try saving a thing.

He had nothing. Only his two hands, which could still feed Fernande and himself. Otherwise he only had this garden waiting for him under the hot sun. He had done little work in the last few days. The grass had grown and crept in from the paths across the vegetable-plots, which he would have to weed. The sun had caught the last batch of lettuce he had planted out. He ought to be up drawing water so it would have time to warm before he watered them in the evening. He must—he must regain his strength and the willpower he had always possessed. Perhaps because he had hoped that Julien's return would be the sign that the War was over for them at last, he had neither strength nor courage, nor even the least desire to start work again that night. That was almost the same as having lost his will to live.

44

When Gaston went downstairs there was no-one in the kitchen. The bead curtain was drawn and the shutters closed. He dissolved a piece of sugar and an aspirin in a small glass of water, drank it, picked up his cloth hat, and went into the garden.

Fernande was sitting on the bench, a big basket of plums by her side. She took them one by one, stoned them, and cut off the damaged parts, which she dropped into a salad-bowl on her lap, and threw the good fruit into a big saucepan on the ground by her feet. As Gaston approached she wiped the knife-blade on the edge of the salad-bowl, which she put down on the bench. From the look she gave him Gaston saw that she had something important to tell him.

He stopped. There was a silence, broken only by the buzzing of the wasps attracted to the plums. As Fernande said nothing, Gaston asked, "Are you going to cook them?"

"Yes. Julien picked them before he went out."

"Don't throw the stones away. Once they're dry they'll burn."

"I know."

Silence.

Gaston started walking. Fernande got up and said, "Micheline came."

"Oh! I didn't hear her, though I didn't sleep at all."

"She didn't come indoors. She was in a hurry. She didn't want me to disturb you."

Gaston felt his throat tighten. He had to make an effort to ask, "What was it?"

Fernande demurred, looked down, and then up again as she whispered, "They've arrested Paul."

Gaston clenched his hands. He walked away, stopped, hesitated, and then came back to his wife and groaned, "They? Who are they?"

"There were two gendarmes and some men from the maquis."

She had waited a bit before replying, but the words came in a rush as though she felt a need to get rid of them quickly.

"It's a dirty trick," said Gaston.

He felt helpless. He had been expecting it since that morning, yet the news provoked hardly any reaction.

"We must do something," said Fernande. "After all, there's only one thing they can have against him—dealing with the Germans. That's not a crime."

She had put into words what Gaston had wanted to shout out loud. It was she who had given voice to his thoughts. Without anger. With a little glint in her eyes which seemed to add, "I'm sorry for you, my poor husband. This is your son."

"What can I do?"

"Nothing. Micheline knows it, too. All the same, she thought she'd better come and tell you. She also thought you might perhaps go and see Vaintrenier. It seems he is the head of the new town council."

Gaston sighed. He imagined Vaintrenier at the town-hall. He tried to visualize the atmosphere there. After what he had seen in town that morning . . .

"I was thinking," said Fernande, "perhaps Julien—I mean, if his fiancée knows people in the Resistance . . ."

She stopped. Gaston had a swarm of black dots dancing before his eyes. He sat down heavily on the bench.

"Aren't you well?" asked Fernande.

"Yes . . . I'm all right."

"Would you like a drink?"

"No, I've just taken an aspirin."

He sighed. Asking a communist to intervene on Paul's behalf! No. He had not thought of that.

"Did you tell Micheline that—"

He could not get the words out. Fernande must have understood, because she said, "All I told her was that she was in the Resistance."

"And what did she say?"

"Nothing. She was crying."

Fernande sat down next to Gaston. It was as though the summer had suddenly become heavy and dull. The wind had died down. The tired trees bent low with the burden of the afternoon. The insects were no more than a continuous hum in the background of the deep oppression of the day. Only the wasps were alive. Irritating. Drumming back relentlessly to beat around their faces. Settling on Fernande's hands every time she put them down on her apron.

Gaston stared blindly into the shade of the drive. Within the void just scooped from his mind, only these monotonous words buzzed around like flies, "They won't want to . . . They won't do anything for him . . . won't do anything for him."

45

Fernande had made a tomato salad; she had cooked French beans from the garden and opened a big jar of rabbit *pâté* that she had made herself. A neighbour had lent her some eggs to make a custard with a can of milk and American chocolate Julien had brought. Apart from the bread, it was a real pre-War meal. Gaston had come in from the garden two or three times to have a sniff and watch the preparations.

"It's going to be a real feast," he said. "But there's always something to spoil our pleasure."

"You'll see, everything will be all right," said Fernande. "If the children can't help, you go and see Vaintrenier tomorrow morning."

Gaston tried to control his feelings, but his anxiety drained his strength. He had watered the garden where most urgently needed, and then had walked over to sit down on the bench. He was still there when Françoise and Julien returned. He stood up and forced himself to smile as he said, "Dinner should be ready. And I do believe your mother has spared no expense. You go on up."

Gaston went down to the cellar and struck his lighter. He still had a stock of good wine. He looked for a bottle from the Jura hills that he had bought ten years before the War. Raising the bottle to eye-level and holding the lighter behind, he could see a little sediment along the side, but the wine itself was clear. The cork must have been good because the bottle was absolutely full. He carried it carefully, keeping it horizontal as though it were still in the rack. When he came in Françoise said, "Oh, you shouldn't have—"

"Oh, yes, after all," said Gaston, "after all."

He turned the bottle slowly upright and put it gently on the table. He wiped the neck with a corner of his apron and went to look for the corkscrew in the small chest of drawers.

"This is a very good one because you can pull the cork without shaking the bottle. With this kind of wine it's a crime to shake it up."

When he had drawn the cork he sniffed at it and pinched it between his fingers to test the quality. When he looked up his eyes met Françoise's, who was smiling as she looked at him. Her eyes were tender, and Gaston found this comforting. It made him feel as though a new warmth had blended with the aroma of the wine now spreading through the kitchen.

"You like taking care of your wine," said the young girl.

"Yes. When I bottled this one Julien was no higher than this table."

"I don't know," said Julien. "You bottled every year, so

how . . . Besides, I've never fathomed how you recognize any in your bins, as you never put labels on your bottles."

"Don't you worry. I know what I've got."

Before the young people had returned he had told himself hundreds of times, "As soon as they're back I'm going to talk about Paul. We must get down to it."

And now things were developing in such a way that he could not get around to talking about it. However, there was Françoise's smile and gentle look. He kept on thinking of this as he said to himself, "She'll help us. If she can she'll help us."

He had been afraid of this girl, and now that she was here, sitting at the same table, he would almost have preferred to talk to her alone. Yet it was she who was the communist. She who had brought in this terrible word, which did not go with her gentle eyes at all. Julien had not joined the Party. He had said so. In spite of this, it was his reaction that Gaston feared the most.

They ate the tomato salad, which Fernande had made with sliced onions and chopped parsley. No-one spoke. Gaston looked at the others stealthily, and every time he met Fernande's eyes he tried to make her understand that it was up to her to say something. Fernande sighed. She shared out the rest of the salad between Françoise and Julien.

"You must eat," she said. "We don't know how long it will be before the food situation is normal again."

"With the Americans here," said Julien, "there's a good chance of being flooded with provisions."

"That won't make any difference," sighed Gaston. "The War isn't won yet. Even the end of the War won't mean that our troubles are over."

He poured a little wine into his glass and, without lifting the bottle upright again, tasted it.

"It hasn't lost any strength. Come on, hold up your glasses so that I don't stir the sediment too much."

They drank to each other. Fernande had accepted a tiny drop, enough to raise her glass to Françoise and Julien's happiness.

The wine went perfectly with the *pâté*. It was a long time since Gaston had eaten such a good dish, but still it gave him no real pleasure. He would have liked to know what his son was going to say about Paul's arrest, and at the same time he dreaded the moment because he felt that from then on the harmony of the evening would be broken. He no longer felt sure whether his looks at Fernande implored her to speak or to keep quiet.

However, she spoke. She had helped herself to only a small portion of *pâté*, and when she had wiped her plate carefully with a piece of bread she drank a mouthful of wine and said, "Julien, you know, there's something that worries us deeply."

The boy looked at her. "Oh, yes, what is it?"

There was a silence. Gaston looked down. Fernande went on, "Micheline came round this afternoon. Your brother has been arrested."

Fernande never used the expression "your brother". She always said "Paul". Julien gave a short laugh. "Sad thing to say, but it was bound to happen."

"Don't be spiteful. You know quite well he has done nothing wrong."

Julien sat up in his chair, put his elbows on the table, and folded his hands in front of his chin. He shook his head as he looked first at his mother and then at his father. "Well, I'll be blowed! Here's a bloke who's been dealing with the Germans all through the occupation, and you find he's done nothing? He's flirted with the Militia and squared himself with all the Vichy organizations that are more or less fascist, and you'd like to see them strike him a medal!"

"Julien," cried his mother, "don't talk like that."

Gaston clenched his teeth and could hardly control himself.

"Don't talk like that," said Fernande again. "You're causing us grief."

"Grief? Do you think he was asking himself what he was doing to you when he came here and talked about the Militia and the sort of low-down deserter I was?"

Gaston was about to explode when he saw Françoise's hand

move slowly over to Julien's arm. "My darling," she said, "I don't know as much as you about what your brother has done. I only know what you have told me. I know that even economic collaboration is criminal, but you shouldn't behave like that. Your parents are suffering great anxiety—which is natural."

"You're not going to support him!"

"I'm not supporting him, but you're tending to destroy him."

"It's the truth that is destructive for him. And if he's coming up for trial they'd better not ask me to be a witness because I'd have to say what I'd heard on one particular evening . . ."

For a while Gaston had been clenching his fists. He banged the table and shouted, "God Almighty! I knew it all along. I knew it all along. What was the use of talking to him? I knew it all along."

His anger prevented him from finding the words. As usually happened, a fit of coughing shook him, forcing him to get up and spit into the grate.

When he had regained his breath he remained standing up in front of the stove, uncertain whether to sit down again.

"Come on, sit down," said Fernande.

None of the warmth or appetizing smells from the beginning of the meal were left in the kitchen. The air was sultry, full of the unpleasant heat of the day which the evening had dispelled from the garden, only to push it inside the house.

"You know I'd refuse to testify against him," said Julien. "But neither would I lift a finger to help him. He's got himself into a mess. It's natural he should stand trial and pay the price."

"I'm sure there are people who deceived themselves in all good faith," said Françoise. "With them the tribunals—"

Julien interrupted her. "All good faith! You're joking. For love of money, yes. But he'll still be cunning enough to get out of it cheaply."

That was enough for Gaston. Fernande, sitting between the table and the stove, was in his way.

"Let me through," he growled.

"But, Gaston, you're not going to—"

"Let me through, I say!"

He shouted these last words. Fernande got up and pushed her chair under the table. When he got to the foot of the staircase Gaston turned round and sent a parting shot at Julien. "Thank you very much. Thank you very much indeed."

He felt his cough mounting. He stopped and went up the staircase as quickly as he could.

46

Gaston stayed for a long time in front of the window wide open to the night which enveloped the garden. He needed to breathe deeply and regain his normal rhythm, to let the blood flow normally again in his veins.

He wiped his forehead several times with his handkerchief.

The evening was oppressive, but his own feelings oppressed him more. He knew now that the fact that the Germans had gone, that he had the right to leave his window open, to go to bed when he wanted, and to get up before dawn, no longer meant anything to him. There was another kind of peace which he would never find again.

Lying on his bed, covered only with a sheet, already too hot, he waited.

He had heard loud voices in the kitchen several times. Was Fernande trying to reason with Julien? Would she really try to defend Paul? Would Françoise try to make the obstinate boy listen to reason?

It would be a waste of time. Gaston knew this. He had been conscious of Julien's determined intention of doing nothing to help Paul. But was not he, their father, in some way responsible for the gulf between his two sons? Had he ever done anything to help them understand each other?

No. He had done nothing. He had led his life in the way he had to, pressed by the urgency of work. His life had never left him any time to think at all deeply about what it could be that kept the two boys apart. What was it? Too big a difference in age? The fact that they had different mothers? The older one's lack of concern?

Yes, all those things, and something else as well. Something that is within men and has no name. Something that eludes you when you are nothing but a craftsman sticking to your trade. And those things are of no importance until one day an unexpected turn of events brings men face to face.

It really was the War that was responsible. Gaston knew this. But he could not wholly understand why. Now that the War was far away, now that people could begin to live again, should it not be possible to forget it all?

If tomorrow he was given white bread again and as much tobacco as he wanted Gaston could begin to live and work again as before.

This was what he told himself, but suddenly the image of the old woman with her kettle came before his eyes; and the image of the houses burnt down and the baker's assistant killed by the door to the passage.

Who could be blamed for all this crime and destruction? Who could atone for the ruin and bear the weight of mourning? The idea was there, confronting him, as though it had just entered the room on the sultry breath of the summer night. It was like a savage beast. There was no doubt about its presence, but hands seized the halter in vain.

The room had never before felt so alive as it had that evening. The War had retreated ahead of this new invading army, which looked anything but warlike. Soldiers walking by, laughing and joking with the girls and chewing away like grazing sheep while smoking effeminate cigarettes. This was no longer war. All it had left behind after its occupation of the town had come to find refuge here tonight, to invade this room where Gaston could no longer be alone. There was no doubt night-time suited him best. The kind of night the War had plunged men into for so many months, cutting them off from the seasons.

This evening it was summer-time again.

Outside it was summer.

A summer that breathed with such strength that its wind rustled all the trees in the garden and banged the shutter.

Gaston got up. The floor was cool under his bare feet. He walked over to the window, opened the shutter, and leant out to fasten the catch as he whispered, "This wind is bringing rain. When it blows up at this time of night we should have rain before morning."

He stayed there for a moment, breathing in deep draughts of this wind which had just blown over the hill, sweeping down across the town like a river sprung between heaven and earth. Already the stars had disappeared over part of the sky. The clouds were invisible, but they were still there, bringing the water the garden needed.

They were still talking in the kitchen, but Gaston no longer felt like creeping quietly downstairs to try to overhear what they were saying about his son.

The close air in the bedroom was livened with light currents and eddies of wind. It was not yet fresh and cool, but it was at least a promise.

47

The three days following seemed endless.

On the first it rained. Gaston had not given a thought to where Françoise was going to sleep. When he got up he asked, "Where are they?"

"But you know that the young girl couldn't stay here."

"So what happened?"

"Well, she's got friends in town, and they offered them a bed."

"Good."

He felt hard, estranged from everything, like the house in the rain that had come to thwart the summer.

Fernande spoke again. "They won't be eating here at midday."

"Really . . ."

So he went out to the shed, where he spent practically the whole day doing odd jobs. His hands applied themselves to one job after another, but his mind was detached from what he was doing and jumped from one thought to the next.

He kept an eye on the drive. In the afternoon he saw Françoise and Julien arrive. They went into the house, but Gaston carried on with his work.

They stayed over an hour with Fernande. Afterwards they came down to see him. They kissed each other, and Julien said, "We've been invited out tonight. We'll come and see you tomorrow."

He began to walk away, then stopped and took a packet of shag out of his raincoat pocket. "Here," he said, "I managed to get this for some American cigarettes."

"Please, no," Gaston started. "I don't need it—"

Julien had already walked away.

On the second day Gaston left the garden only for his meal and a very short nap. The sun was shining again, but the rain had left the earth light and easy to work.

Julien and his fiancée ate with them. Almost in silence. At the end of the evening meal Julien announced that they had found a lorry-driver who was prepared to take them to Lyon.

"Oh, my goodness, you haven't stayed very long," sighed Fernande.

"But we'll come back," said Françoise.

So they left on the morning of the third day.

Fernande walked with them to the garden gate, while Gaston resumed the work which had been interrupted when it was time to say goodbye.

His son had gone away again with this girl about whom he knew nothing except that she was a communist and had a gentle voice and eyes.

When Fernande returned he straightened up, folded his hands around the handle of his fork, and said with a slightly forced smile, "At least they haven't been in our way for too long."

Fernande made no reply except by a movement of her arms, which then fell down again against her pinafore. She was crying silently.

"And we don't know very much about that young girl of his," Gaston went on.

Fernande looked at him. He understood what she was thinking. "I know *you* don't. Because you went up to bed like a brute. But I spent some time talking to her."

She went away. Gaston let her go. He had been unmoved by her tears.

She came back a moment later. She was not crying any more. She approached him and asked, "Have you definitely decided not to go and see Vaintrenier?"

Gaston pulled off his cap and wiped his forehead and bald head. He blew his nose, folded up the handkerchief slowly, and when he had put it in his pocket again he said, "No. It wouldn't do any good. They're all out of the same stable. I don't want to be insulted again."

He waited a while. As Fernande said nothing, yet kept standing beside him without moving, he raised his voice and went on, "I'd just like to be left in peace now. D'you understand? They can think what they like provided they leave me alone. Let me work quietly and die in peace. That's all I ask!"

She looked at him for a few seconds longer and then went away without a word.

Gaston went on throughout the day—work, dinner, rest, work—while the words rang through his head continually: "Die in peace. Die in peace."

So he went on till the end of the afternoon, till the time when there arrived a boy of about fifteen whom Paul employed to do deliveries. The boy leant his bicycle against the boxwood-tree and came over to Gaston. Fernande had heard the gate shutting and came running out.

"The boss sent me," said the boy. "He wanted you to know

that there's no need for you to worry. He came back home a short while ago."

The two old people looked at each other. The boy went on, "Everything's all right. The boss will come and see you soon. He'll tell you all about it. It was a mistake."

The boy waited. Gaston thought he had sensed a note of irony, but said nothing.

"Is there any message?" asked the boy.

"No," said Fernande. "Give them our regards."

They watched the boy take his bicycle and go off. When he had reached the gate Gaston took his tobacco-tin out of his pocket and said as he began to roll a cigarette, "There you are, it was a mistake. Either a mistake or a dirty trick by someone jealous of his success. Ah, but it's not over yet. People still have personal revenges and accounts to settle!"

He stopped to light his cigarette, and Fernande took advantage of the break to slip away. Gaston did not take his eyes off her before the bead curtains in the kitchen door had fallen back into place behind her.

With one hand on his fork and the other holding the cigarette he stood for a long time looking at the road. Between the trees he saw people go by whom he did not recognize. Cars came past too. The town was beginning to live again in a way which was very different from the one they had known during the occupation. And yet it was a dreary summer evening that fell on the garden. He had dug over the dry surface of the soil, turning the damp earth with his iron fork, but it was already dry again, emanating a dull, insipid smell.

Julien had gone away. Paul had come out of prison. They were going to find themselves alone again, Fernande and he, facing the remainder of their lives until the end came. He would be the first to go—that was to be expected. He was the older. The thought was not new to him, but it was the first time he had considered the end with so much serenity.

When he had gone there would still be evenings like this in the garden and in the town, but there would also be quarrels, hatred, wars, the venom of life.

He had received his full share of that venom. Now he had the right to hope for a little peace, even if it meant cutting himself off more from the world.

It should be possible here, at the bottom of the garden. He would have to withdraw inside himself, not think of anyone else or what might happen to his property when he was no longer there.

Gaston shook off the torpor that had overtaken him. The sun had long since disappeared behind the hill. He pulled the fork out of the ground and cleaned the prongs with a small scraper he kept hanging from the strings of his apron, and then slowly walked towards the house where smoke was rising from the fire on which the evening soup was warming up.

PART FOUR

Upon the Garden Earth

48

Gradually the autumn stripped the dying garden bare. The trees on the slopes of Montciel and Montaigu were also losing their leaves. Day by day the earth was advancing towards night.

Gaston was well familiar with that winter darkness which rises up from the earth even while the heavens are still full of light and the woods are russet and gold. He noted its approach from day to day as he worked. He studied the wind. It came mostly from the north. This was a sure sign that a hard winter was gathering up there in distant countries where the War still raged—a war he had seen for such a short while as it swept through the country.

The newspapers were full of the War. They also spoke about its aftermath. It was like a tidal wave of evil, hatred, and wrangling that nothing could appease.

As the autumn advanced and the days shortened he had more time in the evening to think about these things. He looked at the headlines in the papers, but found it difficult to read the articles. Truth to tell, they scarcely interested him. So when the supper had been cleared he would put his elbows on the table and slowly drink the lime or vervaine tea which Fernande had prepared for him.

The two old people spoke very little. When a letter came from Julien by the afternoon post Fernande waited till the meal was over before reading it out loud. Sometimes she stopped as though searching for a word and said, "His writing is becoming worse and worse. There's always something I can't make out."

Gaston said nothing, but he understood that his wife did not always read aloud everything that the boy had written. These letters were short, constantly emphasizing that life in town was not easy. When she had finished Fernande went to the dining-room to fetch a small bottle of ink, a penholder, and a sheet of paper which had above its lined columns the heading of the bakery. She had saved a big packet which she used for all her letters.

Gaston watched her as she wrote. She was slow and often stopped to readjust the pen, which slipped out of place in her rheumatically deformed fingers. She often remarked, "I need a bigger pen. This one is really too small. I can't feel it between my fingers any more."

One evening Gaston said to her, "You should roll some string round it. That would make it thicker, and it wouldn't slide so easily."

She followed his advice, and he noticed that she wrote with much less difficulty.

When she had put down her pen Gaston always asked, "You gave them my love, didn't you?"

Each time she replied, "Of course I did."

Everything continued like this. Life carried on in its small ways. Every day would slowly wear on into its uneventful evening. During the month of September Julien had several times mentioned his marriage, saying that it was to be celebrated in October at Saint-Claude, where Françoise came from. And he said, "There will only be you and Françoise's father."

Fernande had appeared resigned to this. Gaston had sighed, "My goodness, what extraordinary times!"

That had been all. The two old people waited. And then a letter came by the morning post on October 17th.

The sun was shining brightly. Gaston had been tying up the artichokes for over an hour. He was sweating in spite of the north wind, which blew dead leaves along the drive. Straightening up as he did from time to time to wipe his forehead and ease his breathing, he saw Fernande coming back slowly from the gate, reading a letter.

She stopped before drawing level with him. Gaston half shut his eyes to be able to see her better. He could not make out her features because of the shadows over her bent face, but he guessed that she had not stopped merely to be able to read more easily. They received scarcely any letters other than the ones from Julien. He immediately thought of him, and he sensed that something was wrong.

Feeling oppressed, he shivered. Perhaps it was the wind cooling down his sweat, or perhaps it was also a fear that he refused to recognize.

He hesitated. Then, as Fernande began to walk again, he put down his tools and walked over to meet her.

They stopped a few paces from each other. Fernande had let the hand holding the letter fall down against her apron. Her other hand also hung loosely. She raised her head slowly. Her mouth was crumpled and trembling. Tears were running down her cheeks.

Before Gaston had spoken a word she made an attempt to smile, a little bitterly, her head shaking from left to right as though to say, "No, don't worry. It's not serious."

Gaston saw that she was swallowing hard. The skin on her neck was stretching, and as the wrinkles distended they showed up like pale furrows in her sunburn. She seemed to pull herself together, and at last whispered, "I'm being silly. It's silly to cry over a thing like this. It's just as well this way. It's just as well. . . ."

"But what's it all about?"

She showed him the letter. "They are going to get married. They are going to get married in Lyon—all on their own. It will save money. There, that's all it is."

She continued very quickly, as though she feared she might not be able to reach the end of her sentence, "Come along. I'll read you his letter."

She stepped aside to the right to avoid bumping into her husband and walked towards the house at full speed.

Gaston felt only a kind of relief, because for several minutes he had feared there might have been an accident. He was also relieved in a way because the prospect of a journey to Saint-Claude had alarmed him. Now that was over. Julien was getting married. Nothing was going to be done about the occasion, and his sole thought was that he still had, somewhere in the cellar, some wine as old as the boy himself, which he had kept specially for this occasion. This thought aroused no feelings in him. It came to him because it was always natural to think about wine when you spoke of marriage. But then, after all, nothing happened in the normal way any longer in this world, and you had to accept things without astonishment.

He knew that Fernande was crying. He waited a while before rejoining her.

He found her sitting by the table. Her eyelids were swollen. She was staring at the window. Not a muscle of her face moved.

Gaston sat down facing her and waited in silence for her to read the letter. Many minutes passed. The door stood wide open, and the wind blew through the curtain so that the wooden beads clattered against each other. There was a pot of vegetable peelings boiling on the stove. A small jet of steam was constantly blown about by the air currents.

At last she turned towards the table and began in a voice that was weak but hardly trembled, "This is what he says, 'My dear Parents, I know only too well that what I am about to tell you will give you pain, but we have decided to get married here, without inviting anyone, so as to save the journey and avoid the expense. Françoise's father is ill, so that in any case we could not get married at his place. Then, as it is only a year since Françoise's mother died, we could not have a wedding party. We have very little money as it is. Françoise has found a job as secretary to a barrister I know—I sold him some paintings. It's difficult for her to be away for several days. I know the journey would be tiring for you, too. We couldn't put you up as we only have one room and one bed. I have applied for the necessary papers. I hope that the paintings will sell better soon, and we will then have enough money to find a flat. Then you would be able to come for the birth of your grand-daughter—because I hope it is a girl. This will be so much more important an occasion than our marriage, which is nothing but a formality. Françoise is at work, but she asked me to send you all her love—both of you. And I send you mine.'"

Fernande had read it straight through, stopping only to take a breath. She put the letter down on the table. "There you are. He also gives the date. It's the day after tomorrow."

Gaston sighed. He was not deceived by her outward calm. He felt she was struggling not to cry, and he would have liked to say something to lighten her sorrow. He searched for words, but found none. So he sighed, raised his hand, and let it fall again on to the oilcloth, and then stood up slowly and went towards the door.

As he drew aside the bead curtain an idea struck him at last. "We must send them something," he said. "I don't know what. A parcel—or perhaps a little money. I am sure they need it."

Fernande looked at him across the room. Her mouth was not smiling, her face remained closed in, but her bright eyes thanked him.

49

The very next morning Fernande took a big parcel to the station. In it she had put some pears, tinned food, a small jar of melted butter, some jam, and some chocolate. That was all she had been able to find. Gaston had watched her making up the parcel and shaking her head. He knew that was not all she would send. He had never looked after their money, but during the summer they had sold both vegetables and fruit, and he suspected that Fernande had not taken all the money to the savings bank.

The morning of the wedding she said, "I must go to the post-office and send them a telegram. As we can't be there, they should at least have a little word from us."

Gaston had agreed. It was as though all this was only a very remote concern of his. What he noticed most of all was that after she had suffered the first shock Fernande's main reaction was different. She said, "I know it's not very nice for us to see them getting married all by themselves and so far away. But we must think of them. It is not a very joyful affair for young people, a wedding like that."

Once the day was over she began to wait for a letter describing the meagre wedding. Gaston felt she was tense and irritable, and he avoided talking to her. Life went on its round in the garden and the house. There was no obvious change, and yet Gaston felt a foreboding, as though expecting some other event to happen, he knew not what.

The first letter came, telling them briefly about the ceremony. Fernande cried a little when she learnt that Julien had not been married in church. Gaston said, "It doesn't—it doesn't matter at all. Still, they're wrong. You should never fall out with people. You might need their help later on in life."

He had wanted to say, "It doesn't surprise me. A communist!" But he refrained. The more he went on, the more touched he was by his wife's sorrow.

From now on they were really isolated from the rest of the world, and, being alone together in the evenings just as they worked together during the day, they could not put up with everlasting quarrels. Besides, Fernande had not been getting angry for a long time now. It was as though the declining season had numbed their existence. Fernande was stooping more. Her face was more wrinkled, and her eyes were often lost in the distance.

During November they had only one quarrel. It was on a Thursday. Fernande had gone to market, and at eleven, when she came back, she announced, "I have just seen Mme Gresselin, the headmistress of the infants' school. It's a long time since I saw her last. She looks much older."

Gaston only knew Mme Gresselin from having seen and greeted her in the street, but Fernande had met her at closer quarters when Julien was at school. "She must be retiring soon," he said.

"She should have done so already. But because of the War she stayed on a few more years. What can you expect? Everybody tries to earn a little money. Life is so hard."

She stopped. Gaston thought she had opened the conversation just to break the silence for a while. Fernande took out all the things she had bought, went to hang the shopping-bag behind the door in the scullery, and came back saying, "Now that there's hardly any work to be done in the garden, I could try to earn a little too."

She stopped. Gaston looked at her with raised eyebrows. As she did not go on, he asked in the end, "Earn a little? How do you mean?"

"Well, Mme Gresselin told me the school needs a couple of helpers in the canteen. To serve the children and—and to clean."

"Good Lord!" Gaston blurted out. "We may not be rich, but you're not going out to do washing-up as though we were poverty-stricken. No, you're not!"

He had felt hurt by the idea of his wife washing pots and pans, and he had shouted at her.

"Don't get angry," she said. "There's nothing shameful about it. And the little money I earn will help the children."

"Help them? Did anyone ever help us? Why shouldn't Julien start working at his trade or find some other kind of work, rather than trying to live by his pictures? They're living on what his wife is earning! Do you think this is right? And you want to put your oar in too. He needs must have two women to support him—"

"Gaston! Be quiet. You are being unfair. You know quite well he might be called up at any time, and that no-one will give him a job!"

She shouted too, and her attitude only provoked his anger further. He struck his hand with his clenched fist. "I don't give a damn. But I'm not having you going like a beggar to wipe kids' faces and mess about in greasy water. People would think that I make you slave to—"

As always when he shouted too much his voice choked in a thick cough that came from the base of his diseased bronchi with a flood of phlegm. When he had spat and drunk the glass of water that Fernande gave him he staggered back and let himself fall into his chair. It was a long time since he had had such a fit. He had no strength left, and sat, elbow on the table, left hand on his knee, leaning forward in an effort to regain his breath. A whole weight of forgotten exhaustion came to him suddenly. It bore down on him. It seemed to push him towards the floor at which he was staring, unable to utter the least word.

The day was grey and cold. Soon winter would arrive. Winter, which had terrified him so much for the last few years. Was his body really so worn out that it could no longer stand the least difficulty? He had already twice been so seriously ill in the middle of hard winters that he had thought he would not live to see the spring. Would the coming winter be his last? It occurred to him that it was perhaps in anticipation of his death that Fernande was looking for work. Was she afraid of Paul? She had often told him, "You ought to put your affairs in order. What does it cost?"

He raised his head. Fernande was looking at him. Her face was sad, and her eyes seemed to say, "My poor husband, what a state you get yourself into for so little!"

But all she did was to mutter, "All the same, you should try to see my point of view."

He felt too weary to go on with the discussion. He made a movement with his head, signifying neither yes nor no. What did he have to understand? He was afraid of asking. He dreaded hearing his wife say that he would not live for ever, and that he had done nothing to safeguard her existence when he was no longer there. Perhaps that was not what she would have replied, but he preferred to remain in doubt. Above all, he preferred silence. He already regretted the outburst he had been unable to repress and which drove away the peace he had felt for the last few weeks, like sinking one's tired body into a good, soft bed.

He understood one thing that day: the peace he wanted so much could be bought only with silence. He gave up. Fernande did not speak about the canteen until the following Monday, but Gaston knew quite well she had made up her mind.

On the Monday morning, when they had finished their breakfast, she asked, "Would you prefer that I cooked you a meal before I leave, or would you rather I get it all ready so you can eat at midday?"

He did not even ask what she was talking about. "I don't want to change my meal times," he growled. "And I'm quite capable of getting a meal for myself."

Neither did he ask her what time she was leaving, whether she would have anything to eat at her job, how much she would earn, at what time she would be coming back. He had wanted to ask all these questions from the moment he was convinced that she would carry out her intention, but he had sworn to himself that he would not talk about it. Fernande was going to have her own way. She wanted to start living the way she would have to when he was no longer there. In that case it was best to let the silence between them grow. When the time arrived for the silence to stay for ever unbroken it would be all the easier.

Autumn had not yet bared the trees completely, but the rain falling between the low heavens and the earth for the last three days cut off the house from the rest of the town.

This rain announced the coming of winter. It wrenched at the shutters, tore a leaf from the vines or the pear-tree. Sometimes Gaston stared at the sky, sometimes at the glistening, wet earth in the garden, and never before had he experienced so intensely to the depths of his being that heaviness of life which marks the approach of the dead season.

50

So November passed. Fernande went out every morning at about half-past ten and came back four hours later. She always brought back crusts of bread for the rabbits and a can of soup in her basket—soup she heated up for the evening meal.

It had to be accepted. Living like poor people. In truth, they were poor. Gaston admitted this at last. The houses were worthless. The War had swallowed up old people's savings.

So Fernande went to work in the canteen. At a time of life which should have been leisurely she became a charwoman. When she left she was smiling. When she returned she was smiling. But every day her complexion turned more ashen. Her back grew more bent, and she leaned forward more heavily. She never complained. However, Gaston saw her massaging her hands with their twisted fingers. Her left index finger was bent across the middle finger. Her thumbs stayed bent even when she extended her hand, and her wrists were swollen.

"Dishwater doesn't do you any good."

She shrugged her shoulders. "It's nothing—nothing at all. You know this happens every winter."

This was not true. Gaston had never seen her so tired. Moreover, he had never heard her coughing the way she did now.

When he timidly suggested that she should rest she said, "Just let me go on until Easter. When there's work to be done in the garden I'll stop. But their child is going to be born towards the end of March. When that happens I shall send them a little money. Not before. It must be for the baby."

Her face brightened when she spoke about the baby. Her tiredness seemed to disappear magically. So Gaston let her talk.

Julien had written to say that a friend had found them a two-roomed flat near Lyon. But it would not be free until January, and it was not furnished. Gaston at once said, "They've no furniture. But they've only to come here. We don't need two beds in our bedroom. They can have one of them. I expect we can find other things. There's a table in the shed, and there are far too many chairs in the dining-room."

From that day on one or the other would say from time to time, "Look, we could let them have some crockery. Or that little chest of drawers."

"Yes, all they have to do is to arrange transport."

"Even if they have to hire a lorry it'll still be cheaper than buying."

When this started Gaston had made the suggestion so as to

be the first to mention it. But he had felt a slight wrench at the thought of losing so many things that belonged to the house. Later, without knowing exactly why, he found pleasure in discovering new things to give away.

During Fernande's long absences he began to walk around the house looking for some object he had just thought about. He also began to think about the little child who would be born. Paul had no children. There was hardly hope there now, so the arrival of this new little Dubois was important, all things considered.

Neither Paul nor his wife had turned up at the house since the Liberation, but it was not the first time they had failed to appear for several months on end. After all, they had their work to do. Trade must have improved a little. Gaston encouraged these thoughts so as to discount the idea that events had separated his two sons for ever and made Paul keep away from the house. Everything would resolve itself in time.

But time also hurries on the seasons, and winter was advancing rapidly.

On the fourth day of December, with hardly enough light in the sky to indicate morning, a strong northerly wind blew up. The bare branches shook wildly, the vines on the trellis reared up across the window, the house gave a great sigh of anguish, prolonging the fire's roar. And then all was still. Gaston studied the clouds from the window for a few minutes and said, "The north wind is becoming stronger. I think we'll have snow."

"I'll go and fetch another basket of wood," said Fernande, "then we'll be well in hand if it begins to snow."

She went out with her empty basket. A second gust of wind whistled, not so fierce as the first, short squall which caused such a panic before dying down. First it was very light, singing through the young oak-trees. Then it gathered strength, howling around the house and spreading in all directions, beating down the smoke from all the chimneys between the roofs in town, shaking the trees and rattling the trellis.

When Fernande returned she stood for a moment with her back to the closed door before being able to say, "This wind is icy. I thought I'd never be able to breathe again."

Gaston began to unload wood on to the pile by the stove. "You put too much in the basket. It's too heavy for you."

"No. That wind took me by surprise. I only had my woollen cardigan and shawl on. I never thought it was so cold."

She poured out the remains of the coffee left over from lunch, and, holding the bowl with both hands to warm her fingers, she drank it in small sips.

When Gaston had emptied the basket and stoked up the fire he walked over to the window. "Oh, my God," he said. "That blasted wind has already torn three sacks off my artichokes. And I tied up the twine. I'll have to go—"

Fernande interrupted. "Don't be silly. You know that if you went out in this weather you'd spend the rest of the winter in bed. It's not worth chasing after trouble. It comes quickly enough of its own accord."

She put down her empty bowl on the table and opened the door to the dining-room.

"What are you doing?" asked Gaston.

"I'm going to put on my coat. And I'll go and tie up the sacks. I've plenty of time before I have to go to work."

"My God," Gaston moaned, "it's come to this! I'm useless once it's cold outside!"

Fernande slipped on the big overcoat which she had made from a cape left behind by the soldier they had given shelter at the time of the capitulation. She had dyed it herself, and the mixture of khaki base and black dye had given the rough cloth a washed-out brown colour, streaked with lighter yellow. She pulled up the collar, wrapped the shawl round her head, and tied it under her chin.

Gaston watched her as he stood by the window. Then he looked at his artichokes. More sacks were working loose. If the wind grew any stronger they would all be torn away.

"You must take some string and a knife. I think the string I used wasn't strong enough. It was too old. With all the rain we've had, it must have rotted already. There's some stronger stuff behind the cellar door."

Fernande took a small, sharp knife, adjusted her shawl once more, and went outside.

51

As soon as Fernande stepped outside Gaston moved back to the window. He heard her opening the cellar door. She was certainly taking her time in finding that string! And the wind continued its ruthless work. It swept down over the earth's surface, cut across the mounds of soil Gaston had earthed up round the foot of the artichokes, tried to penetrate below the sacks, and there, gathering all its strength like a cunning animal, blew up jerkily. The sacks twisted and turned. If Fernande took much longer all the strings would be broken!

When at last she appeared at the corner of the house Gaston opened the window slightly and shouted, "Tie new string round those that still hold. Do the others afterwards."

She nodded and went on to the plot. The wind seized hold of her, as it did the plants. Her coat flapped. Sometimes it flew right up, billowing above her black skirt. Gaston saw her stumble several times on her clogs and thought she was going to fall.

"I've never known such a cursed wind," he groaned.

When Fernande bent down to gather the huge plants up in her arms and pass the string around them it looked as though she was clutching them so as not to fall.

Gaston followed all her movements. Her fingers must have been numb because normally she worked faster and with more energy. It seemed to give her considerable trouble every time she straightened up. There were moments when she stood absolutely still for no apparent reason. Leaning forward, her rounded back to the wind, she staggered with one foot in the air, making a desperate effort to regain her balance.

In this way she tied up four or five plants. When she reached the next, instead of leaning down as she had with the others, she began by standing up straight, bringing the hand holding the string to her chest. Her hand opened, and the pieces of string escaped on the wind like bright little streamers against the dark earth colours of the world around her.

"Oh, good God, the string!" Gaston moaned. "What on earth is she doing?"

She had made a feeble movement in an attempt to catch the string, but her right hand thrashed in the air, letting go the knife, which fell to the ground. She stood like this for one or two seconds, like a half-uprooted scarecrow still standing up to the force of the wind. Then her knees slowly bent. Her right hand tried to grasp the plant as she fell. Her fingers slipped on the sodden sack. She first fell to her knees, then hesitated a moment before lying down on her left side, facing the small bank of earth.

"Oh, God!" muttered Gaston. "What's the matter with her? What is she doing?"

His throat tightened. For a moment he wanted to believe that Fernande had lost her balance, but she kept lying quite still. Only the hem of her coat was alive, animated by the icy wind.

His hand clutching the window-bolt, Gaston gasped for breath, a vast fear nailing him to the ground.

52

Gaston stood still for a period of time. He could not judge how long. Something happened to him, but he was unaware of it. Remote from the earth and passing time, he was there and he was elsewhere. He saw Fernande lying by the artichokes, and at the same time told himself it was not true. She would be coming indoors to the kitchen, rubbing one numbed hand against the other.

Then, still not understanding what motivated him, he left the window. His strength was back, his clarity too. He put on his big velvet jacket with deliberation and went outside.

While he took off his slippers and put on his clogs he felt the icy air surround and penetrate him. He cringed, hanging on to his determination to persevere as he mastered this body of his which reared up every time it was seized by the cold.

Now he crossed the drive and walked across the plot of earth. His eyes never left Fernande's coat. It seemed as though she was moving. He wanted to run, but the fear of falling held him back.

He leant over her. He hardly touched her. He was there, and he did not dare.

"What's the matter with you? Can you hear me? Can you hear me?"

He had shouted very loudly.

No sound.

Fernande did not move.

Gaston knelt down and tried to get his arm underneath her to lift her up a little. There was a rattle in her throat. She hiccupped again and again. Her face was blue, her bloodshot eyes were half open, and the eyelids trembled as though heaving in the wind.

"Good God! Oh, good God!" stammered Gaston.

He stood up. He felt lost. He looked around. No-one there. Only this cutting wind which took away his breath and lacerated his face with a thousand knives.

He hesitated for a moment. Should he let himself fall down there too and die with his old woman on this sodding earth?

The idea lashed him as though it was part of the wind. A kind of shout rose from the depths of his being. A cry that strangled in his throat and was no more than an unintelligible appeal.

So he leaned down again. With one knee on the ground, he grasped Fernande by the wrist, remembering an old knack he had learnt during the War for carrying the wounded. He pulled. The rattling noise in her throat increased. He pulled again and managed to lift her up sufficiently to insert his back under her inert body. With a huge effort he stood up.

Would his shaking legs hold out?

He took one step. Then another. Fernande's feet dragged along the ground. She had lost one of her clogs. Her left hand was clutching three pieces of string which fluttered in the wind.

Gaston reached the edge of the drive. In order to cross the flagstone border, he leaned forward even further, and, taking care that her body did not swing, let go with his left hand and clutched the clothes-line pole.

At the foot of the steps he had to stop. In spite of the cold he was bathed in sweat. The hand-rail was on his right. In order to be able to hang on to it he would have to change Fernande's position on his shoulders. He clutched the stiff overcoat with his left hand, his right grasped the ice-cold metal, and he took one step up.

There were ten steps. He stopped on each one. He tried to breathe, to take some strength from the wild wind lashing furiously against the house, whirling at full force, then retreating.

These gusts of wind—it was almost as though he could see them there in front of him, filled with a multitude of little black dots.

He knew those black dots. He knew what they signified, and fear overtook him once more. If he fell down here they would both roll down to the foot of the steps. Because of the boxwood-trees no-one would be able to see them either from the road or the track. A strange clarity had followed the detached emptiness of a short while back. Every thought that occurred to him invoked its own batch of astonishingly precise images.

He stopped. He must stop often enough to gather up his strength again. He must breathe regularly. He must avoid the hard gusts of icy air which could knock him down.

He counted the steps. Still four left. He gathered every ounce of strength left within him and climbed up these last four without stopping.

He staggered at the top, and his hand fell on the door-handle which he grasped very tightly.

He paused. The handle turned, the door opened, and the heat from the kitchen rushed out on his face.

He shut the door again. It banged heavily in the teeth of the north wind.

Once inside, he thought of the bedroom and the bed. But there was no fire up there, and he was quite incapable of carrying her upstairs.

Perhaps she had only fainted. He tried to sit her in a chair, but in vain. The lifeless body slung to the left and the right, slumped forward, drained of all its life force.

So, being at the end of his strength, he laid her down on the lino.

53

Gaston had thought that warmth should be enough to bring his wife round again. As she remained lifeless, he tried to make her drink a little brandy, but his hand was trembling so much that he did not succeed. Tears were burning in his eyes. Everything blurred, and when he stood up he had to lean on the table so as not to fall. He looked out of the window many times, but no-one passed by on the road.

He walked back towards Fernande. Began to talk to her again, but she continued to stare at him with her lost eyes, still breathing out with that rattling noise that came through phlegm from the depths of her throat.

Again he was seized with fear.

He took a small, flattened cushion from a chair and slid it under her head, and went outside.

Where should he go? Towards the street? It might be difficult to find anyone. He thought of Mlle Marthe, who lived opposite, but she was very old and hardly went out any longer. He ran down to the bottom of the garden, round the shed, and came to the yard of the house where M. Robin lived. He looked towards the kitchen window and thought he could see a clear shape through the fog of tears and cold that confounded his sight. He hurried on and, raising his arms, began to shout, "Hey! Hey! Hey!"

He choked, and his cough shook through him, forcing him to stop. The window opened and Mme Robin asked, "What's the matter?"

Gaston tried to speak, but his cough strangled him. He could only make signs and could hardly hear the "I'm coming!"

The window closed again. Gaston tried to control himself. He needed to spit, but the wind blew the phlegm back on his coat, and he was unnerved as he searched for his handkerchief to wipe it off.

When M. Robin and his wife arrived he had stopped coughing, but he still could not utter a word. He dragged them along, and it was only when they reached the garden that he was able to stammer, "Come quickly—my wife—my wife—I can't go on."

Mme Robin ran ahead towards the house, and Gaston felt M. Robin's hand grasping his arm to support him. For a moment a black void opened up before him. He stopped, held his breath for a few seconds, and then began to walk on slowly.

When they entered the kitchen Mme Robin was kneeling down beside Fernande, holding her head. Fernande's face was very red. You could hear the quick gasps only just managing to pass through her purple lips.

"She is very flushed," said Mme Robin. "We must find a doctor at once . . . and we'll have to take her up to bed."

Gaston groaned, "Oh, my God! Oh, my God!"

M. Robin helped him to sit down. He seemed so calm.

"I'll run over to our house," he said. "I'll send our daily help over here, and I'll phone your son at once. He will bring a doctor. Have you got his number?"

Gaston shook his head, and M. Robin hurried off.

Gaston now felt relieved of an enormous burden. He was no

longer alone . . . he no longer had to make the decisions. He watched the little woman bustling around in her blue overcoat and with her long, brown, curly hair falling down over her shoulders.

She was speaking. He listened without really hearing her. "I'm going to heat some water," she said. "The doctor might need it. Is there a fire in your bedroom?"

"No. Oh, my God!"

"I'll go up and light it. Is there any wood upstairs?"

"Yes, there should be some."

"And paper?"

"There's some here."

Gaston handed her a newspaper and searched in his pocket for a lighter. "I'll come up with you."

"No, you stay there. You're not standing up for the moment. When my daily help comes over we'll put Mme Dubois to bed."

Mme Robin went upstairs, and Gaston heard her walking about in the bedroom. From where he was sitting he could see only Fernande's head still lying on the floor: the corner of the table on which he leaned his elbow hid the rest of her. She seemed a little less flushed, but her eyelids were still half shut over her lifeless eyes.

Drained of all response, Gaston sat there leaning on one elbow across the table, the other on his knee, staring at his wife's face as he kept on saying, "It can't be possible. It can't be possible."

54

Mme Robin and the daily help had already put Fernande to bed when M. Robin came back.

The daily help was a large Italian woman of about forty, who was stronger than many a man. She had lifted up Fernande, taking her under the armpits, and all Mme Robin had to do was to support her legs to stop her feet knocking against the stairs. Gaston had followed them. The fire was roaring away in the bedroom where M. Robin rejoined them.

"I tried two doctors," he said. "They were both out. So I called your daughter-in-law. She's coming with Dr Letty, who lives next door to them."

"While we're waiting," said Mme Robin, "we could apply a poultice. I'm sure it's her chest. It always helps to ease the congestion, and it will make her temperature go down."

Gaston had sat down in the armchair at the foot of the bed. The grey daylight from the window threw only a dim, cold shadow across the sick woman, hardly enough to make out her features.

"She seems to be breathing more easily," Gaston remarked.

"Yes, you're right. But I don't think her temperature is going down."

M. Robin was holding Fernande's wrist. He went on, "Her pulse is regular, but it's very fast."

The two women had gone downstairs to prepare the poultice. M. Robin sat down opposite Gaston on a low chair on which Fernande arranged her clothes before going to bed.

Now her clothes were at the foot of the bed parallel to the one on which she was lying. Gaston nodded towards them and said, "That's a coat she made for herself out of a soldier's cape —one that youngster from Villefranche left behind. He was called Guillemin if I remember rightly. He helped me bake bread when we were invaded. He was a fine boy. I don't know what became of him."

M. Robin shook his head.

Gaston stopped. He did not know why he had spoken like this, but the act of talking quietly made him feel better.

M. Robin asked, "She was in the garden?"

"Yes. She wanted to go out and tie up the sacks round the artichokes. I'm not up to much these days. But I shouldn't have let her do it. However, you know her. It's impossible to stop her working. Like this canteen. I told her often enough that she was sacrificing her health for the sake of earning a few pennies."

M. Robin stood up and went across to the window. "One of her clogs is still in the garden," he said. "I'll go and get it when I go downstairs."

"Of course," said Gaston. "I hadn't thought of that. I thought I'd never get her back to the house—"

M. Robin interrupted. "I think that's the doctor."

Gaston stood up and walked towards the door.

"Don't bother to go down," said M. Robin. "The woman can show him up."

Gaston stood there undecided for a few moments, listening. He could hear only a faint murmuring of voices. At last there was the sound of footsteps on the stairs, and the door to the bedroom opened.

The doctor was tall and thin and wore big glasses. He said good morning and asked for the light to be switched on.

"I'm afraid we have no electricity," said Gaston.

The doctor looked surprised. "Ah, well, we'll manage," he said. "I have a torch."

He searched around in his bag, and Gaston saw him bend over and peer at the bed. The examination was very short. When the doctor turned round again he said, "No doubt at all. Pneumonia. She must have been sickening for it for several days. Then this morning's cold weather brought it on."

It was only then that Gaston was aware that Micheline, his daughter-in-law, was standing near the door.

"What can we do?" she asked.

"She needs an injection at once for her heart. I haven't the necessary things with me, but the Sisters are just around the corner. For the rest, we'll go downstairs. I'll make you out a prescription."

"I had prepared a poultice," said Mme Robin.

"Put it on. It can only help relieve her."

He hesitated for a moment, looked at Micheline, and went on, "I hope one of the Sisters will be able to come quickly, otherwise I could nip home and—"

"No, no," said Micheline. "I'll see to it. I'll go and fetch the Sister. I'll bring her here."

She opened the door and went into the corridor as she added, "Come on now, we must leave her to rest."

Gaston was the last to leave. Before going out he looked at his wife again and whispered, "Oh, good God! What are we coming to?"

55

Down in the tiny kitchen Gaston looked at the five people who filled all the available space. He stayed at the foot of the staircase, leaning against the dining-room door, and said, "We could bring some chairs in from next door."

But no-one paid any attention to him. The doctor was making out a prescription at the corner of the table and giving instructions to Micheline. Opposite, Mme Robin and her daily help were preparing the poultice.

Everyone was talking. But Gaston was no longer in any state to follow what they said. He could understand nothing but M. Robin's suggestion that he should go and fetch the Sister and the medicine, and that Micheline replied, "Let it be, let it be; I'll take care of that."

The doctor and Micheline left. The two neighbours went upstairs with the poultice. Gaston walked over to sit down.

M. Robin also sat down. "I wouldn't worry too much," he said. "Pneumonia can be cured quite easily, you know. Would you like me to go and fetch some more wood? You'll need quite a lot for the bedroom."

Gaston made a gesture of despair. "What's to become of us?" he said again.

"We'll help you," promised M. Robin. "My wife will come over. And then you have your daughter-in-law coming back. It will be all right. You'll see."

He spoke as though he was talking to a child. Gaston was

aware of this, and he felt that addressing him in such a manner proved that Fernande was lost. He wanted to ask him questions, but he recoiled from the words. He had the feeling that if he spoke about death at this moment he might attract it. All he said was, "I would smoke a cigarette, but I don't think I'm able to roll one."

M. Robin took a packet out of his pocket, and Gaston helped himself. His hands were still trembling. Even the cigarette was shaking in his mouth when he lit it by M. Robin's lighter.

"I'll leave you the packet."

"Thank you. Thank you very much."

"But you must look after yourself. You should have a hot drink."

M. Robin went over to the stove. But there was only water in the saucepan there.

"When the women come down again," said Gaston, "I'll go up and change. My vest is very damp. If I am ill now, that would be the end of everything."

The two women came back, and Mme Robin said, "The poultice should be kept on for quite a while. I'm going over to our house, and I'll bring you back something to eat."

"I couldn't eat a thing."

"You must force yourself. You need to eat. It will make you feel better."

"I think a bowl of soup would be enough for me."

"We're going now," said Mme Robin. "But don't worry, I'm coming back. And if it's necessary I'll send Louisa this afternoon."

The Italian woman indicated her consent, and they all three left. All Gaston could do was to repeat, "What a disaster! What a disaster! What's to become of us?"

As soon as he was on his own again, his anguish returned. He hesitated a long time before deciding to go upstairs to the bedroom. However, he was beginning to feel cold, and the need to change his vest was a stronger factor than his desire to see the sick woman. He was a little frightened of being near her again.

He walked up the staircase slowly. He stopped outside the door for a moment before daring to open it, rigid with fear of finding her already dead. But as soon as he had opened the door he was reassured by the thick, hard gurgling in her throat.

He approached her, touched her hot hand lying on the sheet, and asked, "Can't you hear me? Can you see me?"

Her empty stare disturbed him. It seemed impossible she should have changed so much in less than an hour. He saw her again at the time she had left the kitchen to go out into the garden, and for a long time he tried to remember the words she had spoken as she went out through the door. Had she talked about it being cold? Or about the string? Or was it the knife? That's right, the knife must still be in the garden with her clog. Yes, the clog. M. Robin had promised to fetch it indoors. He had forgotten. That's what people were like—always promising. And his wife had promised to come back. The poultice should not be left on for too long.

He walked over to the window. The clog was still in the garden, a yellow spot on the black earth. But he could not see the knife. It had a black wooden handle. If the blade had been rammed into the ground you might not see it from here. It was a good little knife. They had not made any like it since before the War.

Gaston shrugged his shoulders and walked back to the bed. He was still trying to remember the words Fernande had spoken as she went out through the door. It was of no importance, but this gap in his memory annoyed him.

He looked for a vest in the cupboard, and the door creaked as he opened it. When he had found one he unfolded it and held it out for a moment over the stove. A pleasant smell of herbs rose up. It was one of Fernande's inveterate customs, these dried flowers and leaves amongst the linen.

Gaston was still in the bedroom when Mme Robin came back. She took off the poultice and then asked, "Have you put more wood on the fire?"

Gaston put more logs in the stove.

"You must come down now," said Mme Robin. "I've brought you something to eat."

They went downstairs. On the stove there was a small aluminium can and a red-and-white enamel saucepan.

"You must eat," said Mme Robin. "It will do you good. She is resting. She doesn't need you, and the Sister will soon be here. I'll have to leave you because my husband has to go out soon. He has to be at Poligny before two o'clock. But I shall come back as soon as he has left. There's some vegetable soup in the can. I put some peas and a slice of meat for you in the saucepan."

"But I'm not hungry. I'm not hungry."

The woman hurried off after she had insisted once more that he should force himself to eat.

He took a plate and a spoon from the cupboard. It was true that he had hardly any appetite. But he knew that a little soup would do him good. The soup was excellent—the vegetables had been strained, and there was an after-taste of smoked sausage. He ate all that was in the can. Then he waited a moment before deciding to fetch a fork to taste the peas. At first he took a mouthful straight from the saucepan. They were good and melted on the tongue. He dished up three spoonfuls and cut off half the meat. He thought to himself that it was not very fitting to be eating this way while his wife lay so ill upstairs. Then he told himself it was his duty to regain his strength at all costs. If he found himself having to do everything for himself, and having to climb those stairs twenty times a day as well! He thought about that winter when he too had had pneumonia. He had stayed in bed for over a month. And Fernande had looked after him. But then she was not seventy-one years old. Nevertheless she had often said that those stairs were too much for her. Besides, she was a woman and knew how to look after people. No, he could not see himself looking after a sick woman all on his own, as well as the house, the shopping. . . .

He felt overwhelmed by all that lay ahead. Until now he had been too stunned by this cruel accident to be able to think.

But, as his strength came back with eating, he began to imagine what Fernande's illness would mean to him if it went on for long. He saw himself all alone. Would the neighbours help him? Would Micheline come over often? And that Italian woman. She was strong as an ox, but if she came regularly he would have to pay her.

He had finished eating. He poured himself half a glass of wine. There was no coffee made, and he put two lumps of sugar in his wine and added a little water. It was quite true, he needed it.

He drank his wine, lit a cigarette from the packet M. Robin had left him, then looked at the alarm-clock. It was gone half-past twelve, and the Sister had not yet arrived. It was taking a long time, considering the doctor had said it had to be done as quickly as possible.

He hurriedly cleared the table, put out his cigarette, which he put in his tobacco-tin, and went upstairs to the bedroom.

Fernande's face looked transformed. It was no longer very red. It had turned extremely pale. Her ashen cheeks were hollow, the lower lip was hanging down. Her eyes were shut, and only a feeble moan came from her half-open mouth.

Gaston gently put out his hand and touched her shoulder. "Isn't it going so well? What's the matter?" He leaned forward a little and, raising his voice, repeated, "What's the matter?"

Her eyelids fluttered slightly, but did not open.

Gaston still hesitated for a few moments. Then fear took hold of him again. He left the room, rushed down the staircase and outside, without even putting on his jacket or his clogs.

56

Gaston walked quickly down to the shed in his slippers across the ground that the frost had already begun to harden. When he entered the neighbours' yard he saw the face of M. Robin's son at the window. The boy turned round, and M. Robin immediately came to open the window.

"Come quickly," cried Gaston. "It's not going so well!"

"My wife's coming!"

Gaston turned round and went back towards the house. He was scarcely halfway when Mme Robin caught up with him.

"What is it?" she asked.

"I do believe my poor wife is dying."

His voice broke down over the last word.

"Hasn't the Sister been yet?"

"No. No. I've seen no-one. They let us die all alone."

Mme Robin began to run again. Gaston could not keep up with her. He had not felt the cold when he went out, but now the wind blowing straight into his face prevented him breathing. He felt as though needles were piercing his face and woollen jacket. The cold was coming through the soles of his slippers and freezing his feet.

He had to stop when he reached the kitchen, one hand on his chest and the other resting flat on the end of the table.

He heard Mme Robin's footsteps above his head, then the door opened and the young woman called, "Monsieur Dubois! You must come upstairs."

He climbed the stairs slowly. His mind was empty. He felt neither fear nor the aching affliction of the cold any longer.

The door to the bedroom was wide open. Mme Robin, who was standing absolutely still next to the bed, turned towards Gaston and took two steps in his direction. As he stopped she said slowly, "M. Dubois . . . your wife has passed away."

Gaston looked towards the bed. Fernande was still lying in the same position, except that her mouth was wide open. Her eyes were shut, and she was even paler than when he had left her.

"Oh, my God!" Gaston whispered. "My God! To go like that . . ."

Mme Robin was crying quietly.

They stood there for a long time without speaking, without moving, as though paralysed by Fernande's presence. She was dead. All alone. While Gaston was running through the garden. And now it was over. There was nothing more to do. He waited. He did not even know what he was waiting for.

Cold air was filling the room through the wide-open door. At last Mme Robin made a slight movement in that direction and whispered, "We must go downstairs. I'll go and phone your daughter-in-law."

She went down, and Gaston followed her. They had just reached the foot of the stairs when a footstep grated on the kitchen-door landing. Mme Robin went over to open the door.

A nun dressed in brown with a white head-dress came inside. She was carrying a small leather bag which she at once put on the table as she said, "I've just been called out to—"

Mme Robin interrupted, "It's too late, Sister. Poor Mme Dubois is dead."

The nun did not appear surprised. She clasped her hands together below the rosary which hung round her neck and asked, "How long ago?"

"Only a few minutes, I think."

There was silence. The nun's lips were moving. Gaston thought she must be praying.

After a while Mme Robin asked with an uncertain voice, "I can't understand why you didn't come sooner. It's not far, after all."

"Sooner? But they only telephoned ten minutes ago."

The nun, who was short and rather broad, had a big, chubby, red face. Her brown eyes were bright in the shadow cast by her head-dress. Her lively eyes looked constantly from Gaston to Mme Robin and back.

Mme Robin hesitated again and said at last, "Perhaps there was no-one at your place at the end of the morning."

"No-one? But there's always someone there. You know that."

Gaston's and Mme Robin's eyes met.

The little dark woman was no longer crying. Her face had become hard. Gaston felt that his legs were going to give way, and he fell into his chair as he whispered, "My God! Oh, my God! It's just not possible—to go like that . . . to go like that."

"Do you need our help?" asked the nun.

Gaston made an uncertain gesture as he looked over at Mme Robin, who said in a rather hard voice, "I believe that nuns usually see to these things."

"Of course," said Gaston. "That would be best."

Mme Robin, who was still staring at him, asked, "Should I phone your daughter-in-law?"

"If you could."

The little woman was walking towards the door when the nun asked her, "I would be most grateful if you would also phone the Mother Superior. Tell her what it's about, and she'll send another Sister to help me. Then I'll not need to go back, and M. Dubois will not stay here on his own."

She repeated the telephone number very precisely, and then Mme Robin went out of the door without turning round again.

57

Gaston had explained to the two nuns that they would find all they might need in the wardrobe in the bedroom. He no longer had the strength to climb the stairs. There were comings and goings. Mme Robin, the Italian woman. Then the arrival of Paul and Micheline, bemoaning what had happened.

Gaston understood her to say that the nurse living in the rue de Valière was not at home that morning. She spoke quickly and forcefully. She stopped to lament further and answer the nun's questions. At one point Paul approached his father and said, "We can't leave her upstairs. With all the people who will be coming, it's not convenient. We must put her in the dining-room."

"But there's no bed in there," Gaston remarked.

"Isn't there a single bed in Julien's room?"

"Yes."

"Well, then, we'll bring it down."

"But what are you going to do?"

"Don't worry. I'll take care of everything."

Gaston understood that he had no further say in the matter. His wife had been dead for less than an hour, and already everything was being turned upside down. He felt the ground slipping away from under his feet. Around him was nothing but noise, talk, bustle. As though Death had dragged a frenzied whirlwind in its train, a frightful roundabout—and all he could do was not to interfere.

He saw Paul and the Italian woman taking the table out of the dining-room, where they had pulled the red, flowered curtains and closed the two shutters.

"You're not going to leave that outside," he said timidly.

"Of course not," said Paul. "Don't you worry about the table. We're going to put it in the cellar."

They took it outside while Gaston murmured, "Oh, I'm not worried about the table at the moment."

All this commotion, these wide-open doors not being shut again, brought the winter's cold right into the kitchen. Gaston coughed several times. It was in vain that he stoked up the fire and stayed near the stove. He began to shiver.

Mme Robin came downstairs from the bedroom and offered to take him over to her house. "You can come back when it's all been done."

"No. I want to stay here."

When he saw the Italian woman and the younger of the nuns carrying Fernande downstairs a lump tightened in his throat. They had already dressed her in black and sat her on a chair. He stood up and automatically took off his cap as a great sob shook through him, liberating his tears.

"Oh, God! Oh, God! My poor wife! She shouldn't have been the first to go."

Paul went up to him. "Come on now, don't cry. You'll make yourself cough. We all have to die sooner or later."

"It would still have been better at my age than at hers."

He said this between sobs that rasped up through his throat.

When everything was finished they let him enter the dining-room. The bed stood in the middle of the floor where the table used to be. Fernande was stretched out on the white sheet in her black dress. She was as pale as the napkin they had tied round her face to hold up her jaw. Her lips did not show, and her mouth was no more than a thin, straight, black line. They had laid a doily on a small bedside table. A candle was burning, lighting up one side of her face. There was a saucer by the brass candlestick on which the Sisters had placed a twig of boxwood.

The elder nun came up to Gaston. He knew her by sight, as he had often met her in the street. She also came to the garden to fetch flowers or fruit which Fernande gave to the orphans.

"She was not able to receive the last sacraments," said the nun, "but we will pray for her soul to rest in peace. We knew her. She was a generous-hearted woman. She did not have much, and yet she always knew how to find someone poorer than herself and give them a little. The good God will surely recognize her worth."

She stopped. Gaston raised his eyes towards her. She was about fifty, with a squarish face. The white head-dress strapped around her chin and temples showed up her already hardened features. She prayed in a soft voice, and sometimes her sombre eyes glanced from the dead woman and rested on Paul's or Micheline's face; they were standing next to each other on the other side of the bed. Gaston could not see her fully, but it seemed to him that her eyes, while full of mercy when looking at Fernande, filled with reproach when they rose towards his son or daughter-in-law. Those two did not raise their eyes.

They stood there for some time like this. Then, as someone knocked on the kitchen door, Micheline went out, saying, "Don't disturb yourselves. I'll go and see who it is."

She soon returned, accompanied by Mlle Marthe, who was leaning on the arm of another neighbour. Mlle Marthe was crying. She sprinkled some holy water and came back to Gaston, muttering, "Gentle Jesus, we are as nothing in this world. I saw her walking by only last Saturday when she was going to work. She didn't look ill. And now today she is no longer with us. We are as nothing."

She stopped. There was silence for a long while, and then the elder of the nuns crossed herself and went out.

Gaston stared at Fernande's hands. Those big hands with their swollen joints and twisted fingers lay folded over her chest. Her fingers looked as though they were tied together with a rosary of purple beads. The flickering candle-flame made a spark of light dance on the white metal crucifix at the end of the rosary.

Gaston felt someone taking him by his arm.

"Come now," said the nun, "it's time we opened the window. Come along. Don't stay here and get cold."

58

Gaston remained sitting in his chair until nightfall, looking alternately at the piece of earth where Fernande had collapsed and the grate in the stove. The Italian woman had gone out to fetch Fernande's clog, and she had also found the knife. The wind was still blowing the artichokes about. More string had broken, the sacks blown off, rolling or dragging across the plot towards the pump. The straw was scattered to the wind. Winter raged through the whole garden.

People came and went in the kitchen. Gaston did not even stand up.

Paul had asked him for the family documents in order to complete the formalities, as well as for Julien's address in order to send him a telegram. Gaston had said, "They're in the sideboard drawer in the dining-room. There should be some letters from him with the address on the back of the envelope. Bring the whole drawer in here. It will be easier to look through."

Paul had gone into the dining-room with his wife. They stayed in there for a few minutes. They had found the family documents and an envelope, and Paul had left.

Gaston stood up only when the parish priest arrived. He took off his cap and began to cry again.

The priest's visit was brief. It was growing dark. Micheline, who had seen him off, came back and announced, "There now, it's begun to snow."

Gaston said, "That's about all we needed." And he got up to light the oil-lamp and close the shutters. Tiny snowflakes were dancing on the wind outside the windows.

Paul came back just before seven. His eyes were shining and he smelt of wine. He said he had seen to everything.

"Did you go home?" asked Micheline.

"Of course. The maid is bringing us something to eat. Father will have his dinner and then go to bed. We two can sit and watch for the night."

"Some of the neighbours promised to come too," said Gaston.

"It's not worth it," said Paul. "We're not going to pester people and make them come out in the middle of the night in this sort of weather. It won't bring back the dead."

More people arrived. Then the delivery-boy brought a basket. Micheline heated up the meal, and they all three ate. Before she had left the Italian woman had relit the bedroom stove and made the bed for Gaston. Micheline went up there twice, carrying the small lamp, to put more wood on. Each time she said, "Fancy having no electricity!"

Gaston made no reply. He had wanted to ask Micheline many times why she had not called the Sister when she left that morning as she had promised to do, but he did not dare. He remembered that she had spoken about a nurse when she came back. He had not fully understood, but he was afraid of making his daughter-in-law angry by asking the question. Yet, when their eyes met, Gaston felt uncomfortable.

The meal had been finished almost quarter of an hour when M. Robin arrived, accompanied by two other neighbours.

They went in to sprinkle the holy water, and Paul and Micheline fetched chairs from the dining-room.

"You must have something to drink," said Micheline.

Paul looked at his father and asked, "You've got some bottles, haven't you? I'll go down and get one."

The men protested. They did not want to drink at such a time.

"There's some coffee," said Micheline.

"That's it," said M. Robin. "That's much the best for watching over the dead."

"But you're not going to watch tonight," said Paul. "On no account. You must have some refreshment with us, and then everybody goes to bed. Father as well. Me and my wife'll stay here, but we'll make use of the sofa. No sense in having a sleepless night. Those sort of customs are on their way out."

The neighbours looked at each other, then looked at Gaston, who felt by their eyes they were asking him what he thought. "My goodness," he said, "if Paul and his wife want to stay, what can you say? With this cold weather it's not a good thing walking around at night."

An embarrassed silence followed. Micheline poured coffee for some and herb tea for others. Someone mentioned the War. For a moment the conversation livened up. They spoke about the liberation of Strasbourg and the First French Army fighting at Sundgau. This name cropped up several times, but Gaston had never heard of it before. He was not sure that it was not near Alsace, but he did not dare ask for an explanation. He listened. They spoke about the War and the chance that winter would slow up the progress of the Allies, and yet the War lay far from his thoughts. True that winter had arrived. You could say it had arrived that very morning. Gaston hardly had time to take in the fact before it had taken his wife. And what for? For a few artichokes that would freeze in the end anyway.

Gaston stopped following the conversation of his neighbours and his son. He lived through this day again from the time he had got up. He saw everything that had happened in perfect detail again. Every movement Fernande had made. Every one of her words. When he reached the moment when she had put on her overcoat to go out, the words she had spoken came to him without effort, without even trying to remember them.

So, as he ceased tracing the thread of time, he found a foothold again in that evening. The others were talking about the problem of nationalizing the coal-mines in the north. Gaston only listened for a second, then, raising his hand, he said, "Do you know what she said to me?"

The others stopped and looked at him. Lowering his voice, he went on slowly, "'You see,' she said to me, 'I'm going to put on my coat. And I'll go and tie up the sacks. I've plenty of time before going to work.'"

It had made no impression. The neighbours looked at each other, shaking their heads. Paul said rather brusquely, "Yes, yes, you've already told us. She went out to tie up the artichokes again."

Gaston raised his voice. "I'm not talking about that. I couldn't remember the last words she said to me. And now I've just remembered them. She said to me, 'Before going to work'."

Paul shrugged his shoulders. "You ought to go to bed," he said. "You're tired."

"Yes, I am tired. Work. That's the last word she said to me, you see. The last . . ."

Gaston stood up. The neighbours did the same, saying that since they were not needed they would stay no longer.

As soon as they had left Gaston went to the dining-room and shut the door behind him. This was the first time since his wife had died that he had been alone with her. It was very cold in the room, but in spite of the open window the smell of death was already spreading very strongly. Gaston approached the bed. The candle had burnt down low, and the flame flickered constantly because of the draught through the slats in the shutters. Gaston whispered, "My poor love, there you are already in the midst of winter. And before you went, there you were talking about work. And then it was all over."

He no longer knew how to pray, and he just said, "My God,

if there is a Heaven there should be room for her. If she didn't go to church it was always because she had work to do."

He repeated that word several times. Then, as he was beginning to feel cold, he sprinkled some holy water and quietly left the room.

59

The bed where Fernande had died had been completely stripped. Just the mattress and the eiderdown hung over the foot of the iron bedstead. The other bed had been made for Gaston with clean sheets and a single pillow in the middle.

He stood his little lamp on the walnut lid of the old dough trough between the two beds and walked over to the stove. Opening the doors, he poked the embers and threw on a big log. The wind was not so strong now, and Gaston reckoned that the snow would be falling much more thickly. There might well be a good layer tomorrow, and Fernande would not be there to sweep the steps and scatter ashes. Neither would she be there to fetch wood from the shed or water from the fountain. She would not be there for anything. Not for cooking or shopping. Not for anything. Of course, until she was buried there would be people around to see to it all, but once she had left the house there would be an enormous gap. There had been too much going on today to have left him much time to consider this aspect. Only now that he was alone in the bedroom did all these thoughts enter his mind. In every sphere of his life this huge gap appeared. With Fernande dead, life would be impossible. She had gone so suddenly. Just like that, still strong and working. And the last word she had spoken was about work. Work had taken up so much of their time together that it was natural, really, she should have died that way. But it had been too early. She had been young enough to see him through to the end of his life. If she had been left on her own she would have managed much better than he on his own.

She had left him, and he did not even know if he had any money. She had always looked after their affairs. There were some bonds at the bank, a savings-book. The money from the fruit sold during the summer and her earnings from that canteen should be in the drawer in the dining-room. The funeral was sure to be expensive.

Gaston undressed slowly. When he got into bed his legs were frozen by the damp, cold sheets. That too was something she used to do—take up a hot-water bottle and then come up two or three times to move it to a new place before he went to bed. Tonight no-one had warmed the bed, and in spite of the fire it was a long time before he felt warm.

Normally he put out the lamp before climbing into bed. But tonight he could not make up his mind to extinguish it. He stared at the ceiling reflecting its tiny flickering flame.

And he again told himself that Fernande was dead.

She had left him all alone with his head in a turmoil. Her worries were over. She was still at home, but down below in that freezing room where one hardly ever went ordinarily except to fetch something from the drawers.

They had taken out the table and put Fernande in the middle of the room on Julien's bed. Already she was stiff and cold.

Gaston turned over on his side a little and pulled up his knees. He was disturbed at finding himself stretched out in the position of a corpse. His tiredness overwhelmed him, and sleep advanced slowly. He raised himself on his elbow to blow out the lamp, then lay down again on his side.

He thought about Fernande; he also thought about the dried-out skeleton that Julien had brought along that evening; it was still lying in the loft in the shed.

Fernande still had a woman's face, but in fact she was not very different from that skeleton.

She was down below, and Gaston thought that they would no doubt put him there too some day, when he had lived out his sorrow.

60

The next morning when Gaston got up, Micheline was alone in the kitchen. She had heated up the coffee and milk.

"Paul has gone out," she said. "He's got work to do, you understand. The loads have to be checked on the lorries. Two drivers are going on their rounds this morning, and there's another who should have come back from Bresse last night."

"Yes, of course. I realize that life doesn't stop just because my poor wife has left us."

It must have been light outside, but the shutters were still closed and the lamp burning.

"I'll open the shutters," said Gaston.

"There's snow on the ground, and it's still falling."

He opened them. The garden was white and the artichokes looked like big, unfinished snowmen. The wind had blown the snow up against the stalks and leaves as well as on the sacks that it had not had the strength to tear away. It had stopped blowing. The sky was heavy, and the few snowflakes still falling scattered in all directions. It was a light snow—the kind you see only when it is very cold.

"I'm going home too, to wash and change my clothes," said Micheline. But I'll send the young assistant to sweep the steps and drive. Otherwise there'll be a mess in the kitchen when people start tramping through."

She spoke quickly, and her voice betrayed her irritation.

"I'm causing you a lot of trouble," Gaston said.

His daughter-in-law appeared surprised. She hesitated before replying, "Those who pass on are peaceful enough. It's those who are left behind who have all the trouble."

Gaston walked over and sat down, and Micheline poured out his coffee. He began to break his bread into the bowl, and as his daughter-in-law was putting on her coat he said, "The doctor will have to be paid. I didn't have my wits about me yesterday, and I forgot."

"We'll settle all that later. Paul paid him yesterday afternoon when he went to ask for the death certificate. Don't you worry about it."

She walked over to the door and added, "Have you got any money? You won't need any, but you ought to have a little in the house all the same."

"There's sure to be some in her purse. And there should be some in the dining-room. I'll have a look."

She opened the door and said, "When the assistant comes tell him to go and fetch you some wood."

She left, and Gaston began to eat. The coffee did not taste the same as when his wife prepared it. He ate the coffee-soaked bread slowly, but he could not manage all the coffee in the bowl. As soon as he had finished he rolled a cigarette, but as he was about to light it he had second thoughts. Balancing it on the edge of the table, he entered the dining-room. The candle burning in there was almost new. Fernande's face still looked hollow, and her forehead was shining as though covered in frost.

"My poor love," he murmured. "It's not warm in here. It's a bad time of year to be dying."

He stayed in there only a few moments. The cold and the smell were unbearable. He pulled out the first drawer in the sideboard completely, took it to the kitchen table, and then shut the door again.

When that was done he lit his cigarette and looked for a while at the drawer full of jumbled-up papers. He knew nothing about old documents and was almost unwilling to touch them. No doubt Paul had messed them up when he was looking for the family certificates and Julien's address. However, he must find out how much money Fernande had left because the funeral would be expensive.

Gaston took some old calendars out of the drawer, some bonds, a notebook with recipes, several small blue cash-books in which Fernande had entered what she had sold for several years—rabbits, vegetables, fruit. Another notebook contained addresses that Gaston could scarcely read. He put this on one side, thinking it might be useful when it came to registering the death. That was true. There was still the business of registering, but Paul must have taken care of that. It was usually done at the funeral. He found a big bundle of letters, mostly from Julien. The purse was right at the bottom of the drawer. A big purse made of rather stiff leather with a brown moulded clasp which clicked loudly when opened. The clasp was not shut. Gaston had often seen his wife putting money into this purse and taking some out when it was a matter of paying for wood, for example, or a barrel of wine.

He opened it and took out three ten-franc and two five-franc notes. Gaston thought for a moment. It was impossible. Fernande had kept more money in the house. He knew that she had not been to the bank for several months. Had she given it all to Julien? But she had said so often that she would rather wait till the baby was born. Had she hidden money somewhere else? Gaston took out the few remaining papers—some insurance policies, some old savings-stamps. He looked at everything he had spread out on the table and opened a small cardboard box covered in faded yellow and white material with little red-and-blue flowers. In it were some fairly old coins, certainly no longer of legal currency. Gaston also found the medallion he had drawn when he was called up. It was black enamel on the back, white on the front. Round the circumference a double border of blue and red. In the middle, an inscription, "Long live the conscripts of 1893." In larger figures, the number "156". There was still a piece of faded red, white, and blue ribbon attached to the medal, with a huge baby's safety-pin stuck through it. Gaston turned the medal round and round in his hand. He could see that day in 1893 again. It was spring. The sun was shining, and there were lots of young people laughing. Others were complaining about having drawn unlucky numbers that sent them on overseas service for three or four years. Gaston began to reminisce about his military service, but he did not go on for long. Now was not the time. He must go and search somewhere else. Into the box he replaced a red velvet Sacred Heart on a yellow satin background enclosed behind a deeply convex piece of glass, the whole set in an oval brass frame. A piece of a fountain-pen. A tiny little mesh purse containing only a farthing and two medallions of the Virgin. An old lighter without its striker, another small purse with scalloped edges. There was an inscription on it, but it was too small for him to read without glasses, and he remembered that it was "Cette". He had gone there once for an athletics meeting, and he had brought back this souvenir for his first wife before they had even become engaged.

It was a long time ago, but he still remembered vividly the beach where he had bathed after the meeting. He could see the women lifting their skirts to run barefoot to collect shells as the waves withdrew. For a moment the sun from that day seemed to fill the kitchen, and he almost expected to hear the women shrieking as they ran back to the dry sand when another wave broke.

He sighed deeply, shut his eyes, and sat with them for some seconds closed. When he opened them again the kitchen looked blurred, and he felt tears running down alongside his nose.

He wiped his eyes, blew his nose, and took the drawer back to where it belonged. He kept only the purse, which he managed, though with some difficulty, to stuff into his trouser pocket. He preferred to have the money on him. With all those people coming, one never knew. Next he looked for Fernande's handbag in the kitchen drawer. It was an old one made of black oilcloth that she had mended many a time, tied up with a shoelace. All it contained was a five-franc note and some loose change. In another compartment there were the ration-books and a photograph of Julien with a four-leafed clover stuck on with sticky paper.

Gaston thought she might have hidden the money in the wardrobe upstairs. He could not very well lock the kitchen door, but if he went upstairs anyone might come in and go out again without him being able to hear them. Normally he would not have been so cautious, but he had suddenly felt that someone might take it into their head to steal what little he possessed.

He stood undecided at the bottom of the staircase. Then he

made up his mind. It would take time to search through the wardrobe, but he could lock it now and keep the key in his pocket.

He had some difficulty with the lock, which had not been turned for many years. He was hot. He behaved like a thief, hurrying for fear of being taken by surprise. It was foolish. He knew that, and told himself he was in his own home and still free to do as he wished. In spite of this, he hurried downstairs once he had succeeded in locking the door.

No-one had come. He walked over to his accustomed place and sat down, rolled a cigarette which he lit as he put more wood on the fire. Then, having settled down with his feet in front of the grate, he began to wait.

61

That day was exhausting—the morning a prolonged wait until eleven o'clock. Then the young assistant arrived, bringing a saucepanful of stew, a can of soup, and some apple compote. He swept the steps outside, and Gaston twice had to tell him not to knock the broom so hard against the iron railings. He was an impudent youngster, and Gaston hesitated some time before trusting him with the key to the shed so that he could go and fetch two baskets of wood.

When the boy had left M. Robin visited him and asked whether he needed anything. No, he needed nothing, and if he did his children would help him. He had thought a lot about Mme Robin's attitude towards the business of the nurse and the Sister, and he felt ill at ease. M. Robin wanted to sprinkle some holy water, and Gaston went in with him. He repeated that it was unfair for his wife to die before him. He said the same thing at every subsequent visit.

Julien arrived just before noon. He had caught the only train running that morning. He kissed his father, saying, "Where is she?"

Gaston thrust his chin in the direction of the dining-room and followed behind his son.

Julien leaned over her, kissed her on the forehead, and kneeled down by the side of the bed. He began to cry, his forehead on the sheet.

Gaston looked at him for a moment, and his eyes filled with tears.

When they came back to the kitchen Julien asked, "But what happened? What was the matter with her? Was it an accident?"

Gaston told him everything in detail. The storm. The artichokes. His mother insisting on going out. The trouble he had had bringing her back indoors. Running over to the neighbours. The way they helped him. The doctor's visit. And there he stopped.

"And what did the doctor say?"

Gaston gestured with both hands. "What can you expect? Her strength was failing. He mentioned an injection. I don't know what. The Sister came, but it was too late. She must have been ill for several days. As you know, she wasn't one to take any notice of herself, or always be complaining of this or that. For her, as with me, it was only work that mattered. There was no choice. We had to live. Besides, the War didn't help. Work. That was the last word she spoke to me."

And Gaston repeated Fernande's last words. Then he told how she had been going to the canteen every day. He told him why, and what she had hoped to do with the money she earned.

There he stopped again. Julien was listening to him, sitting at the bottom of the stairs, his back bent and head lowered.

"And the worst thing is," said Gaston, "I don't even know what she did with the money."

He took the purse out of his pocket and showed Julien the contents. "There. That's all. But she must have hidden some elsewhere."

Julien did not even look up to see the notes. He just said, "If only you knew how little I care about that money. It's not possible. To think that she was in the best of health when I last saw her. But then—"

He stopped, wiped his eyes, and raised his head again. Only then did Gaston take in the fact that he had shaved off his beard, and his hair was very much shorter. His cheeks were hollow, and there were dark rings round his eyes.

"You don't look very well."

The boy shrugged his shoulders.

"We are going to eat," Gaston continued. "Micheline sent some food over. And there's still something left over from last night. There's plenty for both of us."

"You eat. I'm not hungry."

"Neither am I, but we must look after ourselves. And it's no good waiting till people start coming in to pay their respects."

They sat down to table, and while they were eating Gaston talked about the little assistant whom he did not like. "When you've finished," he said, "I want you to go down to the shed. See that he's shut the door properly. And while you're there go in and see that he hasn't been messing about with the tools. And there were two billhooks near the wood-pile. Check that they're still there. They are first-class tools—the kind you'd have to pay a lot for these days. Besides, with the War and all, I don't think you'd find the quality. The smaller one—the one to the right and a bit higher up—you know, the one with the split handle. I've been meaning to mend it for some time, but I've never got the time. When the weather's fine the garden takes up the whole day, and when it's bad I can't stay in the workshop without some form of heating. I was always saying that I wanted to make it more weatherproof, but it's no work for a man of my age. Now, what was I going to say? Oh, yes, that billhook—you know the one—well, I bought it when Raginot's place was sold up. You must have been about three or four. Do you remember it? Raginot lived behind the hill at Mancy. Nice old chap. He'd already been using that billhook for thirty years. I knew him when he came back from the War."

Julien did not flinch. He nodded from time to time, and

Gaston continued with his endless story, the billhook remaining the central theme—innumerable anecdotes which joined up again, digressed, followed each other, to end up a sidetrack that invariably led back to the old billhook.

Gaston pursued his stories, jogging along his path of memories, and the further he went the more his anguish seemed to lessen.

However, it returned when the first visitors arrived. Every time he again had to tell the story of how Fernande died. He always used the same words, the same intonations, and all would be well until he reached the point of the doctor's visit. There he experienced considerable difficulty in avoiding the truth, plunging into a vague jumble of words. He said that her strength had failed her, that it was too late anyway. But he was well aware that there was something missing from the story. He had no intention of lying, only convinced of the necessity to avoid details that could be of no interest to anyone. But in order to do this he had to diverge from a well-marked path at a precise point in the progress of his story, borrowing just one fact where the words meant nothing tangible. As he was used to telling long stories out of his wealth of memories, this was a new experience, and he found it difficult to carry through. Right up till the moment the doctor came he used the same words and intonation, almost the same sighs. From then on the story seemed to become very uncertain, and he was soon afraid that Julien might come and ask him some pointed questions.

He felt some relief at about four o'clock when Julien announced, "I'll have to go out for a moment."

"But you must be back by five when they put her in the coffin."

"I won't be long. I'm only going to see M. Robin."

"But—but . . ."

His anxiety, for a moment relieved, came back doubly reinforced. However, there was nothing he could say. He was deeply troubled, and this was made worse by the presence of friends he had not seen for a long time who prolonged their visit. With every new visitor he started the story again, and those who had already heard it followed his recital with shaking heads and hopeless gestures. Would one of them suddenly point out that there was a part of the story where he did not seem to know what he was saying?

His strength was slowly giving out. Several times his coughing overcame him, and he had to remain silent for a while.

Julien was away for only a quarter of an hour. Gaston scrutinized his face when he came back, and it appeared harder. His eyes were not kind. Gaston hesitated for a while before asking, "Well, did you see them?"

"Mme Robin was there on her own."

"And what did she say?"

The boy shrugged his shoulders. "What do you suppose she'd say! What they always say at such a time. She liked Mother very much, and I think she feels her death deeply."

Gaston sighed. Had the little Mme Robin really refrained from mentioning the business of the Sister being late? Or was Julien going to wait till everybody had gone? Wait for Paul to come? Wait till Fernande was buried? Perhaps he himself had been exaggerating the whole thing? After all, what had happened? The Sister was meant to come, and she had not come at once. They had also mentioned a nurse. And Fernande was dead. If the doctor had done nothing it was because there was nothing he could do. That was life, with death awaiting at its end. And death came the day your strength failed. There, that was all. They had both used up all their strength, and perhaps Fernande had possessed less than he. Age had nothing to do with it. She had never looked after herself. She was not going to spend her hard-earned money on doctors. She had even made a truss out of an old corset for her hernia that gave her so much pain. All that just to save a few pence.

And Gaston talked to himself like this, in between all the comings and goings of people whom he did not always recognize and who obliged him again to start telling the story of how his wife died.

At five o'clock the undertakers arrived to put the body in the coffin. Already the kitchen was not very warm, but the door had to stay open for a long time, and the winter cold took possession of the house. The cold, the snow stuck to people's shoes, the approaching night driving away the light—all winter was there, coming right in to take Fernande away.

There was a lot of bustling around in the dining-room, furniture and step-ladders being moved about as the undertakers were hanging up black drapes.

Then the moment came to put Fernande in her coffin. Until then she had been with them—different, but still with them in spite of death. Every time Gaston had been alone with her in the dining-room he had spoken to her as though she were still alive. Now she was really leaving them. She was no longer in her own home in that changed room, and she was still farther away when the men in black put the lid over her and began to screw it down very quickly. Gaston cried, and he also remarked to himself what good tools those men had, and how skilled they were at their work. He felt someone taking his arm. It was Julien who stood crying next to him.

And so they waited while the wooden box was put on trestles and covered with a black cloth embroidered with a big silver-thread cross. Afterwards the men lit two church candles on either side, and the people present sprinkled holy water with a big aspergillum steeped in a metal bucket.

And then, as all the people were leaving, Gaston returned to his seat in the kitchen.

62

Paul had come to attend the placing of the body in the coffin, and Gaston had seen him talking to Julien without being able to hear what he said. He left immediately afterwards. Micheline left a little later, but the visits went on till eight that evening.

The last to come was M. Vaintrenier, who said, "You must

forgive me for not coming sooner, but there's rather a lot to do at the Town Hall."

He had been Chairman of the Town Council since the liberation. Gaston said, "Of course you're forgiven. Life doesn't stop because somebody dies."

It was a formula he had repeated often during the course of the day. Invariably he added, in a lower voice, "It's a sad state of affairs because there's nothing left for me to do in this world."

People would protest, try to make comforting suggestions, but Gaston stopped them by saying, "There's some consolation, you know. I console myself thinking it won't be long before I follow her."

As she left them Micheline had said, "If it's all the same to you we won't come and watch tonight, as we already spent last night here."

When they were on their own Julien said to his father, "Isn't it astounding that no-one's offered to come and watch?"

Gaston felt embarrassed again. He stammered, "What do you expect? It's a dying custom. Besides, Paul and his wife stayed here last night. Tonight, now that you're here—but you mustn't watch up. Especially now that she is in her coffin. If you want to go to bed we'll make—"

Julien interrupted, "It's not worth it. If I want to rest I'll use the sofa."

Gaston did not pursue the matter. He had put the left-overs on the stove to heat up, and the two of them ate in almost total silence. Fernande's chair was empty. Gaston looked at it often. He also looked at his son, who could scarcely take his eyes off the back of that chair, where she had sat for so many years.

When they had finished the meal Gaston took out his tobacco-tin and rolled a cigarette. He lit it, and then pulled out the packet that the neighbour had left him the previous evening. "Here, why don't you have one? M. Robin gave them to me. I was shaking so much yesterday that I couldn't roll one."

As Julien did not react, Gaston pushed the packet farther across the oilcloth, adding, "Go on, take one."

"No, thanks. I've stopped smoking."

"Oh, have you?"

"I sell my cigarettes. Or sometimes exchange them for sugar."

"Ah! For me, it's my only pleasure."

He wanted to ask Julien what work he was doing, how they lived at Lyon, but he thought twice about it. He just asked, "So your wife is coming tomorrow at eleven, you say?"

"Yes. She couldn't ask for two days off."

Julien sat in front of his empty plate without moving, his elbows on the table, his head leaning on his right hand. Gaston felt the silence growing between them. This made him feel uneasy, but at the same time he was afraid that Julien might start talking. A vague fear, but it had been with him since the boy arrived. In the end he said, "I'll do the washing-up. And I'm going to make myself some tea. Would you like a bowl?"

"No, but leave it. I'll make it for you. As for the washing-up, I've got all night to do it."

As soon as he had drunk his vervaine tea Gaston stood up and sighed, "Well, I'm going to say goodnight to her. And then I'll go upstairs to bed."

Julien accompanied him to the funeral room. They stayed there for a few minutes in silence. When they had come out Gaston said, "It's the last night she'll spend in her own home. How insignificant we are in this world! Now I'm going upstairs. I can hardly stand up any more."

63

Gaston did not sleep much that night. He had even been tempted to get up several times. He felt it was not right to leave the boy alone with his mother downstairs. But then he told himself that perhaps it was best that way. There had always been little secrets between them. He, the old man, had never really been part of their intimate relationship. Julien would probably prefer to spend the night alone with her. Gaston heard no sound, but he imagined the boy opening the door from time to time and standing by the coffin for a short while. He tried to recall the death of his own mother, but that was more than forty years ago, and he had forgotten most of the details. He had a better memory for older and less important things, no doubt because they were related to life.

He was also kept awake by the thought of his loneliness. When all this was over he would be on his own. And if he found himself really alone there was nothing left but to die. He had never thought of it before, but now he felt that his wife had always protected him from sickness and death. Paul and Micheline would probably suggest that he came to live with them, but he already knew that he would refuse. He wanted to die here, in his own house set in his own garden. The year he had been ill he had refused to go to hospital precisely because he was afraid of dying. It was that, and the conviction that no-one could look after him the way his wife did. He had not really thought like that at the time, but tonight he knew that it had been one of the obscure reasons for being obstinate about staying at home.

When he rose in the morning his head felt heavy, and he had to take an aspirin. He could see hardly anything ahead except a declining life, with him fumbling along on his own, with nothing to hold on to, no-one to help him stand up on the difficult road.

At ten o'clock Julien had to go into town to order a wreath. He had said that he would wait for his wife at the station, but he must have been held up because Françoise arrived on her own. She stayed for a long time by Fernande's coffin, crying silently. As soon as she had left that room Gaston hastened to say to her, "I'm glad, in a way, that you arrived before Julien. I wanted to tell you . . . You see, it's—you know, my wife liked you very much."

He searched for words. Pursued by his obsession with escaping his loneliness, he had thrown himself into this proposal that he could not put into words. He had not expected that Françoise would arrive on her own, and he had not thought about what he would say.

The young woman looked at him. In spite of her tears, there was still that gentleness in her eyes that Gaston valued so much. When she had arrived she had kissed him with much more tenderness than Julien had done.

Spurred on by the fear that the boy might come back, he at last found the words for which he had been looking. "Heaven knows," he said, "that if I had been the first to go my wife would have asked you to come and live with her. I'm certain of that. So now you understand—"

Françoise moved slightly, shaking her head. Thinking she was about to speak, Gaston waited. A minute, perhaps, went by. Then, as she said nothing, he continued, "It's not always easy to live in a big town. And here, when your baby is born, there's at least the garden."

"I can't decide anything," Françoise said in the end. "But I have a job in Lyon. And for Julien to live here, I don't know. . . . Anyway, you must talk to him."

Gaston said nothing. There was the sound of footsteps on the stairs outside. It was a young girl bringing flowers. When she had gone again Gaston said, "It might have been nice to give her something?"

Françoise called her back and gave her a small tip.

"I'll pay you back," said Gaston as he thrust his hand into his trouser pocket.

"No, please."

She had sat down at the end of the table in the same place where she had sat when she had meals with them.

"Why don't you sit nearer the fire?" Gaston suggested.

"No, I'm not cold."

She sat a little stiffly in her chair. Her pregnancy was hardly noticeable under her wide black dress. Just as Julien had done the previous evening, she was staring at the back of the chair that had always been Fernande's. Gaston had invited her to move over to that particular chair to be nearer the fire. He could not resist imagining her here, replacing Fernande and running the house.

As though guessing his thoughts, she stood up and said, "Perhaps I should get something ready to eat."

"Don't you bother. Paul's young assistant should be bringing something. There's sure to be enough for three. Since yesterday I've had to force myself to eat. I haven't much appetite, you know."

He sighed, and looked again at Françoise's clear eyes. They were almost grey, a little like Fernande's.

He would have liked to talk some more about his proposal, but he could not find the right words. Truth to tell, he did not try very hard. He had already realized that she could make no decision. In front of Julien she was probably like Fernande had always been—ready to accept anything, approving and supporting him in everything he undertook, equally prepared to make sacrifices and be full of admiration for all he did. That was why Fernande had taken to her at once. When they had gone Fernande had said, "I think I'd feel a lot happier if I knew that young girl was with him." That was it. It was Fernande who had seen things clearly. And Gaston told himself that it must be Julien who meant most to her. He, the father, meant nothing to this young girl. She was good and generous—her eyes showed that—but just as he had known how to do it with his mother, Julien had installed himself in her heart. Now there was no room for anyone else.

More than ever now, Gaston felt lonely. In a voice hardly audible he said, "Death is soon over for those who die, but for those who stay behind it's another matter."

64

The funeral took place at three o'clock that afternoon. In spite of the snow and the cold, many people came and the house was perpetually open to the icy wind. Gaston, who no longer had the strength to stand up, stayed in his chair, where people came to him to shake his hand, trailing the snow right up to the stove.

He did not stand up until they brought the coffin through. He took off his cap and whispered, "My poor wife . . . My poor wife . . ."

And the great sob that had been strangling his throat for some time swallowed up the rest of his sentence.

Of course he could not go with the funeral procession in that cold weather far over to the other side of town. So Mlle Marthe, who could not go either, stayed with him. She began by wiping the floor, then she sat down in Fernande's chair, and they stoked up the fire to reheat the house.

Later they talked about Fernande. About the time before the War and the evenings they had spent chatting on the bench in the garden. They went through it all, each one adding a little from their store of memories. It was all filled in, overlapping in a uniform narrative for two voices which could have gone on for ever. They also spoke about the War. Not the one that was going on now. Things happening so far away did not concern them any longer. They talked about the war of 1914–18, then the one that was over for them the day the Germans left the town. Who would have thought it? They had been born just after 1870. People often spoke about the Prussian occupation of the town during their youth.

So there they were, talking without regrets—and without joy—about a whole world of memories in which Fernande had her small place. From time to time Gaston stopped and said, "There now, her worries are over. She won't see her grandson. Neither will I."

The old girl, who was almost the same age as Gaston, did not react like the others. She made no protest. She said every time. "What do you expect? You can't have two lives on this earth."

When the others returned Mlle Marthe went back home, accompanied by Françoise.

Afterwards Gaston told Julien what to fetch. He brought up

a bottle of white wine, which Gaston uncorked with great care, and it filled the room with a strong smell of the cellar.

There they sat, in front of their glasses, Gaston at his place near the window, where he had closed the shutters. Françoise sat in front of the cupboard, which was Julien's usual place. Paul, at the end of the table, half turned towards the staircase so as not to have his back to Julien, who was sitting there. It was Micheline who sat in Fernande's chair.

Paul said, "Lucky you didn't come. It was bloody cold at the cemetery. And standing there at the door shaking hands with people who don't care two hoots isn't my idea of fun."

"That's right," said Micheline. "My feet aren't warm yet."

"You should take your shoes off for a moment," said Gaston.

"No, I've got to get back. I've got work to do."

"You just go," said Paul. "I'd like to stay and talk a bit with Father while Julien's here."

Micheline emptied her glass. Then she stood up. She brushed Gaston's cheek lightly with her mouth, her hat knocking the peak of his cap so that it landed at the side of his head. Before leaving she looked at Françoise and Julien and suggested, "You know you can come and sleep at our house."

"No," said Julien. "We have to get back. There's a train at seven-thirty. We've plenty of time to catch it."

Paul giggled and asked, "Is it your work that's so urgent?"

"Precisely!"

Gaston was disturbed by the tone of Julien's voice, and he said hurriedly, "If they have to get back there's no point in staying here. No point at all."

Micheline was near the door. Julien stood up and went over towards her. Françoise stood up too. Micheline held out her hand and said, "Goodbye, my dear."

"Goodbye, madame," said Françoise.

There was a pause. Gaston looked at Micheline. Their eyes searched each other for a moment. Micheline turned to Julien and said, "Goodbye."

"Goodbye."

She went out quickly.

Silence.

Micheline's heels were clattering on the steps. Then there was no more sound.

Françoise cleared her throat and said, "Perhaps I should go on ahead. If there are things you want to talk about—"

"We don't mind you being here," said Paul.

"Of course not," said Gaston. "We've nothing to hide. Micheline left because she had things to do, but—"

Julien, who was still standing up, interrupted. "Françoise is right. She can go over to Mme Robin's. I have to go in there to say goodbye. She can wait for me there."

Gaston tried to intervene, but was unable to finish the sentence he started. "But why put other people out—"

He had seen that Françoise had questioned Julien with a look. She stood up. It was just as he had thought. She was like Fernande—even a look was enough to persuade her. Gaston felt quite lost and foolish. He no longer knew why he had trusted in that young girl, or even what it was that he had hoped for.

As she approached to kiss him he stood up and took off his cap. His voice was trembling when he said, "Goodbye, my dear. Goodbye. You know my wife liked you very much. She . . . Anyway, think of me sometimes. It's not too bad at Lyon for young people . . ."

He felt he was going to cry, so he stopped. He saw that Paul was looking at him with a sardonic smile, and he coughed to hide his embarrassment.

Françoise kissed him in the same way she had done that morning. Her mouth was near his ear as she said, "Goodbye, Father. Goodbye. Look after yourself."

She put on her overcoat, passed the strap of her handbag over her shoulder, and shook Paul by the hand as he half rose from his chair.

She looked at Gaston again before closing the door. Her eyes were very gentle and shone much more brightly than usual.

As soon as she was gone Julien sat down on the chair she had just vacated and crossed his arms, leaning over the table.

"Well," he said to his half-brother, "what was it you wanted to talk about?"

"Since you're in such a hurry to leave, we really ought to discuss some things that could have waited at least a day or two."

"I suppose so," said Gaston. "But he'll have to come back all the same."

"Certainly not at once," said Julien.

There was a short silence. Gaston looked at his two sons all the time, and grew more afraid they might start quarrelling.

"What I have to say is quite simple," began Paul. "Father cannot live on his own. So he'll have to come and live in our house, and we can make some arrangement—"

Gaston rose out of his chair. He gestured with his hand, which was stretched out over the table: No! No!

"There's no question of me leaving this house," he said firmly. "And if no-one wants to help me I don't need them!"

He had almost shouted that last sentence. He was aware that his strength would not carry him far talking like that, and he hurriedly added, "If there are affairs to put in order with your mother's estate the solicitor will look after it. I know nothing about documents and suchlike, but I expect I have enough to last me the rest of my days without needing help from anyone. And if I survive the winter I've enough strength to see to the garden."

His horny hand banged the table, and the glasses shook.

"Don't shout," said Julien. "You'll make yourself cough."

Gaston looked at him in surprise. Those were his mother's words, and he had pronounced them exactly as she would have done.

Paul drained his glass, stubbed out his cigarette in the brass ashtray, and stood up, saying, "In that case there's nothing further to discuss. However, there are bound to be some matters to settle."

"If it's the funeral you want to talk about," said Julien, "don't worry. I'll pay my share."

Paul's only reply was to shrug his shoulders, and Gaston hurriedly said, "That's my responsibility. I'm not broke."

"No," said Julien, "and if you should need money you could sell the bakery and employ someone to look after you here."

Gaston was about to say that he would not sell his property for all the world, but Paul got in first. He laughed unpleasantly and said, "I was expecting that. Sell up and eat up. Just the sort of thing a bohemian or a communist would suggest!"

Julien jumped up and cried, "The bohemian blasts you to hell and the communist pisses in your face!"

"Julien!" cried Gaston.

But Julien did not listen. While Paul was searching for an answer Julien shouted at him, "I'd rather be broke than snoring away on top of a pile of banknotes gained by currying favour with the Germans."

Gaston saw Paul's face distort. He saw his fists clenching. There was a silence that seemed to last for ever. Then in a very gentle voice, scarcely audible because the kitchen was still ringing with his burst of anger, Julien went on, "I'm ashamed of shouting like this in the house where Mother has just died, but I'm not standing for your sarcasm. My affairs are no business of yours."

Paul was still as livid. The look he sent his father was full of hatred. He pushed his chair back in place roughly, so that it knocked against the table. He walked over to the door, and as he opened it he said, "Goodnight, Father."

"Paul!" Gaston cried.

But the door shut with a bang, and his footsteps could be heard going quickly down the steps.

Gaston waited. He hoped that Paul would come back, or that Julien would open the door and call him back. But Julien sat down slowly, his hands shaking on the table.

"I'm sorry, Father, but—but . . ."

He stopped. Gaston waited a moment, then, as the night was still silent and Julien did not speak, he slowly said, "Now I know what I have to do. Die. Die all alone—and as soon as possible. And when that's over, as long as you don't all bugger things up fighting among yourselves, you'll sell the whole pack as quickly as possible and take your miserable share . . . and we've slaved away all our lives, your mother and I, only to have it squandered and blued in a few months. There. That's how it will end. And don't worry, it won't be long."

He stopped. Julien looked at him. Gaston saw that his eyes had filled with tears, so that, at the very moment that he thought he was strong and ready to control the boy, there he was, beginning to cry too. Julien stammered, "My poor father . . . my poor father!"

Gaston blew his nose and coughed.

"Would you like me to stay here tonight?" Julien asked.

Gaston wanted to cry out to him, "Yes, stay here with your wife. And not only tonight. I'm prepared to give you everything if only you would stay. Everything. I don't want to be alone."

That was what he wanted to shout, but he knew that if he did he would begin to cry again. Instead, calling on every shred of strength in his being, he stiffened himself and said in a firm voice, without a trace of anger, "No, your wife is waiting for you. You belong to her. And try to work for that child your poor mother would so much have liked to see. As for me, I don't need anyone any more. You don't need other people . . . to go where I'm going."

PART FIVE

The Solitary Road

65

That winter was like a long, dream-filled sleep into which Gaston sank as soon as his wife had gone.

The day after the funeral Micheline had come with a charwoman and the young assistant. She had made Gaston the offer of coming to live with them, but as he had refused to leave the house she had not pursued the matter. The house was cleaned and tidied. As Gaston was concerned about the wood supply lasting and complained about having to go upstairs to keep the fire going in his bedroom, they had arranged his bed in the dining-room. In this way, by keeping the stove well stoked and letting the door stand ajar, he was able to get into a warm bed only a few steps from the kitchen where he spent his days. Every morning at eleven o'clock the assistant brought him his meal, fetched a fresh supply of wood and anything else he might need. Paul or Micheline came to see him almost every day, were concerned for his smallest wish, and made sure there was nothing he wanted.

He very soon became used to being cosseted this way, and his wife's absence was bearable.

Time flowed on quietly. He had no problems about money or food. On the contrary, the meals they brought him were far too large for his appetite. He often said, "You spoil me too much. I can't eat all that."

And Paul replied, "You've worked hard enough all your life. And you've had to put up with a lot. So of course we look after you as best we can. You must know that you'll never go short of anything as far as we're concerned."

When Paul, or a neighbour who had come to visit him, reminded him thus of his past life Gaston took a delight in dwelling on it. He loved to talk about it, and when he found himself alone again he continued recounting his happiest experiences or else the hardest. Even when he was completely alone he spoke as though someone was listening to him. "Oh, yes, I remember when I made my rounds with the horse and cart before 1914. That wasn't exactly yesterday, let me tell you. The roads weren't like they are today. And then the winters were much harder. Winters like this one, we had them like that three out of four. The roads weren't always cleared. Or then the horses might have trampled down the snow so that the road was like ice. But my horse was a good one. I always kept it well shod, and with snow-shoes in winter and all that. Well, now, listen to this. I remember one evening I was at Messia and coming out of Toinon Vignet's place—he kept a restaurant. And what did I see? A little boy—he was perhaps eight years old—howling and screaming near my cart. It was lucky I had a steady horse. Next to the boy there were two drunks laughing and joking. 'What's the matter?' I asked. 'That stupid boy,' they said to me. 'We showed him the iron band on your wheels and told him to lick it so that we could see how it should be done. He put his tongue on it. And look, he left a bit of skin behind.' They were two quarrymen. Of course, with the cold weather they weren't working, and had spent the day drinking a few pints. And they told me this as if there was nothing to it. Then I got angry, I can tell you. 'It's not the boy who's stupid, it's you.' One thing led to another, and they threatened me. I took hold of my whip and, my God, things moved fast. They were strong as oxen, but they had forgotten how to move nimbly. One of them ran away with his nose pissing red blood down his lumberjacket, and the other, who was half stunned, wanted to run away too. 'Not so fast, I tell you.' And I took him into Toinon's place to get his name so that the boy's parents would know who to blame. Well, believe it or not, the parents never even thanked me."

He had his whole portion of memories detaching themselves one by one, either leading on to the next or evoked directly by some news they had just told him, however tenuous the link.

When the German offensive in the Ardennes started it looked as though the War was going to take a similar aspect to the campaigns of 1914–18. So this was a period that came back to him bit by bit. It had been a long time ago, and yet it was much nearer than the events at Bastogne.

Paul often brought him newspapers, but his eyesight had weakened so much that he confined himself to reading the headlines. Besides, those newspapers interested him much less than the ones from his own time—that is to say, before 1914. In the bedroom he had found two big bound volumes of *L'Illustration*. One was from 1890, the other from 1897. Hardly an afternoon went by without his taking out these two books and opening them on the kitchen table. There was a whole series of pictures which he could find again easily because he had marked them with pages from the almanac. The first was of the army manœuvres at the frontier on August 16th, 1890. There one saw the mountain regiments attacking the peak of St Agnès, near Menton. The officers with drawn swords, the soldiers with bayonets fixed, the buglers. When he was looking at these it was really another regiment that he saw, the 44th, the Sambre-et-Meuse regiment, whose marching song began to ring through his head. There was also a page in the issue of November 1st that he looked at often. It showed the installation of the furnace for the crematorium at the Père Lachaise cemetery. Gaston shivered for a moment, then bethought himself of the corner of earth where he would lie sleeping one day. In the volume for 1897, when he was twenty-four, there were several pages in colour depicting the life of young soldiers. The barracks, soldiers in red trousers jumping over a wall, drill in the courtyard, foot inspection by a medical major. It was all real, contemporary, hardly as long ago as yesterday. The big September manœuvres also caught his attention. A picture spread over two pages showed a regiment charging across a wheat-field. This happened to him too. And because, at twenty, he had already gained a reverence for the bread that had demanded his nights of work for seven years, he had suffered. He still suffered at the sight today. But curiously it was a sorrow that he liked to experience again.

Some careless person had slipped a page torn from the *Petit Journal* into this volume of *L'Illustration*. It was the cover page, in colours, representing a café terrace in Paris during the summer of the intense heatwave. The customers, as well as the waiters dressed in black and white, were very hot. The date was missing because the page had been torn. This worried him. He ransacked his mind trying to remember the date of that terrible drought, and as soon as he thought he had got it some incontrovertible memory would rise up and throw doubt upon the question.

"But of course not, it couldn't have been in 1891. That's the year we bought Ripan, that big, grey horse we kept only for three months because it bit. And I remember it was raining all the time. Was it 1892? Could be. But then, that was the year my father planted the boxwood near the pump. So it couldn't have been then . . ."

In this way the long hours passed by, turning into days and weeks.

Fernande was not left out of all this. But she had quickly become a silent witness, ageless and ephemeral, who knew how to efface herself, yet come back at the slightest recall. The fact that they had taken her mortal remains to the other end of the town on a cold December day had not purged her from the house. This had happened because it had to, and, without really admitting it to himself, Gaston knew quite well that all she had done was to go ahead of him down a road on which he already found himself. All she had done, having kept level with him for a long time, was to increase her pace and go on without stopping. None of this was of any great importance as it was only a matter of time. From now on time counted for nothing. All this showed the extent to which the passage of years was unimportant. He could just as well live at the age of fifteen, with the lamp lighting up the vault of the oven and his father teaching him how to set out the round loaves, as in the present time, where he was engulfed in a twilight of silence and calm.

Julien's letters, still short and at less frequent intervals, were the only post he received now. He had great difficulty in reading them, and this prevented him from replying.

After all, the boy knew where to find him if he wanted to see him, and Lyon was not all that far away. Julien had been rude to Paul, and now it was Paul who looked after him. Fernande had always held that Paul and his wife were selfish. Today, if she could see what was going on from up there, she must be admitting that she was in the wrong. Naturally, it was his wife's and Julien's presence which had kept Paul and his wife away from the house for such a long time. Julien was living his life the way he wanted. He stayed away. He had found some work, he wrote, which took up all his time. If it was real work one could only be pleased about it. His absence was no burden. No absence was heavy for Gaston. Or, rather, there was no absence. There was only room for those beings with whom he pursued an endless conversation. About whom he never even asked himself whether they were of this world or whether they were already dead.

66

No doubt about it, Julien was like nobody else. When the solicitor had written to him to settle his mother's estate he had replied that he referred the matter to his father's wishes and signed the documents sent to him. So the solicitor came one afternoon together with Paul. He had read a complicated text out loud, and Gaston had had to struggle not to fall asleep. Once this was over Gaston had signed the documents, and then he had asked, "If I understand rightly, it's all in order now?"

So the solicitor had explained to him that, in accordance with his expressed wishes, his two houses would be left to Paul after his death, against the payment by him of a certain sum to Julien. This sum was not very big, but then Paul was providing for Gaston's needs, thus enabling him to continue the enjoyment of his property.

"In that way," Paul had added, "you'll know for certain that your houses will not be sold to strangers. And, of course, Julien has far more need of money than of bricks and mortar."

They had drunk a glass of mature old wine, and Gaston had spoken of the times when he had helped with the grape-gathering at Vernantois.

A few more weeks went by, and then one afternoon Paul arrived and told him that the solicitor in Lyon commissioned to draw up the deed for Julien to sign had returned the papers. Now it was all in order. Paul had explained, "There you are, I've seen to everything. That's saved you a lot of bother and left you in peace. You don't even have to work in the garden, because you'll not be short of anything."

"I'm going to look after the garden. I have got rid of the rabbits, but don't imagine I'm going to let the garden lie fallow."

"You needn't let it go to waste, but at least you've got the means to stop working as hard as you do."

"I'll go on till the end. If I didn't do it I'd be bored."

"You're bored because you are living alone, and if you weren't so obstinate you'd come and live with us, and you'd be much better off."

"No. I have said no once and for all. I don't want to leave my house."

Paul had pursued the matter no further, but Gaston felt that he was really annoyed by his refusal.

From that day onwards Micheline and Paul came to see him less often, and it happened that Gaston had to wait for his meals as late as one o'clock in the afternoon. When he remarked on this to the young assistant the young rogue replied in such a way that Gaston stood up, white with anger, and edged round the table and struck the youngster as he shouted, "You little slut. I'll teach you . . ." He was unable to say any more. A fit of coughing seized him, forcing him back to his chair and leaving him quite weak. When he had rid himself of the choking phlegm he sat motionless for a long time. His hands were shaking so much that he could not control them. The boy had gone, banging the door. It took Gaston over an hour to recover, and he could not eat that day. He never stopped saying to himself, "The little rogue, loitering around in the streets. My dinner gets here all cold and not on time. I'll have to speak to my son."

He said this over and over, more than twenty times, trying to think of a way of getting in touch with his son, who had not been to see him for more than two weeks. It was the beginning of February, and it was still too cold for him to call as far as his place. He kept an eye on the road, waiting for M. Robin to come past, to ask him to telephone.

The afternoon seemed endless to him. He could not make up his mind to close the shutters before it was really dark and it had become absolutely impossible to see a man walking past in the road.

At six o'clock he felt hungry and put the cauliflower in a white sauce and the can of soup that the young idler had brought on the stove to warm up. His anger had cooled down, but still smouldered below the surface. The rogue would be coming back tomorrow with his sly manner and that smile he always wore which seemed to say, "You can say what you like, you old fool, I don't give a bugger for you."

Gaston had often seen this in the eyes of that hooligan, and just the thought of seeing him enter his house made his hands shake.

His meal was almost hot when Paul arrived. His face was red and his eyes were bright. Without even greeting his father he flung out, "What on earth's happened to you? Now you're boxing my lad's ears!"

For a moment Gaston was speechless. Was Paul joking? Had he come to find out what had happened or to blame his own father?

There was a silence during which Paul sat down at the end of the table, tilted his hat to the back of his head, and lit a cigarette. As Gaston remained silent, it was the son who continued, "So what have you got to say? Here you are, not satisfied with being waited upon hand and foot like a prince! Anyone would think you had always led a life of luxury. Maybe when you had the bakery you could make your assistants work by giving them a kick up their backsides, but you'll have to realize that times have changed drastically. We can't allow ourselves to treat the employees as we used to. Here you've got a lad of fifteen. You box his ears, and an hour later his mother's on my doorstep! She talks about reporting me to the trade union and getting the employment officer after me! Puts me in a right mess, it does. If I don't want to find myself in front of a tribunal with all sorts of shit thrown around I'll have to shut their trap somehow. And d'you know what that means? You know what that's going to cost?"

Now Gaston was out of his depth. That youngster had shown him a lack of respect; Gaston had hardly touched him, and now he was being accused of . . . of . . . He no longer knew where he was. As his son was looking at him, appearing to expect a reply, he could only stammer, "But, after all—that little hooligan said—"

Paul interrupted. He raised his arms to the ceiling and let his hands fall down again on the table and began to shout, "Oh, for God's sake! When someone comes to find out about the story don't use those words. You'd be sued for slander. And I'd still have to take the blame. But then, you don't know them. The father was shot by the Germans. The mother is a member of the Communist Party. They're the bosses nowadays. They've got all the rights. Even at your age they'd throw you in prison and think nothing of it!"

Gaston had begun to shake again. He no longer remembered all the things he had intended to say to his son. All he could do was to repeat, "But, after all . . . If that rogue . . . Anyway, what can you expect? I don't understand."

"That sticks out a mile. You insist on living apart from the rest of the world. I can't be dancing attendance on you all the time, after all. Admit that if you agreed to come and live with us a lot of problems would be solved."

Gaston had no reserves left for his anger. He just shook his head, and Paul pulled an ugly grimace. "You're stubborn," he said. "Here you've taken it into your head to cause me all this trouble. A fine thanks for all I've done to see that you're able to lead a quiet life. Well, how are we going to reach some agreement now? I'm asking you. Perhaps you don't realize we've got our work cut out. The boy refuses to come here again; he said so. And I can't force him. It's not his work. He wasn't hired to do it. So I'll have to ask the maid to bring your meals. Only she does the cooking, and she can't be in two places at once, so she won't be able to get here till the afternoon. She'll bring your supper and the next day's dinner. You'll have to heat it up. I can't see any other way out."

Gaston remained speechless. He looked at his hands resting on the oilcloth. They began to shake again as soon as he lifted them. He felt crushed. As though his anger had been thrown into a hole, himself on top of it, and the hole filled in again. He did not even dare look at his son.

He was aware of him sitting opposite, clinging to the idea of bringing him to live in their flat; whereas he was clinging just as strongly to the idea of staying in his own house. Winter would soon be over, and there would be sunny days to lure him into his garden. He knew his son's place. The dark rooms facing either the street or the small backyard. The big kitchen with the maid clattering around and the radio blaring. All the comings and goings. Meals never on time. Noisy streets and noisy neighbours. No, he had made up his mind to stay in his own house, and he would stay here. After all, if they brought him his meals in the afternoon he could at least eat them when he pleased. And he would not have to see that ragamuffin again.

As Paul stood up Gaston asked, "And do you think your maid will be able to fetch my wood in?"

Paul made another hopeless gesture. "Bugger that! I'd forgotten, there's still that business. You must admit you have a knack of making life difficult for us."

"It's quite clear," Gaston moaned, "that your life'll be much easier when I've kicked the bucket."

Paul looked at him with hard eyes and shrugged his shoulders. "Don't talk nonsense. I just hope that the maid won't find it too much for her, fetching the wood. But never mind—when I think how comfortable you'd be at our place!"

67

That visit of Paul's and his anger had made Gaston feel uneasy, and the effect stayed with him for several weeks. He tried to fight against the idea that his son had waited for the deed of gift to be signed before letting him feel what a burden he was. Not a day passed without this thought occurring many times. He pushed it aside, saying, "It can't be true. They've their own life to lead. They're a different generation, and they imagine I should be able to get used to their sort of life. Of course, it would be much easier for them."

Immediately after Fernande had died Micheline had brought him his meals on Sundays, as the assistant had the day off. Now they brought him a little extra on Saturdays, and he managed as best he could. Sometimes the maid was in a hurry. She said, "You've still got enough wood. I'll go and fetch some more tomorrow."

The next day, as though on purpose, she was late. Night fell. She arrived out of breath, put down her basket, and left at once saying, "I must fly. There are guests, and I haven't made the dinner."

The next morning Gaston put on warm outdoor clothes, wrapped a woollen scarf round the lower part of his face to avoid breathing in the damp, cold air which brought on his asthma, and set off for the shed to replenish his wood supply. He took the opportunity to open the cupboards in his workshop and make sure that his tools were not becoming too rusty. Every time he went there he was alarmed to see how the piles of logs were dwindling. This question of heating always made him anxious. Fernande was no longer there to write to the forester and order wood. Paul and his wife no longer came to see him, and he had to ask M. Robin to write the letter. "I've got to saw up that wood and finish before next winter, so please ask him to deliver in the spring to give me plenty of time." After he had said that he added, "I doubt that I'll get through next winter, but in any case I don't want to be without heating."

M. Robin wrote the letter. He often helped Gaston. He asked after Julien, but he never spoke about Paul. Neither did Gaston. It was as though there were a small ditch which they each measured with their eyes, but did not dare venture across. From a kind of pride that he was hard pressed to define, Gaston did not dare ask M. Robin to write to Julien either, begging him to come and see him as soon as possible. Also because, while wanting this visit, he feared it. Paul neglected him. He did not even fulfil the commitments he had undertaken properly when he accepted the conditions of the deed of gift, but Gaston was frightened lest Julien should know. He clung to the hope he felt at the advent of spring. There would be the garden, the wood to saw once it was delivered. It would all fill his days. The nights would be shorter, it would be warm, and he would be able to go outside, out into the street for a bit of a gossip with the neighbours.

The big, pollarded oak-tree near the pump at the bottom of the garden had not been lopped for five or six years. All the branches that had grown amounted to a good deal of wood, and he had promised himself he would tackle that job as soon as the weather permitted.

There were several sunny days at the beginning of March. He began by trimming some of the trees along the drive, carefully collecting the twigs, which he tied into little bundles. He tired quickly, but it was always like that after winter and he knew that work would make him regain his strength quickly. Four days later, as the weather still held fine and the ground had dried out sufficiently to allow him to put up his ladder without it sinking in, he began to trim his oak-tree. He had carefully sharpened his hand-saw, and the work went with a swing. The branches fell one by one, and as he worked he thought about his father, a little chimney-sweep from Savoy who had come here around 1840 and had planted this tree so that the pump would always have shade.

Towards the middle of the morning over half the branches

were on the ground, and Gaston was about to descend the ladder to move it to another place, when he saw his son enter the garden. Paul was not on his own. Two men accompanied him. They stopped at the top of the first plot while Paul headed straight towards his father.

As soon as he was within hailing distance he shouted, "You must be mad, doing that sort of work at your age. You might fall and break a leg—even kill yourself."

"You're not going to tell me off," said Gaston.

Paul smiled. "Of course not, but it frightens me."

"What do you expect. It's over a month since I ordered a supply of wood, and it hasn't been delivered. Every little helps."

"Don't you worry about your wood supply. You know we wouldn't let you freeze."

Gaston had reached the ground in front of his son. He tried to see, between the still, bare trees, the two men who stood inside the garden gate. "Who's that with you?"

"You know him. It's Valentini, the builder. The other's an architect."

"Oh!"

"Yes, I brought them along to have a look at things. You know that part will be taken by the road-widening, so we have to see where we might build from."

Gaston hesitated. He took off his cap to wipe the top of his head and asked almost timidly, "Build? But build what?"

"Well, for the moment some garages for my lorries, and later I could put one or two storeys on top."

Gaston placed his hand-saw at the bottom of the ladder, and, scratching his chin, he thought for a few moments before asking, "Do you mean to say that you intend building in my lifetime?"

Paul made an embarrassed gesture. "Well," he said, "I haven't had any plans drawn up yet, but . . . The present warehouse is a bloody nuisance. You know it's very old. Full of rats . . . And then the rent is steep. So the sooner I set about it, the better it'll be."

Gaston curbed his temper. He felt a stirring in the depths of his soul, words came unbidden that he could hardly restrain.

"As for your tree," said Paul, "leave it. I'll send one of my men to finish it off."

It was perhaps this clumsy attempt which burst the bounds of Gaston's anger. "Shut up!" he cried. "I don't give a damn about that. But what's all this about building? You'd be willing to turn my garden upside down! Muck it up completely, while I've never wanted to change a thing—even to lay on water or electricity! Christ Almighty, you've sworn to make me die before my time!"

Paul looked all around them. The sun had brought people into the neighbouring gardens.

"Don't shout like that—you'll rouse the whole district."

But Gaston was no longer in charge of himself. He had suddenly discovered an aspect of his son that he had always refused to recognize. "I'll bawl as loud as I like. This is still my own home, for God's sake. And you will do me the honour of shoving off with those puppets. Otherwise I'll know where to find a fork-handle that's not worm-eaten!"

Paul feebly tried to protest, but Gaston did not even hear him. "Bugger off," he said repeatedly. "Otherwise the whole district will learn that you leave me to starve, and only come and see me to try and make me come to an untimely end!"

He was carried away, but was clear enough to feel an incipient fit of coughing. He stopped, took a few long, deep gulps of air, picked up a branch about a yard long and as thick as an arm, and made for the two men. Paul ran in front of him and very quickly dragged the architect and the builder outside the garden. Gaston did not stop. With increased speed he reached the gate and double-locked it. The three men had started walking up the rue des Écoles. Brandishing the key in one hand and his cudgel in the other, Gaston yelled, "Come back here, and I'll put the police on your heels!"

But the three men went on walking without turning their heads.

Gasping for breath, Gaston stood leaning against the garden gate for a while. When a window opened in the house opposite he did not bother to look and see whether it was Mlle Marthe or some other gossip, and walked slowly back to the house.

68

As usual, his anger had tired Gaston much more than would the hardest day's work, yet at the same time he felt it had freed him of a great burden.

On his return to the house he sat down for a moment. Then he revived the fire, where there were still a few embers left from the logs he had burnt to heat his morning coffee. It was after eleven o'clock, and he felt hungry. He looked in disgust at the leftovers in the two saucepans which the maid had brought him the previous evening and took them outside and left them on the doorstep as he grumbled, "Canteen muck . . . Doesn't even keep overnight . . . Filthy stuff . . . Pity there's no more rabbits."

He went straight down to the cellar, took some potatoes and two large onions. When he had peeled them he put two spoonfuls of lard in the cast-iron saucepan, and cut up the potatoes and onions into small pieces and put them in. The mere fact of getting all this ready, smelling the hot fat, and hearing it splutter sharpened his appetite further.

"Pity there's no bacon to go with it!"

Since Fernande had died he had never had his potatoes done this way. He added a big clove of garlic, two bayleaves, and a little thyme.

While the fire was burning merrily under his meal Gaston prepared a glass of well-sugared wine for himself.

"Thanks very much," he grumbled to himself. "So he'd like to see me drop down dead. Well, now, we shall see . . . Muck up my garden, would he? I like that. Here I've worked all my life, digging in manure and planting trees to see it all disappear at the swing of a shovel! Blast that! Just because I haven't moved all winter, he thinks I've fallen asleep, maybe. I'll show him . . ."

So he went on, drinking a tumblerful of sweetened wine, stirring his potatoes, and gorging himself on the smell of bay and onions. "It's ages since the house smelt so good."

He talked to himself without stop, as though wanting to keep alight the flame which had just been rekindled within him. He had only needed to threaten with his cudgel, and those three men had fled—and the eldest must have been thirty years younger than himself. The thought of their flight sent a wave of live, warm blood running through his muscles, and made him feel like exerting himself.

"Tonight I'll have finished lopping that tree, and I bet I'll have a pretty pile of branches. And anyone who thinks I'm finished can come and take a billhook. We'll see who's the quickest. Who do they think they are, anyway, with their money and briefcases? Do they call that work?"

He continued talking like this while he was eating his meal. Sometimes he raised his voice as though addressing a large audience.

When he had finished his coffee he poured himself a generous glass of brandy.

"It's neither Sunday nor a holiday, but I think I need this. I'll do the washing-up tonight. I'm going out to take advantage of the sun to get some work done."

He had finished lopping and was beginning to drag the branches towards the shed, when his daughter-in-law arrived. As the gate was still locked she had come down the road that ran the length of the garden, and he did not see her until she was a few yards from the shed. The sight of her irritated him. He laid down the branch he was carrying and took up a stance with one hand in his apron pocket and the other holding the cigarette that had gone out between his lips. Micheline approached, looking mortified and distressed. She hesitated a few seconds and then kissed him on both cheeks. She smelt strongly of perfume, and Gaston noticed that her hair was a much lighter blond than usual.

"Oh, my goodness," she whined, "my goodness, poor Father, what is happening to us?"

"You should know, since you're here. I can't say that your visits have exactly tired me out for some time now!"

He had spoken without shouting, but his voice was very hard. Micheline looked at him in silence, fluttered her eyelids, and burst into tears. "I deserve your reproach," she said. "Oh, how I deserve it. And how I do blame myself for not having known how to neglect my work a little more and given you more of my time. I always try to do too much, and what's the use? I ask you."

Gaston was annoyed by this too-sudden, tearful outburst and interrupted her. "I don't think Paul sent you here to ask me that."

She pretended to be very surprised and frightened. "But he doesn't know I'm here," she declared. "Poor Paul, you should see the state he's in."

"That's no concern of mine. And it's not worth your while coming here and putting on an act for my sake."

"Poor Father, don't shout—you'll hurt yourself. I must explain. But we can't stay here."

Gaston felt harder and harder. He clung to his anger with all his might. Micheline's affectation helped him in this—she had burst into tears far too easily. She sighed far too much, and Gaston found it almost comical the way her chest heaved with each sob, stretching the material of her bodice to bursting-point. He waved his hand towards Mancy, where the clouds were drawing up. "It might rain tomorrow, and I have to take my wood in from the plot before it starts pissing. I haven't time for your whining."

"My God, I'd never have thought you'd be so hard and unfair to me—or to poor Paul, who couldn't swallow a bite at lunch-time."

"Ah, well, I had a splendid meal. I made myself a potato dish. Your saucepans from yesterday are on the doorstep. You can go and fetch them. And don't bother to send me any more food. I'll manage on my own. Anyway, the gate will stay locked."

He turned on his heel and walked back to the tree without taking any notice of Micheline, who remained standing in front of the shed door, her handkerchief in her hand.

"You just go on snivelling," he muttered under his breath. "Then you'll have to pee less. But it won't make you any thinner. Christ."

He kept up his anger, he wrapped himself in it as though it were a tough material, waterproof against tears and sobs from this fat woman who got on his nerves.

With every trip he made Micheline began to speak to him again. "Poor Paul, if only you knew what he has to endure. He was saying, 'My poor old father, who's going to curse me. And I so much wanted to smooth his way in his old age.'"

Gaston made another four trips. It was no longer anger that boiled inside him, but a kind of irritation making him want to snatch a supple switch and whip his daughter-in-law's fat rump.

Unable to bear it any longer by the fifth journey, he placed himself in front of her and, trying hard not to shout for fear his cough might prevent him finishing, he rapped out, "I've heard enough for today. Would you kindly do me the honour of pissing off and not coming back till I go out feet first. When that happens you can do what you like with my land, but while I'm alive you're not going to commit your indecencies here!"

Micheline slowly withdrew, but before finally turning round she sobbed once more, "But it'll make my poor Paul ill!"

"Tell him to drink less and he'll be all right. And tell him not to come and muck me about with his cunning schemes and clowns with briefcases!"

69

The air was refreshed with a few showers of rain, but Gaston did not stop working, sustained by a kind of strength that his anger had engendered. He divided his time between the shed, where he sawed and split the wood from the oak-tree, and the garden, where he started the spring clearing. When the earth had dried out sufficiently he would start digging.

Just before the middle of March he received a letter from Julien announcing the birth of a boy. They had called him Charles Gaston Dubois. Gaston worked even better that day. When M. Robin walked past he asked him to come into the kitchen. He showed him Julien's letter. When M. Robin had congratulated him Gaston asked with tears in his eyes, "Would you like to write a short letter for me?"

"Of course. Shall we do it at once?"

"Really . . . If you could post it for me this afternoon—and if it's not too much to ask—I would like to send them a little money. I'm not much good at buying presents, you know. So I'd rather send them a bit of money. I have some rent from the bakery, and for the moment my needs are not so great."

M. Robin wrote the letter, and Gaston signed it at the bottom with a trembling hand.

"Oh, what a shame," he said. "How happy my poor wife would have been! If the weather looks promising tomorrow I'll go to the cemetery. I haven't been there yet. I haven't felt strong enough. But now . . .

"Would you like me to ask my wife to go with you?"

"No, no. I give her enough bother already with the shopping."

Since Gaston had locked his gate and decided to refuse the meals his son owed him, Mme Robin had taken charge of buying his bread, meat, and milk. Sometimes she brought him a plate of pudding. She did this so sweetly, always saying, "You will be doing me a favour. I made too much, and my husband will scold me if he sees me throwing it away."

The next morning Gaston studied the sky as soon as he was up. The dawn signalled a day of sunshine. A fresh, gentle breeze blew from the East, clearing the mist from the sky. He put two shirts, two vests, and some handkerchiefs that needed washing to soak in the wash-tub, and then, having put on a clean apron and his velvet jacket, he picked up his walking-stick and set out.

Avoiding the centre of town, he crossed the market-place, took the rue Regard and then the Quai du Solvan. He walked at a good, steady pace, glad that there were so few people in the streets. He was going to the cemetery to visit his wife, who had been buried at the beginning of winter, but he did not feel sad. He was going to say hallo to her and bring her some good news.

After walking for three-quarters of an hour he reached the road to the cemetery. An old woman whom he had thought dead several years ago arrived at the same time as he, but she emerged from the rue du Puits-Salé. She was an old customer from the time he kept the bakery. She did not appear surprised to see him, and walked beside him, talking as though they had seen each other the night before.

"Well, so you're going to see your wife."

"Yes," said Gaston. "Winter has lasted a long time. When it's cold it's no good my trying to go out of doors."

"I don't either. I hardly ever go to the cemetery when the weather's bad. However, as I live near by, whenever there's a bit of sunshine I come. Of course, I don't stay long. Just to say hallo, and then I'm off back home. But the dead understand all right. They know me. They know that when the weather's fine I'll stay much longer."

"Is it your husband that you come to see?"

The old woman stopped, placed her hands on her hips with her fingers well spread, and pulled herself up a little to look at Gaston. "My husband? The devil take me, no! It's more than forty years since he came to an end. And he was buried at Bourg, where he was in hospital. I hadn't enough to buy a plot. He must have been dug up again a long time ago. No, no, I've no-one. But I've still a—a lot of friends here, all the same."

They had reached the cemetery gates, and the old woman indicated the graves with a large sweep of the hand. "Your place," she continued, "is up there on the left."

"Yes, above the steps, beyond the big trees."

They took the path to the left, and, walking a little more slowly because it was steeper, the old woman began to talk again. "It's a good place. Not at all damp. And sunny for most of the day. They're much better off up there than near the gates, you might say. It's much healthier, and there's less comings and goings."

She stopped to pick up a vase that the wind had blown down on the white gravel of a small grave. "That's Pauline Richard," she explained. "The one who used to be landlady of La Civette. Did you know her?"

"Why, of course I knew her!"

"She was a good woman. She's not among her own sort here. Mostly the nobs and snobs in this part."

She jerked her chin towards the enormous graves in blue and black marble, great vaults surmounted by columns and statues, others enclosed with wrought-iron gates. She stopped in front of a mausoleum that a subsidence in the earth had tilted towards the right. "There you are," she remarked. "They're no better than a simple stone. All these elaborate contraptions. One day they can't stand up any more, and they tumble down. And I wonder if the dead are really any better off underneath."

Surprised at first, Gaston listened to her now as though she were talking about living people. She sometimes gave a little laugh which did not seem at all out of place here where life seemed much stronger than death.

For the sun, already hot, filled the cemetery with life. Grey lizards scuttled across the stones and disappeared down cracks, gnats flew around in the light, and the lilacs planted near the cemetery wall were already a delicate green with the first buds.

When they reached the trees the old woman took a small

paper bag out of her basket—it contained bread-crusts. She broke them up and scattered them between two graves, saying, "This is for the birds. They come and are a bit of company for the dead."

Gaston started up the narrow, grey stone steps, and the old woman followed him. When he reached the path at the top he walked as far as a mound covered in dead flowers.

"They haven't yet fixed the stone," he remarked. "The earth doesn't settle quickly in the frost."

"All it needs is a bit of rain and it'll soon be done."

He sat down on the edge of the next grave and, with both hands on his walking-stick, he said, "I'll rest a while, and then I'll clear off all that muck."

The old woman stood still for a few minutes. Her hands were crossed in front, and her black basket hung down against her legs. Only her lips were moving, although no sound came.

"Ah, well," she said in the end, "I'll go away and leave you two together. I'll go round and give the others a bit of company."

She walked away slowly, and Gaston saw her stop by the graves, stand quite still, set a vase upright again, pull out a tuft of grass, or replace a crucifix. When she had disappeared he looked at the yellow earth with Fernande at rest below, and he said, "That's right, this is a good corner. And now the cold weather is over."

He sat like that for quite a while. "And do you know, Julien has a son. Ah, well, some of us leave and others arrive. That's the way of things."

He laid down his walking-stick, stood up, and began to gather together the flowers that winter had flattened against the earth. He left only the two garlands of beads. Julien's and his own.

"My poor wife," he continued, "I've had plenty of sorrow since you left me. And I wonder if it's worth the trouble putting up a stone. When I see how peaceful you are here."

He did not feel sad. It even seemed to him he felt just as comfortable here as at home. It was a garden where no-one would come any more and speak unkindly to you. Otherwise they did not come, or else they came as friends like that old woman who had gone off for her bit of small talk with the dead.

When he had cleaned up the grave he went to wash his hands under the tap a little farther up. He came back to pick up his walking-stick and said, "I've just seen that Félix Ramillon and his wife are quite near you. And farther along there's Cretot's daughter. They're all people you knew well."

He poked out a dandelion growing between two clods of earth with his stick and set off down a side-path, mumbling to himself, "I'll go back to the gate a different way. Then I'll see a few more people. I know more here now than I do in town."

70

After this visit to the cemetery Gaston applied himself to his work again. He felt much more calm, as though he had moved forward with the certainty of being truly on the right road. He no longer needed that anger which had spurred him. He felt strong enough to continue on his own till the end. His work he kept well in hand, and it was this that sustained his life. This was all there was to be done, the two of them continuing hand in hand, one sustaining the other without bothering too much about counting the days.

Two weeks sped by, with a weather that drew the sap to the tips of the branches and forced the grass to reach up through the earth. Grass appears all too soon, but has that good quality of spurring one on to sow and plant. Gaston began by digging over the vegetable beds behind the house, which, protected from the north, were the best for the early sowing. He emptied a compost heap and spread the manure from his wheelbarrow.

By the beginning of the third week he had on the whole passed the peak of that fatigue which the year's first labours always generate. He had fallen into the rhythm, and although he was alone in the work now, he reckoned he was not behindhand. One morning he was delighted to see young Picaud, the forester.

Lucky I know the house," said Picaud. "I tried to open the gate, but it was locked."

"That's right, I don't leave it open any longer. People who really want to see me know the way."

"Are you afraid of burglars?"

Gaston hesitated. He blew his nose to give himself time to think, and then said, "No. The lock is jammed, and I haven't had time to mend it."

The forester spoke about Fernande's death and apologized for not having come to the funeral. Gaston made a gesture with his hand to show it was of no importance. Then he asked how his order for wood was coming on.

"I'll be bringing it next week, but I thought that if you wanted to chop up some more bundles of kindling I could bring those down at the same time."

"Well, thank you, but it's not kindling I'm short of. It's logs I need, and not the kind that are pissing with sap."

The forester gave a loud laugh. "I can only deliver what I've got. And that's this year's wood."

They discussed the matter for a while, but the forester had no other wood in reserve, and Gaston would obtain nothing better. Picaud was already on his way, when he changed his mind suddenly and retraced his steps. "I've thought of something," he said. "Four or five years ago we felled two big limetrees which were in the way of access to another cut. We pared off the branches, but I was never able to sell the trunks, which were damaged. Of course, it's not the best kind of wood for heating, but if you want to prepare them they're sawn into lengths, and you only have to split them with wedges and a sledgehammer. Lime splits like nothing on earth. We'll get them on the lorry, and that'll give the rest of your wood time to dry out a bit."

Gaston thought of the long walk into the forest. While he

hesitated Picaud said, "Of course, I know that using a sledgehammer is no work for a man of your age, however easy the lime splits."

Gaston straightened his back. The words had stung him. "What are you talking about? D'you think I'm a cripple? I've managed all the work ever since my poor wife died—and you can see for yourself that it hasn't suffered."

He pointed around at the garden.

"Well, it's up to you to decide," said the forester.

"It's decided already. Just tell me where it is."

"It's not as far as the place where you once fetched branches. This place is just above Perrigny, on the slope of the small hill facing south where the valley begins."

Going down on one knee, he drew a map of the route Gaston had to follow with his finger in the dust.

"Yes, yes," said Gaston, "I know it. I've been there often to look for mushrooms. Well, now, that was in your father's time . . . and I believe your grandfather was still alive then, so it's not exactly yesterday. . . ."

He rambled on with a long story which turned into another and which he continued to himself after Picaud had interrupted him to say, "I must run. I've deliveries to make. You only need take an axe for the opening cut and your sledgehammer. You'll find something to do for wedges up there."

"Don't worry. I've done more of that kind of work than you'll ever do, even though you are a woodcutter."

He watched him walking off—a big fellow who waddled as he swung his arms to and fro. He would show him whether swinging a sledgehammer was work for a man of his age!

"Youngsters get used to machinery, so they lose their strength before they're even forty. In your grandfather's time the master felled trees in the forest like everyone else—even though he was the boss. Nowadays you give orders and drive lorries. And when someone tells you about the olden days you haven't even enough respect to listen."

He had started work again and talked to himself for a long time in this fashion. He spoke without rancour, even with a new kind of pleasure which gradually took on shape and depth.

Now and again he would straighten his back to study the sky and estimate the wind. It came from the north-west, and as it had blown from that direction for more than the last three days, you could be sure there would not be a drop of rain for the rest of the week.

The rest of the day passed very quickly. Gaston never stopped picturing the road to himself, searching his memory for the smallest path in that forest he had traversed so often. This journey into the past warmed his blood, drove a current of energy right through his veins, making him forget the present.

He went to get his sledgehammer ready before nightfall, sharpened his axe and his billhook. Later, when he was back in the kitchen, he greased his boots and the old leather gaiters which would protect him from the dew. He ate his meal and made the coffee so that he would only have to heat it up in the morning.

That evening he went to bed without needing to light the lamp.

71

There was scarcely a hint of light in the sky when Gaston walked out of the house. He had tied his axe and sledgehammer together with string and carried them on his left shoulder. His billhook and food and drink were in his haversack. He held his walking-stick in his right hand; the iron tip rang out as it hit the tarmac.

The weather was calm, but he knew that the wind would rise when the sun rose, and he wanted to set to work as early as possible. It is never easy to walk with your head into the wind and the sun in your eyes. Besides, he preferred to cross the town before people began to come out of their houses. He met only a few workmen from the dairy. Later some cyclists passed him on their way to the optical factory.

When he had passed the railway bridge he slackened his pace. The road was beginning to go uphill between the houses, and there was no point in getting puffed. His legs felt strong, he possessed a good reserve of energy and wanted to avoid that cough which always left him exhausted. So he stopped to rest a few times and used the opportunity to survey the town stretched out before him, all grey and blue in the cold morning light. His eyes lingered over the cemetery.

"My poor old wife," he whispered, "you may well say I'm mad wanting to tackle this sort of work at my age. But what d'you expect. You know one can't burn that sopping wet wood they deliver. If only people were a little more conscientious, but that bloody war has killed off all honesty. All that's left for old people is to die alone. When I told you that you wouldn't believe me. But it's true."

Every time he stopped he changed the position of his haversack, shifted the tools to the other shoulder and the walking-stick to the other hand. In his head he carried the map that the forester's stubby finger had traced on the earth.

When he reached the old Roman road he veered off to the left and took a path that crossed at right angles and climbed along the right edge of the wood to emerge on another road, well before Saint-Étienne-de-Coldre. He had to stop half-way up. The slope was steeper. He turned round. He overlooked the village of Perrigny. The road to Haute-Roche was on his left and dipped downhill behind the corner of the wood. That was exactly the way Picaud had explained it. Gaston set off again. When he reached the road above he turned right and counted three hundred steps before beginning to look for the path.

Brambles had overgrown the bank, but he made out the old path to the cut from the slight depression in the ground.

"I was bloody well right to bring the billhook. And just as well I put on my gaiters, too."

He began by cutting a long ash pole, trimming the twigs,

but leaving a fork at the end. Then, holding the brambles clear with this, he cut them with his billhook as near to the ground as possible. He dragged them across to the other side of the path in bundles and tipped them down the bank.

When the passage was clear he could see that only ferns grew on the road to the cut. It would be enough to tread them down to make a path over which he could transport his wood easily. He took off his jacket and hung it with the haversack on a maple-tree a few yards from the path and walked towards the tree-trunks just visible above the ferns. He counted eight big pieces sawn into three-yard lengths and said to himself that if he cut even half that amount it would give a good supply. The forester had said that the trunks were less than a hundred yards from the public road, and he had not been wrong.

Before he cut his wedges Gaston wanted to see what the wood was like. He trod down the ferns all around the first trunk, cut away a few brambles, and swung the billhook into the thick of the wood. Two cuts on the slant, and a piece as large as a hand jumped up, revealing a white and healthy-looking wood.

"It looks all right on the surface."

He looked at the sawn end of the trunk. The centre was slightly soft, even slightly rotten, but the sapwood was intact.

"Shouldn't look a gift-horse in the mouth."

The sun had risen above the summit of the hill, and its first rays ran like a stream through the tree-trunks, lapping against the dew-covered ferns across the earth. The wood was golden like a burnished autumn. Only a few green flames pierced through in places. The wind had risen, but howled across the summit of the trees.

Gaston found an acacia-tree without difficulty. This furnished him with wedges, which he cut very quickly. He wanted to try out his strength and see if the sledgehammer was still a tool for his age.

And so he attacked the first trunk. The work was not easy, to be sure, for the dry, dense wood had aged in the sun and rain.

"It's well seasoned," he kept on saying. "I know the kind.

It's difficult to split, but the grain is dense, and that makes a good fuel."

The first cut was the hardest. If the crack went beyond the centre he would try to split it in two. Like that, the work would be easier later on. If it stopped there he would have to start again on the side and lift out lengths, piece by piece. As he had feared, the crack did not go beyond the rotten centre. Gaston laughed a little wildly. The wood was resisting. It wanted to fight. Ah, well, he'd show it some fight.

"God, we'll see who's got the upper hand!"

A kind of friendly fury animated him. He talked to the wood as though it were an old companion. However, he bashed away with the sledgehammer, bellowing a deep-throated yell with each stroke. The sledgehammer splintered the wood bit by bit as the wedges sank deeper with each blow. The tree-trunk growled and whimpered like a wounded creature. When he had forced the second crack the length of the trunk Gaston came back to the attack, took up his axe and, swinging it in a wide arc, drawing his chest almost parallel to the ground, he drove the iron head into the base of the two cracks. One blow was enough to cleave the axe-head into the wood at the end of the trunk. He let go the handle, took up the sledgehammer, and climbed on top of the tree-trunk in order to be able to strike with greater ease. At the third blow against the steel, which rang out across the valley, the wood began to lift. Gaston gave a short laugh and simply said, "Right!"

He climbed down and, throwing all his weight on the axe handle, he forced a response from the wood—a long crackling of stretched fibres tearing one by one.

The first piece wrested from the tree was there at his feet. The opened trunk still quivered with the torn fibres, which slowly settled into place again.

"A pretty sight!"

He lifted the end of the piece, ran his hands along it until he felt it rocking. There he flexed his knees slightly, balanced the load on his shoulder, and carried it, taking short steps, as far as the edge of the public road.

The hardest part was over. He now knew that the rest of the tree would yield easily. It had realized that any form of resistance was useless. Here he was, the old man whose ability the forester had doubted, the old man whom they wanted to bury before his time by taking his land away from him with the excuse that he no longer had the strength to cultivate it and make it pay, and he had mastered this lime-tree with all its knots.

He was hot, and he put on his jacket again. Now that he had the measure of the work and had estimated his own strength, he no longer felt any need to hurry so much. The walk and the first bout of work had given him an appetite. He might just as well have some of his food in advance. He unhooked the haversack and set off to look for a sunnier stretch of bank along the road to avoid the chill of the woods and to eat a bite.

72

The sun was already high when Gaston had finished his snack. It was pleasurable to regain the woods, where, in spite of the absence of leaves, the branches softened the light. He set to work again at an easy pace, convinced now that he would manage the job in his own good time. In order to vary the job and to give his hands a rest, he carried off each piece of wood immediately after cutting it.

When he had finished the second piece of timber he walked down to where his jacket was hanging and looked at his watch. It was not quite eleven o'clock, and he reckoned he could cut up another trunk before eating. For the time being he drank half a glass of wine mixed with water, and then took up his axe again.

As he trod the ferns underfoot he thought he heard something stirring behind the tree-trunk. He stood still. "Might be a rat or some other sort of filth," he growled.

He cleared a way and examined the trunk. It had deteriorated even more than the others. Not only was the centre rotten, but there was a hole as big as a fist. On the whole, that was an advantage, as it would split all the more easily.

Gaston took note of a crack already formed in the trunk, and with a powerful blow drove his axe into this. There was a creaking sound which prolonged in a most unusual way and became a spitting noise like that of soaking wet wood on the embers of a fire. "Good God! It's crying before it's anywhere near the fire!"

He let go of the axe handle, took up the sledgehammer, and struck two rapid blows on the back of the axe-head. This time the spitting noise turned into a hissing sound, and Gaston felt worried. "Oh, God, I wouldn't be at all surprised if there wasn't an adder inside."

He stepped back, regretting that his axe was so firmly entrenched—it would have been a much better weapon than the sledgehammer. But at the same time he thought it best to catch the beast as it came out of the hole, rather than letting it slide off into the ferns. The hammer poised in his hands, he waited a few seconds. He had just about decided to knock at the tree-trunk again when a triangular head stuck out and dropped like brownish-red slime down the cut edge of the trunk, which still bore the black marks of the cross-saw.

"Christ! It's a red one!"

The sledgehammer fell, crushing its head. The body spurted and twisted on the ferns. Gaston had already stepped forward to finish it off when another adder came out, much faster than the first. In the time it took to lift the hammer, the beast was already on the grass. The heavy mass of iron stopped it, striking the middle of its body. Gaston raged, "Blast! It's spawning them!"

He hardly had time to withdraw a pace before another appeared, then yet another followed hard on its side, while still more came out from the ferns behind the fallen tree-trunk. "Oh, Christ, it can't be true . . . but it can't be true."

Involuntarily Gaston stepped backwards, and he felt his foot crushing another reptile. He had the instinct not to lift his foot again. The left heel was on the middle of the body of an enormous adder whose head was striking at his leather gaiter while the tail whipped across his boot.

"Filthy muck!"

There was hissing on all sides. Gaston felt himself drenched with sweat. He struck at the nearest adder with his hammer, and when he had practically cut it in two he came back to the one underfoot. It was vain to lean all his weight on that foot. He felt the body of the beast sinking into the moss and ferns. If he lifted his foot it might try to bite above the gaiters. Trying to crush its head with his right foot, he lost his balance, but, using his hammer as support, he managed not to fall. Freed, the creature coiled up to attack. Gaston saw its small, lively eye shining. He would have to be quicker than this coil of brown energy with death in its tongue. Hardly lifted above two feet, the cudgel fell.

Now that he was free, Gaston looked towards the stump whose shadowy mouth continued to spew out snakes.

This time fear overtook him completely. He seemed to be living a nightmare. He ran without stopping for the road. There he paused and thought of his jacket, his axe, and all the things he had brought to the forest. He wiped the stinging sweat from his eyes with the back of his hand and peered through the undergrowth towards the stumps. Even from this position he could still see movements.

"Damn and blast that filthy muck! Blast that muck!"

A terrible agony constricted his throat. His head rang, just as the hollow wood must have rung where the adders lay sleeping.

Should he go back as far as his jacket? Then he thought of the billhook. The best weapon would still be a supple and strong stick. If he had his billhook he could cut one.

Without making any noise, watching carefully where he placed his feet, and holding the sledgehammer half raised, he advanced towards the jacket. He reached it down, along with the haversack and the walking-stick, and went back to the road. He was soaked, and his limbs were trembling. Only the thought of his good axe embedded in the tree-trunk prevented him from fleeing. He made himself breathe deeply and thought for a few minutes. Then, bearing in mind that he would have to be ready to beat about him when he retreated, he put on his jacket and hitched the haversack over his shoulders.

His hands were still trembling so much that it was difficult to undo the lace which closed the haversack. Although he had tied it in a bow he pulled the wrong end, making a hard knot that he could not undo again. His thick nails scratched against the material, and in the end he took out his knife and cut the lace.

He stayed in the middle of the road, and while he was doing this he kept an eye on the surrounding area. When he had extracted his billhook he hooked it on to his belt and picked up the pole he had used to hold back the brambles. Keeping it between both hands he beat the grass along the ditch where he wanted to go in and cut a hazel-bush. As nothing moved, he advanced carefully, cut down the hazel in two blows of the billhook, and dragged it on to the road. He chose two good branches, cut them off, and stripped the twigs. When he had stowed his billhook back in the haversack he tried out the two sticks, making them whistle through the air and beat the bank where the grass was laid flat under their blows. He adjusted his cap firmly on his head and swung the haversack round on his back again, and went slowly towards the path to the cut.

Eyes on the watch, he advanced noiselessly, his right hand stretched out in front holding the supple weapon ready to strike. From time to time he would measure the distance still separating him from his axe. Deeply embedded as it was in the tree-trunk, he knew he would need a good while to pull it out. A good while and both his hands. So he would have to drop his sticks only a yard from that black hole which would spit out snakes at knee-height.

"Dirty, filthy muck," he kept on muttering under his breath.

Half-way there he saw a reddish, shining dart slide through the grass. The creature had come from behind and overtaken him. He quickly took a few steps forward and beat about with his stick. But the ferns were stiff and broke the force of the blows—the adder escaped. If he had been able to pass near that one without seeing it it proved that others too had made for the road.

He stood stock-still for a moment, turning only his head and body to look around. The silence in the forest scared him out of his wits. Even the wind seemed to have stopped. No birds. Nothing. A great emptiness.

The thought that this was unnatural dawned on him. He tried to push the idea out of his mind. After all, it was not the first time he had killed so many adders. True, but he had never before seen so many together. He had heard talk about old tree-stumps where they might congregate in large numbers to hibernate, but this was rare. Was there not something unusually weird about it all? And then this silence? He was sure that thousands of small eyes were staring at him. Suddenly an army of snakes would pounce upon him. He looked up to make sure there were none in the trees.

He felt ridiculous, and yet he could not overcome his fear.

His eyes came back to the axe. After all, he could not abandon it there. It was a first-rate axe, strong and made of good steel. It had been his since just after the other war.

No, thank you, he was not going to leave his axe among the snakes, certainly not!

He walked on a few paces. Changing his tactics, he stamped the ground, preferring to see the creatures moving on his approach, rather than passing them by without even suspecting they were there. He progressed in this way till he was a few yards from the tree-trunk at a spot where there still lay two of the wooden wedges he had used for splitting the trunks.

All the adders must have left the tree-trunk and scattered in the forest.

To make sure Gaston held his two sticks in his left hand and, picking up one of the wedges, he aimed at the stump and threw with all his might. He hit the tree just below the hole. There was a heavy thud, and immediately two triangular heads stuck out of the hole, while another adder, coiled up at the foot of the trunk, reared up and darted with its forked tongue. Gaston was too far away to hear it hissing, and yet it seemed as though the whole forest was hissing around him. He looked panic-stricken, his eyes flew like a moth from one point to the other. Was the forest really alive? Was it his imagination? Had he lost his mind to the point of seeing adders everywhere? He still hesitated, his body torn between two forces—the one pulling him towards the axe and the other pushing him towards the road.

"Filthy muck!" he shouted, his voice choking.

But he ran, stopping when he thought he saw a movement, ran again, and quickly reached the road.

Still holding his sticks, he took his sledgehammer and the walking-stick. He turned back for a last look towards the wood, where he thought he saw several adders making in his direction. So, spurred by a fear he could no longer control, and intuitively avoiding the short-cut, he kept to the edge of the wood, staying carefully in the middle of the road.

73

It was in vain that Gaston tried to sleep that night. The adders were there, even more so than in the forest. They came right up to him, cold, silent, and relentless. As soon as he began to fall asleep they approached even nearer. He tried to flee, but the reddish-brown creatures were all around him. He hit out. He killed them by the hundreds, but still more came. He woke up with a start, covered in sweat, and when he managed to drive away the visions of his nightmare it only made room for others a little less crazy, but which he could not rid completely from his mind. He thought about his axe. The foresters would find it when they went to pick up his wood. They would see the adders and would assume that he had run away like a panic-stricken child. He also happened to think about his haversack, which he had left in the kitchen. Without realizing it might he not have brought back one or two snakes who would come and attack him when he was asleep? The idea was ridiculous. He knew that. And yet it occurred to him again and again.

Sometimes he suspected himself. He suspected his own reason, wondering whether he had not succumbed to his exhaustion and fled from the forest after having seen only one single adder.

It occurred to him to go back and fetch his axe, but when he rose that morning he realized it was impossible. The struggle and his flight had shaken him so much as to leave him with no strength in reserve. He could scarcely swallow a few mouthfuls of coffee. He was filled with a disgust, and his mouth tasted so bitter that even tobacco smoke seemed unbearable.

He worked as usual in the garden, driven by that kind of instinct he had always possessed which forbade him to be inactive when the weather allowed any kind of work. But his heart was not in it. Nothing moved forward. The day weighed down on him and his surroundings, as though a great exhaustion had flattened the earth. The sky, which was bathed in that light that gives life to plants and birds and insects, looked more dismal to him than the frozen mists of a winter sky. His legs carried him, his hands and arms urged through movements he had performed thousands of times in the course of the years, but it was all extraneous to himself.

That day he ate only bread and cheese for lunch. Very early in the evening he drank a big bowl of vervaine tea and went upstairs to bed. His accumulated tiredness made him sleep right through until dawn practically without dreaming. But he had not regained his strength, and the following days seemed endless. His work did not progress. For the first time in his life he was haunted by the thought that this work was devoid of all meaning. He tilled, he planted and sowed . . . and what would he do with the harvest? Would he get as far as the harvest? If he succeeded in pushing his futile life that far, would he have the strength to gather in the crop? Had he not signed papers guaranteeing him the means of existence until this misery was over at last?

Many times he had to make a great effort to reject the idea of seeking out his son and saying to him, "Do what you like with the garden as long as I don't have to bother with food, heating, and washing."

The past came back to him, but only with memories that surprised him by their clarity. They rose from the subtle depths of his mind. When he was a small child he had known an old assistant who had worked a long time for his father, and who was given shelter and food until he died. The old man lived in a corner of the flour store behind the stables, on piles of empty sacks which were soaked in his sweat. Every one of his wrinkles was a black crease of dirt. The old man must have felt he was disgusting to other people because he refused to come to table and ate his soup all on his own. During the summer he would settle in the sun in a corner of the yard, and in winter he sat leaning against the warm wall between the flour store and the bakehouse. Cockroaches and crickets were his only companions. When they talked about the old people's home he became very angry, began to cry and tremble as he shouted, "I shall go away. I shan't bother you any more. I'll go and die under a bridge!"

The bakers said that this was a kind of blackmail, but they always gave in and left the old man to himself; almost the only friendship he had was for the horse that he groomed until his dying day. Gaston did not remember his death, except that he often heard tell that they had found him one morning curled up on his sacks in the same position that he always went to sleep in every evening. It was during winter. There had been slippery ice on the roads, and the previous night the horse had broken an ankle at the end of the rounds. When he found out that the horse had been slaughtered the old man lay down to sleep without eating his meal and never rose again.

This was not a story that Gaston had told very often, but now he could not stop thinking about it. He would start again from the beginning, trying to remember forgotten details. He could see the old man's face—and his wretchedness. He could even recall the smell rising from the pile of sacks where he slept.

Was he going to end up like that? Obstinately insisting on living alone and rejecting anybody who tried to approach him?

It rained the last two days of that week. Two long days which he spent in his corner by the fire, looking at the windswept garden. His eyes were often drawn to the spot where Fernande had fallen. There were still some frostbitten artichokes left, which the first sunshine had blackened. From a sense of decency, which was quite spontaneous, he had refused to touch this plot. The whole garden had been dug over from the bottom end to the far side of the house, and this narrow strip of earth ran like an embankment from the flagstones bordering the drive to the fence alongside the road.

He looked at it, sighed, and then whispered, "My poor old girl . . . what's to become of me?"

He had never, even in the long solitude of this last winter, experienced the absence of his wife with such sorrow. Because up till now he had not been forced to make up his mind about any problems. The only time that he had made any change in his way of life, by throwing out his eldest son, it had been done in a fit of anger.

He did not really regret that anger which had allowed him to regain some of his strength, but it seemed to him that it had already vanished and gone like a twig at the mercy of a torrent of storm water.

So he sank into his chair, watching the rain streaming down the window-pane, curled himself up inside his thick, woollen jacket, awkwardly waiting, both hoping and fearing he knew not what from the days to come.

74

One morning the following week the forester arrived with the delivery of wood. As soon as Gaston saw the big lorry loaded up with logs come to a halt outside the garden, his fear of appearing ridiculous was reawoken. He thought of locking himself up inside the house and letting the men unload the wood outside the fence, but told himself that if he did not pay the forester that selfsame day he would see him again sooner or later. Besides, Picaud was already on his way down the side-road.

"I'm coming!" Gaston shouted.

He picked up the key and made for the gate. He could see his lime-wood on the top of the load from some distance, longer than the rest and lighter in colour where it had been split.

The forester's assistant was on top of the lorry, ready to start unloading. "Shall I put them in the road?" he shouted.

"Wait a moment," said Picaud.

Gaston unlocked the gate and shook the forester's proffered hand. "There you are," said the forester. "We've brought you the wood you cut yourself as well. I'd never have thought you would have managed that much."

"Indeed," Gaston sighed, "I'm not all that young any longer."

They talked for a moment about the quality of the wood. Then the forester said, "Didn't you forget your axe?"

Gaston felt a mixture of fear and hope all at the same time. "Yes. I remembered it when I reached the bridge at Perrigny. But I was too tired to go back. I thought you might find it."

The man took the axe from the driver's cabin. The steel had rusted. Part of the head was brighter where it had been embedded in the tree-trunk.

Gaston thanked him. He did not dare meet Picaud's look. He walked over to lean the axe against a stone on the drive, and as he came back Picaud asked him, "Well, shall we put it in the street. You're going to take it in today?"

Gaston shook his head. Could he possibly manage to drag all this wood down to the shed on his own in one day? He thought quickly and said, "Listen. The nearest plot hasn't been dug yet; if you could bring your lorry right up to the fence the wood could be thrown across. Then even if I can't manage the lot before nightfall it'll be safer than in the street."

"Easily done."

Picaud climbed into the driver's cabin, started up the engine, drove forward, and then backed. Then he joined his assistant and helped him throw the logs into the garden, as near as possible to the drive. While the men were unloading Gaston took back his axe and fetched the cart. When all the wood was on the ground he took the two men into the house and poured them a glass of wine. He looked at them stealthily, wondering whether they would say anything about the adders, or if, on the other hand, they were keeping quiet only to make fun of him, telling everyone in town that Gaston Dubois had abandoned his axe to the snakes.

As the men were about to leave Gaston was unable to bear it any longer and asked them, "Didn't you find anything else up there in the cut?"

They looked at each other. "No."

"Because I killed two adders. I left them near the tree-trunk."

"Ah," said Picaud, "not much chance of finding them a week later. We often kill them in the cuts, we do. But we only have to turn our back, and the buzzards and falcons come and get them."

Gaston suddenly felt relieved. He accompanied them outside, and asked again, "They were the red kind, two beauties. Are there many of them up there?"

"They're not exactly in short supply. A slope facing straight south—that pleases them, as you can imagine. Especially in spring."

"At this time of year," said the assistant, "you have to be careful because they're spawning. Then they're at their most vicious."

The men told several stories about adders. Then Picaud climbed into the driver's seat as he said, "It's not that we wouldn't like to stay on, but we've still got deliveries to make, and we can't afford the time."

Gaston thanked them again and watched the lorry driving away and disappearing round the bend.

He went back inside, closed the gate, but as he was about to turn the key in the lock he hesitated, shrugged his shoulders, and just pulled out the key and slipped it into the pocket of his apron.

He had watched the two men unloading the logs, which he now had to pile into his cart and take down to the shed at the bottom of the garden, where he would then have to saw and split them before next winter. And because of the steeper slope at the end of the drive, he would not be able to load more than ten or so at a time.

He started working, but a voice inside him kept whispering that he would never finish.

With the third load he was so tired that he could not pull the cart up the slope, and had to carry the logs separately to the shed until the cart was half empty. He was about to start pulling again when Mme Robin appeared. "But you'll never manage all that," she said. "You shouldn't be doing that kind of work at your age."

Gaston was deeply moved by the compassion in her voice and eyes. He was old. He was at the end of his strength. It must show on his face for someone to talk to him like that.

Up till now he had been kept going by a kind of faint hope that prevented him collapsing. And now, because of the strength shown by the two foresters, because of those few gentle words from the young woman who had taken pity on him, because of perhaps an accumulation of thousands of small details, here he was suddenly feeling drained and empty. He held on like grim death for a few more seconds, then he let the shaft of the cart fall, put a hand to his forehead, and whispered, "Yes, it's beyond my strength . . . beyond my strength."

His voice rose in pitch and strangled. He made a desperate effort to stifle a sob that broke bitterly from his lips. "I'm finished . . . finished for good. . . ."

Without shame, without thinking of anything other than his strength that he would never regain, he began to cry.

75

Gaston let himself be guided back to the house.

After this long period during which he had rigidly shut himself away from everything which might approach him from outside, after this seclusion into which he had retired, imposing on himself a working rhythm that no longer corresponded to what his body could tolerate, he gave up. He listened to the friendly words without response. When Mme Robin told him he was wrong to shut himself away in solitude when his eldest son had undertaken to help him he shook his head. "They do as they please . . . as they please. . . . I can feel I'm at the end of my tether."

This was his way of saying that he felt life slipping away, a way of avoiding a word which frightened him a little.

Mme Robin informed Micheline and Paul, who came to see him that same evening. They arrived just as Gaston had lit his fire. Micheline placed a big basket covered with a napkin on the table, kissed Gaston, and began to sob as she said, "Oh, my goodness, poor Father, how hard you have been on us. We've been waiting every day, hoping you'd get in touch."

With his elbows on the table and his head lowered, Gaston merely said, "I'm finished . . . finished. . . . You can do as you like."

They spoke to him for a long time. He did not really listen to what they said. It was like a gentle, monotone song, making him feel sleepy. He stared at the basket and the white mass of the napkin. However, when Paul asked if he had decided to come and live with them he straightened up and summoned a remainder of energy. "No. Don't start that again. I'm not leaving this place except feet first."

"You're an obstinate cuss," growled the son.

But Micheline leaned over towards Gaston and said in a gentle voice, "Now look, Paul, if our poor, dear father wants to stay in his own house we mustn't argue. When you're his age you'll feel the same. You become fond of things. We're all the same. I understand that very well."

She uncovered the basket and took out a can, which she placed on the stove. "This is vegetable soup—nice and thick, the way you like it—and the vegetables have been sieved very finely. In the saucepan there's peas and bacon. I also brought you some cold chicken, some figs, some jam, and cheese."

"But I don't need all that."

"You must eat. Then you'll see, you'll get your strength back. You'll see how well we're going to look after you."

"My strength will never return. Though I'll need some to finish bringing in my wood at least, and chopping it up. And then I've begun on the garden—"

Paul interrupted him, "I'll send a man round tomorrow to bring your wood in, and I'll send someone to cut it up. As for the garden, we'll also help you with what you have started. All you'll have to do is to direct them. As for the rest, if you would only listen to me . . ."

Gaston gave a long sigh. There was silence. He looked at Paul, then at Micheline, next at the basket and all the things spread out on the table. He turned towards the window. The last glimmer of daylight was insufficient to show up their faces. "You really ought to light the lamp and close the shutters for me," he said to his son.

Micheline lowered the lamp and lifted the lamp-glass clumsily. It rang out against the shade. She lit the wick, which Gaston then had to adjust. He had been thinking about Fernande as he watched his daughter-in-law. How competent she had been in all her actions! The peace he had enjoyed when he was able to rely on her to cope with all their worries!

Paul had closed the shutters. He sat down again and lit a half-smoked cigarette, which he then crushed out in the ash-tray. He offered one to his father, who refused. "No, I've just smoked one. Even tobacco, you know, gives me hardly any pleasure now."

There was another painful silence. The thought of the garden, where Paul wanted to start the building works, hovered between them almost palpably. Gaston could feel it. Paul looked at his father, and then asked, "What's the garden worth, now that you can't cultivate it any longer?"

Gaston shrugged his shoulders. "I know. The earth dies quickly when you don't spend any time on it."

"Well, then, d'you believe that's a good thing—grass and weeds growing everywhere and spreading across where you're still cultivating a bit to keep yourself occupied?"

"Of course not."

He did not get any further or ask Paul what exactly he planned to do. He said only, "You speak of the earth, but there are also the fruit-trees. They don't take much work, and fruit is very profitable, after all."

"If that's all there's involved you know well enough that I wouldn't do you out of any profit you might make with the fruit. And then, what's in the beds in front? The big plum-tree. That's old. It's—"

"It's old, but it still yields well. And the plums are good."

He was attached to this old tree he had planted and cared for over so many years. "And besides," he continued, "there are some peach-trees now at their best."

"Listen. I'm not arguing. It's up to you to work out how much you make a year, and I'll pay whatever you say."

Gaston could see the garden before his eyes. He remembered the summers with the produce being gathered. The labour he had expended on this earth. He also imagined his feelings on seeing the weeds gain control. He knew he would not have the courage not to try to deal with them. His health would be spent in that struggle, which he might not even win. "You know that I don't need any money," he said in the end. "All the same, seeing it all churned up—"

"Don't exaggerate. You know we only want a small strip."

When Gaston did not reply Micheline asked, as she folded the napkin and put it in the empty basket, "Would you like to give me your washing tonight, or would you rather the maid took it in the morning?"

"I did a little washing last week, but pumping the water makes my back ache."

"There you are," said Paul. "There's another detail you hadn't thought about. But if I start building the first thing will be to pipe in the water-supply. Even if you don't want it brought into the house, you could always have a tap at the end of the garden."

"I'm not having a trench dug up to there!"

Gaston had almost shouted, and Paul hastily said, "No, of course not. We'll do it the way you want. All I ask is that you let me start on the garages . . . that's all."

Gaston stood up to go and put a log on the stove—the kettle was not singing so loudly. He did this slowly. It was not that he needed time to think it over. He had already made his decision. He was only granting himself a short reprieve. As long as he did not reply, the entire garden belonged to him. He knew that the words he was about to speak would be final. They were there, ready to be spoken, but he lacked the strength to pronounce them.

When he had closed the stove again he leaned down to rake the embers and clear the ash. Having hung the poker back on the brass rail, he watched it swinging. He could feel his son and daughter-in-law watching him all the time. The poker was still swinging just a little. When it had come to rest Gaston turned around slowly towards his son, coughed for a while, and finally said in a wavering voice, "All right. As you need it so badly, do it. I'll try and put up with it in the short time that's left to me."

76

Yet once more Gaston Dubois had overestimated his authority. Yet once more he had sized up the situation like an old man who knows nothing about modern times. He had imagined a few workmen arriving one morning and tearing out the fence, from which he would be able to recover the stakes. He would keep the best and cut up the rest for good, solid logs. During the four weeks that passed before the work started he spent most of his time in the first vegetable plots. He accustomed himself slowly to the idea of having a yard up front. Behind the house he prepared a place for the workmen to bring the topsoil when they dug out the foundations. He had organized everything in his mind.

Then on a Monday morning he was dragged out of his sleep by the rumbling of an engine which periodically made the house shake. He lay still in bed for a moment, trying to guess from where the noise might be coming. Full daylight penetrated the slats in the shutters. The rumbling came from the street. Gaston leaned out of the window. His hands clenched the windowsill, and all he could do was to whisper, "Good God! Oh, good God, it can't be true!"

He was quite unable to move, incapable of saying another word.

The fence had already gone. There was a lorry parked in the street, and a huge machine—what it was called, Gaston did not know—tore up the earth in his garden. A long, jointed arm bent itself double, unfolded itself, brandishing a tool whose jaws bit into the good, black earth, lifted it by the barrow-load, and poured it into the back of the lorry.

"Good God, it can't be true!"

He ran down the staircase and, without even taking the time to put on his jacket, he reached the garden.

He had been able to see only a part of the yard from the window, but as soon as he reached the drive he could ascertain that the whole left side of the garden had already been ripped up over a distance of more than thirty yards. He could see only two men, not counting the one in the cabin of the long-armed monster. The torn and twisted iron gate lay in the middle of the road alongside the garden. The drive itself had been torn up, and Gaston had to work his way around the quagmire to reach the road. As soon as he was within hailing distance of the two men leaning against the lorry he shouted, "But what are you doing? You must be mad!"

The workmen looked at him. One of them took a few steps towards him. He was a thin little man with black hair and moustache, probably about forty years old. He had not been able to understand what Gaston had shouted. When he had joined him he asked, "What was that you said?"

He had a strong Italian accent.

"I said you must be mad. What are you doing? You're wrecking everything!"

The man seemed surprised. He turned round towards his mate, who had not moved. Gaston pointed at the lorry half full of topsoil with stakes and bits of wire sticking out. "What are you going to do with that?"

"We're taking it to the tip."

"To the tip? Earth of that kind? And why d'you want to take it away? You should only take away the subsoil. Stop it at once! This can't go on."

The man walked over to the side of the machine, jumped on to the running-board, and began to talk and gesticulate. The long, metal arm laid its huge jaws on the ground, the engine slowed down to a tickover, and the Italian came back followed by the driver.

This one was French, hardly any taller than his companion, but broad and massive. He wore a blue cotton vest, leaving his shoulders with their knotted muscles exposed. His hands and forearms were black with engine grease. "What's going on?" he asked.

Gaston explained once more that he could not understand, that this was not the way he had envisaged it would happen.

The man said, "I'm just doing what I've been told. One and a half yards had to be dug out before starting on the foundations. That's what it says in the plans."

"One and a half yards," stuttered Gaston. "But—but this topsoil. I'd made room for it over there behind the house."

The men looked at each other. Then the driver said, "But how d'you think the lorry could get down there?"

"I thought—anyway—but it can't be done, it can't be done."

Gaston had not even dared to mention the wheelbarrow. He looked at the big machine whose engine was spluttering as the steel plates on the sides shook. He looked at the lorry with its double wheels almost as tall as himself. Never before had he felt so weak, so small, as poor as at this moment.

"And my fence," he muttered again.

"We put the gate in the side-road. We can carry it over to the house if you like."

Gaston scarcely managed to respond. He felt crushed. There he had come to send the men and their machine away, and now he felt overwhelmed with weakness. As he stood there, silent and still, the driver went back to his cabin. As soon as he was in his seat the engine roared into action, the little chimney alongside the cabin belched out blue smoke, the caterpillar tracks grated as the arm rose up in the air opening its jaws with their long, shining teeth.

For many years now Gaston had dug over this earth every spring with his fork. The machine's teeth were made of the same steel, they shone as well, but they bit into the earth with a power that was a thousand times greater. A kind of evil fury. Every wound made Gaston feel ill, as though attacked by the steel himself.

The Italian had stayed near him. They looked at each other for a moment. Then Gaston asked, "The trees—if you could—you must leave them in the road. I'll cut them up."

"Of course. That's easily done."

They looked at each other, and Gaston thought he detected a gleam of pity in the man's black eyes. The man asked, "Shall we carry the gate down for you?"

"My God, we can't leave it over there."

The man called his mate, and between them they took the gate and carried it without stopping once to the shed. Gaston knew he could not even have lifted it. Nevertheless, he remembered the day he had put it up. He still had the bakery then. He had done it one evening with his assistant's help; and it had been no more difficult than for these two men.

When they had leaned the gate against one of the beams in the shed Gaston said to them, "Would you like a glass of wine?"

The two men followed him into the house, where Gaston took out some glasses and a bottle of wine, saying, "You must call in your friend."

"No," said the Italian, "he can't stop just like that. Machines are hired by the hour. They're expensive."

Gaston raised his glass. "Here's good health to you."

"And to you too," said the Italian.

The other one raised his glass too and said a few words that Gaston could not understand. "Isn't he French?"

"No. And he doesn't talk. He's a prisoner. But he's not German. Seems to be Polish, conscripted into the German army. There's only one thing he understands."

The Italian turned towards the other and laughingly said, "War kaput . . . War over."

The other began to laugh, and raised his hand as he said, "War kaput, War over."

It was true. The War had been over for more than a week. The Germans had surrendered on May 8th. Gaston had read about it in the newspapers that M. Robin brought him, but this event made no difference to him.

Since 1939 the War had swept through the town twice. Each time the house and the garden had been spared. Now today the War was over, but he felt there was something else that was over too. And then other things were only beginning. New times were starting, and he did not understand them. A time which took no account of the old man he had become while waiting for he knew not what.

Fernande was gone. The garden was going, and there he was in the kitchen, drinking a glass of wine with an Italian and another man, whose country they were not sure of.

Certainly, the world was no longer what it had been.

"We must go," said the Italian.

They emptied their glasses and went out. Gaston followed them. The lorry was full, and the man who did not speak

French climbed into the cabin. The engine rumbled, and the lorry set off down the road. The Italian had gone off too, and when Gaston turned round he saw him climbing into another lorry exactly like the first, but which he had not noticed because it had been parked farther up the road in the recess by the *école normale*. The empty lorry came and took the place of the one that had just taken away the fence and the first load of that good, black earth which Gaston had enriched with so much manure, and so often drenched with his sweat. He watched the heavy machine going back and forth for a moment longer, and, exhausted, he walked slowly back to his house.

77

That summer was longer and more dismal than a winter. Gaston drifted into lazy inactivity in his house, which he never left except to draw his water, go to the shed, or cut up his wood for an hour or two every day. Sometimes he would take his tools out of the cupboard, oil them, and put them back in place. He knew that these planes, chisels, drills, were no use to him, but he went on looking after them as he had always done as a matter of course. Each one had its own story, which he would tell himself. So a moment from the past would return and enliven his loneliness with its happy faces.

He had given up the garden. The part that the building works had spared became overgrown slowly with the grass that he had fought back for such a long time. Paul had sent one of his workmen two or three times to help Gaston, but these visits had stopped and Gaston had said nothing. He had even given up complaining.

When he looked towards the street the cement walls which rose up from the ground the whole width of the garden filled him only with a kind of disgust. When the weather was not too hot he went to sit near the pump, behind the boxwood-tree, which hid the yard from view. His hands clasped over his walking-stick, his body sinking into itself, and his neck drawn down between his shoulders, his eyes half closed below the peak of his cap, he spent several hours reviewing the course of his life. His youth was the time he returned to most willingly, trying to remember names, faces, places, and dates which sometimes became a little confused.

He was sitting there one afternoon in the month of August, half asleep, when Françoise arrived. He heard her calling near the house. "Anyone there? Anyone there?"

He recognized her voice at once, and his heart contracted so much that it was difficult for him to shout, "Here I am!"

He stood up and walked along the drive, which was now no more than a narrow path amongst the grass where a few stubborn flowers grew here and there. Françoise came down towards him, and when they met Gaston took off his cap, kissed the young woman, and whispered, "My goodness . . . my goodness . . ."

His throat tightened. He struggled to drive back his tears. They walked back to the house, where Françoise had left a black pram with its hood down. A big baby with curly, blond hair was lying in it with bare legs and chubby cheeks, looking at the sky with its big blue eyes.

Gaston leaned over. He wanted to speak, but a sob broke within him so that he said in a shaking voice, with a tone rising until it was no more than a strangled cry, "It isn't true. It isn't true. My poor wife . . . If she were here . . ."

Françoise had picked up the baby and brought it nearer to Gaston. He felt clumsy. He let go his walking-stick and stretched out his trembling hand towards the child's bare arm.

"You see how he resembles Julien," said Françoise.

Gaston took off his cap again to kiss the child, who laughed and waved his hands.

They stood there for a few minutes, embarrassed and not knowing what to say. Gaston was smiling, but the tears kept on flowing down his white-stubbled cheeks. He wiped them, blew his nose several times, and muttered, "We must go up. We can't stay here."

Françoise followed him, carrying the baby. They sat down in the kitchen, where the shutters were closed.

"It's chilly in here," said Gaston. "Won't the little one be cold?"

"No, he's quite all right."

"He's full of life."

He looked at the child, and it was Julien that he saw. In the same place, on Fernande's knees. "And Julien?"

"He wasn't able to come. There's too much to do in the house where he's working."

Gaston looked down. He wanted to speak, but what he had to say was not easy. He was about to make up his mind when Françoise asked, "And how about you, Father, how is it going?"

"Me . . . Oh, I . . ."

After a long silence, while he clutched the edge of the table with his hand, and without having really made up his mind, the words came tumbling out, "I'm finished. I know there wasn't anything much left for me to do, but all the same . . . all the same. They're pushing me into the grave before my time. Into my grave. You've seen what they're doing up there in front. They've turned everything upside down. Everything. And they've shut me up here behind that cement. When the north wind blows there's an unbearable draught. I won't be able to keep warm this winter. It's dreadful. They had no right to do this to me. They could have waited till I was gone. I haven't much time left, anyway."

He stopped. He had spoken loudly, and the baby was looking at him, intrigued.

"Oh, Lord, I've frightened him."

"No, no, he's listening to you."

"Perhaps it's time for him to have something."

"No, he's just had his bottle. I'll go and put him in his pram. He'll fall asleep."

She went down and came back very quickly. Gaston had not moved. He had other things to say, and he felt he must speak. He listened to the young woman explaining that she had called at Saint-Claude and was staying in Lons-le-Saunier only for a few hours to see him and show him his grandson. Her voice was still gentle, and her eyes showed a great tenderness. When she stopped Gaston wanted to speak. He muttered, "You must tell Julien . . ."

But he did not go on. The words choked him, but refused to come out. "He must come and see me," he tried again. "He must—it's important. I can't explain, but he must come. I shouldn't have done what I did. It's important for him as well. For him and for you."

He wrung these painful words out, one by one. "Do you understand?" he asked.

"Julien will come and see you. He'll come as soon as there's less work."

"But what about a Sunday? Couldn't he come on a Sunday?"

Françoise lowered her eyes. She seemed to hesitate before replying. As she lifted her gaze again her eyes were shining more brightly. She quickly explained, "You understand, with the baby, I had to stop working. Julien feels as I do. We don't want strangers looking after him. So, as we haven't much to live on, Julien works at a pastry-cook's on Sundays."

"That's not a bad thing at all. Perhaps he'll then go on and really take up his old trade again. It might be better paid than decorating, and then he might hope to save."

Françoise replied with merely an evasive gesture, and Gaston understood that this was still not his son's idea. However, he could not prevent himself from adding, "If only you could come back here."

But that was as far as he went.

It was quiet and cool in the shady kitchen. Nothing had changed since Fernande's death. Yet Gaston was alone. He knew this. The thought was with him every moment. Françoise had come, but she was going away again, taking the baby with her. He would never see it again.

Nothing had changed inside the little house, but as soon as you opened the bead curtain and went outside on the landing there was the new yard, the cement wall, with its reinforcing iron rods sticking up like pikes. The cement had devoured the garden and killed the trees.

"You've no idea how they make me suffer."

Gaston had spoken without thinking. No doubt because it was a sentence he repeated to himself many a time during the long days when he was alone.

He stood up, walked over to the scullery, and came back with a saucepan. He lifted the lid. "Here, smell that."

"But you must throw that away. It's gone bad."

"Of course I'm going to throw it away. But that's what they brought me yesterday. Sometimes they don't come for three days at a time."

"But they ought to—"

Gaston raised his hand in interruption. "There's nothing to be said about it. Nothing!"

He took the saucepan back into the scullery, and then returned to sit down. Seconds went by. They looked at each other without speaking, and Gaston stiffened because he was afraid of giving in to his misery again. He continued in a harder voice, "There's nothing to be said. It's my own fault, so I'll have to manage on my own. Luckily I have good neighbours. You should go and see Mme Robin. She'll tell you—she'll tell you a lot. How they make me suffer . . ."

He turned his head and stared at the empty grate. Tears rose into his eyes again. His voice trembled once more as he repeated, "You must tell Julien—you must tell Julien that—"

He stopped. The baby had begun to cry down below, and Françoise ran outside. Gaston hesitated a moment and then joined her. She had picked the child up into her arms and wiped two large tears off his round cheeks. He had stopped crying already.

"What was the matter?" asked Gaston.

"Nothing. He must have felt lonely. Or it could have been his teeth. He doesn't cry very often, you know."

When the baby saw Gaston he smiled and waved his fist.

"My goodness, he'd be happy here in the garden. It's still

peaceful down at the bottom, and the air is so much better than in town."

He watched the baby for a moment without speaking and added in a more serious voice, "Poor little fellow. Who knows what he'll find in life. The world's not the same. The other day M. Robin talked about that bomb they dropped on Japan. Of course, it meant the war was over. But what does that mean? Here am I, at the end of my life. And when I see all this madness I've no great regrets about leaving."

"We must hope that this war is the last. If not, it wasn't worth all the misery."

"My dear," sighed Gaston, "that's what we said in 1918. And you see . . ."

Françoise had put the baby down to sit in the pram.

"We could go down to the bottom of the garden," Gaston suggested. "I always sit down there. It's peaceful there at least."

The young woman pushed the pram down the drive. The grass made the going difficult. She had to stop and lift the front in order to turn it round. It was easier to pull it.

"If my poor wife had seen her garden in this state, my God, she wouldn't have believed it. Would you like to take some flowers with you? That's about all that's left from the time she was here."

"I don't want to take any with me. They will be faded by the time I get home, and I've already enough to carry with the baby. But I'll pick some all the same. When I leave I'll go by the cemetery. It would be nice to bring her flowers from her own garden."

"To be sure, she'd be happy. To be sure. I can't walk that far any longer, I haven't the strength left."

They had reached the place where Gaston had left his chair. "I'll go and find you a seat," he said.

"No, it's not worth it. You stay with the baby. I'll go and pick some flowers, and then it'll be time for me to leave."

"You'll find some secateurs and raffia behind the cellar door."

Françoise went off. Alone with the baby, Gaston pulled up his chair near the pram and sat down. The child looked at him. There was a rattle at the foot of the pram. Gaston picked it up and shook it in front of the child, who began to laugh.

"Oh, the little mite," said Gaston. "You're a real little Dubois. Hey, you see how happy you'd be here in the garden. If your mammy were with you . . . If your mammy were with you . . ."

Once more he tried to control himself, but he had not the strength. As he continued playing with the child, whose chubby hands clung to the rattle, the old man began to cry silently.

78

After Françoise's visit Gaston lived with the image of the child smiling to him. The memory was much closer to him than others he constantly evoked, but more hazy. Blurred with tears. Now he no longer cried. He lived like a sick plant whose sap slowly congeals as the season advances.

Letters from Julien and Françoise were less rare. Since the fence had come down the postman brought them right up to the house. Gaston lay in wait for him. He was a large man of about fifty, with a red face and a black moustache. He fancied a drop of wine. Gaston would offer him a glass and ask him to read the letter. The man read slowly and sometimes stumbled over a word. When he had finished he invariably said, "There, that's all."

And invariably Gaston would ask, "He doesn't say anything about when he's coming?"

"No, he doesn't say anything about that."

When the first frost set in Gaston had to stay in the kitchen. Every morning from ten o'clock onwards he would stand by the window, the peak of his cap touching the pane, and look up the drive towards the road. By eleven o'clock he knew that the postman had passed without bringing any letter, and he would sit down again in his chair.

The days passed by this way, and Gaston went out only to fetch wood and water. He never went up to the bedroom any more, but one morning he heard a heavy thud which made him jump. He rose and climbed upstairs. It was raining, and the heavy sky gave no more than a grey, dull light into the room, which left the corners in shadows. At first he could see nothing unusual. He looked above all at the ceiling, fearing that a tile might have shifted. At last, as he walked towards the bed, he saw a white area in the faded, blue-grey wallpaper. The paper was torn, and a piece of plaster was missing.

"It's the photograph. The photograph."

He walked round between the bed and the wall. A big, gilt frame was on the floor, with the glass broken. It was Gaston himself who had framed this photograph of his parents, which had been taken in the drive in the garden on one summer's morning which he could remember in every detail.

Gaston wiped his hand across the damp wall. Then he picked up the frame, which he carried over to the window. He repeated, "The photograph . . . The photograph . . ." That was all.

He stayed there looking at it for a long time. Then, as he felt the damp, cold air penetrate his body, he returned to the kitchen.

All that day he lived with his parents, remembering their gestures, their speech, the way they lived, and, above all, the work in the bakery which they had taught him. Because of this, perhaps, because of this house and garden in which he had come to live after them, it had seemed to him that they had never been really dead. They had continued their life in his memory, in this place where nothing had changed. And now this morning, because the rain had soaked through the wall and loosened the plaster in this room that he never opened any more, the big photograph had fallen down. Was this a sign that everything was coming to an end? That everything was already over?

Gaston was tormented by this thought until the evening. He grumbled and moaned about the winter, which had arrived before autumn was even over; he grumbled about the weather, about the house; and he cursed the building which Paul was having constructed and which he blamed for making the garden much colder.

That evening he went to bed very early.

In spite of the hot-water bottle he had put in his bed, he found it difficult to keep warm, and this prevented him from falling asleep.

The next morning he awoke drenched in sweat and breathing very fast. It was not light yet. However, he got out of bed, lit the fire, made himself some tea, and changed the damp sheets.

Fear spurred him on to do everything quickly. He had several fits of coughing which tore the phlegm from the depths of his chest.

"That's all I needed, all I needed . . . And I'm all on my own."

Before going back to bed he had opened the shutters. Leaning back against his two pillows, he watched for the dawn. The rain had changed into a fine drizzle that he had felt on his hands and face when he had leaned out of the window. All he could hear was the drainpipe dripping into the big galvanized tub. "If I can't go out the tub will overflow, and the water will run down into the cellar."

The darkness stuck to the window-panes, a blue-grey darkness pierced only by the distant lights from the factory which could just be discerned beyond the walls of the *école normale*.

The sky grew paler imperceptibly.

It was not the advent of day, but a slow metamorphosis of the night. It was this drizzle, up till now invisible, which gradually established itself behind the window-panes.

When Gaston arose to put more wood on the fire the roof of the school was shining and even paler than the sky. But the garden was not there. Darkness refused to raise its siege. It clung to the ground all around the house, which had no connection with the rest of the world. Only a few yards of garden separated the house from the road, but it was enough to make Gaston feel utterly alone with his burning fever. It was as though a fire raged in his chest, and yet his back was clammy, and he was shivering constantly. He stayed for a moment by the stove, his hands clenching the brass rail, his back turned to the heat from the grate, his thighs right up against the doors behind which the wood was moaning. Because of the heavy weather, the chimney was drawing badly, and the wood burnt slowly.

"Fine thing, being all alone . . . I might die . . . die from sheer wretchedness."

He said this without a trace of anger; more because he needed to speak and chase away the silence and the night. He said it because these were the only words that occurred to him. And these words evoked Julien's face from the shadows, and Françoise's gentle smile even more strongly.

He had pulled on just his long underpants and his woollen jacket on top of his nightshirt. "Even so, I ought to get dressed. You never know."

He went back to the bedside, put on his trousers and socks, and returned to the kitchen. He was not hungry; another bowl of tea was enough. He rolled a cigarette, but the first puff made him cough. He let the cigarette go out of its own accord between his fingers, shook off the ash, and stowed the end in his tobacco-tin. "If I can't even smoke any more, what's there left for me?"

He did not want to go back to bed. It seemed to him that staying in bed would only provoke the illness. He went to look for a blanket, wrapped himself up in this, and returned to sit near the fire. He stared at the side-road slowly appearing out of the mist. Strictly he was not expecting anything. Only M. Robin walked that way, but he never left the house this early.

His eyes began to hurt from staring so fixedly, the lids became heavy, blinked a little, and then shut. He coughed from time to time. When he stood up to spit in the grate or to throw on another log he felt his legs bending under his weight. Black dots danced before his eyes.

At the end of the morning, when Mme Robin came to see him, Gaston had dozed off in his chair. He jumped when he heard the knocking. As the door was locked he rose to go and open it, and he had to lean against the table. The effort provoked a more violent bout of coughing than before. When it subsided and his eyes were full of tears and his ears buzzing he heard the young woman say to him, "We must tell your son. He'll call the doctor. You can't stay like this."

Gaston had wiped his eyes, but his vision was still blurred. "Oh, no. No, no, it's nothing. If only you would make me a mustard plaster."

"But that's not enough. You must see a doctor."

He found a little strength again. "No. They'll send me into hospital. I don't want that. I don't want that."

"But you must at least go to bed."

"No. I feel better by the fire."

Mme Robin prepared the mustard plaster, went to fetch a basket of wood, and then she again spoke about calling the doctor. Gaston obstinately refused. When she left he cried, "Don't call anyone. No-one. I don't want it."

The fear of his illness tortured him, but the fear of having to leave the house was even stronger.

Mme Robin came back to see him several times and stayed with him for a good deal of the afternoon. He forced himself to talk, to appear strong, to control his cough.

"There you are," he said towards the end of the afternoon, "I'm better, much better. I knew there was no need to disturb anybody."

The young woman left, and as soon as she was out of the door Gaston went back to bed without undressing and pulled two blankets and a big eiderdown over himself.

79

His temperature rose during the following night. He could feel it at work inside him. He had left the small lamp alight by the bedhead, but at about four in the morning, as the flame was dying down, he wanted to get up and fetch a candle. He sat up slowly on the side of the bed, put on his trousers, and waited a few minutes. The fire must have gone out because it was cold in the room. He pictured all the movements he would have to make to relight it, and the work involved seemed impossibly hard. When he tried to stand up he felt giddy. The whole house rocked, the floor disappeared from under his feet, and he had to sit down again. "Finished," he whispered, "finished."

He tried again twice, then, riveted with fear of falling, he clung to the back of the chair where he had hung his velvet jacket and managed to relieve himself in the chamber-pot.

After that he climbed into bed again. Sweat was pouring off his face and body. His nightcap was soaking and cold, but he did not dare take it off.

When his exhaustion had lessened he began to think almost serenely about dying here, like this, with no-one to help him. He would be snuffed out like the lamp drained of its oil, whose tiny flame flickered, lighting only the marble of the bedside table and the corner of the sideboard near by. He lay there with this thought until the flame darted up in a final burst, went out, leaving a glowing red dot no bigger than a cigarette-end. When the red dot had disappeared Gaston raised himself on his pillows and began to cry, "Bastards! Bastards! They'll leave me to die. They'll leave me to die like a dog. Bastards! Bastards!"

He fell back, exhausted. His head sank down amongst the pillows, and his eyes stopped scanning the darkness.

When he woke up Mme Robin was standing at the bedside. The previous evening Gaston had given her the key, and this was his first thought now. "You were right to take the key," he whispered. "It's not going so well, you know. I don't think I would have managed to get up and open the door."

He felt almost comfortable lying there in bed, and her presence in the house reassured him. "Do you think you could light my fire?" he asked.

"I've already done it, M. Dubois. And I've brought you some coffee."

He drank a bowl of hot, milky coffee, thinking how frightened he had been of this illness, which was already getting better. "Perhaps I can get up."

Mme Robin made him stay in bed. "I'm going to fetch my charwoman, and we'll change your sheets. But don't you move while you're waiting."

She hurried off and returned with the Italian woman, who helped Gaston over to sit by the fire.

"You shouldn't have gone to bed with your clothes on."

"I was cold. Besides, for getting up . . ."

He stopped. He fought against his cough for a few seconds, but he had to give in. This bout revived the burning in his chest, and he began to sweat again. The women made him undress and go to bed. His breathing was quick and shallow. Once he was in bed he heard the women talking in the kitchen without being able to understand what they were saying. He also heard the door opening and then shutting again, and he called out, "Are you there?"

The Italian woman came in to him. "Madame has gone out, but she's coming back."

Gaston wanted to ask whether she had gone to call a doctor, but he kept quiet. The woman stayed near the bed, looking embarrassed, not knowing what to do with her hands. He closed his eyes and waited.

When he came round again he realized he had slept for a long time. The sound of voices coming from the kitchen had woken him. "What is it?" he cried out.

Micheline entered and immediately said, "Don't worry, Father. We're here. And the doctor's coming. It's nothing. A touch of flu. It's quite normal with this weather, you know."

Gaston looked at her through half-closed eyes. She seemed very distant to him, and her voice reverberated in a strange way. When she had spoken about a doctor coming he felt a small dart of anger, but he said nothing. He no longer had the strength to cry out, and he feared the cough which brought on the pain in his chest.

However, he found a renewed strength after the doctor's visit when Paul said to him, "You'll have to come to our place. The car is waiting outside. We will carry you."

"No! I don't want to, I don't want to."

He had not cried out very loudly, but enough to bring on his ailment. When he had coughed and spat he felt so weak that he did not even attempt to resist. He could only tell them what to take with him in a bag. His razor, his shaving-brush, the leather thong for sharpening the blade, the case containing his money, and a few papers.

"If there's anything else you need I'll come and fetch it."

"You might have looked after me here," he whispered again. "You must tell Julien to come . . . his wife. . . ."

Paul raised his voice. It was hard, and he hissed, "Be quiet. You're in no state to decide. There's no-one free to stay here with you, and you'll be warmer over there."

"Don't shout," Gaston begged, "don't shout."

He felt as weak as a baby, and this feeling was emphasized when he was wrapped up in a blanket and they carried him off. One of his son's drivers, a big fellow of about thirty, took him in his arms and lifted him, saying, "Don't be frightened, Grandpa. There's no danger. We'll reach the car in next to no time."

With his mouth and nose covered by the blanket, Gaston only felt the damp, cold air pricking at his eyes. They filled with tears at once, and he saw the house and what remained of the garden through an iridescent, yellow mist. "The sun's come out . . ."

"The sun," said the driver with a laugh. "There's been no sun for ten days."

They moved around the new building, which now had two

floors. Gaston saw an enormous grey bulk pitted with black shadows passing in front of his eyes.

When they reached the car the driver began to laugh again as he said, "I could have carried you like that as far as Montciel—even farther."

The man climbed in next to Gaston; Micheline sat in front next to Paul, who was driving.

"Did you close the shutters properly?"

"Yes," Paul shouted, "don't worry."

"And the door, did you lock it?"

"Of course," said Micheline. "There's no need for alarm."

Every jolt of the car echoed through him. He tried to look at the street, but his tears made everything blurred. His voice was hardly audible as he whispered almost constantly, "Oh, God, to go like this . . . leave your house. . . . To go like this . . . abandoning everything. . . ."

He was carried into a room at his son's place which was far too big, with too high a ceiling, and badly lit from two windows facing a narrow courtyard. There was a big, square enamelled stove, and Gaston at once noticed a bucket of coal. As soon as he was lying in the very low bed he gasped, "Open the window. I can't breathe. Coal fire in a bedroom . . . it's unhealthy."

"Oh, no," cried Paul, "that's because you have been breathing the cold air. You'll get used to it."

"Don't shout like that. I'm not deaf. Besides, it hurts."

Paul shrugged his shoulders and left the room, followed by his driver.

"Don't you worry," said Micheline. "The maid is going to bring you some tea. And the nurse is coming at four o'clock to give you an injection."

"Do I need injections?"

He could not understand his daughter-in-law's reply. She spoke with her back turned towards him as she rummaged around in a cupboard. He added to himself, "Do I need an injection for where I'm going?"

80

The following day Gaston lost all sense of time. When he emerged from sleep at some hour during the day or night, all he could see was a faint light of no definite colour dimly illuminating the wall and blankets. When he stirred his hands he saw them moving far away from himself, blurred and transparent. His chest hurt. It was not the burning sensation he had feared so much, but like a weight, a sheath which tightened now and again, preventing him breathing.

When the pain subsided he tried hard not to move so as to avoid rousing it again.

There was a constant movement of images on a plane between himself and what he could still see of this room, between himself and the faces that approached him. Sometimes they were very sharp, sometimes very hazy, sometimes they were superimposed on each other. One followed the next, passing slowly, or else they began to slip by in a jolting, jerky rhythm.

The clearest and most compelling were linked with his childhood, his youth, and his daily work. The dough in the kneading trough. The light from the bake-oven and the furnace spitting out long flames. The shovel he used for the loaves, with its endlessly long handle scraping across the burning-hot oven bricks. The loads of wood. The hot bread; its crusty smell came back to him, inundating the room. Sometimes the dough he was kneading with his bare arms became grey, then brown, then almost black. His movements changed too; the prongs of a fork replaced his arms. It was no longer dough, but garden earth turned over, raked, hoed, dug, spread with manure and leaf-mould a thousand times. The smoke no longer smelt like the dry wood burning brightly in the bakehouse furnace, but was acrid with plants torn up in autumn and burnt in huge piles on misty mornings. Sometimes children's shouts and laughter rose up, calling in reply to Fernande's voice. Julien ran through the smoke towards school. Could it be him? Was it not his little boy, who had grown bigger in the house where they were now all living together?

In the end it was all extinguished, like the autumn bonfires when a heavy drizzle falls in the evening. And then the fog lifted, a watery sun appeared, the early morning wind re-kindled the fires, and other memories surged through in ever-quickening pace. The dead and the alive intermingled. The dead from the War or from work. Laughter was farther away than the sighs, happiness less alive than sorrows. Here and there the theme of a song came back in snatches, but only feebly because of the distance. It was from a grape-harvest festival where they had sung about the golden corn, the poplars, and cherry-time. It was never more than a very timid echo soon stifled by the groans of men mixing dough or tilling the earth.

Then, more strongly even than all the others, the vision of the adders crawling all over the place came back relentlessly again and again; they slithered underfoot, crept under the door, coming to imprison Gaston's frozen legs, and he would be jerked restlessly. This memory was linked with the forest, the felled trees, the trimmed branches, the work he had done on his own or together with Fernande.

Because Fernande was always there, quiet but alert, a still profile, the tired features hardly disturbed by the other memories.

She was there with each job that Gaston started again and again without respite. She was there for the earth, for the bread, for the wood, for the thick snow on the steps and the garden. She belonged to every season, every effort, every torment.

Her silence was part of this life which began again relentlessly. She stayed alive even when Gaston could see no more than her soldier's coat lying near the artichokes on the frozen garden earth.

Soon there was nothing but the fog of an endless twilight where the only living thing was Fernande's bright eyes and slight, sad smile.

The smile stiffened. The shadows withdrew. In the end they

disappeared at the moment Gaston regained enough clarity to remember that Fernande had died before himself.

Then another smile was born out of the fog.

Françoise.

Was Julien not coming with her? Were they not coming to take him back home where he would get better? Back to his house and garden?

Had they sent for Julien and this Françoise, whose voice was as gentle as Fernande's?

There are faces, looks, movements, voices that can heal. There are beings whose mere presence makes pain and sorrow go away. But such beings are never there when you call them!

He would have to find the strength to call! To cry out a name.

To think that he used to be so strong, and now he could not even pronounce a single word.

As the light grew dimmer sounds also diminished. However, when he awoke after several hours' sleep he occasionally regained a clarity that allowed him to hear even the careful footsteps on the bedroom floor. He could understand all that was said around him, and he tried to reply. But no sounds would come from his throat, and the slightest effort left him breathless.

He was at his son's place, in a room so large and tall that he could see neither the ceiling nor the walls. His bed was in the centre of this enormous void where voices had a strange resonance, where every sound was distorted, amplified, and broken into echoes around the walls, to be lost in this night endlessly winding in search of a dawn.

Night went on its way, but always into other nights as thick and dark.

He too went his way through the middle of this night, carried on a surge which rocked this too-big and too-deep bed.

How many days since he had left his house? Where was his garden? Had the door been shut properly? Was the fire out when he left the kitchen? And the shed? The tools? Would the oil protect them against damp until spring?

The billhook was in the haversack. Tomorrow he was setting off for the mountains with Fernande. They would find the cart again in the forest . . . branches. . . . They would trim the branches . . . A big load. And people would say, "Gaston Dubois, he still knows how to trim branches. And there's a good load on his four-wheeled cart."

The ground was soft under their feet in the forest where they walked, as light as the earth in the garden, as yielding as the dough rising in the trough. The ground was soft, warm as dough and as cold as snakes.

There he lay. Himself. Gaston. All alone in this night without stars. In this night where no winds blew. Where the earth itself no longer pushed up the sap into the heart of plants.

There he lay. Himself. Gaston. All alone on this road that led nowhere.

The night grew lighter. The night closed in.

He was warm inside, but all around him lay a frozen winter which would finally pierce his limbs.

He was warm inside, but slowly the warmth trickled away, evaporated, dissolved in the cold streaming down from the heavy sky and oozing from the rich earth.

The drizzling rain soaked into him, the water rising from the ground froze his legs.

There he lay, all alone, and no-one came to help him find the way he had lost.

Were they all going to abandon him?

Were they going to leave him at the mercy of this frozen universe where there was no room for life?

Within him rose outrage, cries, appeals.

Was there another world beyond the frontiers of this world where he had suffered so much?

The priest had come. Gaston was able to recognize him by his black frock, but above all he knew this was a priest because never since Fernande's death had anyone come so close to him or spoken with such gentleness. He could not understand the priest's words, neither could he speak himself. It seemed that this face stayed quite close to his own for a long time. Then the silence and cold wrapped themselves round him again.

Time had stopped. Nothing moved, nothing lived around him.

Hours and hours went by like this, and all he could do was make the huge effort demanded by every breath he took. Because he was now breathing more and more briefly, more quickly, but also less painfully.

He gasped for air, his mouth dry and open, his throat inflamed. Less and less air entered his chest. All the flour and pollen dust he had breathed during his life was still in his lungs, dried out and burning.

The flames from the bakery oven and the hot sun glazing down over the garden had left a fire behind in his chest which consumed the little air that his throat allowed to penetrate with each desperate cry through his inflamed tubes.

Everything remained dark. Then suddenly an invisible hand snatched a fragment from this night. Tearing the silence apart. Footsteps drew closer. A face moved closer and closer, something cool touched his forehead. A voice whispered in his ear, "Father . . . Father . . . please forgive me."

The word plunged into the depths of his being and rose again like an echo. But his tightly-bound throat stopped it.

The face retreated. Another face leaned over him, and a rough hand shook his shoulder. Paul's voice thundered so that it hurt, "Father! It's Julien! Julien. Don't you recognize him?"

The voice continued less loudly as the face went away. "You see. It's over. He can't even see any more."

Gaston wanted to shout. It was as though his strength was suddenly born anew. He raised himself a few inches, his chest filled with air, but the cry from his throat was no more than a rattle.

A long sigh rose again from the depths of his chest. A sigh like the one he breathed every evening when he had performed the last actions of an endlessly long day's labour.